THE CAMDEN MURDER

THE CAMDEN MURDER

Mike Hollow

Allison & Busby Limited
11 Wardour Mews
London W1F 8AN
allisonandbusby.com

First published in Great Britain by Allison & Busby in 2022.
This paperback edition published by Allison & Busby in 2023.

10 9 8 7 6 5 4 3 2 1

ISBN 978-0-7490-2884-8

Typeset in 11/16 pt Sabon LT Pro by
Allison & Busby Ltd.

FSC
www.fsc.org
MIX
Paper | Supporting
responsible forestry
FSC® C171272

Printed and bound by
CPI Group (UK) Ltd, Croydon, CR0 4YY

For Rebekah,
a sparkle of sunlight in a still troubled world

CHAPTER ONE

Frederick Bernard Long felt a faint thud on his head – or more precisely, on the top of his police-issue steel helmet. He stopped and pulled it off, then muttered a few choice words under his breath: words that he knew thirty-odd years ago would have earned him a clip round the ear from his mother, God rest her soul. A generous splattering of white was immediately recognisable in the half-light against the dark blue of the helmet. 'Blasted pigeons,' he added out loud to his initial more discreetly voiced imprecations. His younger colleague stopped beside him.

'Hang on a moment, lad,' said Long. He bent down to pull a tuft from the patch of grass at the foot of a plane tree set among the paving stones, then wiped off the offending mess. At least it was easier to remove from steel than it was from the cloth covering of a peacetime police helmet. He wondered idly why the miscreant bird had singled out him rather than Dalton. Perhaps it was his height. Even for a policeman it was conspicuous, and standing out from the crowd had caused him trouble all his life. It wasn't just pigeons that picked on you.

He'd always been tall for his age. Well above the average man's height at fifteen, when he finally stopped growing he stood six foot three in his stockinged feet, as skinny as a rake and with a tendency to stoop to avoid attention until his dad, an ex-army man, beat it out of him and told him to stand up straight like a man. His time serving in the ranks as a conscript in the Great War had put some muscle on him, and the monotonous diet had added a few useful pounds, so that by the time he was twenty he was a fit and presentable young soldier.

Long had taken to the military life quite easily, discovering that a regimented existence with rules and regulations for everything suited him. Being moved up to the front line was no picnic, of course, but it had to be done, so he just got on with it. He was content to be a private, with no hankering for promotion even to lance-corporal, and he'd got by quite well, steering clear of trouble whenever he could. Until, that is, some fool of a young officer looking for a man to run messages back to battalion headquarters thought it would be amusing to single him out for duties as a runner, purely because of his name. And so, overnight, he was dubbed 'Runner Long' and saddled with one of the most dangerous jobs in the army. The young officer was killed soon afterwards, and Long volunteered for training as a machine-gunner, but the name dogged him until the end of the war.

Nowadays running of any kind was something he

tried to avoid. While his height and his boot size were the same as they'd been back then, his weight and girth had steadily increased, and his constable's tunic was seven inches larger at the waist than it had been when he joined the Metropolitan Police fourteen years ago. Pounding the beat at the regulation speed of two-and-a-half miles per hour suited him better than chasing villains down the street, and he relied more on experience and cunning than on athletic prowess to fulfil his duties to the satisfaction of his sergeant. Besides, he had Dalton at his side, a constable twenty-one years his junior: wet behind the ears, of course, but as lean and fit as he'd once been himself. Yes, if any running should be needed, Dalton could do it.

They were on early turn, which meant they'd been out patrolling the streets of Camden Town since six o'clock this morning, and now it was not far off eight. Their regular beat took them up Royal College Street and across the bridge over the Regent's Canal, followed by a right turn into Baynes Street, a short lane of small terraced houses, at the other end of which a wide bridge carried the trains running in and out of Camden Town railway station.

It wasn't long since the first glimmers of light had signalled the approach of dawn, and all was quiet. There had been no bombs since before they came on duty. The blackout wasn't due to end until eight minutes past eight, but Long at least had walked this area for so many years that he was confident he knew his way around in the darkest of nights as well as he did by day.

The delay in their progress caused by the pigeon incident probably proved more significant than he would have expected, for without it they might have missed what happened next. Just as they reached the turning into Baynes Street they heard the hurried slap of shoe leather on cobbles, then almost immediately the figure of a tall, slightly built man in a white jacket and peaked cap came hurtling towards them in the twilight and clattered into them. A milkman, judging by his uniform. It was fortunate perhaps, thought Long, that he himself had taken the full force of the collision. He imagined that the ballast he carried under his tunic would have made the other man's experience something akin to running into a brick wall. If Dalton had been in the way instead, the milkman would probably have sent him flying.

'Steady on, now, sir,' he said, bracing himself as he stopped the man with a hand to each shoulder. 'What seems to be the trouble?'

The stranger's chest was heaving as he struggled for breath. He stared at Long for a moment, looking disoriented, as if surprised to have run straight into a policeman. 'Thank goodness I've found you, Constable,' he gasped, righting his partly dislodged hat. 'Round there – come quickly . . . It's on fire.'

Tugging at Long's tunic sleeve, he led them back the way he'd come until they reached the entrance to a cobbled yard set back from the street. It was surrounded on all sides by two- and three-storey brick-built warehouses and stores, and both Long and Dalton knew it as a builder's yard, disused since the builder in question had gone bankrupt at the beginning of the war.

'This way,' said the man. 'Behind that wall.'

They followed him as he dashed towards one of the buildings, PC Dalton keeping up with him more easily than his colleague. A wall about seven feet high screened part of the yard from sight, but as Dalton neared it he saw the cause of the alarm.

He stopped dead in his tracks. He couldn't bear to look at it, but neither could he look away. The horror of the scene gripped him and wouldn't let him go. It wasn't just the flames prancing on the blazing car in feverish mockery of the blackout, it was what he fancied he could see among them. As the breeze caught the smoke for a moment, he glimpsed what looked like the silhouette of someone seated at the wheel, as still as if taking a nap before resuming their journey.

If he'd been in a movie, he thought, he'd have sprinted to the vehicle, yanked the driver's door open and dragged the helpless victim clear in the nick of time. But no, this was real life, and he couldn't get within twenty feet. He might as well try walking into a furnace.

PC Long caught up with him. There wasn't much he hadn't seen in his time, and he felt a twinge of sympathy for Dalton, but there was no way round it: this sort of thing was just part of the job, and probably always would be.

'It's all right, lad,' he said. 'There's nothing we can do for whoever that is – or was. Best thing you can do is run round to the phone box in St Pancras Way and dial 999 for the fire brigade. And if the phone's out of action, run on down to the fire station. It's only four or five minutes' walk from here to Pratt Street, so a fit young fella like you can run there in no time at all. And phone the station too. The last air raid was hours ago, so if we've got a car on fire with someone dead inside, it's suspicious – they'll have to get the CID in. Now be off with you.'

Dalton sped off, relieved to be spared.

Long turned to the man who had brought them to the scene and who now seemed rooted to the spot, as if transfixed. 'Come along now, sir,' he said. 'I expect the fire brigade'll be here in two ticks, and we don't want to get in their way.'

'Yes,' said the young man absently. 'Is it all right if I go now?'

'In a moment, sir. I just need to make a note of your particulars.'

'Why's that?'

'Because you're a witness, sir. We may need to talk to you later.'

'Oh, I see. All right then.'

Long took him a few steps away and stopped. 'We should be all right here, sir.'

'Couldn't we do this somewhere else? I – I don't really want to see that fire.'

'I understand, sir, but I have to keep an eye on the scene. Perhaps you could just stand with your back to it, so I can still see.'

The man shifted his position accordingly while Long took a notebook and pencil from his pocket and turned to a new page.

'Now, then,' he said, 'if you wouldn't mind giving me your name.'

'Of course. It's Rickett – Joe Rickett.'

'And you're the milkman, I assume, dressed like that. On your round, were you?'

'Yes, that's right – Express Dairy.' He gestured across the yard. 'That's my basket over there, with the bottles of milk in it.'

'Right. And does your route normally take you through this yard?'

'No, it's just that I overslept a bit this morning, so I had to dash out. And then I . . . well, to be honest, I, er, felt the call of nature. You must know what that's like in your job.'

Long gave him a blank stare and waited with pencil poised for him to continue.

'So anyway,' the milkman hurriedly resumed. 'I slipped in here and nipped round the back to find a suitable place – somewhere a bit secluded, you know.'

'And you found this car on fire?'

'Yes. It was burning away like mad, and I could—' He gulped. 'I could see someone in it, and there was nothing I could do to save them – it was so hot I couldn't get anywhere near it. So I ran off straight away to get help, and that's when I bumped into you.'

'The person in the car – could you see who it was?'

'No. There was smoke as well as flames, and it was making my eyes sting. I couldn't tell who it was or even what they looked like.'

'Were they moving? Did you hear anything?'

'No. Whoever it was must've been dead by the time I got here – no one could survive a fire like that.'

'So what time did you see the car?'

'I'm not sure, but it must've been only a few moments before I found you and your colleague. What time is it now?'

Long checked his watch. 'Seven forty-nine.'

'Well, I suppose it must've been about a quarter to eight, then.'

'Thank you, sir.'

'Look, can I go now? I've got to get on with my round – people expect their milk to be delivered on time, even when there's a war on.'

'Just one more question, sir. Did you see anyone else?'

'Near the car? No, there was no one else around.'

Long reviewed his notes. 'Right, that'll be all for now. Where can we get hold of you if we need to talk to you again?'

'At the dairy, or if I'm out delivering they'll tell you where.'

'And your home address?'

'Elm Road – number 28, upstairs flat.'

'Very well. Thank you for your assistance, sir.'

'Just doing my duty,' said Rickett. 'Good day to you, Constable.'

He hurried off without another word, picking up his basket of milk on the way. He didn't look back.

CHAPTER TWO

The milkman had not long disappeared from view when a fire engine, its bell clanging, swung round the corner and shuddered to a halt. PC Dalton jumped down from the running board and ran over to Long while the crew rolled out a hose.

'I got through on the phone all right,' he said. 'The fire brigade boys picked me up on their way. Seems we were lucky to get anything – this was the only pump they could spare. It can't do foam, but they said they'll put the fire out the old-fashioned way, with water.'

'And the CID?'

'Yes, they agreed with you, it's suspicious, so they're getting someone up here from Scotland Yard as quick as they can. I've told them where we are. And we're to tell them the station's going to fix up somewhere for them to stay.'

'Right, lad,' Long replied. 'Now, these firemen don't need two of us watching, so I'll stay here and keep an eye on 'em. You go and check those warehouses – bang on a few doors and see if there's a caretaker or anyone around. I doubt there will be, if this place has been empty for a year, but we need to check if there were any witnesses – those buildings are the only ones that overlook this yard.'

Dalton took a deep breath.

'Run along, then,' said Long. 'No time to lose.'

Dalton departed, feeling weary, and his older colleague watched as the firemen directed a fine spray of water over the blazing car. They soon had the fire under control, and when it was extinguished an athletic-looking man of about forty in the uniform of London Fire Brigade joined him.

'Jackson's the name,' he said. 'I'm the station officer. Looks like everything's in hand now. You'll be needing to report this, won't you?'

'I shall, Mr Jackson, but we've got a detective coming, and I'm sure he'll want to ask you all sorts of things.'

'Very well, I'll hang on here. I expect he'll be very interested to know how a car comes to be on fire in the night in a disused builder's yard, especially one with a dead body in it.'

'Any idea how the fire started?'

Jackson looked back at the burnt-out remains. 'A simple enough question,' he said, 'but one that's not always easy to answer. The way things are these days, normally the first thing I'd think of would be one of those dratted incendiary bombs. Causing us no end of trouble, they are – but I probably don't need to tell you that.'

'No, I think we've all seen what they can do. But it's

not very likely in this case, I'd have thought. I was up at five this morning and the all-clear went just before that. I haven't heard any German planes overhead since then, and you can tell by the sound they make, can't you? It's different to ours. So I don't imagine there was one hanging around dropping incendiaries by the time this fire started. Could it have been a delayed-action one?'

'I don't think so. We've certainly had plenty of delayed-action high-explosive bombs these last few weeks, but as far as I know they haven't been using delayed-action incendiaries.' Jackson moved towards the car, with Long following him. 'But here's the funny thing.' He put a gloved hand to the driver's door handle and eased it open.

'What's that?' said Long.

'Well, I thought this door might be jammed, but it isn't – it opens quite easily. So if the driver's sitting there and the car catches fire, why on earth didn't the poor blighter just get out?'

CHAPTER THREE

Detective Inspector John Jago edged the car forward a couple of feet in the early morning gloom and pressed down on the brake pedal to halt it. Again. They'd already been caught in a bottleneck in Tottenham Court Road, crawling past the wreckage of some poor soul's haberdashery shop blasted into the road in the overnight air raid, and now they were stuck in another jam. He drummed his fingers impatiently on the steering wheel. He could see the problem: they were inching towards a junction that appeared to be the meeting point of at least five main roads. That must have been a challenge for drivers even in peacetime, he thought.

On the traffic island just ahead stood the remains of a fingerpost that would once have identified where these roads led to, but was now fingerless, pointing nowhere. In this case he knew the damage couldn't be blamed on enemy action. The reason behind the zealous removal of road signs at the end of May had been the government's desire to prevent invading Nazi hordes from finding their way around the country. Jago, however, had always suspected a flaw in their reasoning. Confronted by a lack of road signs, wouldn't enemy forces just grab the nearest passing civilian and force the information out of them? As he watched a man climbing the steps from the underground public lavatory beneath the traffic island, he was tempted to jump from the car and employ the same interrogation tactic himself, but the queue moved forward.

As if a five-way road junction with no signs wasn't already a recipe for chaos, he could now see that a furniture lorry and a brewer's dray had collided over to the right, and a police constable was directing all traffic to continue straight ahead.

'Where are we, Peter?' he said.

Detective Constable Cradock was sitting in the passenger seat beside him, poring over the *A to Z* street map of London. 'Nearly there now, guv'nor,' he replied. 'If I'm not mistaken, we're in Camden High Street.'

'Good.'

'We just need to turn right at the next junction.' Cradock looked up and noticed the road accident that lay between them and their destination. 'Oh.'

'Oh, indeed. So how do we get to Baynes Street if we can't turn right? You'll have to direct me.'

'Yes, sir, leave it to me.'

'And when we get there, make sure you keep that map book in your pocket. I fancy we're going to need it here.'

'Yes, sir.'

Cradock buried his head in the map again, and Jago took in their surroundings. Directly ahead, where two of the five roads met, was a small branch of the Midland Bank, its windows boarded up as a result, he assumed, of bomb damage. On the next corner to the left of it was a larger building bearing the name of the National Bank, and to his right stood a third bank, the Westminster. 'Look at that, Peter,' he said. 'A bank on every corner.' He glanced round the rest of the junction. 'And a pub on every other corner – the Britannia, the Halfway House, and the Mother Red Cap. What does that tell us about Camden Town?'

'I don't know, sir. They're rich but they spend all their money on drink?'

'You could be right. Doesn't look like a rich sort of place, though, does it? All a bit run down – but I dare say we'll know a lot more about it before the day's out.'

'Yes, sir.'

The traffic ahead of them began to move, and they managed to cross the junction. They passed the Midland Bank and saw next to it the red-tiled frontage of a Tube station that must once have borne in large letters the name Camden Town Station. Now, however, the first four letters of that name had disappeared – as had about a third of the station, smashed to pieces by a bomb. Jago could only hope it hadn't penetrated below to the tunnels: people sheltering from air raids in that way had paid with their lives. He'd heard on the grapevine that the bomb that hit Balham station a month or so ago had left a hole big enough to swallow a double-decker bus and killed dozens. The papers hadn't named the station, of course, they'd only mentioned an underground railway station in London being hit and said there were 'some' casualties, but a friend who lived over that way had told him what it was really like.

Cradock's voice interrupted his thoughts. 'Turn right here, sir – Dewsbury Terrace.'

Jago swung the car round into a narrow street and continued following Cradock's directions on a zigzag course that took them past a big Aerated Bread Company office block built in the modern style, then across the Regent's Canal, past the Camden Town railway station and finally to their destination. As he turned into Baynes Street he could see the murky water of the canal down a short slope to his right. A colourfully decorated narrowboat chugged slowly into view, a woman at its stern glancing round and discreetly emptying a chamber pot over the side. Not a good place for a swim, then.

He checked his watch. Barely half an hour had elapsed since his new boss, Detective Superintendent Hardacre, head of Central Branch at Scotland Yard, had dispatched him to investigate a suspicious death in Camden Town. He did a rough calculation in his head: the distance was only three miles or so, which meant an average speed of six or seven miles an hour. Not very impressive, he thought, but it said something about the state of the roads in London these days.

A little farther along the right-hand side of the street was the entrance way he'd been told to look out for. He drove in and found a yard surrounded on all sides by a hotchpotch of dilapidated sheds, huts and unidentifiable buildings. Above it the sky was choking on the smoke belching from the forest of chimneys, both residential and commercial, that seemed to make up Camden Town.

He parked beside what looked like a small office with broken windows. There was no sign of the reported burnt-out car, but he did see a police constable and a man in a fire brigade uniform. The constable approached them as they got out of the car. 'Good morning, sir,' he said, with a grave salute. 'I was told to wait here for you.'

'Good morning, Constable,' Jago replied. 'I'm DI Jago and this is DC Cradock. And your name is?'

'Long, sir. PC 182N. Kentish Town station.'

'You're the man who reported the incident?'

'Strictly speaking no, sir. There were two of us actually – young PC Dalton was with me, and he was the one who phoned in with the details. After he'd done that, I sent him off to finish the beat and I thought I'd better stay here to guard the scene. Before he went, I got him to check all these buildings in case there were any other witnesses, but he didn't find any. Not surprising, though – this place has been empty since war broke out. It used to be a builder's yard. And before you ask, sir, I haven't touched anything, nor has anyone else, except the fireman over there opened the driver's door. He's hung on here to wait for you, so I expect he'll tell you about that himself.'

'You say "other witnesses". Does that mean you were acting on information from a witness?'

'Yes, sir. The milkman was on his round, delivering

22

down the street here. He reported seeing a car on fire, and we responded immediately.'

'Name?'

Long pulled his notebook from his tunic pocket. 'Said he was Joe Rickett, sir. Works for Express Dairy and lives at 28 Elm Road, upstairs flat. Got caught short, sir, that's what he said, so he popped in here to, er, relieve himself, and found the car on fire. Was dashing off for help when he ran into us.'

'Where did he run into you?'

'Down the end of the street, sir, where it meets Royal College Street.'

'And what time was this?'

Long turned the page in his notebook. 'He found us at seven forty-six, sir, and said he'd discovered the car on fire just moments before that, about a quarter to eight. Said it was burning like mad. He could see someone in it, but what with the smoke and flames he couldn't tell who it was or what they looked like. It was so hot he couldn't get near enough to do anything – he reckoned whoever it was must've been dead already. I asked him if he'd seen anyone else at the scene, but he hadn't.'

'And what time did you see the fire yourself?'

'Me and Dalton ran straight to the scene, sir. We would've been there by seven forty-seven. There was nothing we could do except call the fire brigade.'

'Thank you.' Jago glanced over his shoulder as a squeal of brakes heralded the arrival of a police car. The door opened, and Nisbet, the Scotland Yard photographer, got out.

'Be with you in a jiffy,' he said, pulling a camera and tripod from the back seat. 'That's it over there, I suppose – I'll just get all my stuff ready, then I'll make a start.'

Long's face suggested a certain disapproval of the man's informality as he turned to Jago. 'Would you like to see the car now, sir, or would you like to speak to the gentleman from the fire brigade first?'

'Fireman first, please,' said Jago. He gave the photographer a polite smile. 'Good morning, Mr Nisbet – do carry on.'

PC Long brought the waiting fireman over, and Jago extended a hand in greeting. 'Hello,' he said, 'I'm DI Jago and this is DC Cradock – we've been sent over by Scotland Yard.' He was still reluctant to identify himself as 'from Scotland Yard'. It might be true, given that he and Cradock were now seconded there, but he couldn't shift the sense that it sounded pretentious. 'And you are?'

'The name's Jackson,' said the fireman, grasping Jago's hand and shaking it. 'I'm the station officer at Camden Town fire station. I thought I should wait for you here in case I could be helpful.'

'Thank you – I'm sure you will be. Perhaps we could take a look at the car now – lead on, Constable.'

Long took them across the yard to where a wall extended to one side of an anonymous grimy building, and as they passed its end a separate enclosed area came into view. The rear edge was bounded by a brick-built Victorian warehouse, three storeys high, now serving as the bleak backdrop to the remains of a burnt-out car.

There was something desolate in the silence of the scene before them. Halfway up the building, the triangular frame of the warehouse hoist had swung out on its hinge and now loomed over the car like a hangman's scaffold.

CHAPTER FOUR

'That's it, sir,' said PC Long with a cursory nod in the direction of the car. His remark was superfluous, but Jago acknowledged it.

'Yes. Nasty business.'

Cradock waited for what he thought was the appropriate moment of respectful silence, then gave a polite cough to break it. 'Shall I get the murder bag from the car, sir, and start dusting for prints?'

Jackson broke in before Jago could reply. 'If my experience is anything to go by, Inspector, you're not likely to find any after a fire like this. It'll probably have destroyed them, and even if it hasn't, our hoses will've washed them away. Have a go, of course, but I wouldn't expect much if I were you.'

'Go ahead, Peter,' said Jago. 'We have to try.'

'Very good, sir.'

As Cradock went to fetch the bag, Jago was distracted by the sound of another, quieter car. It was a sedate and solid-looking grey Rover saloon, a model that he'd heard was popular with doctors. He didn't recognise this particular one, but the man who got out was indeed a member of that profession – Dr Gibson, the pathologist from St George's Hospital.

'Sorry I couldn't get here any sooner, old chap,' said Gibson as he slid out of the car. 'I came as soon as your Mr Hardacre gave me my orders. He does that, doesn't he? Give orders, I mean.'

Jago declined to make any comment on his new boss's manner in front of PC Long, but responded with a faint smile and an almost imperceptible wink as he introduced Gibson to the station officer. 'I was just about to ask Mr Jackson one or two questions,' he said. 'Would you mind waiting for a moment before you start your examination, Doctor? Just while Peter checks for fingerprints.'

'Not at all,' said Gibson. 'I'll listen in.'

Cradock returned with the bag and took out the fingerprint equipment and two pairs of rubber gloves, one of which he gave to Jago.

'I understand you opened the driver's door, Mr Jackson,' said Jago as the four men walked over to the burnt-out car, leaving Long to keep unwanted intruders away from the yard. Jackson nodded. 'But you haven't touched anything else – correct?'

'That's right,' Jackson replied. 'And I was wearing gloves, so I don't think I'll have contaminated any evidence.'

'Thank you.' Jago turned to Cradock. 'OK, Peter, you can get started.'

Cradock wriggled his hands into the rubber gloves and strode ahead briskly to the car. He reached out to open the door, but then hesitated and turned his head away. When Jago arrived beside him he could see why. The body in the driver's seat was charred beyond recognition, its fists clenched and arms bent in a way he'd seen in fire victims before. And then there was the smell: indescribable, but unforgettable.

'Sorry, sir,' Cradock gasped, struggling not to retch. 'I haven't seen one like . . . like that before.'

Jago said nothing. What was he supposed to say? Play the older, wiser man – 'Don't worry, son, you get used to it'? He'd seen plenty of death in its ugliest forms, in war and in peace, and he'd never got used to it. The sight of men on fire, struggling to escape the wreck of their tank at Cambrai in 1917, was as real to him still as the shrapnel he carried in his body from that same battle. He turned away and breathed deeply to steady himself. 'Just carry on when you're ready, Peter.'

'I'll be all right, sir. I'll get on and do it.'

Cradock began dusting the car for fingerprints, while Nisbet took his photographs. The speed with which the photographer completed his work made Cradock feel that his own task was the more difficult one, but he applied himself dutifully, secretly delighted to be responsible for this key part of the investigation. He soon became convinced, however, that the man from the fire brigade was right. Whether it was due to the effects of fire and water or not, his efforts were proving fruitless. 'Sorry, guv'nor,' he said. 'There's nothing here that we could use.'

'We can only do what's possible,' said Jago. 'In any case, even if the car had been covered in prints, we might not know which were the driver's and which weren't if all we've got is a body with half the skin burnt off. Pack your stuff away, and we'll let Dr Gibson have his turn.'

Gibson began his initial examination of the body as soon as the photographer had left. 'This won't take long,' he said. 'Most of what you'll want to know I'll only find out when I examine him properly at the hospital.'

Jago glanced at the body. 'Or her? Are we sure this was a man? The body's so badly burnt I'm not sure I can tell.'

'I think we're looking at a man, but I won't be able to confirm that until I get the remains back to the mortuary.'

Sooner you than me, thought Jago. He could imagine few more unpleasant ways of spending a morning than being cooped up in a freezing mortuary with a corpse in that state.

'And I'm sorry I can't offer you an estimated time of death,' Gibson added. 'Calculations based on normal rates of post-mortem cooling don't apply when the body's been burnt like this.'

'Of course.'

'But if Mr Jackson can tell you approximately when the fire started, you won't need my help on that – if the driver was trapped in the car, time of death will be very soon after that.'

Jackson was doing his own examination of the car, his head under the bonnet, but looked up when he heard his name mentioned. 'If you want to know when the fire started,' he said, 'judging by the intensity of it when we arrived I'd say it'd probably been burning for seven or eight minutes, maybe ten.'

'And what time did you get here?' said Jago.

'Seven fifty-four.'

'So the fire could've started at seven forty-four or a bit later?'

'Yes, but it's not a precise science, more a matter of experience, so I could be wrong. Now, I'm going to have a look in the boot, if you don't mind.'

'Please do,' said Jago, as Jackson moved to the back of the car. He turned to Gibson. 'That tallies with what our witness reported – he said he found the car at a quarter to eight, and it was burning like mad. Our officers were on the scene by seven forty-seven, and it was already too late.'

'There you are, then, Inspector,' Gibson replied. 'Estimated time of death between seven forty-four and seven forty-seven, which is a jolly sight more precise than what you'd normally get from someone like me.' He paused. 'Forgive me – that sounds rather callous. What I should say is that in a case like this, Mr Jackson's advice is more valuable than mine, and at this stage I've no reason to dispute his finding.'

'At this stage?'

'Yes. Clearly that assumes the deceased was killed by the fire – but if he was already dead when it started, time of death would obviously have been some time earlier, and how much earlier could be difficult to establish. We'll have to wait and see what the post-mortem throws up.'

The pathologist's final words caused Jago to swallow involuntarily, but he took the point. 'Of course, thank you. I appreciate your help – and that goes for both of you. Now, Mr Jackson, what can you tell us?'

'Well, to start with, the make of the vehicle. Judging by the little badge on the bonnet, it's a Standard. But if you want to know which model, you'll have to ask someone who knows more about them than I do.'

'Did you find anything of interest in the boot?'

'Just the usual sort of things. Take a look.' He waved a hand towards a starting handle and the remains of a few tools lying in the boot, their wooden handles mostly burnt away. 'Just basic stuff for emergencies, I should think.'

'Thank you. And could you give me your opinion on how the fire started?'

'I'll do my best. I expect you know this, but if a vehicle catches fire it's usually going to be because of a fuel leak – some petrol leaks out, say from the fuel pipe to the carburettor, and a spark sets it alight. You can get a spark from one of the plugs or from a cable, or, for example, if the owner's done some home-made wiring like rigging up an electric lamp in the engine compartment and the insulation's chafed on a sharp surface. But let me show you something. Would you excuse us, Doctor?'

Gibson moved away from the body, and Jackson took his place. He pointed at the middle of the car's dashboard. 'See that, Inspector?'

'The ignition lock?'

'That's right. The key's still in it, and it's in the off position. I was having a bit of a poke around under the bonnet just now, and I can see the fuel pump's definitely mechanical, not electrical.'

'I see. So the pump only works when the engine's running.'

'Exactly, which means if there was a leak somewhere and a fire started, once the engine stopped there'd be nothing pumping petrol out through the leak and the supply of fuel to the fire would be cut off. Once it reaches the upholstery, of course, the fire'll spread, but this lot seems to have gone up faster than I'd normally expect to see in an electrical fire. Also, the fact that the key's in the off position suggests that if the fire started while the car was moving, or even if it was stationary with the engine running, the driver turned the engine off. So then, why didn't he jump out instead of sitting there and burning to death? There's no sign of a collision, so it doesn't look like he was trapped.'

'Could he've been taken ill or had a heart attack or something while he was driving, when the fire started?' asked Cradock. 'Suppose he just managed to stop but then died before he could get out.'

'It's possible,' said Gibson. 'But it would certainly be an unfortunate coincidence if he passed away in the very moment between bringing the car safely to a halt and getting out.'

'And it'd be a bit odd too,' said Jackson, 'for someone taken ill like that to drive into this yard and park in a corner where no one could see him rather than just stop in the street, wouldn't it? I imagine you detectives would have a question or two about that.'

'I think we would,' said Jago.

'But one thing's for certain – it'll be a hell of a job confirming his identity, whoever he is, burnt like that.'

'Well, that may depend on whether the car's his or not. Look at the number plate there – it's just a piece of pressed metal, so you can still read it after a fire, and we should be able to trace it.' He turned to Cradock. 'Peter, go and ask Long where that phone is that they used, then get down there as fast as you can and call the county council. Find out who it's registered to – it's LL 3826. And call Kentish Town nick too, while you're at it, and get someone to bring this car to the station yard, so we can keep an eye on it.'

'Yes, guv'nor,' Cradock replied. He ran off in the direction of the yard entrance, where Long was still on guard.

'You may need to rely on dental records too, John,' said Gibson. 'Teeth and bones generally resist the fire longer than other parts of the body, so when I get him on the slab I'll check whether he's had any work done. If he has, you'll just have to hope he's a local man with a local dentist, otherwise it could take you a while to find them.'

'Yes, thanks,' said Jago.

'And there's one other thing that might help you – or rather three things, actually.' Gibson bent over the body again. 'Here – three metal items that survived the flames. A key ring with what looks like a front-door key and another smaller key that I can't identify, a little medallion that he had on a chain round his neck, and thirdly what I think must be a wristwatch, although it doesn't seem to have any hands or glass.'

He handed the items to Jago, who weighed them in his hand.

'Thanks,' he said grimly. 'Whoever he is, he won't be needing a watch any more.'

CHAPTER FIVE

Jago was still chatting with Gibson when Cradock returned, looking a little flushed and out of breath from the run.

'I've got it, guv'nor,' he announced, taking his coat off and leaning against the wall.

'Well done, Peter. What did the council say?'

'They put me through to a clerk who checked that number plate while I waited. He said the car's registered as a Flying Standard Eight saloon.'

'And who does it belong to?'

'Not to a named individual, unfortunately. It belongs to a company – Baring and Sons Confectionery, of Albert Street, Camden Town. They're the ones who make those nice chocolates.'

'On which I dare say you're an expert.'

'Well, I've tried them, and—'

'Yes, but have you contacted the company?'

'Yes, of course, sir. I got the number from the operator and spoke to someone at Barings. They confirmed it's one of their company cars, and it's assigned to someone called Les Latham, who's an employee of theirs.'

'Address?'

'Yes, I got that too. They said he lives at 71 Belmont Street.'

'Good work – let's go.'

The houses in Belmont Street looked old and tired. Jago parked the car outside number 71 and mounted a few steps to the front door, followed by Cradock. The house had three storeys, and the three bell-pushes beside the door suggested that it had been divided into flats to create rental income for the owner. He pressed the one marked 'Latham' and waited.

The woman who eventually opened the door was of medium height and slim and, by Jago's estimation, in her early forties, her make-up and tightly permed hair giving the impression that she took more care of her appearance than the landlord did of the building. The breeze from the street wafted a spidery trail of smoke from the cigarette in her hand back into the house.

'Good morning. Is Mr Latham at home?' said Jago.

'No, he's out,' she replied. 'I'm Mrs Latham – who are you?'

'We're police officers – I'm Detective Inspector Jago and this is my colleague, Detective Constable Cradock.' He showed her his warrant card and National Registration identity card.

She glanced briefly at them. 'Do you mind me asking what you're here for? I'm not accustomed to having visits from the police.'

'It might be better if we could come in first, if you don't mind.'

She hesitated. 'All right, then. We live up on the top floor – follow me.'

They climbed the stairs to her flat, where she showed them into the living room. It was small but tidy, and some of the furniture looked new. Another woman, older and wearing a flowery pinafore and frayed slippers, was wiping the top of a glass-fronted cabinet with her back to them, holding a duster in her right hand and a cigarette in her left.

'Sorry, Mum,' said Mrs Latham, 'I've got visitors. Police. Can you leave us alone for a bit?'

'Course, dear. Whatever you say, Rose my love,' said the woman. There was affection in her voice, but also, it seemed to Jago, more than a trace of weariness. She turned round, revealing a lined face and lank, thinning hair. 'Nice to meet you, officers – always a pleasure to see a policeman. Hilda Crow's my name – Mrs Hilda Crow. If you need me for anything, I live just round the corner – Ferdinand Place, behind the bus garage, number 33.'

She moved towards the door, walking unevenly as though suffering in her hip, and departed, leaving a faint cloud of cigarette smoke trailing in her wake. Rose Latham offered Jago and Cradock chairs but remained standing herself.

'So, what do you want my husband for?' she asked. 'He's gone to work.'

'I see. What does he do?'

'He's a commercial traveller, although he prefers to call himself a sales representative. He works for Baring and Sons, the confectionery people – visits shops and persuades them to buy their chocolates and sweets and things.'

'Does he have a car for that?'

'Yes, he does. It's not actually his, though – it belongs to the company. Why do you want to know?'

'I'm sorry, Mrs Latham, but I'm afraid there's been an incident involving a car, and we think it may be your husband's. Do you know the registration number of the car he'd be using today?'

'The number plate, you mean?'

'That's right.'

'No, I don't. He's had so many cars with his jobs, and to be honest I'm not that interested. I don't suppose Barings would let me use it even if I wanted to. Come to that, I doubt whether Les would either – he's a bit old-fashioned like that. I do know the letters, though – they're LL. I remember them because he always says they stand for Les Latham or "Lucky Les". But I can't remember what comes after it – the number's too long.'

'Could it be LL 3826?'

'Could be, I suppose, but I can't say for certain.' She halted for a moment, as though her mind had wandered, then snapped back, a new note of urgency in her voice. 'But you said something about an incident. What do you mean?'

'I'm very sorry to have to tell you this, but I'm afraid there's been an accident.'

'What kind of accident?'

'A very serious one.'

'You mean – Les?'

'We don't know for sure, but a car matching the description of your husband's was found in Camden Town this morning. There was a body in it.'

She sat down with a gasp, her eyes fixed in shock. 'Not Les – please tell me it's not him.'

'There's no easy way to say this, Mrs Latham, but I'm afraid we don't know – we've found no identification on the body, you see.'

There was a pause before she spoke. 'Are you saying you want me to identify the body?'

'Normally I'd say yes, Mrs Latham, but in this case . . . well, the fact is there's been a fire. The car's burnt out. I'm sure you'll understand that means it can be difficult to identify anyone in the vehicle. I won't be asking you to look at the body.'

She was silent, as if unable to take in what he was saying. When at length she spoke, her voice was quiet but firm. 'I appreciate your kindness, Inspector, but in the last war I was a driver-mechanic with the WAAC – you know, the Women's Army Auxiliary Corps – I drove an ambulance and I saw a lot of poor soldiers with terrible burns. Most of them died, and it was a mercy they did. I don't think you can show me anything I haven't seen before.'

'Thank you, Mrs Latham. It's very courageous of you to offer, but I'm afraid I have to say the condition of the remains is such that no one, not even you, would be able to recognise who the person is, and in cases like that we don't allow close relatives to see them.'

'All right. I understand, Inspector – I just wanted to be helpful.'

'You can still help us. Tell me, please, does your husband wear a medallion?'

'A medallion? Yes, he's got a little St Christopher that he always wears on a chain round his neck – the patron saint of travellers, you see. He reckons it brings him good luck.' She paused and bit her lip. 'I gave it to him years ago, and I got it engraved on the back. To L from R, it says – well, that's all there was room for.'

'Thank you – that does match the description of a medallion found on the body. I'm very sorry.'

Rose Latham buried her face in her handkerchief, crying gently. Jago waited in silence, pained by the number of times he'd had to break harsh news to anxious wives, husbands, parents. At length she stopped, wiped her eyes and nose, and looked up.

'There's a watch, too,' she said. 'He always has that on. It's a Bravingtons – a rectangular one. It's a funny-looking thing, because it's got no hands or dial – just a shiny metal case with two little holes where you can see the numbers jumping round to tell you what time it is. He thought it was very modern – probably made him think he'd got the latest thing and it would impress his customers.'

'I see. That matches the watch we found.'

She nodded slowly. 'It must be him, then. I've never seen anyone else wearing one like that, and if you've got the medallion too, it's got to be Les.'

She looked as though she were about to cry again but controlled herself. 'Please excuse me. This is all a terrible shock.'

'I'm very sorry to be the bearer of such news, Mrs Latham.'

'No, that's all right. I know you're only doing your job. But what happened?'

'I can't say until the pathologist's done his post-mortem examination and reported his findings, but I'll come back as soon as we know. For now, I'm wondering whether you saw him when he set off this morning.'

'No, I can't say I did, really. He must've got up without waking me, because when I stirred he was gone.'

'And can you remember what time it was when you stirred?'

'Yes, it was twenty past seven. I hadn't heard him at all, but that's not unusual for me. Les was going up to Cambridge for a few days – that's the area he covers, Cambridgeshire – and when he's doing that he's always up early, so he can beat the traffic jams. I've got used to it, I suppose – I sleep through it unless he's really noisy.'

'How early would that be?'

'It depends, but he's usually up by about half past six, I think. He has to walk round to the garage to get the car – I don't mean a garage of our own, I mean a proper one with petrol pumps and everything. The company's very fussy about that – he's not allowed to keep it at home because they don't let him use it for private motoring. They say it's got to be locked up overnight in a garage that they've approved, so he has to pay five bob a week to keep it there.' She stopped abruptly, as if suddenly struck by the triviality of her words. 'I'm sorry – you don't need to know all that, do you? It's the shock – it's got me all at sixes and sevens.'

'Don't worry, Mrs Latham. It'd be helpful if you

could tell us where this garage is, though.'

'Oh, right, well it's in Crogsland Road. You go down to Chalk Farm Road and turn right, then right again, and it's on your left after Kirkwood Place. You can't miss it – there's a blue sign on the front, "Bowen's Garage", and a pair of petrol pumps outside. I think Mr Bowen lives over the shop – well, in the house next door actually, but pretty much on the premises.'

'Thank you. And forgive me for what might sound a rather odd request, but I wonder whether you could possibly tell us who your husband's dentist was.'

'Dentist?'

'Yes. We might need to use dental records to help us complete the identification.'

'Oh, I see, yes. Les and I both use the same dentist – Mr Lonsdale, in Camden High Street.'

'Do you have a telephone in the flat?'

'Yes – Les needs it for his work. It's just through the door there.'

'Could my colleague make a call? I'd like him to contact Mr Lonsdale.'

'Of course. His number's in the little address book beside the phone.'

'Thank you. Peter, call Mr Lonsdale, please, and ask him to get in touch with Dr Gibson. I'd like him to get Mr Latham's records over to the hospital as soon as possible.'

'Yes, sir.'

Cradock left the room.

'Is that all you need, Inspector?' said Mrs Latham. 'Only, if you don't mind, I think I'd like to be on my own for a bit now.'

'Of course,' said Jago. 'But there is just one other thing you might be able to help us with before we go. Do you have a photo of your husband that we could borrow?'

'Yes, of course.'

She crossed the room to the sideboard and returned with a framed photograph. 'This is us at our wedding,' she said, handing it to him.

Jago took the photo and examined it. The quality suggested it was an amateur shot taken on a cheap camera, and it had faded with age, but he could still see that Rose Latham looked young, fresh and natural in a traditional white wedding dress. The man beside her was tall and good-looking, with a confident bearing.

'How long ago was that?' he said.

'Twenty years. We met just after the war. Les wasn't long back from it – he'd been in the army, and we got married in 1920. Such plans he had then – getting a good job, having a family.' She paused. 'It didn't all work out, though. He wanted children, but somehow it never happened. But at least he did very well in his job – six pounds a week he gets. Yes, he's done very well for himself.'

She leant against the wall and stared out of the window, as if she could see her past life played out on the other side of the glass.

'I'm sorry, Mrs Latham. Do you have anything more recent?'

She drew herself up with a sigh. 'I'll see what I can find.' She went back to the sideboard, opened a drawer and rummaged in it. 'Here you are,' she said, producing a couple of photographs and handing them to Jago. The quality of both was much better. The first showed a man in shirtsleeves and flannels standing proudly with arms akimbo on the front steps of a house, framed by the columns of a porch.

'Was that taken here?' said Jago.

'Yes, when we moved in, a couple of years ago. We only had this one floor of the house, of course, and rented, just like now, but he was very pleased with himself. I think he liked the idea of being the king of the castle and all that, and I suppose a picture of himself standing outside the front door made him feel like he owned the whole house. His mate Jack took it, I think.'

'Jack?'

'Yes, Jack Henderson, a pal of his at work.'

The door creaked open as Cradock returned to the room and reported that he'd contacted the dentist successfully.

'Thank you,' said Jago. 'I was just asking Mrs Latham if she had a photograph of her husband that we could borrow. This was taken a couple of years ago.' He handed the doorstep photo to Cradock and studied the second one. This was a good studio portrait. 'Do you know when this one was taken, Mrs Latham?' he asked.

'That one was early last year,' she replied. 'I think he said he needed it for work or something.'

Jago studied the portrait. It was strange, he thought, how much a person's face told you about them. Seeing Latham's for the first time made him feel he was beginning to get to know him. It was likeable, with an engaging smile and friendly crinkles at the eyes, a face that looked straight into the camera, signalling openness and sincerity. The face of a man, he thought, from whom you probably *would* buy a second-hand car. And a face that no longer existed. 'May

I take it with me?' he said. 'I'll make sure I return it.'

'Oh, yes – I've got a couple of spares as well as that one, so no need to worry. He didn't just have the one copy.'

'Thank you. I won't deprive you of your wedding photo, but may we take the other one – of your husband outside the house?'

'Of course.'

Jago handed the portrait to Cradock, who took his own look at it and then put both photos carefully in his pocket.

'Thank you, Mrs Latham,' said Jago. 'We'll leave you in peace now. If you need us for anything, though, please get in touch immediately.'

'I will,' she said, and dismissed them with a feeble wave of her hand.

CHAPTER SIX

'Well, we've got a name for him now, sir,' said Cradock as they took the two flights of stairs back down to the ground floor. 'Lucky Les Latham – but not so lucky this morning, eh?'

Jago let the remark go without comment. Cradock probably didn't mean to sound so callous, he thought. Perhaps it was just the bravado of youth.

They reached the street door and let themselves out. Jago glanced back up to the flat they'd just left and saw Rose Latham standing at the window, staring down at them. He wondered whether she was intending to wave them goodbye, as people sometimes did, but she made no movement. He made none in return and switched his gaze back to street level.

'Did I miss anything while I was out of the room phoning the dentist, sir?' said Cradock, whose own attention appeared to be more focused on an attractive young woman walking by on the other side of the street. He dodged suddenly to avoid colliding with a lamp-post.

'You'll be missing a few teeth if you don't watch where you're going,' Jago admonished him. 'But I think all you missed up there was Mrs Latham saying her husband was earning six pounds a week, so I reckon he must've been doing pretty well in his job.'

'It's certainly more than I get,' Cradock replied glumly.

'Yes, but he was older than you, wasn't he?'

'And he wasn't a policeman.'

'Would you rather have his job, then? Running round all over the place trying to persuade shopkeepers to sell your chocolate bars?'

'Maybe.'

Jago laughed. 'You'd be no good in a job like that – you get so peckish all the time you'd be eating half the stock.'

Cradock's expression suggested he felt hard done by, but Jago ignored it. 'The only other thing she mentioned,' he said, 'was that her husband was pally with another traveller at Barings, name of Jack Henderson, so we'd better have a word with him and see what we can find out. But first we'll pay a visit to Mr Bowen at his garage.'

They got into the car and set off for Crogsland Road, following Rose Latham's directions, and soon spotted a building with a sign saying 'Bowen's Garage', as she had described. It was a cheap-looking structure made from corrugated iron, with a ridged roof and a large opening at the front to admit vehicles. A pair of petrol pumps stood guard in front of it, and a gate to the left led down to a yard, where Jago glimpsed the end of a curious type of wooden shed that he couldn't identify.

As they approached the garage entrance a man in grease-stained overalls came out towards them, wiping his hands on a rag. He was about fifty, Jago guessed: tall and well-built, with neatly cut greying hair.

'Morning, gentlemen,' he said. 'How can I help you?'

'Mr Bowen?' said Jago.

'That's me.' He gestured up towards the sign. 'And this is my business, as you can see. Servicing, repairs and fuel.' He glanced to where Jago's car was parked. 'Playing up, is she?'

'Actually we're not here as customers, Mr Bowen,' said Jago. 'We're police officers.'

They showed him their identification cards, which Bowen examined closely. 'Right,' he said. 'All the same, how can I help you?'

'We'd like to have a word with you concerning Mr Les Latham. We understand you looked after his car.'

'Yes, that's right. What's he's done now then? Got himself in trouble?'

'I'm very sorry, Mr Bowen, but I'm afraid I have to tell you Mr Latham is dead.'

'Dead? Oh, dear – poor fellow. What happened?'

'His body was found in his car – there'd been a fire.'

'You mean a fire in the car?'

'That's correct. Were you responsible for servicing it?'

'Hang on a minute – are you suggesting it was my fault?'

'No, I'm not. I just want to know whether you service his car.'

'All right, then, I do.'

'And you're not aware of anything wrong with it that could've caused a fire?'

'Certainly not. Are you?'

'No, Mr Bowen, but we're treating it as a suspicious death, so we're trying to piece together what happened, and any information you can provide might help us do that.'

'A suspicious death? What does that mean?'

'At this stage it means we don't know what happened. Now, I understand Mr Latham kept his car here overnight. Is that correct?'

'Yes, that's right – it's one of the rules at his company, apparently.'

'When did you last see him?'

'It was this morning – he came to pick up the car, as usual.'

'What time was that?'

'I don't know exactly, but at a guess I'd say it was about ten past seven. I open up about seven, and I hadn't long started work when he arrived.'

'And then he set off in the car?'

'That's right, yes.'

'In that case it looks as though you may've been the last person to see him alive. Do you know where he was going?'

'No.' Bowen was beginning to sound anxious. 'I haven't a clue. He just said goodbye and went, and that's all.'

'Are you sure?'

'Yes, I am.'

'How did he seem when he left here?'

'Same as always – you know, seemed to be looking forward to the day.'

'Not worried about anything?'

'No, no – but I don't think I ever saw him worried about anything. He wasn't that sort of bloke.'

'Was there anyone else with him?'

'No, he was on his own, as usual.'

'And what did you do when he left?'

'Me? Oh, I got to work on that ancient Vauxhall over there – I'm trying to do it up so I can sell it. No one's making cars for civilians any more because of the war, so you can't get a new one for love nor money. That's pushing up the demand for good second-hand ones, of course, so I'm hoping if I can get that old bus going I'll find a buyer.'

'Was anyone here with you?'

'No, I work on my own nowadays. Trade's been poor since the war started, you see. So many people've had their cars requisitioned, and the ones who managed to hang on to theirs can't get the petrol now it's rationed, so half of them've just laid their cars up for the duration. I keep my ear to the ground as far as business is concerned, and from what I hear it's been bad for all the garages round here. I think Les was very thankful that he still had his car – he loved driving.'

'So apart from his love of driving, what kind of man would you say Mr Latham was?'

'Oh, just a normal kind of bloke, as far as I know. Cheerful, like I said, and friendly, and he always looked very smart, but I suppose in his line of work he had to be. He was a salesman – a commercial traveller – so he must've had to make the right impression. Good at his job too, by all accounts – his wife told me he could sell ice cream to Eskimos.'

'You know Mrs Latham, then?'

'Well, I can't say I know her that well. I've met her, you know, once or twice when she was with him when he brought the car in.'

'I see. What else can you tell me about Mr Latham?'

'Nothing, really. He always paid me on time, but then again that would've been the company's money, not his. Always very polite, considerate – said thank you and all that. But I can't say as I really knew him – we weren't mates or anything like that. Our relationship was strictly business. Still, I'm very sorry to hear he's died. Will that be all now? I don't think there's anything more I can tell you.'

'Yes, that'll be all for now, thank you – we'll let you get on with your work. Goodbye.'

Jago turned to leave.

'Oh, by the way,' said Bowen, 'can you let me know if you find out how it happened? The fire, I mean. If word gets round that a car I service caught on fire . . . Well, I don't want people thinking it was anything to do with me – that wouldn't be good for business at all.'

Jago glanced back at him. 'Don't worry, Mr Bowen. We'll let you know.'

CHAPTER SEVEN

It was time to see what conclusions, if any, Dr Gibson had been able to draw from his post-mortem examination of the body. This was a part of his investigations that Jago never enjoyed, and as he and Cradock drove down to St George's Hospital at Hyde Park Corner he was hoping the pathologist's report would be brief.

At the hospital they were met by Gibson's lab technician and general assistant, Mr Spindle. They'd met him before, but his first name hadn't featured in their introductions, and they remained in ignorance of what it might be. His appearance, as when they'd first seen him, was sombre. Despite his white coat, there was something decidedly funereal about his manner that left Jago feeling the man might just as easily have found his niche in life as an undertaker.

'Good morning, gentlemen,' he said in a lugubrious tone. 'Dr Gibson said you were coming in connection with the unfortunate case of the car fire. Not a nice way to depart this sorry world, if I might say so.'

'Correct,' said Jago. 'I can't say I envy you in your work.'

'Indeed, sir. We've had them all in here, of course – strangled, drowned, garrotted, shot, not to mention poisoned, beaten, and run down by trams. If there's one thing working here all these years has taught me, if you don't mind me saying so, it's that death's a great leveller. You can be a duke or a dustman in life, but once you get here on the slab you're just a dead body, as naked as the day you were born, and your soul's departed. Wondering where it's going to end up, I don't doubt. Now, if you'd like to come with me, I'll take you to the post-mortem room.'

They followed him down a corridor, Jago musing on the fact that Spindle even had a curiously solemn way of walking, like a begaitered bishop on his way to inspect a parish. They arrived at the door to the post-mortem room and Spindle ushered them in.

In the centre of the room stood Dr Gibson, also in a white coat, bent over the unmistakable charred victim of the fire. He straightened up on hearing the door open and turned to face them.

'Ah, hello again,' he said with a broad smile. 'So, you've come to see what delights I've turned up for you.'

Not for the first time, Jago was puzzled at how an apparently normal man could take pleasure in such gruesome work, but the evidence was there before him. Horses for courses, he supposed.

'Oh, yes – I can't wait,' he replied, inwardly blaming his involuntary shiver on the chilly temperature in the white-tiled room. 'Could we possibly discuss your findings somewhere a bit warmer than this?'

'Yes, of course – let's go to my office.'

They adjourned to a small room along the corridor. It was marginally warmer than the post-mortem room and offered a motley collection of chairs for them to sit on. As Gibson closed the door behind them the faint wail of an air-raid siren could be heard in the distance.

'Doesn't sound too close,' he said. 'I think we'll be fine here, unless you'd rather go to the shelter.'

'If you think it's OK here, we'll stay,' said Jago.

Gibson laughed. 'Believe it or not, our air-raid shelter is the outpatients' department. As far as protection's concerned, the windows have been sandbagged, but that's about as far as it goes. It's right next to where the water mains come into the building too, so if anything hits us it'll be a toss-up whether we get buried under the rubble or just drowned. But in any case, when the raids are on we're too busy to take shelter, so most of us don't bother now.'

Jago recognised the macabre humour of the trenches in Gibson's words, but he also knew it was a way of dealing with the horror. He remembered the old fears that had surfaced in himself when the Blitz started in September, and he wondered whether the doctor had felt the same way. Now, however, was not the time to ask.

'Let's get down to business, then,' he said. 'First of all, we think we know who the man on your slab is – we've traced his address through the car's registration number, and his wife's confirmed he wore a medallion and watch like the ones you found on the body.'

'Good,' said Gibson. 'It's Mr Les Latham, isn't it?'

'How did you know that?'

'You told the dentist.'

'Ah, of course. So he's been in touch already?'

'Yes, he's been and gone – came straight down here. He brought Mr Latham's records with him and had a look at the dead man's teeth – there were five fillings, all of which corresponded with his record of work he'd done on said Mr Latham.'

'And his judgement's reliable?'

'Conclusive, I'd say. I'm no dentist, but he seems to know his stuff. I should note that with regard to my own "stuff", before he got here I'd managed to examine the deceased's pelvic bones and established that they're definitely male.'

'Thanks very much. So now at least we can be confident that we have a male body, and that it's the mortal remains of Mr Les Latham.'

'Exactly – beyond reasonable doubt, as the lawyers like to say. And while a name won't make any difference to what I'm able to establish, there's certainly an administrative advantage in being able to label the body correctly. Isn't that right, Spindle?'

His assistant nodded sagely. 'Undoubtedly, sir. We like to get their names right.'

Jago responded with a polite smile. 'So, what else have you established?'

'Where would you like me to start?' said Gibson.

'With the cause of death, if you don't mind. Judging by what we saw at the scene and what Jackson from the fire brigade said, I think we can rule out a motoring accident. The car was parked, the ignition was switched off, and there was no collision damage to the bodywork.'

'That certainly sounds plausible, but the mechanical details are not really my field.'

'What about natural death, Doctor?' Cradock interjected. 'Like a heart attack. You were going to check.'

'Yes, I did check, and I couldn't find any evidence of sudden death by natural causes.'

'So to my mind that leaves just suicide or murder,' said Jago. 'What do you think?'

'Well, let's consider the possibility of suicide first.'

Jago grimaced. 'I'm long enough in the tooth to know anything's possible,' he said, 'but I have to say I find it difficult to believe it was suicide. I mean, deliberately setting fire to yourself as a way of ending it all – it's such an awful way to go, and there are much less painful ways to do it.'

'I agree,' said Gibson. 'Actually, suicide by burning's almost unknown in Europe, but there have been cases where men or women have poured petrol or paraffin over themselves and set light to it, and burnt to death. And then there are the deaths that look like suicide but are actually murder. You remember the Rouse case?'

'Yes – about ten years ago, wasn't it?'

'That's right. A blazing car with a body in it burnt beyond recognition. It was Alfred Rouse's car, and they thought it was his body too, but it wasn't – it turned out he'd picked up some other fellow, offered him a lift and plied him with whisky, then killed him, leaving people to conclude it was himself who'd perished in the flames. He nearly got away with it too.'

'Nearly, yes. But in our case it's different, isn't it? The company's confirmed it's Latham's car, and the dentist's confirmed it's his body, so he obviously hasn't faked his own suicide.'

'Quite. It's not a fake suicide, and I don't think it's a genuine one either.'

'So you've established that someone burnt him to death intentionally?'

'Not exactly. As a matter of fact, murder by burning is comparatively rare, but I don't believe that's what this was anyway – I think it was just plain murder. The thing is, I found no carbon monoxide in his bloodstream and no smoke particles in his air passages. They can only get into your body if you're breathing, and that means Mr Latham must have stopped breathing before the fire started.'

'So he was already dead?'

'Exactly. And I think the idea of a man starting a fire after he's died can be safely ruled out.'

Jago smiled at the doctor's wit but couldn't quite bring himself to laugh. 'I assume the idea of someone else trying to make it look like suicide still can't be ruled out, though.'

'You're right – it may have been an attempt to do that. I mean if you do away with someone and you don't know about things like carbon monoxide or smoke particles, it might seem an obvious way to cover your tracks. And if you don't read the newspapers and follow the trials, you'll probably have no idea of what we pathologists can find out nowadays. Anyway, if this particular blaze was an attempt to pull the wool over our eyes, I can tell you our murderer has certainly failed.'

'So if it wasn't the fire that killed him, have your clever tricks come up with anything to indicate how he was murdered?'

'Well, I haven't found any lethal skull fracture consistent with a blow from a hammer or a similar weapon, so we can rule that out. Nor are there any wounds to indicate he was shot or stabbed.'

'Could he have been strangled?'

'That's more difficult to establish. There have been cases where a victim was strangled and then burnt, but whether one can find the evidence of such a strangling after the fire depends on how severe it was. In some cases even after a very intense fire we can identify ligature marks, for example, but burns can generally obscure signs of strangulation, and certainly of things like bruising. In this case I couldn't find any signs of strangulation, nor did I find the hyoid bone was broken, which is common in stranglings.'

'So on balance you'd say he wasn't strangled.'

'I can't rule it out categorically – all I can say is the hyoid bone wasn't broken.'

'What about suffocation?'

'That's another possibility. It could render the victim unconscious or kill him, either of which would enable the murderer to start a fire in the hope of covering their tracks, although in this case the absence of smoke particles and carbon monoxide would require the victim to have been suffocated to death before the fire started. Unfortunately evidence of suffocation would not have survived the fire damage. You only have to glance at the body to see that.'

Jago ignored the invitation: he'd already had one glance, and that was one more than he'd have wished. 'So,' he said, 'to sum up, all we can say is he wasn't shot, stabbed, strangled or beaten to death, but he might possibly have been suffocated, and it definitely wasn't the fire that killed him. And we're to treat this case as suspected murder, because a dead man can't start a fire.'

'I can't put it quite that way in my report,' Gibson replied, 'but I think it would not be inappropriate for you to pursue your enquiries on that basis.'

CHAPTER EIGHT

'Right,' said Jago as he and Cradock came out of the hospital, fortified by a bite to eat with Gibson in the refectory, 'we need to bring Mrs Latham up to date with the results of the post-mortem. She knows her husband's dead, poor woman, but now we'll have to tell her we think it was murder. Never the best thing about this job, is it?'

Cradock murmured his agreement as they got into the car.

'I want to call in at Kentish Town station on the way too,' Jago continued, 'and find out whether our esteemed colleagues there have got anywhere for us to sleep tonight. I don't fancy bedding down on the canal towpath at this time of year. Get your map out and tell us how to get to Holmes Road.'

Cradock navigated them successfully, and half an hour later they pulled up outside the police station. They went in and introduced themselves to the desk sergeant.

'Ah, yes, sir,' said the sergeant. 'We've been expecting you.'

'Good. I assume you're fixing up somewhere for me and DC Cradock to stay while we're here.'

'That's right, sir. We've booked you into a little hotel that we sometimes use for visitors. Well, it calls itself a hotel, but it's more of a boarding house really. There's a room each for you, and it's bed and breakfast, with an evening meal on request – all very cosy. It's just over the road at 17 Raglan Street, so you can always pop round here and eat in the canteen if you prefer. The landlady's called Mrs Minter and she's all right when you get to know her. Anything else you need to know about the accommodation arrangements, sir?'

'No, thank you, but can you tell me where the nearest Ministry of Transport office is? I want to ask someone a few questions about petrol coupons.'

'That'll be at what used to be the junior school in Hawley Crescent – if you go back down Kentish Town Road it's the first turning on the right after you cross the canal. The school got taken over when all the kids were evacuated last year and now it's the Ministry of Transport depot, and the ARP use part of it for sleeping accommodation for their people.'

'Thanks. Are there any messages for me?'

'Yes, sir. Detective Superintendent Hardacre wants you to report to him at Scotland Yard at nine o'clock sharp tomorrow morning.'

'Thank you. I think we'll go and drop our stuff off at this "hotel" of yours now.'

'Very good, sir. Oh, by the way, one of our men's

phoned in with a message that might be of interest to you.'

'Oh, yes? And what's that?'

'He said a Mrs Gladys Wilson stopped him as he was passing her house, sir. Seems she'd dropped a milk bottle.'

The sergeant paused, as if for dramatic effect.

'And?' Jago enquired. 'Is this a police matter?'

'Oh, yes, sir. Fortunately it was an empty one, so she didn't lose a pint of milk, but she'd just washed it and was putting it out for the milkman when it slipped through her fingers and smashed on the doorstep.'

'Right. Could you just get to the point, please?'

'Sorry, sir. I know you've got a body in a burning car to sort out, but that's the point – you'll be interested in this. She cleared up the glass and took it round to the alley to put it in her dustbin, but then when she took the lid off the bin she found an empty petrol can in it and reported it to our man on the beat.'

'And what did he do with it?'

'He's taken it into custody, sir. Or at least, he's bringing it back here now. Thought it might be a clue, seeing as how the woman lives down at the end of Baynes Street, number 22, where the railway bridge is, and that's near where that car was found on fire, isn't it? He says it's the regular sort of square two-gallon can that people carry about in the boot of their car in case they run out. Interesting, wouldn't you say, sir?'

'I would, yes. How long will it take your man to get here?'

'About fifteen minutes, sir. But he phoned just before you arrived, so he should be here in a few minutes.'

'OK. Well look, we'll take our things over to Raglan

Street and come straight back. Tell him to wait here if he arrives before we do.'

'Yes, sir.'

Jago and Cradock took their modest luggage from the car and walked round to the address in Raglan Street. As the desk sergeant had intimated, to call the property a hotel was perhaps overstating its merits. It was a drab-looking terraced house, its only embellishment being a small bay window on the ground floor. The landlady answered their knock at the door and looked them up and down suspiciously, as if they might be impostors. After demanding to see their identity cards and warrant cards, however, she appeared satisfied and admitted them. They received the keys to their rooms together with her firm instructions about use of the bathroom, time for breakfast, and what she considered an appropriate hour by which they should return quietly at night. When she'd finished they were allowed to carry their luggage up to their respective rooms.

'Thank you,' said Jago when they came back downstairs.

'You're welcome,' she replied in a curiously unwelcoming tone of voice, as if it pained her to express such a sentiment. 'I'm sure your stay here will be very comfortable.'

'I hope so, yes, but we must be off now.'

'Not so fast,' she said, stepping into his way. 'If you expect me to cook you your breakfast, you'll hand over your ration books to me now. I'm sure you know the regulations – no ration book, no food.'

'Of course. Very sorry.' He took his ration book from his pocket and surrendered it, and Cradock did the same.

She examined the ration books carefully, as if expecting

a pair of Metropolitan Police officers might be passing her fakes, then pocketed them. 'Right, they seem to be in order, but have you ordered your new ones? These expire on the fifth of January, and I don't want to get caught out.'

'Caught out?'

'Yes – last time the ration books ran out, in June that was, I had someone staying here who hadn't got round to applying for his new one. It turned up so late, I didn't have it in time for his first week of rations, so he was expecting me to feed him with no food. I don't care who you are – I'm not having that happening again.'

'I'll make sure it doesn't happen, Mrs Minter, although I very much hope we won't still be here in January.'

'Please yourselves,' she sniffed. 'You can have them back when you leave. And another thing – since you're police officers, I allow incoming phone calls, and if you're not here I'll take messages. All outgoing calls will be timed, and will be paid for by you, in cash. Is that clear?'

'Very clear, Mrs Minter,' Jago replied. 'We're obliged to you.'

She acknowledged his expression of gratitude with another sniff and a curt nod of her head. Jago doffed his hat, and he and Cradock walked back to the police station.

'She doesn't look like she'd stand for any nonsense,' said Cradock. 'Worse than my mum.'

'I expect she's learnt from experience,' Jago replied. 'Bad experience, judging by the sound of it.'

At the station they found a young constable waiting for them, with a petrol can standing on a rag on the floor beside him. The air was pungent with the smell of motor fuel.

'Here he is, sir,' said the desk sergeant. 'The man with the can.'

'Yes. Thank you, Sergeant,' said Jago. He turned to Cradock. 'Check it for prints, please, Peter.'

'Yes, sir,' said Cradock. He fetched his equipment from the car, moved the petrol can and the rag carefully to one side of the room and set to work.

'Now, then, Constable,' said Jago to the young uniform man. 'Are we going to find your prints all over this can?'

'No, sir. I knew there'd been that car fire and that it was suspicious, so as soon as I saw the petrol can I asked Mrs Wilson, the lady whose dustbin it was in, for a rag and I wrapped my hand in it before touching anything.'

'Good man.'

The constable's face relaxed into a smile of relief that he hadn't done anything wrong. 'Thank you, sir.'

Cradock finished dusting the can and looked up from his crouched position on the floor. 'Clean as a whistle, guv'nor – no prints on it.'

'You mean nothing at all?'

'That's right, sir. A bit surprising, isn't it?'

'Indeed, unless this Mrs Wilson is so house-proud that she wipes the contents of her dustbin clean before handing them over to a policeman.'

'But not surprising if whoever dumped it had just set fire to a car with a man in it, eh, sir?'

'Indeed.'

'It's a bit gruesome, though, isn't it? Burning to death, I mean. I can see why it's not a method many people choose when they want to do themselves in. A touch too messy for my liking, but I suppose it appeals to some.'

There was a casual lightness in Cradock's remark that almost brought a rebuke to Jago's lips. It was a terrible way to die. But he couldn't blame the boy – he was too young to have seen men burnt alive, and Jago hoped he never would.

CHAPTER NINE

The uniform constable had no further light to shed on the petrol can, so Jago headed for the door. Cradock picked up the can and followed, but after a couple of paces Jago looked back at him and stopped. 'That thing stinks to high heaven, Peter,' he said. 'Run back and get that rag, and stuff it in the top of the can to stop the smell getting out. If we come back to Mrs Minter reeking of petrol she'll probably refuse to let us in. And if you're hoping to get extra helpings with your breakfast you'd better keep on the right side of her, just in case.'

'Yes, sir,' said Cradock. 'I just hope she's got good mattresses on those beds of hers. You never know with places like that, do you, even if she does call it a hotel.'

'No,' said Jago as his young colleague disappeared in search of the rag. He waited by the door. Cradock's parting remark had sent his thoughts wandering to another hotel, the Savoy, where his American journalist friend Dorothy was living by courtesy of her paper, the *Boston Post*, all expenses paid. Now that was a real hotel. He wondered what kind of living and working conditions he might be enjoying now if conscription in the Great War hadn't interrupted his own journalistic aspirations at an early stage. Who was to say where he'd have ended up? But then again, if he'd stayed on a local paper like the *Stratford Express* and had to travel anywhere with his work, he'd probably still have been relying on the hospitality of establishments like Mrs Minter's, grateful just to have a roof over his head and a mattress of any description.

He unconsciously patted the inside pocket of his jacket to check that the note was still there. It had come in the post from Dorothy a few days ago, inviting him and Cradock – and his old friend Rita if she could drag herself away from her cafe in West Ham – to join her as her guests for a Thanksgiving dinner at an American restaurant near Piccadilly Circus. She'd said more than once that she'd introduce him to American food one day, so he guessed this would be her way of entertaining English friends to some traditional transatlantic fare. The date of this gathering was Thursday the twenty-eighth of November, just two days away, and the fact that he was quite unnecessarily carrying her invitation around with him forced him to admit, albeit only to himself, how much he was looking forward to it. Life seemed to grow surprisingly mundane when he didn't see her for a while.

Cradock returned, and it was time to suspend these reflections. 'Right, Peter,' he said, 'put that can in the boot and get in the car. I want to call on that Mrs Wilson who found it.' He checked his watch. 'But first we need to go and tell Mrs Latham what we think happened to her husband.'

They drove to Belmont Street, where they found Rose Latham in a subdued mood. She showed them into the living room with barely a word.

'I said we'd come back once we had the pathologist's findings,' Jago began.

'Yes,' she replied. 'I don't suppose the news is good.'

'I'm afraid it isn't. We asked your husband's dentist to examine the teeth of the man who was found dead this morning, and he's confirmed that the fillings and so on match the records of treatment he's given to your husband in the past few years. I'm sorry to have to tell you that we're now convinced it is your husband's body.'

She nodded with an air of quiet resignation. 'I thought you'd say that. What with the medallion and the watch, it couldn't have been anyone else. Thank you for coming, though. It helps to know. I've always been concerned about him driving in the blackout – it's so difficult to see where you're going. There's been so many accidents.'

'Actually, Mrs Latham, we're not convinced it was an accident, so there are one or two things I'd like to ask you.'

'Not an accident?'

'No.'

'You surely don't think he killed himself, do you? Les would never do that – he loved life too much. He wanted to get everything out of it he could.'

'No, I'm not saying that.'

'So you mean . . . you're saying . . . someone killed him? Deliberately?'

'At the moment that seems the most likely explanation, I'm afraid. We're now treating it as a case of suspected murder.'

'But that's impossible. I don't believe it.'

She sat down abruptly on a chair, shaking her head slowly. She took a small lace handkerchief from her sleeve and dabbed at her eyes. Jago waited in silence until she seemed to have composed herself.

'I'm very sorry, Mrs Latham,' he continued, 'but as I said, I have to ask you a few questions.'

'That's all right. Go ahead.'

'Thank you. I'm just wondering – was there anything on his mind recently? Did he seem troubled about anything?'

'Troubled? No. I'm the one who worries. Les was always bright and breezy, confident. Everything seemed to be going well for him.'

'Can you think of anyone who might've wanted to harm your husband?'

'No, I can't – he was everybody's friend. The life and soul of the party. I don't know a lot about his work, of course, but I don't recall him ever mentioning not getting on with someone.'

'Was there anyone in his past who might've wished him ill?'

'Not that I know of, no.'

'Anyone in his family?'

'He didn't have any family. His parents are both dead, and he didn't have any brothers or sisters, nor cousins as far as I know.'

'As far as you know?'

'What I mean is, I don't know everything about his

past – you never do when you marry someone, do you? You only know what they tell you.'

'I see. I'd like to ask you a little more about this morning – you said when we were here before that your husband was going to drive up to Cambridge today.'

'Yes, that's right.' She paused, gazing ahead as if her mind was elsewhere. 'I suppose I'll have to phone the place he stays and let them know he won't be coming, won't I?'

'Don't worry. If you can let us have the number we'll do that.'

'Oh, thank you, that would be kind. I've got it right here.' She reached into her handbag and pulled out a small address book, then thumbed through the pages until she found what she wanted. 'It's called the Fairview Commercial Hotel, in St Barnabas Road, and the phone number's Cambridge 4071. It's run by a lady called Mrs Roberts, I think.'

'Thank you. And once he'd picked up his car at Mr Bowen's garage, would he've set off straightaway for Cambridge?'

'Well, no, actually. That's why I was a bit worried – I was wondering where he'd got to. He said yesterday evening that he had to see someone in the morning before he set off, so when I woke up and saw he was gone, I was expecting he'd be back for his stuff.'

'What stuff?'

'His suitcase with his clothes and everything for the next few days. It was all still here when I got up, so I thought he must've been planning to fetch the car, see this whoever it was that he had to see, then come back here in the car to pick up his things and go.' Her voice trembled as she put the handkerchief to her eyes again. 'But he didn't come.'

'I'm very sorry, Mrs Latham, but would you mind if we took a look at these things your husband would've taken with him?'

'It's only his socks and shirts and collars and things.'

'Nevertheless, I'd appreciate being able to have a quick look.'

'All right, then. They're in the bedroom – Les uses one corner as a kind of office for when he's at home.'

She led them to a room at the back of the flat. Jago glanced round it and saw a wardrobe, a chest of drawers, and a double bed on which lay a fastened suitcase. In the corner near the window were a kitchen chair and a small table laden with numerous papers, a cardboard box and a large notebook. Next to the box stood a jug of water and a glass. 'Is that something your husband used?' he asked, pointing to the glass.

'Yes – when he was working.'

'Do you mind if we take it away with us? I'd like to check it for fingerprints.'

'Why do you need his fingerprints?'

'It's just so that if we find anything relevant to this case and want to know who's touched it, we'll be able to eliminate his own prints.'

'Of course, take it away then, if it'll help.'

'Thank you. I'd like to start with a look in that suitcase.'

He opened the case on the bed. Inside were the clothes and shaving gear one would expect a man to take on a business trip. He moved some of the clothes aside and found an engraved silver case containing two sealed packs of playing cards. 'Your husband liked a game of cards?' he said, showing it to Rose.

'Yes, but not with me. That's pretty, isn't it? I haven't seen it before.'

'May I take it with me? I'll be sure to return it.'

'Yes, of course.'

Jago put the case into his pocket. He sifted the remaining clothes in the suitcase and noticed the corner of a small photograph protruding from beneath a folded shirt. He pulled it out: it showed only a thatched cottage. 'Any idea why this should be here, Mrs Latham?'

She took it from him and glanced at it, then shook her head. 'No. No idea, I'm afraid – never seen it before. Take that too, if you like.'

She handed the photo back to him, and he slipped this too into his pocket as he turned his attention to the wardrobe.

'May I take a look in here?' he asked.

'Yes, of course, that's where Les kept his work clothes.'

Jago opened the wardrobe door and found five suits hanging on the rail: more than he owned himself and, judging by the feel and weight of the cloth, better quality than his own. 'Very nice suits,' he said.

'Yes. He was always careful about his appearance. He said people won't buy from a salesman who looks like a tramp. You have to make the right impression, he said – it's one of the tricks of the trade.'

'Nice hats, too, sir, eh?' said Cradock, reaching for a shelf in the wardrobe on which sat an assortment of headgear. 'This looks like a very smart bowler.'

'Yes,' said Rose. 'That's what he wears for work. He's got that straw boater there for the summer, and he's got a nice flat cap for the winter – he wears that for driving, so he'll have taken it with him this morning.'

Jago edged his way round the bed to get to the table. 'Do you mind if we take these papers away with us, Mrs Latham?' he said. 'We may need to have a look at them, and I don't want to take up your time now.'

'Yes, of course. They'll just be things like orders and invoices, I expect. And that box, that's probably got some of his samples in it – chocolate bars or whatever to show to his customers.'

Jago looked into the box and found its contents seemed to confirm what she'd said. He picked up the notebook and began to leaf through it. 'Can you tell me what this is?'

'Yes,' she said. 'He's always looking at that before he goes away. He calls it his journey book – it says where all his customers are and which order to visit them in.'

'I see.'

Jago began to flick through the pages but stopped when three small paper items fell out of the back and onto the floor. He bent to pick them up. 'Petrol ration books,' he said.

'Really? I expect Les needed them for his work – he was always driving. Part of the job, of course, but he didn't mind that. He loved his cars, did Les – he could never wait to get his hands on the latest model.' She paused for a moment, hesitating awkwardly as if unsure what to say next. 'So yes, they'll be for his work.'

'Of course. I'll take these with me, and the book too.'

'Be my guest,' she replied. 'None of it's any use to me, but if it helps you find out what's happened, you're welcome to it.'

Jago handed the items to Cradock and looked round the room for anything else of potential interest. The only object that caught his eye was a second cardboard box on the floor next to the wardrobe. He knelt down and removed the lid: the box was full of beer mats. He pulled out a handful and held them up for Rose to see. 'Beer mats?' he said.

'Ah, yes,' said Rose. 'I think he collects them – he's got a stamp collection too. Why is it men always want to collect things? You don't find women doing it. I can only imagine it's because he spends a lot of time in pubs and hotel bars when he's travelling and he just picks them up, but it still beats me why he does it.'

'He probably wants to get one of every kind,' said Cradock.

'Exactly,' said Rose. 'But why? What's the point?'

The expression on Cradock's face suggested that to him this was an entirely plausible and adequate reason for collecting beer mats.

Rose shook her head slowly to signal her incomprehension. 'It's probably because he's a man, and that's all there is to it. But I must say, one thing I've always liked about Les is that he might spend a bit of time in pubs, but I've never seen him drunk. Not once, bless him. Jimmy says Les has never been one to drink too much.'

'Jimmy?'

'Oh, yes, sorry – Jimmy Trent. He and Les were mates in the army, back in the Great War. They still meet up for a drink from time to time at the Oxford Arms in Camden High Street when they're both around.' She paused as a thought seemed to dawn on her. 'I'll have to tell him, won't I? I don't know if I can do that. It'll be a terrible blow for him – they'd been through a lot together, those two. Look, Inspector, you don't think maybe you could . . .?'

'Yes, we'll tell him – there's no need for you to. Just tell us where we can find him.'

'Well, he's a boatman – you know, he works on the narrowboats, up and down the Regent's Canal. That means he's here in Camden Town quite often, so if you want to catch him, best to check at the locks – I think he moors his boat in the pound down there when he's here. Or if it's the evening, try the Oxford Arms. Otherwise just ask anyone on the canal and they'll tell you where he is. They all seem to know each other.'

'OK, we'll do that. Is there anyone else we should contact?'

'What about his work? They'll have to know, won't they?'

'Don't worry – we'll look after that. I'll be calling them later today to let them know what's happened.'

'Thank you. I can't think of anyone else apart from Jimmy and Barings. Like I said, Les's parents are both dead, and he was an only child, same as me. We didn't have any children, so I suppose we were the end of the line. And now—'

At this thought she began to sniffle and got her handkerchief out again. She waved her hand at him apologetically.

'I think that'll be all for now, Mrs Latham,' said Jago. 'We'll take these things with us and return them to you when we've finished with them. Do get in touch with us if you think of anything else that might help us – just call Kentish Town police station, and they'll pass it on. In the meantime, thank you for your help, and again please accept our condolences.'

Rose Latham nodded her acknowledgement, the handkerchief still clutched to her face.

'We'll let ourselves out,' said Jago, heading for the door as Cradock gathered up the glass and papers from the table. They stepped out onto the landing and he pulled the door shut behind them with a sigh. This wasn't the first time he'd had to do this, and it probably wouldn't be the last, but once again he was left feeling inadequate. What use were a policeman's condolences to a woman who'd gone to bed a wife and woken up a widow?

CHAPTER TEN

'Well,' said Jago as they settled into their seats in the Riley, 'that threw up a few items of interest, didn't it?'

'Yes, sir,' Cradock replied. 'Although I wasn't sure why you wanted to take that picture of a house away. Is it significant?'

'I've no idea, but it just struck me when I saw it that it was the only photo in that suitcase and it wasn't one of his wife, it was one of a house.' He took the photograph from his pocket. 'A nice little thatched cottage, mind, but still. Perhaps he was going to visit someone.' He flipped the photo over and saw a word written on the back: 'Shangri-La'. 'What's that, then?' he said. 'Does it mean anything to you?'

Cradock read it aloud. 'I'm not sure. It rings a bell, though.'

'Really?' It seemed to Jago that not many things rang a bell with Cradock. 'Tell me more.'

'I think it might be something from a film I haven't seen.'

'You remember things from films you haven't seen?'

'No, sir. But this was something Emily told me about when I took her to the pictures. She'd seen it, you see.'

Jago listened more attentively. He was aware that since Cradock had started walking out with his old friend Rita's daughter their budding relationship had involved going to the cinema, but his young assistant had always been somewhat cagey about what took place when they were there. 'What film?' he said.

'You mean the one we saw, or the one I hadn't seen?'

'The one you hadn't seen.'

'It was called *Lost Horizon*, I think, and Emily said the man in the paper reckoned it was the greatest film ever made. There was a place in it called something like Shangri-La – in Tibet, I think, some kind of perfect place where no one could find you and everyone was kind and lived for hundreds of years.'

'Hmm, a mixed blessing, then. A utopia?'

'A what, sir?'

'Never mind. The idea appealed to Emily, though, did it?'

'I don't know, sir – she didn't say. She said it was her favourite film, but that's because the hero was played by Ronald Colman, and she likes him. She said I ought to grow a moustache like his.'

Jago pictured Ronald Colman's sophisticated pencil moustache grafted onto Cradock's youthful face and thought his colleague would be wise to ignore her advice, but decided to let him discover that for himself. 'So maybe that's the name of the cottage in the photo,' he said.

'Someone's idea of the perfect place to live. A bit more imaginative than "Dunroamin", at any rate. But I'm just curious that he should be carrying it with him when he goes off to work.'

Cradock thought this an opportune moment to switch the conversation away from his love life with Emily. 'And speaking of Latham going off to work, sir, that journey book thing could be useful, couldn't it?'

'Indeed, it could. For one thing, it might tell us who he was planning to visit today. Those petrol ration books are interesting too.'

'Why's that, sir?'

'Because they haven't been stamped, that's why. Didn't you notice?'

'Sorry, sir, no. Is that important?'

'You don't have a car, do you, Peter? If you did, you'd know that when you go to the Post Office to get your petrol ration books, the clerk writes your car registration number on the front and then stamps it. So how did the Post Office come to issue these ration books without stamping them? It's highly suspicious.'

'You mean maybe he didn't get them from the Post Office?'

'Exactly.'

'Black market, perhaps?'

'It looks like that. It suggests that either they literally fell off the back of a lorry and he found them in the street, or more likely someone pinched them from His Majesty's Government and they came into Latham's hands illegally. I think we need to go to that Ministry of Transport depot and find out whether they're missing any. But first we ought to pay a visit to the lady who found the petrol can in her dustbin.'

He started the engine.

'Right,' said Cradock. 'And by the way, sir, the box of beer mats – was that significant?'

'No,' said Jago. 'Of course not.'

CHAPTER ELEVEN

On arriving in Baynes Street they drove past the entrance to the yard where the blazing car had been found and carried on to the far end, where the railway bridge crossed over the road. They stopped outside number 22, which was the last house on the right, overshadowed by the grimy brick arch of the bridge. Cradock jumped out of the car, opened the boot and retrieved the petrol can while Jago gazed up and down the rows of small terraced houses whose front doors all opened directly onto the street. Gladys Wilson's, like those of her neighbours, looked miserably neglected, its black paint peeling.

They knocked on the door and waited. It eventually creaked open, revealing a short, wiry woman who looked fifty but was probably younger. She invited them into the house once they'd identified themselves, Jago first, followed by Cradock with the petrol can.

'I'm afraid you'll have to take me as you find me,' she

said. 'My old man's away serving with an anti-aircraft searchlight regiment in South Wales, so I'm all on my own here, and what with the bombs and looking after his chickens it's all getting a bit too much.'

'We won't trouble you for long, Mrs Wilson,' said Jago. 'I'd like to thank you for having the good sense to report what you found in your dustbin this morning to the constable.'

She gave him what he assumed was meant to be a sweet smile, but it revealed teeth as neglected as her house.

'I wonder if you could just tell me what happened,' he said.

'Of course, dear. I was out in the scullery doing a bit of washing up – I'd left last night's stuff over, you see, since it's just me on my own here at the moment. I had an empty milk bottle, so I washed that too and took it through to the front door to leave it on the doorstep for the milkman.'

'Is that Mr Rickett?'

'That's right. He's lovely – he's been our milkman for a few years now. Very reliable, he is, and he always keeps an eye on the old people – you know, making sure they're all keeping well.'

'Thank you. I'm sorry to interrupt you – do carry on, please.'

'Right, well, the bottle was still wet, see, so it slipped through me fingers and smashed on the path. So there I am, broken glass all over the place. I picks the bits up, wraps them in some old newspaper, then takes it round to the alley at the back to put it in the dustbin, but when I takes the lid off, what do I find inside it but a petrol can I've never seen before.'

'This one?' said Cradock, holding it up for her inspection.

'That's the one. So anyway, I thought someone must've just dumped it in there because their own dustbin was full. No skin off my nose, I thought – I'll pop it in the salvage box. I mean, you know how the government keeps going on at us about saving all our scrap metal and waste paper and what have you. Well, I like to try and do my bit, so I keep some old cardboard boxes outside next to the dustbin for all that stuff, so the council can take it away and make it into tanks or Spitfires or whatever it is they do with it all.'

'Did you touch the can?'

'No. I was going to take it out of the dustbin and put it in the salvage box, like I was saying, but then my next-door neighbour came out to put something in her bin and she said had I heard about the fire there'd been in a car round the corner. I said no, but it dawned on me maybe an empty petrol can in my dustbin might have something to do with it, so I left it where it was and when the copper came by on his beat I stopped him and showed it to him. He seemed very interested and took it away.'

'Did you see anything else unexpected in your dustbin?'

'No, but it didn't occur to me to start rummaging around in all the old rubbish in case there was something else in there that shouldn't be.'

'Have a look please, Peter,' said Jago.

'Yes, sir,' said Cradock. He tipped out the battered metal bin's contents onto the ground, holding his head back in a vain attempt to keep his nose clear of the smell.

'Here, don't go making a mess,' said Mrs Wilson.

'Don't worry,' Jago replied. 'He'll put everything back in again when he's had a look.'

Cradock completed his search and reported nothing unusual found, then began to return everything into the bin.

'Wait a minute,' said Mrs Wilson. She jabbed a finger towards the bin. 'What's that there?'

She stepped past Cradock and fished into the dustbin to pull out a square of white material streaked black with grease.

'That's not mine,' she said. 'Look, it's a man's hankie. I haven't touched any of my husband's since he went off with the army months ago, and I certainly haven't thrown any of them out. And look at the state of it. Someone else must've put that in my bin.'

'Thank you,' said Jago. 'I'll take that away with me, if you don't mind.'

'Course not – it's not mine, is it? But that petrol can – do you reckon it was something to do with that fire?'

'I don't know, Mrs Wilson. But tell me – when do your dustmen come?'

'Thursday mornings, as a rule, although sometimes the air raids mess up their schedule.'

'Of course. And one last question – is there anything else you saw or heard that might shed any light on who left the can in your dustbin?'

'No, dear, I can't help you there I'm afraid.'

'In that case thank you very much. We'll be in touch again if there's anything else we need to ask you.'

'Any time, dearie. Mind how you go.'

CHAPTER TWELVE

Mrs Wilson remained standing in her front doorway while they made their way to the car, and when Jago glanced back she gave him a smile and a wave. The kind of woman, he thought, who considered it impolite to close her door on you as soon as you'd left her house, and who waved you off until you were well under way. It was only when he and Cradock got into the car that she closed the door and disappeared from view.

'So,' he said, 'what did you make of Mrs Wilson?'

'She's a sweetie,' Cradock replied. 'Reminds me of my mum – a bit cranky, perhaps, but harmless as far as I could tell. Looks like she may've done us a favour finding that petrol can in her dustbin, too. Makes you think maybe someone used it to set fire to that car, doesn't it?'

'Possibly. But there's no proof, is there? And we've no idea who put it there, or why.'

'What about that milkman?'

'Dumped the petrol can in Mrs Wilson's dustbin? Why would he do that?'

'Supposing he started the fire?'

'You mean he set fire to the car, then ran all the way up to Mrs Wilson's house at one end of the street carrying a petrol can, then all the way back to the other end and into the arms of our two constables, all the while dressed in his Express Dairy uniform and no doubt with his milk cart parked on the street by the yard for all the world to see? It doesn't sound like a very smart way to go about murdering someone. In any case, why would a milkman want to burn a commercial traveller to death in a disused builder's yard halfway through his round?'

'You're right, sir. I just thought it was worth considering the possibility.'

'Quite right, Peter, but I think with what Long's told us and the unsolicited character reference we've just had from Mrs Wilson we can probably rule him out. Unless some incriminating evidence comes to light I think we can assume he's just a passing member of the public spotting a fire and doing his civic duty reporting it to the police. Anything else?'

'Er, yes, sir – that hankie. D'you reckon whoever dumped the petrol can used it to wipe all the prints off? It would explain why the hankie was so mucky, wouldn't it?'

'Yes, it would. But it's not going to help us much. You probably noticed yourself there was no convenient monogram embroidered in the corner to give us our firebug's initials – it's just a man's hankie that could be his but could equally be one he'd pinched from someone's washing line.'

'Pity.'

'Yes, and in any case, as I'm sure you were about to say, the fact that it's a man's hankie doesn't necessarily mean it was a man who used it.'

'Of course, yes. By the way, sir, I was wondering – why did you ask her what day the dustmen come?'

'That's simple. I was just thinking the answer might tell us something about whoever it was who chucked that can in the bin. Leaving it there on a Tuesday if the bins aren't going to be emptied till Thursday, that's quite a risk – two whole days for Mrs Wilson to find it. If he lived nearby he'd probably know what day the dustmen come.'

'So you mean he's probably not from round here?'

'It's only a possibility – but then again it could be he's local but hadn't made a plan for how to dispose of the can and was acting on impulse.'

'Or just panicking?'

'Indeed. Either way I don't think it helps us much. I think we'd be better off going down to that depot before they close for business. I want to know what they can tell us about unstamped petrol ration books.'

It was after five o'clock by the time they arrived at the depot. On the outside, the building was still every inch a school, but on the inside it looked like an exhibition for flimsy partitioning: any classroom not already packed with stores seemed to have been hastily carved up into offices with thin hardboard walls. A sign at the entrance indicated that the Ministry of Transport wasn't the only official body represented on the premises. There was competition, it seemed, from Air Raid Precautions and the Ministry of Supply to name but two, but Jago guessed it must be the same up and down the country with so many new services mobilised to fight the war. The fact that there were at least signs to follow was something to be grateful for.

They soon found a door marked 'Ministry of Transport'. Jago gave a brisk knock and, when there was no response, pushed it open and peered in. The room beyond was gloomy and its furnishings were sparse: two desks, a few chairs and a row of cabinets, all of which looked as though they'd lain forgotten in some government store since the last war. It was inhabited by two women. One, who looked in her late thirties, was signing papers with a fountain pen. The other, tapping rapidly at the keys of her typewriter, was younger. Both wore the anonymous grey jackets and skirts which Jago assumed were the convention for women in the Civil Service.

'Excuse me,' he said. 'I'm looking for the manager of the depot. Can you tell me where I might find him?'

The older of the two women examined him with a penetrating gaze made the more forbidding by the tight bun in which her dark hair was drawn back. 'Here,' she said. 'And it's not him you've found, it's her.'

Jago sensed the weariness in her voice. 'I'm terribly sorry – I wasn't thinking.'

'Don't worry – you're not the first person to assume I can't be the manager because I'm not a man. It's the world we live in.'

'Quite. Well, let me introduce myself – I'm Detective Inspector Jago, and this is Detective Constable Cradock.'

'Come in, gentlemen. It's not often we have detectives visiting. Take a seat.' She waved her hand towards the only two empty chairs in the room. 'My name's Mallard, Miss Sarah Mallard, and this is Miss Shanks, my secretary.'

The younger woman looked up briefly from her typewriter to give them a hesitant smile of greeting, then resumed her work.

'You may not be surprised to learn,' Miss Mallard continued, 'that I'm only in this job because my predecessor has been elevated to a position of greater glory in the Ministry of Transport. I've no doubt normal service will be resumed when he returns at the end of the war, but for the time being the ministry has no alternative but to appoint women to fill the gaps, so you'll have to make do with me. So what is it that brings you here?'

'I'm hoping you might be able to spare us a few minutes of your time, Miss Mallard, to help us with our investigation.'

'An investigation? Yes, of course – if you think I can be of some assistance.'

'Thank you – I'm sure you must be very busy.'

'We are, Inspector, and we're short of staff these days, so we're putting in extra hours to get the work done. Now, what is it you need from me?'

'It's just a little information. Might we have a word in private?'

'Of course.'

She dismissed her colleague with a nod of her head, and the younger woman left the office.

'Thank you,' said Jago. 'I'd like to pick your brains on

the subject of petrol ration books and the system you have for handling them. You store them here, I believe.'

'That's correct. Motor spirit ration books – that's their official name. We do store them, but as you probably know, we're not the people who issue them to the public – our job is to supply stocks of them to post offices and the council taxation offices. Then drivers just have to go and present their car registration book to get three months' worth of coupons that they can use to buy petrol from a garage.'

'Thank you. Now, we've been looking at some recently in connection with our enquiries, and I'd like to know whether they'd have been distributed from this depot.'

He handed her the ration books from Latham's flat, and she examined them, jotting down the numbers on a piece of paper.

'Let me see now,' she replied. 'These books have got one coupon for one unit and two coupons for two, making a total of five units, so they'd be issued for cars of eight or nine horsepower. I expect you know a unit is still one gallon at the moment?'

'Yes, I do.'

'That could change, of course. Specifying the allowance in units instead of gallons means the government can change the amount of petrol people are entitled to without having to print millions of new coupons. Anyway, if you'll come with me, I'll check these numbers in our records.'

She led them out of the office and down a narrow corridor.

'So how many people do you have working here?' said Jago.

'It's about thirty at the moment,' she replied, 'so my job keeps me very busy. You know, even my own mother finds it difficult to believe I'm a manager in charge of so many people – but then she grew up in a different world, where women didn't do that kind of thing. She's in an old people's home now and becoming weaker in both body and mind, so I can't blame her for not keeping up, but some of my male colleagues in the Civil Service . . . ' She stopped at a door with a number twelve screwed to it and opened it without knocking. 'This is where we keep the records. Do go in.'

The walls of the small room were lined with filing cabinets and heavily laden shelves, but there was only one desk, at which a young man was seated, pen in hand, bent over a large ledger. His face suggested he was barely into his late twenties, but his ginger hair was already thinning, matched by a feeble ginger moustache that Jago recognised as the kind young men grew in the vain hope of looking mature. He rose to meet the two visitors, revealing his gangly frame, and removed his tortoise-shell glasses to fiddle with them awkwardly as he waited to be introduced. He struck Jago as a man trained to speak only when spoken to.

'This is Mr Hepworth,' said Miss Mallard. 'He's a clerical officer in the records department.'

Hepworth acknowledged their arrival with a nod, then glanced at his manager as if to check whether she wanted him to introduce himself, but she was already continuing.

'These gentlemen are police officers, Mr Hepworth, and they've come to ask us for a little help.'

'Good afternoon, Mr Hepworth,' said Jago. 'We're checking up on some petrol ration books. Do you deal with those?'

'Er, no, not ration books. I deal with vehicle registration books – what most people call their log book. We've been very busy with them since the air raids started to get so bad.'

'Really?'

'Absolutely – it's dreadful. For example, you might want to buy a second-hand car from someone, but the owner can't transfer the log book to you because he's been bombed out and it's been destroyed. So we have to do all the work to make sure that's correct, check our records and issue a replacement one. We're so busy now, it can take anything between three to four weeks to get it done, and people get—'

'Three *and*, Mr Hepworth,' said the manager, interrupting him, 'not three *to*. Between three *and* four weeks.'

'Sorry, Miss Mallard,' he mumbled, but she had turned away, raising her eyebrows to Jago as if suggesting that correct use of English was as important to the successful prosecution of the war as presence of mind and calm leadership, at least in the civil service.

'I'd like to see the ration book stock ledger, Mr Hepworth,' she continued. 'Could you fetch it for me, please?'

Hepworth went in search of the required volume and returned with a sturdily bound ledger, which he placed on the desk. Miss Mallard opened the ledger, found the page she was looking for and leant over it, running her finger down row upon row of numbers and dates. She did the same on the next page, then stood up straight and shook her head. 'No. The serial numbers on the ration books that you brought fall within a sequence listed here, but we don't have a record of any with those particular numbers having been issued.'

'And what does that mean?'

'It could mean either that they've got lost somewhere in the system or that we never received them from the ministry.'

'Lost in transit, you mean?'

'Yes. I believe they're printed in the Midlands and then transported to the various local depots, like this one, and I suppose whether that's by road or by rail, everything's vulnerable to war damage these days, so it's quite possible a batch could have been destroyed or gone missing.'

'And if they were lost in transit they could also have been found in transit?'

'I'm not sure what you mean.'

'Found their way into the wrong hands.'

'Oh, I see. Well yes, in theory, I suppose.'

'Or could it mean they were stolen from here?'

'Yes, I suppose that too is a possibility, in theory, but it's extremely unlikely that they would have been stolen from the depot itself – my staff are very trustworthy. It's also possible, of course, that they're forgeries, although I must say if they are, they're very good ones.'

'Is there anything you can do to help us find out more about the status of these ration books?'

'Well, in the first instance I shall ask the ministry whether they were dispatched, and if they were, I'll check whether they've gone missing in transit or here at the depot. As you can imagine, with every driver needing petrol coupons we're rushed off our feet, and sometimes things that go missing turn up again misfiled or stored in the wrong part of the depot. I'll let you know as soon as I get a reply, and in the meantime I'll remind the staff of the need for vigilance in our handling of these coupons.'

'Thank you.'

'Do please bear in mind, though, that we're having to cope with an inordinate volume of work. People expect us to do the impossible with very limited resources, and it's not surprising if the occasional administrative error occurs. When it does, we find ourselves the target of the most unreasonable complaints, but really, we're working under extraordinary strain.'

She paused, as if to observe the effect of this account of her plight, but Jago couldn't help thinking that her workload and that of her colleagues, onerous as it might seem to her, was not quite comparable with the perils of a fireman battling to save lives and burning buildings in the middle of an air raid. He kept his thoughts to himself, but feared his expression might have betrayed him.

'I tell you,' she said, 'we're run off our feet here, Inspector. So if you think civil servants spend all day drinking cups of tea and go home at four o'clock in the afternoon, you're mistaken – very mistaken indeed.'

CHAPTER THIRTEEN

The Oxford Arms was a cosy little Victorian pub nestling on the corner of Camden High Street and Jamestown Road, only a stone's throw from the Regent's Canal. A few early-evening drinkers were already slaking their thirst in the public bar, and when Jago enquired of the barmaid whether one of them was Jimmy Trent, she discreetly pointed out a man in rough working clothes seated at a table on the far side. Jago bought a couple of pints of beer for himself and Cradock, and as they approached the table, the man lifted his weather-beaten face and eyed them suspiciously.

'Mr Trent?' said Jago casually, doing his best not to sound intimidating.

'Yes. Who wants to know?'

'I'm sorry to interrupt you, but I wonder if we might join you for a moment. We're police officers – I'm Detective Inspector Jago and this is Detective Constable Cradock.'

'Ah, right – I thought you looked like coppers.'

Jago knew from long experience that there was a sector of the population that always claimed to be able to spot a plain-clothes policeman. Some even attributed this gift to their keen sense of smell, but he didn't want to prejudge Trent's character. 'Is it that obvious?' he said.

'No, it's just when two blokes you've never seen before come into your local and ask if they can join you, it usually means trouble. Not always police trouble, of course, but trouble.'

'Well, just to put your mind at rest, we're not here to get you into any kind of trouble. I'm hoping you might be able to help us.' He glanced down at Trent's glass, empty save for a mere inch or so of beer at the bottom. 'Can I get you another?'

'Don't mind if I do – a pint of bitter, please.' He drained his glass and handed it to Jago, who went to the bar and got it refilled.

'There you are,' he said on his return, placing the beer on the table in front of Trent and sitting down. He raised his own glass. 'Cheers.'

'Cheers,' Trent responded. 'So what's this all about?'

'Well, we're here with some bad news, I'm afraid.'

Trent looked alarmed. 'Not Annie?'

'Annie?'

'My missus – nothing's happened to her, has it?'

'No, no. It's about someone who I understand is an old friend of yours – Mr Latham.'

'Les, you mean?'

'That's right. I'm sorry to have to tell you this, Mr Trent, but your friend died this morning.'

Trent's face was expressionless. He let out a long breath

and shook his head slowly. 'Well, that's that, then, isn't it?'

'You sound as though you're not surprised.'

'Oh, no, it's not that. I'm very surprised. I suppose it's just that when you've seen a lot of friends die, you kind of accept it as normal. I think it was the war did that to me. You know – when your time's up, there's nothing you can do about it. One minute you're here, next minute you're gone. I shall miss him, though – we were good pals in very bad times. Can you tell me what happened?'

'He was found dead in his car this morning, and the car had been destroyed by fire.'

'An accident? An air-raid?'

'No. We believe he was murdered.'

Despite the calmness with which he'd reacted to the mention of Latham's death, Trent seemed taken aback by this new information. 'Murdered. Who by?'

'That's what we're investigating, and it's why we'd like to talk to you – since you were friends, we're hoping you might be able to shed some light on what kind of man Mr Latham was and help us to find whoever took his life.'

'Well, I'll certainly help you any way I can. It doesn't seem real, though – he was always such a character, you know, a larger-than-life sort of bloke.' He paused, as if dwelling on this memory of his friend. 'But wait a minute – how did you know to find me here?'

'Mrs Latham told us you and her husband used to have a drink together from time to time, and she suggested we look for you here.'

'Oh, that's all right then.'

'When did you last see him, by the way?'

'I couldn't say exactly, but not for a few weeks – he's

away quite a lot, and I'm up and down the canal all the time.'

'How long had you known him?'

'Hmm . . . getting on for twenty-five years, I suppose. I got to know him in the army during the war, when we discovered we were both from the same part of the world. He was a Camden Town boy and I – well, I was born on a boat and I'll probably die on a boat, so you could say I'm from nowhere and everywhere. But me and my family before me, we've always worked up and down the canal, and I'd spent a lot of time loading and offloading here. Somehow we both made it through the war, although mine was a bit longer than his, and when it was all over and he was back home and I was on the boat again we used to meet up here in the pub whenever I was passing through – we'd have a drink together and play some cards.'

'You said your war was longer than his – why was that?'

'Oh, nothing, really. It just took us off in different directions, that's all. We were both in the trenches to start with, in the Middlesex Regiment, but then I was taken out to be batman to an officer who got posted to the Royal Sussex, and Les got himself a job as driver to some bigwig staff officer. I would've been demobbed when the war ended, like Les, but no such luck – about a month before it ended my officer was ordered out to North Russia, so of course I had to go with him. They said it was something to do with a civil war, but I never really understood what it was all about. All I know is it was colder than I've ever been in my life, before or since, and by the time I saw Les again it was late in 1919.'

'Was he working as a commercial traveller by then?'

'Lord love us, no. Les had a terrible time trying to find a steady job after the war – first time we met up, the best he'd been able to get was a bit of casual labouring at Lawford's Wharf here on the canal. He was living in Rowton House.' He paused knowingly, but Jago showed no sign of recognising the name, and Cradock's face was conspicuously blank. 'It's a big place in Arlington Road – you can't miss it. A hostel for homeless men. He said they had more than a thousand men sleeping there – you could rent a little cubicle with a bed and nothing else for sevenpence a night. It had things like toilets and places to wash that I've never had on my boat, but it wasn't what Les was hoping for in life. He said he felt ashamed to be living in a place like that and he'd be out of it the first chance he got.'

'He was very motivated to find some better work, then?'

'I'd say he was, yes. He was a determined sort of bloke – knew what he wanted, and always seemed to reckon he knew how to get it.'

'Can I just take you back to what you said about playing cards with him?' Jago took from his pocket the card case he'd found at Latham's house and nudged it across the table. 'Do you recognise this?'

Trent smiled. 'Oh, yes, it belongs to Les. Pretty, isn't it? I don't suppose it's real silver, but even if it's only plated, it's certainly something he could never have afforded back in those early days. He loved his cards, though, and he liked to act a bit classy, so I expect he treated himself to that when he started getting regular money.'

'Was he a serious card player?'

'Yes, he was. We both got into the habit when we were in the army – there wasn't much in the way of entertainment, so any spare time we had, all the men just smoked and played cards. I'm sure you'll recall that, if you were a soldier yourself.'

Jago nodded. He remembered it well.

'Do you play?' Trent continued.

'No,' said Jago, shaking his head. 'It lost its appeal for me after the war.'

'I suppose we never broke the habit. Poker was Les's game, and he took it very seriously.'

'And you too?'

'Not really, no. I think when Les played with me it was more for practice.'

'Practice?'

'Yes. We both learnt a lot of card tricks in the army, see, and Les liked to keep his hand in, so we'd meet up for a drink and a game here, and we'd see who could get away with the most tricks – trying to catch each other out, like. He was much better at it than me, though. It's what got him his first proper job, you know, after the war.'

'And what was that?'

'You know Goodall's?'

'The card makers?'

'Yes. Biggest in the world, they say. They had their factory just round the corner from here until about ten years ago. Huge place it was – they used to have a thousand people working there, making a couple of million packs of cards a year – imagine that. I reckon that's what got Les interested in working for them. It was obvious, I suppose – if they made that many cards, there must be millions of people playing, and that meant a lot of people in need of buying some. In the end he got a job with them as a commercial traveller, and whenever he visited a potential new customer he'd demonstrate the cards by doing some fancy shuffling and a few tricks – pick any card, that sort of thing. They loved it and usually bought some. Some of those tricks are dead easy, but Les used to say people only see what they're expecting to see, so if they're expecting magic, that's what they'll see.'

'Did Mr Latham use his card skills for personal gain?'

'What do you mean?'

'I'm just wondering whether he played for money. Did he with you?'

'Once or twice, maybe, but no – you don't have money to spare if you work on the boats, and well, I couldn't afford it.'

'What about other people? Did he play with them for money?'

'I think he did, yes – the thing is, he liked a taste of the good life, and you need a bit of cash for that, don't you? I think that's why he never tried selling things like encyclopaedias or brushes – playing cards and then chocolates, they were his lines. He knew the best way to make money is to sell stuff that people want to buy, and he found plenty of customers. I think he wasn't averse to making a bit of money on the side, too. But don't tell Rose I said that – I don't think she knows.'

'Making money on the side? You mean by winning it at cards?'

'I think so, yes.'

'Well, thank you, Mr Trent, you've been most helpful.

Now, if we need to talk to you again, could you tell me please where we can find you?'

'Mostly on my boat – the *Jasmine*. We live on her, see, as well as work on her.'

'That's you and your wife?'

'That's right – Annie. She's one in a million, but . . . it's a bit difficult at the moment.' He hurried on. 'We're tied up in the pound below Hawley Lock. The motor's playing up and I've got to get it fixed, so if you need me in the next couple of days you'll probably find me there, and if you don't, like as not I'll be here, in the pub. If I'm away, though, well, you'll just have to wait till I come back, unless you want to come looking for me up and down the canal.'

Jago pushed his chair back and got up from the table. 'Thank you, Mr Trent – we'll bear that in mind. That'll be all for now.'

Trent jumped up from the table too. 'Oh, by the way, Inspector,' he said. 'If you do happen to come to the boat and Annie's around, please don't mention the cards – she, er, well, you know, she doesn't approve.'

'I see,' Jago replied, and gave him a friendly but non-committal smile.

CHAPTER FOURTEEN

Having ascertained from Mrs Minter that she could have their cooked breakfast on the table by seven o'clock, Jago gave Cradock his reporting instructions and was pleased to find his young colleague already present, albeit somewhat bleary-eyed, when he came down to eat the next morning.

'Morning, sir,' said Cradock sleepily as Jago took his seat at the table. 'What time is it we've got to see Mr Hardacre?'

'That's not till nine o'clock,' Jago replied, 'so I reckon if we get this down us in short order we'll have time to pay a quick visit to Mr Bowen at his garage on the way – assuming he was telling the truth when he said he starts work at seven. I'd like to see how he reacts when we tell him we think Latham was murdered. I'm wondering whether he can tell us anything more about that petrol can, too, so we'll take it with us.'

'Very good, sir.'

Cradock's eyes lit up when Mrs Minter brought their breakfast to them. It appeared to be as traditional and comprehensive as the current rationing would allow: a bowl of porridge to start with, followed by a fried egg and bacon, and as much toast and marmalade as he could decently manage, accompanied by a mug of tea. They downed the meal as quickly as possible and drove to Crogsland Road.

Bowen's claim proved reliable. When they arrived at his garage they found him already at work underneath a car, from which he wriggled out on his back as they announced their arrival. He was dressed in the same greasy overalls as the previous day and wielding a large ring spanner in his right hand.

'Good morning,' he said, getting to his feet. 'And what brings you gentlemen here so early in the day?'

'Just a few questions, Mr Bowen, if you can spare us the time.'

'Of course. Is this about Les Latham again?'

'It is, yes. I said we'd let you know when we found out what had happened, so I thought I'd better come round and tell you – I'm afraid we now believe Mr Latham was murdered.'

'Murdered? Good Lord – that's not what I expected to hear.'

'What did you expect to hear?'

'Oh, I don't know, I suppose I just thought it must've been some kind of fault on the car – an accident, like. I was worried it might've been something I'd missed when I did the service.'

'Well, you can put your mind at rest on that score. Our evidence confirms it was murder.'

'But that's crazy – who'd want to murder a man like him, a middle-aged commercial traveller going about his business?'

'That's what we're trying to find out. Can you think of anyone who might've wanted to kill him?'

'No. But then again I don't really know that much about him. Like I said, the only dealings I had with him were here, to do with his car. But what about his poor missus – how's she doing?'

'She seems to be coping well under the circumstances, as far as I can tell.'

'Well, if you see her, can you pass on my condolences and best wishes to her? I'm not very good at sending sympathy cards and that sort of thing, and nowadays you never know whether the post'll get through anyway, do you? Poor woman – it must be awful for her to lose her husband like that, so suddenly, especially in days like these when everything's so uncertain. I don't envy you, having to break news like that to people.'

'It's part of our job, unfortunately. Now, there's something I'd like to ask you that's more to do with your job. There's a petrol can I'd like you to have a look at.'

Cradock took his cue and fetched the can from the car.

'Here you are,' said Jago, passing it on to the garage owner. 'What can you tell me about that?'

Bowen took the can and turned it over. 'Well, it's a petrol can, as you said, standard two-gallon size, same as any other – the only thing a bit unusual about it is the brand on the front, ROP. Some people used to say that stood for Rotten Old Petrol, but actually it was Russian Oil Products – a petrol company. I think it was set up over here by the Soviet government sometime in the twenties, to sell imported Russian petrol. They had a depot further up the canal from here, and of course there were rumours that they were all spies, but I don't know about that. All I know is they weren't very popular with the other oil companies.'

'Why was that?'

'Simple – they undercut everyone else's prices. It was about threepence a gallon cheaper.'

'Do you sell it?'

'No, I've always stuck to Shell. Besides, the war put a stop to price-cutting, didn't it? Now it's all pool petrol, and all the companies have to do what the government says and sell at the same price.'

'Did Mr Latham buy petrol from you?'

'Yes, he was one of my regular customers.'

'Did he have one of these ROP cans?'

'I think he did, yes, but I couldn't tell you whether it was this one in particular – they all look the same, so it could be anyone's.'

'Were you in the habit of filling a can for him?'

'Er, no. I mean, I used to – he had to drive a long way with his work and he always liked to have a spare bit in a can in case he couldn't find a garage to fill up. But not since the rationing came in – I'm not allowed to put petrol in anything except a car's tank, as I'm sure you'll be aware, what with you being a policeman.'

'Indeed, but it's something a garage proprietor might do as a favour to a regular customer, isn't it?'

'That's as may be, but I didn't, all right? I run an honest business here – I stick to the rules.'

'Good. And are you aware of any other garage owners

in the area who are perhaps a little less scrupulous than you in their business affairs?'

'Shady operators, you mean?'

'Yes, I'm thinking of fraudulent practices concerning the sale of petrol, for example.'

'Well, you hear about that sort of thing going on, of course – I suppose there'll always be someone trying to bend the law to line their own pockets. There was that bloke running a garage over in Harrow who got caught putting paraffin in his petrol, wasn't there? Anything up to thirty per cent, so they said, and his customers had no idea. That's not going to do your engine any good, is it? He got investigated by the Petroleum Board and ended up with a forty-pound fine.'

'And in this area?'

'Well, I dare say there's plenty of rackets going on somewhere, and like I said, I try to keep my ear to the ground, but I haven't heard of anything like that round here.'

'Has anyone ever offered you any suspicious petrol coupons?'

'What do you mean by suspicious?'

'Coupons they might have come by illegally.'

'Like nicked, you mean? Well, that's something you hear of too – people stealing coupons and trying to sell them on to drivers. Your blokes always let us know if there's any stolen ones in circulation and what the serial numbers are, so we look out for them, don't we? I can't say I've personally had anyone turning up and trying to buy petrol with them, though.'

'Right. And you've never heard of Mr Latham being involved in anything like that?'

'No, I can't say I have.'

'Thank you. Now, I understand from Mrs Latham that her husband was very fond of cars, so I was wondering whether he did much of his own maintenance.'

'Not on that car, no. I'm not saying he couldn't, mind – he knew all about cars – but it wasn't his, you see. It belonged to the company, and they insisted that any repairs or maintenance had to be done by a proper mechanic in a proper garage. I suppose they didn't want their employees tinkering about with the cars and spoiling them, or worse still doing some repair that caused an accident so the company ended up being held responsible. Why do you ask?'

'Well, it's just that we found quite a number of tools in the boot.'

'What kind of tools?'

'There was the starting handle, of course, and a jack and a wheel brace, but I also spotted the remains of a hammer, a few spanners, a couple of screwdrivers, a jemmy and some pliers. Did he usually drive around with all that?'

'I don't know if he always did, but when I've had the car in for servicing I've noticed he carried quite a few tools. Probably for roadside repairs – he certainly knew enough about cars to do that sort of thing in an emergency.'

'You'd need a hammer for roadside repairs?'

'For some things, yes. Let's say your starter motor bendix gets jammed in the flywheel ring gear – the easiest way to release it is to hit the starter with a hammer.'

'And what about a jemmy?'

'Well, he probably had that for an emergency wheel change – those hub caps can be a devil to get off, you know.'

'I see. Right, well, thank you very much – that's been very helpful. We'll be off now.'

'You're welcome,' said Bowen. 'Anything else you need, just drop by again.'

Jago raised his hand slightly in acknowledgement of this offer and started back towards the car, followed by Cradock. Almost immediately, however, he stopped and turned back. 'By the way, Mr Bowen, there was something else I meant to ask you – I noticed an odd wooden structure in your yard last time we were here and I couldn't work out what it was. Can you enlighten me?'

'Ah, yes, come with me.'

Bowen led them down to the yard at the back of the garage. The structure in question was a large shed with horizontal shutters, one of which was open, revealing a wooden grille. Beneath it were what looked like windows, but instead of glass they were fitted with chicken wire.

'Do you mean this one?' he said.

'Yes, that's it,' Jago replied. 'What is it?'

'I think I know, sir,' Cradock butted in before Bowen could reply, eager to show that for once he knew something his boss didn't. 'Is it a pigeon loft? My Uncle Bert used to have something like that.'

'That's right, son,' said Bowen, 'and I hope you're not going to ask me whether I'm rearing them for the pot. People seem to think the only reason why anyone would have a lot of pigeons in their back yard would be to top up their meat ration with the occasional pigeon pie, and I'm getting tired of explaining that they're homing pigeons and they're very important. Come and see.'

Cradock dropped back so that he was behind Jago,

who suspected this move was intended not so much to show respect as to duck out of the conversation, since it was likely that his assistant's interest in pigeons was strictly related to their potential as a pie filling.

Bowen led them to the loft, opened a door and took a pigeon in his hands, holding it gently and stroking its head with the side of his finger. 'See that, Inspector?' he said. 'Beautiful, isn't it?'

'Yes,' said Jago, to be polite. As far as he was concerned, homing or not, a pigeon was still just a pigeon.

Bowen held the bird out towards Cradock. 'You take a look too, Detective Constable. What do you think?'

'Oh, yes, er, beautiful.'

'Some people think the only thing pigeons can do is decorate Lord Nelson's hat with their droppings in Trafalgar Square, but they're actually very intelligent birds. If you train them, they can bring a message home from hundreds of miles away without getting lost. They save lives, too – did you know the army's using them, and the RAF?'

'Er, no,' Cradock replied, aware that he'd already exhausted his scant knowledge of pigeons and their lofts.

'Well, I'm a member of the National Pigeon Service, and we provide homing pigeons to support the war effort. That means every RAF bomber that flies out on a sortie has two pigeons on board in case it gets shot down. If it does, the crew can release a pigeon carrying a note of their position, and it'll fly back home, forty miles an hour, and the men can be rescued. They're amazing creatures. Terrible to think it was only the beginning of this year the government was telling people to shoot as many as they could to stop them ruining the crops. At least now they've had the sense to make it illegal to kill a homing pigeon. I think we should all be proud of these birds.'

'I can see you care about them.'

'I do. I've got no wife and no children, but these little creatures are like my family. People forget that wars affect them too – think of what it was like for all those horses at the front in the fourteen war. Even the animals in the London Zoo down the road in Regent's Park have been bombed. It's a miracle none of them's been killed. Even so, a zebra got loose, and I heard it was halfway to Camden Town before they managed to round it up.'

Cradock tried to suppress a chuckle at the thought, but Bowen eyed him pityingly. 'Yes, it sounds comical, but that poor creature must've been terrified when the bombs were falling. I don't know about you, but I hate to see animals suffering, and it's not their fault we're at war, is it? Now, if you don't mind, I've got work to do.'

'Yes, of course,' said Jago. 'And we can see how important that work is. We've no further questions for now, so we'll be on our way, and thank you very much for your help.'

'That was surprising, wasn't it?' said Cradock once they had said goodbye to the garage owner and were out of earshot. 'I mean, you might expect someone running a business like that to be a rough and ready sort – you know, hard-nosed and all that. But he was a bit of a softy when it came to those pigeons. Cooing all over them as if he was their dad, wasn't he?'

'Never underestimate the love a man can have for his animals, Peter,' said Jago as he unlocked the car door. 'I've seen grown men, hardened soldiers, weeping over the death of a horse. It's the same with dogs – some of them are so faithful and loyal, they seem to love their master, and he loves them back. It's a real bond.'

'Not my idea of fun, though. Taking them for walks all the time? More trouble than they're worth, if you ask me. You haven't got a dog, have you, sir?'

'No, and I never have. I don't think CID working hours and dogs are compatible.'

'So duty comes before love, eh, guv'nor?'

'Yes – sometimes it does.'

Cradock looked at him as if expecting him to elaborate, but Jago said nothing and his face was inscrutable.

CHAPTER FIFTEEN

The air in the gloomy, ochre-walled corridor leading to Detective Superintendent Hardacre's office attacked Jago's sense of smell with a particular pungency. It suggested a recent battle between cigarette smoke and disinfectant, and the slight predominance of the latter suggested in turn that the Scotland Yard cleaners had been at work in the early hours of the morning.

Jago knocked on the door at nine o'clock precisely, and a sharp voice from within ordered him to enter. Hardacre was seated behind his desk, hunched over a sheet of paper, with a fountain pen poised in his hand. He raised his head enough to register his visitors' presence, then glanced up at the clock on the wall and gave an indeterminate grunt. Apparently satisfied that their timekeeping was acceptable, he motioned Jago and Cradock to take a seat. Before their trousers had even touched the chairs he dipped his head again and ran his forefinger along the last few lines of whatever it was he was reading, presumably for the sake of speed, then scribbled a signature at the bottom, seesawed a wooden rocker blotter over it to dry it, stuffed the paper into a folder and tossed it into his out tray.

He removed his wire-rimmed spectacles and rubbed his eyes, then slurped from a mug of tea. Jago wondered what time his boss had started work that day, and whether he and Cradock would also be offered a drink. On the first count he had no idea, and on the second his expectations were low.

'Right,' said Hardacre. 'A car on fire in Camden Town with a body in it – so what've you got to report?'

'A milkman found it, sir,' Jago began, 'out on his round at about seven forty-five yesterday morning. It was in a disused builder's yard by the Regent's Canal – he reported it to a couple of uniformed men on the beat, and they went straight to the scene. They could see there was someone in the car, but the fire was so fierce there was nothing they could do – they couldn't get anywhere near it.'

Hardacre shook his head. 'Poor blighter. Reminds me of the war – did you ever come up against those German flamethrowers?'

'Not at close quarters, sir.'

'I did. Flanders, summer 1915. You don't forget that in a hurry. Have you identified the body?'

'Yes, sir. His name's Latham – he was a commercial traveller for a company that makes chocolates.'

'Not a great loss to the war effort, then.'

'No, sir. Possibly a considerable loss to his wife, though, sir.'

'Yes, yes, I dare say. Much left of him?'

'No, sir. The body was badly charred – in the end we identified him by his dental records.'

'Right.'

Jago was struck by the detective superintendent's manner. Whatever he might have been thinking, outwardly he seemed no more moved by the idea of a man burnt beyond recognition than he might be by hearing that someone's carrots weren't cooked enough.

'I don't like cars on fire with bodies in them,' Hardacre continued. 'I had a case like that once myself and it was the devil's own job to work out whether it was an accident or murder or what. Very confusing. Right now I'm waiting to hear whether the borough police down in Ramsgate are going to call us in – they've got the same kind of thing on their hands. Not a car, but some bloke found burnt to death on the floor with his bed still blazing away beside him, and they can't work out what happened. Could've been an accident – he was seventy-three, so maybe he was smoking in bed, fell asleep and set the lot on fire. But then it turns out he was a millionaire, so there's a possible motive for someone. Then up pops something else – last year he married his secretary, forty years younger than him, and six weeks later they separated. It gets more interesting, doesn't it?'

'Are you thinking there might be some connection, sir?'

'No, I'm not. What I'm saying is you never know till you start digging. And when you do, you can bet your boots you'll find the same thing at the bottom of it every time – it'll be sex or money, or both.'

'Well, we've started digging, sir, and we've ruled out accident and suicide.'

'So it's definitely murder?'

'Yes, sir. The pathologist says he was dead before the fire started – possibly suffocated, but we can't be sure.'

'Right. What else do you know about him?'

'Not a lot yet – it seems he was a keen card player, though.'

'For money?'

'So it appears, yes.'

'That's the sort of thing that can put someone's nose out of joint – not everyone likes losing money to a card sharp. You want to look into that.'

'Yes, sir, I shall.'

'Anything else?'

'He was a cheerful sort, apparently, and his wife says he was the life and soul of the party, everybody's friend.'

'Yes, well, somebody clearly hadn't taken a shine to him, though, had they? Any suspects?'

'Not yet, sir. Apart from his wife, we've spoken to the garage owner who looked after his car, and one of his friends, but none of them's come up with anything that might point to a particular suspect. We're going to visit his employers this morning and see if they can tell us anything.'

'Any other lines of enquiry?'

'Yes, sir. We found some petrol ration books among the deceased's possessions, and it's beginning to look like they may be stolen. We've been in touch with the local Ministry of Transport depot, and they're checking for us.'

Hardacre shook his head in disbelief. 'Good grief – is there nothing these people won't steal?'

'These people, sir?'

'The Great British Public, lad, that's who. It seems like anything that's not screwed down gets nicked these days – and plenty of stuff that is screwed down too, for that matter.' He turned to Cradock. 'I told your guv'nor here the last time I saw him that I hate thieving and I hate thieves, and now I'm telling you too – just so you know, right? We got four young toe rags remanded at Tottenham yesterday – do you know what they did?' Cradock's reply, if he'd dared to speak, would have been no, but Hardacre didn't wait for one. 'They managed to get hold of a car somehow and went out in the blackout offering people free lifts, then robbed them at gunpoint. And if that wasn't enough, they broke into a shop and stole a load of wireless sets and shot a woman dead in an off-licence. Disgusting – and all four of them of an age to be called up. They should be out there somewhere fighting for their country, not terrorising innocent people here. If there's any justice they'll swing for it, but like as not some soft-minded judge'll just have a kindly word with them, then pat them on the head and let them go.'

Jago's private reflection was that if the young men in question expected that degree of leniency from a judge they'd be disappointed, but he kept it to himself: the detective superintendent was now firmly mounted on his hobby horse.

Cradock braced himself against the back of his chair as Hardacre fired a final salvo. 'So you mark my words, sonny. Your job is to get these villains off the streets and behind bars, where they belong – they start out thieving and they end up as murderers.'

'Yes, sir,' he said meekly.

Hardacre turned his attention back to Jago. 'So this commercial traveller of yours, he's a wrong 'un too, is he – nicking petrol coupons?'

'We don't know that yet, sir, but we're looking into it.'

'Good. And you say you're going to talk to the people he was working for, right? You might find he was pinching stuff from them too. What are they called?'

'Baring and Sons, sir. They're based in Camden Town, which is where the deceased lived.'

'And where did he do his commercial travelling?'

'Cambridgeshire, sir.'

'Hmm, plenty of thieving going on there too, I shouldn't be surprised. I got a report last week – seems that while we're busy here guarding damaged buildings in London to keep the blasted looters off 'em, there's more villains heading out into the country to do their breaking and entering where there's not so many coppers around to see them. You can't win, can you?'

'No, sir, but we can try, can't we?'

'That's the spirit, Jago. We just need to make sure we nick more of 'em this week than we did last week, and then we're winning.'

'We'll do our best, sir.' Having steered the conversation into a safe haven, Jago thought now would be a good time to make their excuses and leave. 'Will that be all, sir?'

'Yes, off you go. Just make sure you get this wrapped up quickly. The public expect Scotland Yard to solve murders, so now you're here, you'd better make damn sure you do.'

CHAPTER SIXTEEN

'Right,' said Jago as they stepped out of the Scotland Yard building into the bright winter sunshine, 'now that I've told Mr Hardacre that we're going to visit Baring and Sons, we'd better get on and do it, but there's someone else I'd like to see on the way.'

'Oh, yes, who's that then, sir?' said Cradock.

'I'm thinking of Hilda Crow – I'd be interested to know what she can tell us about Latham. Her daughter seemed to send her packing pretty quickly when we turned up, didn't she?'

'Yes, but she's his mother-in-law. She probably won't have a good word to say about him.'

'You mustn't let your view of mothers-in-law be clouded by what the comedians say about them. I'm sure some of them must be very nice – and besides, you might have one yourself one day.'

Cradock gulped. Walking out with Emily was nice,

but the thought that this might one day result in him being married to her, with his boss's old friend Rita as his mother-in-law, was suddenly a daunting prospect. If Emily shared all her secrets with her mum, he could just imagine Rita casually dropping the juiciest of them into the conversation the next time she saw Jago. 'Oh, I can't see that happening,' he said, 'not yet awhile, anyway,' but the hint of a tremble in his voice belied the confidence of his words.

'We'll see, Peter,' said Jago. 'But it'd probably be good to steer clear of mother-in-law jokes all the same, just in case. In the meantime, I think it might be profitable to explore Mrs Crow's impressions of her son-in-law when his wife's not around to hear them. Let's see if she's in.'

Ferdinand Place was a narrow cobbled street with a monotonous row of terraced houses on one side and the high back wall of the Chalk Farm bus garage on the other. When Hilda Crow opened the door to them she looked exactly the same as when they'd last seen her: the same apron and slippers, and a successor to the previous day's cigarette in her hand.

'Oh, it's you,' she said. 'I didn't expect to see you again so soon.'

'Well, you were kind enough to offer us your assistance, Mrs Crow, so we thought we'd drop by while we were passing.'

'Right, well, come in then.'

She led them through the gloomy house to a small living room that looked as though it hadn't seen a paintbrush in years. The curtains were faded and the furniture was worn.

'Sit yourselves down then,' she said. 'Can I get you a cup of tea?'

'No thank you,' said Jago, taking a seat. 'We'll only be a moment. We'd just like to know a bit more about your son-in-law, Mr Latham.'

Hilda made an attempt at fluffing up a thin and reluctant cushion, then settled into an armchair with it. 'Rose told me you think he was murdered – is that right?'

'Yes, I'm afraid it is.'

She shook her head. 'I don't know – as if there wasn't enough trouble in the world already. Who'd want to go around doing something like that? There must be someone out there with a screw loose. Anyway, I'll help you any way I can, but what's there to say? He was my Rose's husband. There can't be much I know about him that she couldn't tell you herself.'

'Yes, but we're talking to anyone who knew him well. How would you describe him?'

She thought for a moment, her hands clasped over her lap. 'Well,' she said, 'He's not the sort of bloke I would've chosen for a husband, but we're all different, aren't we? I don't suppose he'd have chosen me for a wife.' She chuckled at her own comment, then began to cough. 'Sorry, Inspector – I've got a bad chest. I've been taking some of that Camthol linctus stuff, but nothing seems to shift it.'

'That's all right – take your time. What else can you tell us about him?'

She gave another cough and continued. 'He was

ambitious, I suppose – yes, I'd say he was definitely ambitious, and he seemed to be doing well in his job, although you never know whether a man's telling you the truth about his work, do you?'

'Do you have any reason to believe Mr Latham was not telling the truth in some way?'

'Oh, no, I'm just saying that's often the way it is. Anyway, Rose seemed to be happy with him, or at least she put up with him, and that's more than you can say for a lot of marriages.'

'How long have you known him?'

'It must be twenty years or more – since the first time she brought him home.'

'And how did he strike you?'

'Well, when he was first courting her I thought he was a cocky young devil – a bit too big for his boots. He was what I'd call a Flash Harry – you know, liked his fancy clothes. I always got the feeling he wanted to make a good impression, but I suppose if you're a salesman you've got to do that. He liked his cars, too – he was always talking about what he was going to get one day. This car, that car – half the time I didn't know what he was talking about, but I could see he knew what he wanted. I suppose Rose was one of the things he wanted too, and he got her. And now look where it's got him – he's dead, and she's left on her own, and I won't be here for ever, will I?'

'Does she have any brothers or sisters?'

'No. She was my only child – I might've had more, only my husband deserted me when she was two and never came back. Why are men so unreliable?' She paused as if expecting Jago to answer, but when he didn't she sighed and carried on. 'Left me in the lurch, he did, good and proper. I had to get by as best I could and bring her up single-handed. I went to the court and got a maintenance order against him, but it was only ten bob a week, and apart from paying that he never lifted a finger to help. I couldn't even tell you where he is now. The magistrates told us we ought to live together again, but what did those silly old fools know about it? No, that was a waste of time – he was always a ne'er-do-well and always would be, and I was better off without him. The only help I got was from my old mum and dad, bless 'em, but they're long gone now. All I've got left is Rose – if it wasn't for her I reckon I'd have done myself in years ago. I can't stand being in the house by myself, so I go round and do a bit of dusting and what have you for her, just for the company and someone to talk to. It suits her too, I think – she's never been one for housework.'

'I'm very sorry, Mrs Crow. It must've been a difficult life for you.'

'Yes, well, you live and learn, don't you? I swore I'd never let that sort of thing happen to Rose, so I brought her up to know what men are like. I reckon if a few more mothers did that, there'd be a lot more happy women in the world, not selling themselves down the river for a tuppenny-ha'penny wedding ring. I thought I was in love when I met my husband, and I thought he was in love with me, more's the pity. I married him on an impulse, and that was my big mistake. It turned out to be a short and miserable marriage followed by a lifetime of hard slog and heartache, but at least she's had a better time of it than I did. I made sure she knew how to look after herself, and I don't think she stands for any nonsense.'

'Did you approve of your daughter's marriage?'

'Approve? I'm not sure I was given the choice. My old man had done a runner all those years before, so young Les didn't have to come and ask her father's permission to marry her – not that there's any law says you've got to, but I still think it's nice. Anyway, he didn't come and ask my permission either – they just turned up together and told me they were getting married, so whether I approved or not never came into it. Rose certainly seemed set on it, so even if I had disapproved of him I don't suppose it would've made a ha'porth of difference. I think he was what she was looking for. As far as I can tell, all she's ever wanted in life is a good-looking man, a home of her own, some nice clothes and a bit of spare cash – and when she married Les, that's what she got. But as for whether he got what he wanted, well, you'd have to ask him, wouldn't you?'

Jago expected her to follow this apparent wisecrack with a cackle, but instead she just gave him a feeble smile.

'And more recently,' he said, 'how did they get on together, from your point of view?'

She raised her eyebrows and pouted in a way that suggested no one could answer such a question with more than a guess. 'As well as any other couple, I'd say. I've never seen them having a row or anything. They had a lot in common, you see – they both wanted the same things in life.'

'Children?'

'Well, that's not the sort of thing you ask about, is it? But I think they were OK without – it didn't seem to bother her, at any rate.'

'So would you say it was a happy marriage?'

She eyed him cautiously. 'I don't think it's my place to comment on that. What goes on behind closed doors is none of my business. But don't get me wrong, Inspector – he didn't knock her about, if that's what you mean, not as far as I know. I just think he had a bit of a mean streak.'

'What do you mean by that?'

'You're not going to catch me telling tales about my daughter's marriage, Inspector – if you want to know more, you'll have to ask Rose. Go and ask her about Bob – and don't tell her I said so.'

'Who's Bob?'

'I told you, ask her – if she wants to tell you she will, and if she doesn't, she won't. That's her business, not mine. But look, they may've had their ups and downs, like any couple, but I don't think Les could've found a better wife than Rose, and she could've done a lot worse herself.'

'Very well. Before we go, could I ask one more question?'

'Of course.'

'Can you think of anyone who might've wanted to harm your son-in-law?'

'Harm Les? No, I don't think I do. Not that I know anything about his friends or his life at work or what he might've got up to in his own time. But he seemed to be doing well in his job, quite a success. I could imagine maybe people being jealous of him, but harm him? No, I don't think so.'

She placed her hands on her knees and leant forward slightly towards them with a fixed grin that signalled she had nothing more to say and it was time for them to go.

CHAPTER SEVENTEEN

'So is it Baring and Sons now, sir?' said Cradock as they left Hilda Crow's house. He glanced back over his shoulder and caught the twitch of a curtain in the downstairs window. 'Looks like she's keeping an eye out to make sure we've really gone. And what do you reckon about this Bob, then? Sounded a bit mysterious, didn't it? Are we going to ask Mrs Latham about it?'

'Definitely – but I'm jumping to no conclusions. Mrs Crow strikes me as a bit of a gossip, so there may be nothing in it.'

'Yes, funny old bird, wasn't she?'

'People might call you a funny old bird if you'd been through what she has,' Jago replied. 'Life isn't all sunshine and roses, you know, and a bad experience can leave a mark on you for life just as surely as a broken nose.' He stopped, realising this was the kind of thing Cradock had probably heard from his mother. 'And yes,' he continued, 'it is Baring and Sons next. I want to talk to Jack Henderson, that pal of Latham's at work that his wife mentioned. He might be able to tell us things she doesn't know.'

'Secrets, you mean?'

'Perhaps, but not necessarily. I'm interested in finding out what he was like to work with, and how people thought of him in the company – people at work sometimes see a side of you that your friends and family don't, and they can be a better judge of your character because they see how you react under pressure.' He gave Cradock a knowing look that the younger man found unsettling. 'Working together can bring out the worst in people too, you know.'

Cradock's eyes widened. 'You think someone at the firm killed him, sir?'

'I've no more idea than you do at this stage. For all we know, anyone we have a nice friendly chat with today could be a suspect by tomorrow, but we'll start with the people most likely to be able to tell us something about him – his friend Henderson and whoever runs the company too, if he's there. We might pick up some useful information.'

Cradock thought for a moment. 'And, er, if we meet the boss, do you think he might give us some free samples?'

'I said pick up information, Peter, not pick up free chocolate, even if it is as nice as you say it is. Policemen who accept gifts from suspects don't go down very well in court.'

'Yes, sir, I just thought perhaps, you know—'

'I do know, and I'm afraid if you want some of

their products you'll have to buy them for yourself. Do things by the book, Peter, or you might end up with someone throwing the book at you – and that's not a pretty sight.'

'So do you always do things by the book, sir?'

Jago studied Cradock's face, trying to spot any hint of irony. He smiled. 'Do as I say, Peter, not as I do. Now, come along – let's see what Baring and Sons have to say for themselves. We'll start at the top if we can.'

Barings' factory and head office were about a mile away, housed in a sleek, modern building in Albert Street. Jago and Cradock went in through the main entrance and identified themselves as police officers to the commissionaire on duty in the foyer, who made a brief internal phone call. Two minutes later a primly dressed secretary with a severe expression came down to meet them and escorted them to the lift. She said nothing as they ascended together to the top floor, then took them through an anonymous door opposite the lift into what he assumed was her own office. She knocked on a connecting door and opened it. 'Detective Inspector Jago and Detective Constable Cradock, sir, from Scotland Yard,' she said, showing them in.

'Ah, yes – come in, gentlemen.' The figure who rose from behind an imposing mahogany desk was a white-haired man, lean to the point of gaunt, and dressed meticulously, albeit in the style of an earlier era. 'Joseph Baring,' he said, 'managing director. Do take a seat, please.'

Jago noticed the drawn expression on his face as he sat down: the strains, perhaps, of war or business, or both.

'Would you like coffee?' Baring continued. 'My secretary is very efficient, and she probably has some brewing already.'

Jago had turned down Hilda Crow's offer of a cup of tea, and there hadn't even been a whiff of such consideration from Hardacre, so now he had no compunction about accepting their host's hospitality. 'Yes,' he replied. 'That would be most kind of you, thank you.'

Baring dismissed the waiting secretary and resumed his seat behind the desk. 'I'm sorry to be meeting you in such sad circumstances, Inspector,' he said. 'I was out yesterday afternoon, but your telephone message was reported to me as soon as I returned. What a terrible business. Am I right in understanding that Mr Latham's body was found in a burning car?'

'I'm afraid that's correct, yes.'

Baring shook his head sorrowfully. 'Dreadful. We've lost a few people since the war started, on active service and here on the home front too, but the death of an employee is always still a shock. There's one thing I must ask you, though – does your involvement mean you suspect there may have been foul play?'

'It does, Mr Baring. At the moment we're treating it as a case of suspected murder.'

'Oh, dear. That makes it even worse, doesn't it? The thought that he's not just a random casualty of war, that someone's deliberately killed him – that's particularly unsettling. Who would do a thing like that?'

'That's what we're trying to establish, sir.'

'And Mrs Latham – how is she taking it?'

'As bravely as can be expected, I think.'

'Good for her. We've arranged to have some flowers sent, of course, although I fear the shortage may mean they're not quite up to what we'd usually send. It must be a very distressing time for her. Mr Latham had no other dependants, as far as I'm aware, but she'll be well looked after. I'm pleased to say that like some of the other chocolate manufacturers, we were among the first businesses to set up an occupational pension scheme for our employees at the beginning of the century, and its provisions for widow's benefits are quite generous.'

The door opened and Baring's secretary came in, depositing a tray on his desk with coffee for three.

'Thank you, Miss Jenkins,' said Baring. She replied with a silent smile and departed. 'Help yourselves, gentlemen,' he continued.

Jago took a fine china cup and saucer from the tray and added milk from the jug to his coffee, followed by Cradock, who tried to suppress his delight at spotting a small plate of chocolate-covered biscuits. He looked questioningly at Jago, as if wondering whether to take one would amount to police corruption, and upon receiving a discreet nod of permission, grabbed one as if his life depended on it.

'Thank you,' said Jago, taking a sip of his coffee. 'So, Baring and Sons sounds like a family business – is it still?'

'Oh, yes,' Baring replied. 'I'm the third generation. My grandfather, Josiah Baring, founded the company in 1872. He was a Quaker – he believed all people are created equal by God, and that we employers have a responsibility to treat our staff with respect and dignity, and to look after their welfare. That doesn't mean we pay everyone the same money, but we pay them fairly, according to their skills and responsibilities.'

'How long had Mr Latham been with the company?'

'About ten years, I believe, but if you want to know more specific information about his service, I'd better pass you on to his manager, Mr Todd.'

'Thank you, that would be helpful.'

'I'll ask Miss Jenkins to take you to him. But please, if there's anything else I can do to help you, or any questions he can't answer, come straight back to me. I want to do everything I can to help you get to the bottom of this most unfortunate incident – and if that means treading on a few toes, you'll have my full backing. We all need to pull together to see justice is done on behalf of our sadly departed colleague.'

'Thank you, sir. Is there anything you need to know from me?'

Baring seemed to hesitate before answering. 'Er, well, there is, actually. Do you mind if I ask a rather delicate question?'

'Not at all.'

'It's just this – you said it's a case of suspected murder. I realise that may mean Mr Latham's merely the innocent victim of a drunken lout or a homicidal maniac, but it also raises the possibility – theoretically of course – that there may have been some reason for the attack that might . . . well, not to put too fine a point on it, that might imply some complications, perhaps even some culpability on his part. Do you have any indication that there might be any such, er, complications?'

'We've only just started our investigation, Mr Baring, so it's impossible to say.'

'Of course, of course.'

'Are you thinking about possible repercussions for your company's reputation?'

'To be frank, Inspector, yes, I am. We have eight hundred and thirty employees who depend on this company for their livelihood. I'm sure I don't need to tell you that in business reputation is everything, and our commercial travellers are the ones who embody that reputation in the eyes of our customers. If there's so much as a hint of impropriety or any lack of moral probity in our representatives, the customers will no longer trust them, and that could have the most damaging consequences.'

'Well, all I can say is we're not aware of anything of that nature at the moment.'

'Thank you. But please, don't misunderstand me – the truth is more important than the ups and downs of our business. You must get to the truth of the matter, and if that proves to be an embarrassment to this company, so be it. We shall take it as a harsh lesson and do whatever we must to restore our reputation for integrity.'

CHAPTER EIGHTEEN

Joseph Baring buzzed for his secretary. 'Ah, Miss Jenkins,' he said, as she stepped back into his office, 'please take these gentlemen down to Mr Todd – they need to speak to him.'

Jago and Cradock followed her downstairs to another, smaller office, where she knocked on the door. It was opened by a young woman in a fashionable powder-blue tailored suit. She had strikingly good looks, and her confident manner suggested that she knew it. After explaining that she was delivering the two visitors at the behest of Mr Baring, Miss Jenkins left, her nose slightly tilted upwards, as if to avoid an unpleasant odour.

'Good morning,' said Jago. 'We're police officers – I'm Detective Inspector Jago and this is Detective Constable Cradock. We'd like a word with Mr Todd, please.'

'Ooh, detectives, eh?' the young woman replied.

'That sounds very exciting.' She turned her head slightly towards Cradock. 'It's good to know there are men like you keeping us safe in the blackout. My name's Violet – Violet Edwards, Mr Todd's secretary. Let me take your things.' They handed over their hats and coats, and she hung them on a hat stand in the corner of the room. 'I'll just check that he's free.' She knocked on a door, opened it and leant into the neighbouring office. 'Mr Baring's sent a couple of policemen down to see you, sir.' She led them into the office and hovered behind them, notepad in hand.

'Thank you, Violet,' said Todd. 'That'll be all for now.'

'Very good, sir.' She turned neatly on her heels and paraded out of the door like a fashion mannequin, Todd following her with his eyes as she went. 'Good morning, gentlemen,' he said when the door had closed behind her. He gestured vaguely towards a couple of bentwood chairs, and they sat down. 'Is this to do with poor Les Latham?'

'I'm afraid it is, Mr Todd. You've heard already, then?'

'Yes, I have – I was about to tell my secretary when you arrived.' He paused, as if the thought of breaking the news of Latham's death to her was troubling him. 'We're all going to miss him, you know. It wasn't just that he was a nice man – he was one of our best commercial travellers, and they're what keeps the whole company going.'

'A key role, then?'

'Oh, yes. I've heard it said that the reason why Barings

were so successful early on was that they had some top-class commercial travellers, very skilful by all accounts, and I like to think the same's true today. They're the people who bring the business in and generate the sales – and sales mean profits.'

'So a man like Mr Latham would've been valued by the company?'

'Oh, yes, definitely. He was at the top of his game.'

'A nice man, and successful too, then. Can you think of anyone who might've wanted to harm Mr Latham?'

'Harm him? No, I can't.' He looked more closely at Jago. 'You mean you think someone deliberately killed him? I was assuming it must've been an air raid or some kind of accident.'

'I'm afraid I've just informed Mr Baring that we're treating it as a case of suspected murder.'

Todd's face registered shock. 'Murder? But that's impossible – not Les. He was a very popular member of staff – I always found him a charming fellow.'

'Yes, but it would seem someone didn't share your view of him. Did he have any enemies that you're aware of?'

'I can't think of anyone, certainly not in this company at least. Of course, I don't know about people in the outside world who may have crossed his path. You can never tell with people, can you?'

'Do you know much about his past?'

'No, not really – I only know him as one of my team of travellers here at Barings. I believe he's been here for eleven years.'

'And you?'

'I've been here for five.'

'You mentioned he was part of your team. What's your own role in the company?'

'I'm the regional sales manager for the south and east of England, so that means I'm in charge of all the travellers covering that area. Les Latham reported to me, same as all the others.'

'How did you find him as an employee?'

'I regarded him as an asset to the company and I had my eye on him for promotion. He worked hard and got good results, and I felt I could trust him.'

'Trust him in what way?'

'Well, you know, just to do an honest job. The ground he covered meant he must've put in the hours I'd expect him to, and I never had any reason to query his expenses – it's not unknown for commercial travellers to wangle their expense-sheets, you know, but I never saw anything to suggest Les did.'

'Was he happy in his work?'

'I think so, yes. He was good at his job, did well, had a company car and got out on the road, so I don't think there was much to be unhappy about. He liked the products he was selling too, and that's important for a salesman.'

'Yes, I've been told he liked selling things people wanted to buy.'

'Of course – who doesn't? I mean, it makes sense, doesn't it? There's a limit to how much people want to spend on brushes or dusters, but chocolate? Everyone likes that – we're giving them a treat. I tell you, this place is doing more for public morale than the BBC itself.'

'I can imagine your products being popular in wartime.'

'You bet they are – we're going flat out to meet the demand. There's no doubt about it – the whole country's working like stink and losing sleep every night because of the air raids, so our chocolate's a great way to get a bit of extra energy. If you're up on a roof all night watching out for incendiary bombs or racing around in a fire engine putting fires out, one of our bars can be just what you need to keep you going.'

'I see.' Jago could tell this was a man skilled in selling.

'They're healthy too,' Todd went on. 'Did you know a box of our chocolates contains milk, fruit, honey, treacle, butter and nuts?'

'No, I can't say I did. And sugar?'

'Yes, and sugar, of course, but our chocolates aren't just confectionery, they're food, full of nutritional goodness. And for all that,' he concluded with a verbal flourish and a wag of his forefinger, 'we're still only charging the same price as we did before the war – two and ten a pound.'

'Well,' said Jago, 'you've almost persuaded me to eat more chocolate, Mr Todd.'

'I'm sorry, you must forgive me. You know how it is – once a salesman, always a salesman. But I'm sure you haven't come here to talk about that. Look, pardon my curiosity, Inspector, but people are saying Les died in a car fire. Is that right?'

'His body was found in a burning car, yes.'

Todd shook his head slowly. 'Terrible. And you're sure it's murder? Definitely not an accident?'

'We believe that's the case.'

'Could he have done it himself? Taken his own life, I mean.'

'Do you have any reason to think he might've done?'

'Well, no, but it happens, doesn't it? Pressure of work and all that – you never really know what's going on in another man's mind. I just wondered. What about his wife, Mrs Latham – has she been informed?'

'Yes, she has.'

'The poor woman. She'll be lost without him. What did she say?'

'I can't discuss that, I'm afraid.'

'Of course, please excuse me. I must sound more curious than I ought to be, but it's just such a shock for everyone.'

'Indeed. Tell me, did Mr Latham have any particularly close colleagues?'

'I think he got on fine with all of them, but the closest as far as I know was Mr Henderson – Jack Henderson.'

'Ah, yes, Mrs Latham mentioned that he was a friend of her husband's. What's his role in the company?'

'He's another traveller in my team, covers west London and Middlesex. He lives locally, same as Latham, and I think they used to see each other outside work.'

'I'd like to have a chat with Mr Henderson. Is he in the office today?'

'Not at the moment, no – he's out calling on customers.' He glanced at his watch. 'But he should be back in half an hour or so, so if you want to see him I'll catch him when he gets back and tell him to wait for you. You'll find him in the office three doors down from here, on the right as you go out. Would that be OK?'

'Yes, that'll be fine, thank you.'

'Is there anything else I can help you with?'

'No, I don't think there is, thank you.' Jago got to his

feet. 'We'll be on our way now, and we'll pop back to see Mr Henderson.'

'Just one thing before you go, Inspector,' said Todd. He opened a cupboard and produced a familiar-looking blue box. 'May I offer you a complimentary box of our chocolates to take with you?'

Jago feared the temptation might be unbearable for Cradock, so he answered quickly before his young colleague could speak. 'That's very kind of you, Mr Todd, but I'm afraid we'll have to say no. We're expected to pay for our own chocolates, you see, so it'd be frowned upon if we accepted them.'

'Of course, how silly of me. Well, goodbye, gentlemen. Let me see you out.' Todd put the box down on his desk and stepped past them to open the door. His secretary was just outside it, a manila folder full of papers in her hands.

'Oh, Mr Todd,' she purred, 'you gave me a shock – I was just putting those records together for you. They're all here.' She threw what Jago suspected was intended to be a seductive smile in the direction of the two police officers.

'Thank you, Miss Edwards,' Todd replied. 'Put them on the desk, please.'

'Just one last question, Mr Todd,' said Jago. 'Can you tell me where you were between seven and eight yesterday morning?'

'Yes, of course. I was here in the office.' He laughed uneasily. 'You'll probably think I'm addicted to my work, coming in that early, but the thing is, Mr Baring's asked me to prepare an urgent stock report, and it takes a lot of time to go through all the figures. My secretary can

141

confirm that – you were with me, weren't you, Violet?'

'Oh, yes,' said Violet.

'Well, Inspector,' Todd continued, 'I don't suppose I've been of much help to you, but if there's anything else you need to know, please don't hesitate to come back. Poor Latham. "Lucky Les" – that's what he used to call himself, you know, but it looks like the poor fellow's luck has finally run out. Anyway, I won't detain you, gentlemen. Goodbye.'

'Goodbye, Mr Todd,' said Jago, and he and Cradock followed the young secretary back into the outer office, where she stepped across to the hat stand.

'Goodbye, then, officers,' she said, handing them their coats and hats. 'I hope you didn't have to use the third degree on Mr Todd. I'm sure he'll come quietly.' She giggled, and Jago had the distinct impression that she'd fluttered her mascara-laden eyelashes at Cradock. She turned to Jago with a conspiratorial glance. 'What was that about Mr Latham, though? Is he in trouble?'

'I'm sorry, Miss Edwards,' he replied sombrely, 'but we have some bad news. I'm afraid Mr Latham's been killed.'

'No!' she gasped, her manner transformed: she looked genuinely shocked. 'But that's awful – what happened?'

'He was found dead in his car yesterday morning.'

'Oh, poor Les. I don't know what to say.'

'Did you know Mr Latham well?'

'Not what you'd call really well, no. We were work colleagues, so I knew him, of course, but nothing more than that,' she replied, with what seemed like a hint of wariness in her eyes. 'Why do you ask?'

'We're just trying to find out more about him, about

142

his life at work and outside. Did you see anything of him outside work?'

'Of course not,' she replied quickly. 'Anyway, why do you want to know that sort of thing if he's been in an accident?'

'Because the evidence suggests it wasn't an accident. We believe he was murdered.'

'Murdered?' She uttered a sort of whimper and then burst into tears. 'I'm sorry,' she said, 'you'll have to excuse me.'

Before Jago could reply, she had rushed from the room, leaving the door to bang shut behind her.

CHAPTER NINETEEN

Miss Edwards did not return. After waiting for a couple of minutes out of politeness, Jago decided their visit was concluded. 'Come along, Peter,' he said, 'there's no point waiting for her to come back. We'll see ourselves out.'

The modern style of the Baring and Sons building made it easy to find their way back to the entrance: the long corridor led them straight to the lift, which in turn took them down to the ground floor.

'Now, then,' Jago continued as they emerged from the building onto Albert Street, 'I've deprived you of a free box of chocolates, so let's go and find a cafe – I'll buy you a piece of cake to make up for it.'

Cradock's face lit up. 'Oh, thanks, guv'nor, that's very kind of you.'

'Don't mention it – it's the least I can do for a poor starving lad like you.'

They headed up the street and turned into Parkway,

144

a long thoroughfare in which shops of every kind jostled for space, and stopped at the first suitable establishment they came to: a small privately owned place with a sign outside promising cakes baked on the premises. As soon as they were seated at a table, Cradock eagerly studied the menu. 'Look at that, sir,' he said, pointing to the short list of offerings printed on it. 'Home-made fruit cake. I'll have a piece of that, please, if that's all right.'

It was like taking a kid out for a treat, thought Jago, but there was something endearing about the simple transparency of Cradock's enthusiasm. 'You're welcome,' he replied. 'But don't get too excited – they may not be running to big slices these days.'

'Good point, sir. Do you think perhaps we ought to have a sandwich as well?'

'Just to be on the safe side, eh? All right, then.'

Jago cast an eye around the room while Cradock made a further study of the menu. Apart from a couple of elderly women hunched in quiet conversation over a table in the corner, they seemed to be the only customers. The list of sandwich fillings, curtailed no doubt by the war, was as short as that for cakes, and Cradock didn't deliberate for long before choosing cheese and pickle. Jago took his own brief look and decided to have the same. As soon as he put the menu down, the waitress bustled over to their table: she seemed glad of something to do. She took their order and bustled away again, and within minutes was back with sandwiches, cake and a pot of tea.

'Well, then, Peter,' said Jago when she'd gone. 'What did you make of the regional sales manager?'

'Todd, you mean?' Cradock replied. 'He seemed all right. You could tell he was a salesman, though, the way he went on about those chocolates – made me feel like maybe I should take what he says with a pinch of salt. Sounded like he was quite a fan of Latham too, but then I suppose people always say nice things about you when you're dead. I got the impression Latham wasn't the only one he'd got his eye on, though – did you see the way he looked at that secretary of his?'

'I certainly did,' said Jago, pouring tea for both of them as Cradock began to attack his sandwich. 'Unfortunately I wasn't able to observe you at the same time. Where were your eyes?'

Cradock swallowed and brushed crumbs from his lips. 'Nowhere, sir. She's not my type.'

'She's certainly not like Emily, and I must say I think any sensible young man would be better off with an Emily than with a Violet. But she certainly seemed to take a shine to you, didn't she?'

'I don't know what you're talking about, sir.'

'Come now, Peter – keeping her safe in the blackout? I think I got you out of there just in time.'

Cradock blushed and changed the subject. 'The news about Latham took the wind out of her sails, though, didn't it?'

'It did, yes. I was surprised by how she took it, considering they were only work colleagues.'

'Me too. Up till then I got the impression she was the kind of girl who can take care of herself, if you know what I mean. Perhaps she had a soft spot for him – she might be called Violet, but she doesn't strike you as a particularly shrinking violet, does she?'

'No, indeed. A rather forward young lady, if anything. It'd be interesting to know whether she ever tried to work her charms on Mr Latham.'

'Wouldn't surprise me, sir – you know what they say about commercial travellers.'

'I'm not sure I do, Peter. What do they say?'

'You know, sir – they're like sailors. A girl in every port. They travel around to all their customers, away all the time staying in commercial hotels, plenty of temptation, and they reckon the wife'll never find out. They're notorious for it.'

'You think he had a mistress?'

'Maybe. Good-looking fellow, snappy dresser, with the gift of the gab too – if a bloke can sell ice cream to Eskimos, what chance does some girl in the back of beyond have?'

'Don't tar them all with the same brush – I'm sure they're not all like that. But having said that, it is possible. That fellow Rouse, the one who was convicted of murder, he was a commercial traveller. A real philanderer too.'

Cradock's face suggested he was wrestling with his memory. 'Is that someone who gives lots of money away, like that American bloke who built all the libraries?'

'Mr Carnegie, you mean? No – that's a philanthropist. A philanderer's someone who's generous in a rather different way. It means a man who . . . well, not to put too fine a point on it, a man who spends too much time with women he shouldn't be spending time with – other men's wives, for example. One of Rouse's big mistakes was

147

saying he had a personal harem. When the police dug into his past they turned up all sorts of shady goings-on – a wife here, a mistress there, a close lady friend somewhere else. I'm beginning to wonder whether beer mats weren't the only thing Mr Latham collected.'

'Sir?'

'Women, Peter – women.'

'Ah, yes, sir,' Cradock replied, embarrassed to feel his face flushing. 'So do you think he could've been leading some sort of double life?'

'I don't know, but it's certainly a question we need to look into. I think it's time we took a trip up to Cambridge – we need to find out what kind of life he lived when he was away from home. When we get back to the station I want you to ring the Cambridge police and ask if we can come up tomorrow and conduct some enquiries on their ground. We don't want to get up their nose by turning up out of the blue outside our jurisdiction. And besides, if you talk to them nicely they might be able to lend us a car – with all this business of petrol coupons I'm feeling we should perhaps travel by train and save the country some fuel.'

'Very good, sir – will do. If we go up to Cambridge tomorrow, though, isn't that when your, er . . . isn't that when Miss Appleton's invited us for that special American meal at Piccadilly Circus?'

'Yes, but that's not until the evening. There used to be a fast train from Cambridge at half-past five that got in to London a bit before seven, so find out if that service is still running and hasn't been cut for the war effort. If it is, we just need to make jolly sure we catch it. And by the way, put a clean collar on for the day so you look presentable – there won't be time to go home and change into your glad rags before we eat.'

'You don't mean we've got to wear dress suits for this meal, do you, sir? I haven't got one of them.'

'Certainly not. I haven't got one either, but I shall be wearing my best suit, if only to keep our end up – we don't want the people of Cambridgeshire or the local constabulary to get the idea that the Metropolitan Police are a bunch of scruffs.'

Cradock wondered whether an outing for Jago's best suit was really about impressing the natives of Cambridgeshire or perhaps more about making the right impression on the lady hosting their meal, but he valued his life too dearly to betray even a hint of such thinking. 'Yes, sir, definitely, I'll do my best,' he said, and changed the subject. 'Actually, I'm surprised we didn't find a dress suit in Latham's wardrobe, what with him having such a flashy taste in clothes. And talking of finding things, there's another thing I was thinking about too.'

'Really?'

'Yes, sir, it was what that bloke Bowen was saying about those tools in Latham's car. He said you might need things like a hammer and a jemmy if your car breaks down in the middle of nowhere.'

'Like Cambridgeshire, for example?'

'Yes, sir. But that list of things in the Larceny Act – what it calls "implements of house-breaking" – that list has things like jacks and jemmies in it, doesn't it? So what if Latham's other life included a bit of quiet burglary on the side? Like what Mr Hardacre said – breaking into houses out in the country where there's no bobbies about? Just a thought, sir.'

'Well, we've no evidence he was getting up to anything like that, but on the other hand it does seem that Mr Latham was a man of many parts, some of which perhaps we've yet to discover.'

CHAPTER TWENTY

Jago paid for the food and drinks, and he and Cradock returned to Baring and Sons, where they made their own way to the office Todd had mentioned. It was clearly intended for members of staff somewhat lower in the corporate hierarchy than Todd himself. For a start there was no secretary waiting to intercept them, and the furniture and fittings looked less cared for than his. Moreover, the number of desks indicated that it was a shared office, although only one of them was occupied when they entered it.

Jack Henderson introduced himself and dragged over a couple of chairs for them. He was as smartly dressed as Jago imagined his late colleague would have been. He remembered what Rose Latham had said about the importance of making the right impression, and idly wondered whether salesmen received a special clothing allowance from their employer, just as he and Cradock got their plain clothes allowance from the Metropolitan Police.

If they did, Latham's suits suggested Baring and Sons must be more generous than his own employers, as did the one Henderson was wearing. Jago took in the rest of the man's appearance. He was tall, with a confident manner, clear blue eyes, a broad smile revealing good teeth, and a full head of dark hair that looked as though it was naturally wavy but had been tamed by a regular application of Brylcreem. Clearly he was a man who liked to make the right impression too.

Henderson shook both detectives firmly by the hand and invited them to sit. 'Mr Todd said you wanted to talk to me about poor Les Latham. I must confess I'm still a bit dazed by the news – it's all been such a shock. He was one of those people who're always so full of life and energy, it's hard to take it in when someone tells you he's . . . he's not here any more. And now Mr Todd tells me you think he was murdered. I can't believe it.'

'I'm sorry, Mr Henderson,' said Jago. 'I'm told that you were a close colleague of Mr Latham.'

'Yes, we were pals – we worked together for years. If there's anything I can do to help you I'll be more than happy.'

'Thank you. I'm hoping you might be able to tell us a bit about him.'

'Of course. What would you like to know?'

'I'd like to know what kind of man he was, in your opinion.'

'Well, the main thing to say is that he was a great salesman. Been in the job for years, knew it inside out. Loads of ex-servicemen went into sales work after the last war, officers too, but a lot of them didn't last long – they just didn't have what it takes. Les, though, he was a born salesman. He loved selling, and I reckon he could sell just about anything, as long as he believed in the product – that's very important, you see, because if you don't believe in it you'll have a hard time persuading your customer to.'

'Was he an ex-officer?'

'Oh, no, not Les. He was more your salt of the earth type. He was in the army, same as me, but he had a cushy job driving officers round in a staff car. Typical of Les to land a job like that. I don't know how he got it, but he was the sort of bloke who always seemed to know someone who could fix things for him, put in a good word, that sort of thing. Good at calling in favours too. He probably knew someone who'd be able to help him – or maybe he knew something that he could turn to his advantage, as you might say. A lot of men at the front would've given their right arm for a job like that.' He paused. 'Well, not literally, of course – they wouldn't have got a job as a driver if they only had one arm. Although knowing Les, he probably could have. But anyway, whatever he did to get it, he was lucky he did. It probably helped him get the commercial traveller job, too – there's a lot of driving involved, of course, and he was very experienced at that. There wasn't much he didn't know about cars and engines.'

'Can you tell us a bit about his job here at Barings?'

'Certainly. I suppose the first thing to say is it's not what you might think. When you talk about a commercial traveller, a lot of people think of some poor old bloke with a suitcase full of brushes trying to flog them to housewives on their doorstep.'

'I suppose that's true, yes.'

'That's what we call "working on the knocker". That's how Les and I both started out, foot-slogging round the streets, but it's not what we do now. Our job's about selling to the retailers. We visit the people who run the shops – everything from chain stores to village grocers – and present our range of products to them, especially anything new we've brought out. We take their orders, then supply the goods to them. Lots of these people've been our customers for years, so we're not doing some kind of fly-by-night job – you know, sell them some dodgy stuff, take their money and run. No – we build a relationship with our clients for the long term and we help to make them successful.'

'And I understand Mr Latham's job used to take him up to Cambridge.'

'Yes. Each traveller covers a different territory, you see, and Les's was Cambridge and the surrounding area, so he visited shops in the town itself and in the villages round it. Most weeks he'd drive up there for a few days while he did his rounds, then come home again.'

'And I think Mr Todd said your territory is west London and Middlesex?'

'Yes, that's right. It means I can live here in Camden Town, not far from the office – I've got a little flat in Lyme Terrace, overlooking the canal. It's not exactly the Ritz, but it's very handy – I can drive to my clients and be back home nearly every evening. Good for my beauty sleep, you know.'

'I see. So can you tell me where you were yesterday morning, between seven and eight o'clock?'

'What? Am I a suspect?'

'No, no – it's just a routine question.'

'Well, I'm afraid my answer's pretty routine too – I would've been getting out of my bath and having a spot of breakfast. The all-clear had gone at about five, if I recall correctly, so I came back into the house, which thank the Lord was still standing, and tried to get an hour or two's sleep in my own bed. Not that I did, of course – I think I was too cold to get back to sleep, but at least I was out of that confounded shelter. Horrible things, they are. But anyway, I'm sure you don't want to know all that. What else can I tell you?'

'Can anyone else corroborate your account?'

'If you mean was I sharing the bath with anyone to save water, the answer's no. I wasn't even sharing breakfast. I'm a confirmed and contented bachelor, and I live alone.'

'I see. There's something else you might be able to help me with. Tell me – was Mr Latham happy in his job?'

'Yes, I think he was. He enjoyed being out on the road – said it gave him a real feeling of freedom. Besides, nothing got him down – he was a real optimist, and that's the most important thing if you want to succeed in this business. You've got to believe you're going to go in there and get a sale. The same goes for any business, I should think – you need to know what you want, have the confidence to believe you'll get it, and take whatever risks you must to succeed.'

'Someone we spoke to earlier today described him as ambitious. Would you agree?'

'Yes, definitely. He used to say life was a game and he was lucky, so he was going to win – and have a bit of fun on the way. The thing about Les, you see, was he just loved selling – that's probably why he was so good at it. He never seemed to get fed up with it, even though we've been through some tough times over the years – ups and downs like the Depression, when people don't have so much to spend on chocolates and the like.'

'And now? I expect the war's affected your work.'

'I should say so. The company can't get as much sugar as it used to, so that's certainly affected us – that and the petrol rationing.'

'Yes, that must be difficult in a job that involves being on the road a lot. But if you're a commercial traveller you can get extra petrol, can't you?'

'Yes. We couldn't at first, but we kicked up such a fuss the government changed the regulations. Now we can get a bit more, but it depends on what car you've got.'

'I believe Mr Latham's car was a Standard – a Flying Standard Eight.'

'Yes. Very proud of it he was – said it could do eighty-two miles an hour, although who needs that on our roads? But the important thing as far as the petrol ration's concerned is that it's an eight-horsepower car, which means the government allows you coupons for an extra thirteen gallons on top of the basic allowance of five. That makes eighteen gallons a month, but it's still not enough to get round all your customers as often as you should.'

'I see.'

'Of course, what he really would've liked is a Rover. He thought they were a cut above the Standards and the Austins, just like he was a cut above the average salesman – and I think that Viking ship the Rovers have on their radiator badge took his fancy. Trouble is, I don't think Rover are making an eight-horse saloon these days – the nearest thing's the Rover Ten Special, but the company has a strict policy on the cars it provides. Eight horsepower for travellers, ten for area managers, twelve for regional managers. Above that, I think they probably just get what they want.' Henderson paused for a moment, lost in his own thoughts. 'Mind you,' he said, 'if Les had managed to get the Ten Special he might still be here.'

'Why's that?'

'Oh, it's just that I think that's the model that has the body panels and floorboards sprayed on the inside with asbestos to fireproof it. Quite a strong selling point, I should think, even without those incendiary bombs they keep dropping on us. Anyway, maybe if he'd had one of them he would've got out in time to save his life. We'll never know, will we?' He glanced up at the clock on the office wall. 'Look here, Inspector, I'm terribly sorry, but I've got an appointment with a customer that I really have to keep, so I need to go. Was there anything else you wanted to ask?'

'There are one or two things, but they can wait. We're going to be busy all day tomorrow, but perhaps we could call in the day after tomorrow, if that's not inconvenient for you?'

'That'll be fine – I'll be out in the morning, but should be here in the office in the afternoon.'

'Very well, Mr Henderson, we'll see you then.'

Jago and Cradock left his office and walked back along the deserted corridor. Cradock was looking puzzled. 'Sir,' he began, 'what he said just then—'

Jago put a finger to his lips. 'Not yet, Peter. Wait till we're outside – walls have ears, you know.'

Cradock fell silent until they were out of the building

and not at risk of being overheard. He was about to finish his question, but Jago spoke first.

'Look at that lovely sky,' he said, stopping a few steps away from Barings' front door.

Cradock looked up. 'Sir?'

'So bright and blue – could almost make you forget it's November, couldn't it? We might not see another sky like that till next spring, and who knows where we'll all be by then, eh?'

'Yes, sir.'

'Just the day for a trip to the seaside – but unfortunately we have a job to do, so I suggest we do the next best thing.'

'What's that, sir?'

'We'll leave the car here and take a little walk beside the still waters of the Regent's Canal and see if we can find Hawley lock – I fancy seeing whether Mr Trent's at home on his narrowboat, and it must only be about half a mile from here.'

'Righto, sir.'

They set off towards Camden High Street, in the direction of the canal.

'So what was it you were going to say, Peter?' said Jago.

'Oh, yes,' said Cradock. 'I was just going to say that what he said just then – Henderson, that is – it didn't make sense. He said if Latham had been in a car with asbestos or whatever it was to fireproof it, he might've got out in time to save his life. But he couldn't have – he'd been murdered.'

'Yes, but we know that because Dr Gibson's told us Latham was already dead before the fire started. What Mr Henderson's just said is what someone would say if they didn't know that – they might think he'd been murdered by being shut into a car that was then set on fire.'

'Oh, right, yes.'

'Of course, what we don't know is what Mr Henderson actually knows or doesn't know about how Latham died.'

'You mean you think he could be lying?'

'I don't know. I just believe in maintaining a healthy scepticism until I have convincing evidence.'

'I see, sir, yes – I think.'

'Did anything else strike you?'

'One little thing, yes – what Henderson said about Latham liking the Rover because it's got a Viking ship on its badge. What do you think he was getting at?'

'I'm not sure – it seems a very small thing to influence your choice of car. Perhaps he thought Latham saw himself as some kind of latter-day Viking chieftain – you know, conquering all in his path.'

'Right,' said Cradock. 'I suppose it must be dog eat dog in that kind of business, when you've got to out-sell the competition, but even so, those Vikings . . . I mean, it wasn't exactly a vicarage tea party when they turned up, was it? Not the nicest way to get to the top in your job, even if you're a salesman. Couldn't happen in the police, could it?'

Jago glanced sideways to check whether Cradock's face betrayed any hint of sarcasm or merely playful cheek but found no evidence of either. 'I think it'd be frowned upon, Peter, from below if not from above. But you have to admit, those Vikings certainly knew how to get things done.'

'Henderson said Latham was ambitious, didn't he, and so did Mrs Crow. So if he *was* trying to get to the top, do you think he might not've drawn the line at being a bit rough on the way?'

'Sharp elbows, you mean?'

'Yes. He might've made a few enemies, mightn't he? And didn't the Vikings burn their dead kings in their boat?'

'I'm not sure they actually did that, Peter. And besides, even if they did, I don't think a self-respecting Viking chieftain would've willingly embarked on his final journey to Valhalla in a Standard Eight.'

CHAPTER TWENTY-ONE

Jago had never been to Venice, but he'd seen pictures of its elegant buildings and wondered at the thought of a city whose streets were canals and whose buses were gondolas. He had no expectation of finding such aquatic delights in Camden Town, and if there were any residual romantic notions lingering in his mind they were soon dispelled by his first close-up acquaintance with the Regent's Canal. True, the narrowboats were painted in delightful patterns of blue, red, green and yellow, and looked scrupulously clean in the winter sunlight, but everything around them presented a dismal contrast. The banks of the canal were lined by smoke-grimed warehouses and a dingy hotch-potch of commercial premises, while the oily surface of its stagnant water shimmered in what seemed to him a weak and mocking parody of the boats' rainbow-coloured decorations.

Their police warrant cards having gained them access to the canal's towpath, Jago and Cradock walked along it in search of Jimmy Trent's boat. When they reached Hawley lock the canal widened and they could see the *Jasmine* moored halfway along the northern bank. Across the water, a ramshackle brick structure bearing the name of Henly's Garage rose bleakly from the canal-side, an ungainly emblem of the area's grim functionality.

'What are you hoping to get out of Jimmy Trent, sir?' said Cradock. 'Assuming he's at home, that is.'

'I'm interested in what Henderson said about Latham being so ambitious,' Jago replied. 'That's the sort of thing that can make enemies for you. The way he talked about that cushy job he said Latham got in the army made it sound like it wasn't necessarily all above board. Trent knew him back in those days, so I'd like to know whether he can tell us about any strings Latham might've pulled to get the job.'

'Or palms he might've greased?'

'Precisely – anything's possible if an ambitious man happens to be a bit unscrupulous too. We'll see what our boatman has to say.'

Trent's head emerged from the *Jasmine*'s cabin as they approached, and he stepped onto the bank to welcome them. 'Hello – you're looking for me, are you?' he said.

'That's right, Mr Trent. We'd just like to ask you a few more questions about Mr Latham. May we come aboard?'

'Be my guests. Watch your heads, though, and mind how you go – there's not a lot of space down there.'

They entered the cabin, followed by Trent. It wasn't much bigger than Jago's Anderson shelter at home:

barely seven feet wide and similar in length, with not even five feet of headroom, and yet this was presumably where a whole family had to live, every day of the year.

'Cosy, isn't it?' said Trent.

'Decidedly,' Jago replied. 'How on earth do you manage?'

'Well, for one thing, it helps if you're not too tall – boat people tend not to breed their kids to be policemen. But apart from that, you just have to make every inch count. Take a seat there on the side-bed, and I'll perch down here.'

The bed in question was little more than a wooden bench, only four feet long, if that, but the two detectives squeezed onto it as best they could.

'Where do you put children in a place this size?' said Cradock.

'It depends how many you've got. When you make the bed up where you're sitting you can get three little ones in, with the cross-bed at the end there for Mum and Dad. If you've got any extras they have to sleep on the floor.'

'What about when they get too big to fit?'

'The way boat people've always done it is when the kids are too big or too old to sleep all in the same cabin they get sent away to work on someone else's boat – in my case that was when I was eight.'

'Do you have children yourself?' Jago asked.

'We've got a daughter who's married and a son who's away in the army. We had another two, but we lost them both when they were little – Daisy died of measles and Bobby drowned in the canal. Now it's just me and Annie. She's out on the bank at the moment, shopping for something to cook for our tea – should be back soon. I don't suppose you came here to talk about my family, though. What is it you want to know?'

'I'd like to know more about Mr Latham's war service. One or two people we've been talking to have described him as ambitious, and you said yourself he knew what he wanted and always seemed to know how to get it. I'm interested in that job you said he got in the army, as a driver. Since you told us that, someone else has suggested he might've manipulated his way into the job, possibly to improve his own chances of surviving the war. Are you aware of anything that might confirm that?'

'Ah, well, I, er, wasn't going to mention that.'

'Mention what?'

Trent hesitated. 'I don't know whether I should tell you, really. I mean, Les was a mate of mine.'

'Nothing you say can harm him now, Mr Trent. And it may help us to find out who killed him, so I'd appreciate it if you'd tell us.'

'All right, then. The thing is, Les was very friendly and all that, but if you're saying was he ambitious, I'd say yes, he was, and sometimes that brought out another side to him.'

'A mean streak?'

'Yes, you could call it that, I suppose. I'd say more of a nasty streak – he wanted to get on, and he'd do things that I wouldn't do if he thought it'd help him. Nasty things.'

'Was that how he got that driver job?'

'Yes, I think maybe it was. I don't know the whole story – probably no one does now – but there was something he told me when we met up again after the war was over. We'd had a pint or two together one night in the pub, and I said he'd managed to land on his feet when he got that job, lucky bloke – it'd got him out of the trenches. He said yes, it was lucky, but it was because he'd made a smart move too. He said sometimes you've got to make your own luck, so I asked him what he meant, and he told me this story.' He hesitated again.

'Go on,' said Jago. 'I'd like to know.'

'Well, he'd been sent on some errand to battalion headquarters, and while he was there he overheard a junior officer talking to the lieutenant-colonel. The junior bloke – a lieutenant, I think Les said – sounded all het up about something. Seems it was all about some malarkey he'd got up to with another officer that he shouldn't have, and the lieutenant-colonel said they'd have to hush it up for the sake of morale and the lieutenant's family, so Les tucked it all away in his mind. A few months later this same Lieutenant So-and-So turns up as a new officer in Les's company, and Les has a bright idea.'

'Let me guess – he blackmails him?'

'I think so, yes. He didn't use that word – he just said he'd managed to turn that little bit of knowledge into five pounds for what he called his personal post-war recovery fund.'

'Did he mention the officer's name?'

'Yes, he said he heard the lieutenant-colonel say something like, "Look, Binnie, you can't afford to go making a fool of yourself like that – the high command tends to take a dim view of that kind of thing." So he was

Lieutenant Binnie, I suppose, but Les never mentioned his Christian name.'

'Do you know whether he got more money out of this man later?'

'No, Les didn't say, but I wouldn't be surprised. He did say the lieutenant had kindly put in a good word for him, though, when some staff officer was looking for a new driver. So that's how he got the job and got out of the trenches.'

'I see. Well, thank you, Mr Trent, that's very interesting. Was he involved in your own escape from the trenches, by any chance?'

'What, did he fix it for me to be a batman? No, that was just something that happened. Some people reckoned I'd landed a cushy number, but really I was just taken to be some officer's skivvy. A "soldier servant", that's what they called it in those days, and that's exactly what it was. At his lordship's beck and call morning, noon and night, cooking his food, washing his clothes, polishing his boots, fetching his water – you name it, I had to do it. And all that for one and six a day. Officer's slave, more like. I wasn't used to living like that – before they took me away for the army I was a number one – that means master of my own boat, like my old dad before me, not working on someone else's. Yes, it was a hard life on the canal, and it still is, but I was a free man, and I prefer to stay that way.'

'How is business, now that we're at war again?'

'Oh, up and down, you know. The government's put some money into the canals because of the war, so there's more traffic now, which is good for people like me, and we're getting jobs like carrying metal to the munitions factories. But even so, it's not what it was – everything's changed. I mean, I never thought I'd switch to a motor boat, but that shows how much I know, doesn't it?'

'Ah, yes – how's your repair coming along?'

'It's not fixed yet – we're waiting for a part, and it's not so easy to get spares now there's a war on. Makes me wish we still had old Tom – he was the horse we used to have for pulling the boat. He died last year, and we realised we'd have to bite the bullet and move with the times. I loved old Tom. He knew this canal so well, he didn't really need me to lead him – he could find his own way along just as well without me. He'd just plod along with me beside him, thirty miles a day, pulling a seventy-foot narrowboat with forty tons of coal on it, and Annie at the back, steering.'

'Do you always carry coal?'

'Sometimes, from the mines in the Midlands down to London, then back up again with a backload of grain. If you've got a contract you might carry the same thing all the time, but when you're running your own boat the customers just take you on for one load at a time, so you have to take what you can get. Not that I mind. In fact I prefer it that way – no contracts to tie you down, just a straight three quid a trip, cash in hand. So basically we carry whatever anyone wants us to. It might be timber, or stone, or cocoa beans up from Limehouse for that company Les worked for.'

'Baring and Sons?'

'That's the one, although nowadays it depends on whether the ships've got through from Africa or wherever. We can't carry as much as we did when we had

Tom – the diesel engine takes up a bit of space, not to mention the fuel tank – but now we've got the motor we can keep going for longer. All night long, if we want to, because we don't have to stable the horse for the night any more. With old Tom, shifting a load of coals from the Midlands to London used to take a week, but when we switched to the diesel we could do two trips a week. Not because it's faster – the law says we can only go at the same pace as a horse – but the motor boat can go for longer. Mind you, that's all gone by the board since the air raids started.'

'Tell me, do you ever carry petrol?'

'No. Some do, but not me. There was this thing that happened, back in Queen Victoria's time, where the canal goes round the top side of Regent's Park – my dad told me. There was a boat, see, the *Tilbury*, carrying gunpowder for the coal mines, but it had a couple of barrels of petroleum on board too, and my dad said they reckoned the fumes had been leaking out into the cabin, where the stove was burning. I don't think that petroleum stuff they had in the old days was the same thing as petrol like we have now, but it was just as dangerous. Anyway, you can probably guess what happened – the whole lot went up with a bang. All three men on board were killed, and the bridge they were going under got blown up.'

'I imagine the chances of anyone carrying petrol and gunpowder on the same boat would be slim today.'

Trent laughed. 'I should say so – you'd need your head examining.'

'Speaking of petrol, is that something Mr Latham ever talked to you about?'

'What, you mean petrol in general? I expect he must've done from time to time, what with the price going up.'

'I'm wondering whether he ever talked about difficulties in getting hold of it – one of his colleagues told us it's been a job for commercial travellers to get as much as they need.'

'Oh, yes, he did mention that once or twice. I remember one chat we had that stuck in my mind – probably because it was to do with some Russians.'

'Really? I'd be interested to hear more, if you don't mind.'

'Certainly. So, it was September last year when the petrol rationing started, wasn't it? Right at the beginning of the war?'

'That's right.'

'Well, I was talking to Les, and he said he was worried, because he used a lot of petrol for his work, driving around here, there and everywhere, and if the government started rationing it he might be out of a job. He said he might need to find some way of getting hold of some extra. That's when I thought of the Russians.'

'The Russians in general, or did you have some particular ones in mind?'

'I meant the ones down the canal, with that wharf.'

'I'm sorry, Mr Trent, you'll have to explain.'

'Ah, yes, of course. Well, there's a wharf on the canal, near Northampton, where I was offloading some stone for building one day, a year or two before the war started. I got talking to a bloke there and it turned out he was a Russian – spoke English, of course. I told him I'd been to Russia in 1919, and he was quite pally – I didn't tell him I was there with the army to fight the Reds, of course, because I thought what with the Reds winning, he was probably one himself. But anyway, he worked for an oil company that stored petrol on the same wharf and he was very interested in the canal and all the locks and things. When he found out I was a boatman he asked if I could show him round next time he was down this way and tell him all about it.'

'So you gave him a guided tour?'

'Well, I don't meet many foreigners in the normal run of things, but I like to be friendly, so I said yes. I showed him the locks at Camden and told him all about the stuff we transport on the canal and all that. He seemed very pleased with it all, and when we finished he said he'd like to give me a couple of bottles of vodka by way of a thank you. I said that's very kind of you, but I've tried it and it doesn't agree with me. He seemed to think that was very odd. So then he says would I like some petrol – again, as a present, like. I said sorry, but I don't have any use for petrol – my boat's pulled by a horse, and I certainly haven't got a car. He said never mind, then, shook my hand, and said if ever you get a car or start drinking like a proper man, just come and see me at the wharf.'

'And did you take him up on his offer?'

'No, but when this rationing thing started, next time I was calling at that wharf I looked the Russian bloke up and told him about this friend of mine who's a commercial traveller and getting worried about running short of petrol, and the Russian said maybe he could help him. So I told Les where he could find him.'

'And did Mr Latham get in touch with him?'

'He didn't mention it, so I asked him one day and he

said no, he hadn't. Then a bit later I noticed they seemed to have closed down their business at the wharf and gone, so I suppose he missed his chance.'

'Do you remember the name of the company?'

'Yes, that's easy – they were Russians selling oil and petrol, and the company was called Russian Oil Products.'

'Ah, yes,' said Jago. 'I think I've heard of them. Thank you, Mr Trent.'

'You're welcome – any time. I'd better be getting on, though – I need to go and find out whether that part's come in yet, for the motor. It's funny, you know – here's me still rushing around trying to get the boat fixed and talking about Les, but he's not here any more. He used to have so much energy, but now . . .' He broke off, seemingly lost in his thoughts. 'But perhaps he's well out of it, what with the mess we're all in with this war. It's poor Rose I feel sorry for – she's the one who's got to keep soldiering on. I've been to see her, by the way – to pay my respects, like.'

'How was she?'

'Oh, bearing up, I think, as well as can be expected under the circumstances. Her eyes were all red when I got there, though, like she'd been crying. I was thinking maybe I ought to ask her if she had, but before I could she said sorry, like, said she'd just discovered something that'd upset her.'

'Did she say what that was?'

'No – she just said she'd found something in Les's stuff that she wasn't expecting. She didn't say anything more about it, but I could tell she'd had a bit of a shock.'

CHAPTER TWENTY-TWO

When he'd finished his questions for Trent, Jago clambered out of the *Jasmine's* cabin and onto the canal bank, followed by Cradock. As he put his hat on, he noticed a middle-aged woman in a threadbare overcoat trudging towards them with a shopping basket on her arm. She was heading for the boat, but seemed to take no interest in the two strangers who had just emerged from it.

She drew level without deviating from her path, so Jago stepped to one side and raised his hat to her. 'Mrs Trent?' he enquired.

She stared at him blankly, then with only the slightest of nods she edged past him onto the boat, setting her basket down by the cabin doors. Trent stuck his head out. 'This is my wife, Inspector,' he said. 'Annie.' He took her hand. 'In you come, dear.'

Once she was in the cabin, Trent came out and joined

Jago and Cradock on the bank. 'You'll have to excuse her,' he said. 'Annie's not very talkative at the moment. She's not herself, see.'

Jago recalled him saying that things were difficult and wasn't sure whether this new comment was an invitation to enquire further, but while he was still wondering whether to ask, Trent continued.

'I'd better explain,' he said. 'Let's just move down the bank a bit.'

He took a few paces along the towpath and then, judging that they were far enough from the boat to be out of earshot, he stopped and faced them. 'She's a good woman, you know – normally she'd be as bright as a button and very friendly, but she's had a difficult time. She's got a couple of cousins, you see, one of them with a new baby. They live up in Coventry.'

At the mention of the city's name, Jago guessed what might be coming next, but he didn't want to interrupt.

'We took a load up there a couple of weeks ago,' said Trent, 'and when we'd got it offloaded at the wharf, Annie went to visit the one with the baby, to help her, like. She was going to stay for a day or two while I brought another load back down this way with a mate of mine. So we did that, and then I went back to drop him off and pick up Annie, but as we got near Coventry I could tell something wasn't right. You can always see three church spires lined up in a row – that's how you know it's Coventry. But now we could see something else – there was smoke everywhere. It was only when we got there we discovered there'd been this terrible air raid.'

'You hadn't heard about it?'

'No, but then we wouldn't, would we? When you're a boatman on the canal it's not like living in a town – it's a world of its own, and you're cut off from what's going on outside it. I've never had a wireless on the boat, and a newspaper's no use to me.' He looked embarrassed. 'It's the reading, see. I'm not that good at it – that's why I don't like contracts. When I was a kid we never got any proper schooling, on account of always being on the move. I had the odd day here and there, but not enough to learn things like reading and writing. I just have to get by the best I can without it.'

'Was your wife caught in the air raid?'

'Yes. She hasn't spoken a word about it, but her cousin told me hundreds of planes came over in the night, and the whole sky was lit up red from the fires. She said it was terrifying, bombs falling all the time. And when the all-clear went in the morning and they came out of the shelter, the whole city centre had gone, blown to pieces and burning, with a horrible stench of gas and sewage everywhere. She said she didn't see a single street that hadn't been bombed. By the time I found Annie, she was in a terrible state – not speaking, just shaking. She hasn't been the same since. She gets on with her chores and steers the boat, just like she's always done, but she doesn't talk like she used to. When she's not working she just sits and stares. It reminds me of those blokes who got shell shock in the war. They were the same – just staring. You were a soldier, weren't you? Did you see that?'

'Yes, I did. I'm very sorry about your wife – it must've been an awful experience for her.'

'It was, but I don't know how to help her. I'm just hoping she'll get over it and get back to her old self, but that didn't happen for all those lads in the war, did it?'

For a moment it looked as though Trent was on the verge of tears, but he steeled himself. 'I'll have to take her to the panel doctor. Like as not he'll just prescribe a tonic and leave her to it, but I can't afford anything fancier than that. I don't know what's going to become of her.' He glanced back at the boat. 'Look, I'd better go and see what she's doing. Please excuse me.'

Jago watched Trent disappear back into the narrowboat and shook his head.

'Poor bloke,' said Cradock.

'Poor bloke indeed,' Jago replied. 'Sounds like she's going to need more than a tonic.'

'Yes, and he's got a lot more on his plate than worrying about whether she'll find out he's been playing cards.'

CHAPTER TWENTY-THREE

The sky was growing a little overcast as the two detectives made their way along the towpath back to the road. At the lock a boatman was vigorously winding on the mechanism that controlled the gates, perhaps with a view to mooring his narrowboat for the night in the pound. Jago wondered what boat people did for shelter during the air raids. Their wooden boats would offer no protection against bombs, so he could only guess that they must run to the nearest public shelter, if there was one. Another reason not to envy their way of life. Still, Trent seemed to be content with it.

'Well, then, Peter,' he said, 'what did you make of that? Not often you get to see the inside of a canal boat, is it? First time for me, anyway.'

'Me too, sir. I was mainly thinking I'm glad I didn't grow up on one. Kicked out of home to go and work somewhere else when you're eight? No thank you.'

'Ah, but that was before you were born – things've probably changed since then.'

'I should hope so too.'

'And what about Mr Trent?'

'Well, I thought what he said about Latham and that officer was interesting.'

'It was, wasn't it? Quite revealing. A bit of blackmail and extortion on the side to land yourself a nice cosy job in the middle of a war and get yourself out of harm's way – not exactly Viking warrior stuff, but it's not playing by the rules, is it? He seems to have had rules of his own, especially when it came to looking after number one. And when I say number one I don't mean Trent and his boat – Latham doesn't seem to have done much to help his old pal, does he?'

'No – Trent probably thinks Latham didn't know the meaning of hard work, tootling round the country in his little car with his chocolates. And what about those Russians? That's a bit mysterious, isn't it?'

'On the face of it, yes. I think that might be worth looking into. What I'd like to do now, though, is extend our walk a bit further – I want to ask Rose Latham what exactly it was she found that gave her such a shock.'

When they got to the flat in Belmont Street, Rose Latham looked surprised to see them but invited them in. 'Have you found out who did it?' she asked anxiously as they sat down in her living room. 'I couldn't sleep last night – I kept thinking about it, but my mind just kept going round in circles.'

'I'm sorry to hear that,' said Jago. 'It must be a very difficult time for you.'

'It is, yes. Everyone's been very kind, though. The neighbours have popped round, and one or two people have put notes through the door saying how sorry they are to hear the news, but I haven't had time yet to go round and thank anyone.'

'Ah, that reminds me – Mr Bowen at the garage asked us to pass on his condolences to you.'

'Oh – er, right. If you see him again, please say thanks from me. It's very thoughtful of him.' She seemed distracted for a moment, but then continued in what sounded like a resolute tone. 'But I can't just sit around all day brooding on it – there's a lot to do when someone passes away, isn't there? And there's still bills to be paid, so I suppose I'm going to have to deal with money and all that – I always left that sort of thing to Les, but it'll have to be me now.'

'Do you have any income of your own?'

'Have I got a job, you mean? No, I've never worked. Les always said he'd earn enough for the two of us. He was a bit old-fashioned like that, but he always did, so we've never had any money problems.'

'I'm told the company has a good pension scheme.'

'So they say, but I don't know how much I'll get yet.'

'Did your husband have any life insurance? He had to do a lot of driving, after all.'

'Yes, he did. You're right about the driving – he was on the road one way or another every day of the week, and when the war started there were so many accidents in the blackout, my mum said I ought to make sure he had some good life insurance. Personally I've always thought it's bad luck to do that kind of thing – you know, tempting fate – but I asked him about it, and he said he would, just in case.

I haven't managed to find the policy yet, though.'

'As you said, there's a lot to do.'

'There is, but it's probably good to keep myself busy. Somehow it doesn't seem to matter any more whether everything's clean and tidy now that I'm on my own, but, well, you've got your self-respect, haven't you? Can't just let things slide. I've started tidying things up, going through the wardrobe and sorting out Les's stuff. Everyone's collecting clothes these days, aren't they, for refugees and bombed-out families and what have you. There's a church down the road doing it. I thought I'd take some of Les's old things down there.' She paused for a moment. 'I might try and sell those suits, though – they're good quality, and I should be able to get a few bob for them. Those hats of his, too – I mean, a bowler's no use to me, is it?'

Her question hung on the air, unanswered.

'Speaking of tidying up, Mrs Latham,' said Jago, 'we were talking to Mr Trent this afternoon, and he mentioned that you'd found something among your husband's possessions that came as a surprise to you. I wondered if you could tell us what that was.'

Rose bit her lip, hesitating. 'Yes,' she said. 'There was something. I, er . . . well, to tell you the truth, I don't know what to make of it. You know how we're supposed to take important documents like birth certificates and things to the shelter with us when there's an air raid on?'

'Yes.'

'Well, Les used to have an old leather briefcase for that, and he always took it down to the shelter, so I was looking for it when I was going through some of his stuff yesterday. I found it at the bottom of the wardrobe, under some old clothes. He used to keep it locked, because he said he had some other things in it too – important papers to do with his work, he said. He never liked me looking at his things – his work things, I mean. He said I wasn't to, it was commercial, confidential, so I didn't. Anyway, he said the company'd told him he had to keep them locked up. I couldn't see the key anywhere, so I phoned Barings and spoke to his boss, Mr Todd, but he said they'd never asked him to keep any papers locked up – said I must be mistaken. I thought I can't leave things like my birth certificate locked up like that with no key, so I took a screwdriver to it and forced the lock – it was a flimsy old briefcase, so it was quite easy.'

'What did you find?'

'Some of the things I'd expect to find, like the birth certificates, and our marriage certificate, and quite a bit of cash – thirty-two pounds ten, to be precise. But then I found . . . well, let me show you.'

She crossed to the fireplace and pulled what looked at first like a small notebook from behind the clock on the mantelpiece, then handed it to Jago. One glance told him it wasn't a notebook. The cover identified it as a Post Office Savings Bank book. He looked inside. It had Latham's name and home address at the top of the page, and it listed a series of deposits totalling three hundred and twenty-seven pounds but no withdrawals. There were also a few loose pieces of paper in the back, which he slipped into his trouser pocket for safe keeping while he turned the pages. 'I see,' he said. 'So this is what came as a surprise to you?'

'Surprise? I was shocked. I had no idea – have you seen how much he's got in that account? He's been salting cash away for years without telling me. And why? I don't understand. It makes me feel like I didn't really know him. It's not nice, finding out your husband's got secrets when he's not here to explain them. Do you know anything about this?'

'No, I don't, Mrs Latham. But I think I'd like to find out if I can. May I hold on to this for a while?'

'Please do. I suppose I get all his money now he's died, do I?'

'I imagine so, but it may depend on whether he made a will. I'm afraid I can't advise you on matters like that, though – you'd need to speak to a lawyer. But you're sure he never mentioned anything about these savings?'

'He never breathed a word. And now what am I supposed to make of it? For all I know, he could've been saving up to surprise me with a new house or a trip to America – or he might just as well've been planning to run off with someone else. And now I'll never know.'

'Do you seriously think he could've been thinking of doing that?'

'Leaving me, you mean? I'd like to say no, but I know what you men are like. You're all the same – any bit of skirt that comes along can turn your head, then you're off like a lamb to the slaughter.'

Jago's face must have betrayed his surprise at this outburst, as she continued immediately, 'But that's just it, isn't it? Now I've seen that damned savings book, I'll never be able to stop thinking about it and I'll never be able to get him to explain just what he thought he was getting up to behind my back.'

She spun away angrily to face the wall, her fists clenched,

and took several deep breaths before turning back to him. 'I'm sorry, Inspector, you'll have to excuse me – I think my emotions are a bit raw at the moment. My mum says I'll probably be like that until there's a funeral, and then I'll start to feel better once it's done. But what happens about a funeral? For Les I mean. How long do I have to wait?'

'It depends on the coroner. He has to release the body for burial.'

'The coroner? But that could take ages – they must be working every minute of the day, with all those people getting killed in air raids.'

'It's not as bad as you might think, actually. The government's said coroners don't have to hold inquests if they're satisfied a death's due to war operations, and of course that covers people killed in air raids. A case of suspected murder's different, though – there still has to be an inquest for that.'

'So I just have to wait for the coroner, do I?'

'Yes. In a case like that, the inquest's normally adjourned until any criminal proceedings are completed. Once that's over, the coroner decides when to release the body to you for burial or cremation, as you prefer.'

Rose shook her head and smiled briefly to herself. 'You know, for a man who never seemed particularly religious to me, Les was quite worried about what way he should go when the time came, if you know what I mean. No one in his family had ever been cremated – but then it used to be illegal, didn't it, so that's hardly surprising. Me, I've always been clear I want to be buried the proper way, so that's what I'm going to do for Les. He thought getting cremated would be cheaper, and less of a palaver, but at the same time I think he was worried – just in case it turned out there was a life after death. We went to his aunty's funeral years ago, and you know how the vicar says "The dead shall be raised incorruptible"? I didn't think anything about it, but Les said to me what happens if I'm cremated, then? There'll be nothing left to be raised. I reckon he thought if he was cremated – well, he'd have literally burnt his boats.' She forced a weak laugh. 'He never did decide what he wanted, but I suppose now he can have it both ways – cremated in his precious car and then buried too.'

Jago was surprised at her remark. There was something callous about it that didn't quite fit with the conventional image of a bereaved wife grieving the loss of her husband. But perhaps she had good reason, he thought. He waited for her to finish reflecting on the wit of her own observation, then cleared his throat. 'There's something else I'd like to check with you before we go, Mrs Latham.'

'Oh, yes,' she replied. 'What's that?'

'It's about your husband and the kind of man he was. We've been talking to people who knew him and we've heard quite a lot about how friendly he was, and so on, but one or two people've mentioned what seems to have been another side to his character, even saying he had a nasty streak. Would you have anything to say about that?'

Rose Latham's face was serious as she thought before replying. 'That's a difficult thing to talk about, Inspector. We always take a chance when we marry someone, don't we? There's a risk to it – time can change people, and you don't know how things might work out when you start off. When Les and I got married, I really thought I was the most important thing in his life – I suppose most brides do, don't they? But to be brutally honest, I'd say over the years we've grown apart. I blame his job – all the time he was away on the road. I began to feel I was taking second place to his "career", as he liked to call it. That seemed to come before everything, including me. But all he was doing was selling chocolates to shopkeepers – it's not exactly finding a cure for cancer, is it? And all I was doing was getting more and more lonely.'

'But then you found someone who paid you more attention?'

'I suppose you could say I did, yes.'

'One of the people we've been talking to mentioned a name to us – could you tell me about Bob?'

Rose's expression changed. Her face looked suddenly anxious. 'Who told you about him?' she asked warily.

'I'm afraid I'm not at liberty to say, but I'd like to know about Bob.'

'What is there to say? He was loving, affectionate – he was devoted to me, and when I was feeling lonely he just had a way of cheering me up.'

'I don't want to intrude on your privacy at a time like this, Mrs Latham, but I have to ask you – was this relationship a friendship, or was it an affair?'

Her eyes widened. 'What are you talking about? An affair? I'm afraid you've got hold of the wrong end of the stick, Inspector. Bob wasn't a man – he was a dog, a puppy. He kept me company when Les was away, and I think he was what kept me from going off the rails when I was feeling so lonely.'

'I'm sorry, Mrs Latham – my mistake. Could we get back to what you were saying about your husband's character?'

'Of course. But that was it, you see. That dog loved me, but I think Les hated him. He said Bob barked too much, but he was only a little puppy and it wasn't a noisy bark, more like a yelp really. The funny thing is he only did it when Les was in the house. They say dogs can tell, don't they? Les wanted me to get rid of him, but I said no, that dog was the only creature on this earth that cared for me. We had a row about it.' She paused, looking distressed. 'You remember that thing the government set up just before the war started, to look after all the animals?'

'The National ARP Animals Committee? Yes, I do – the police are part of it.'

'In that case you'll remember what they said – if war came and we had to be evacuated we wouldn't be allowed to take our pets with us, so the kindest thing would be to have them destroyed. That was like a green light for Les. When he saw that in the paper he said, "Right, that dog's going." I said no, and I swore at him. "I'd sooner lose you than him," I said. He said, "If I had a gun I'd shoot the dog myself." Then he just got up, put the lead on Bob, marched him down to the vet and had him put down.'

She paused and wiped her eyes with her finger. 'It broke my heart, Inspector – I never thought Les could be so cruel. After that I couldn't bear the sight of him. Whenever he was here I couldn't wait for him to get back to work and disappear from my life for a bit.'

Jago said nothing, studying her face in the silence.

'But hang on,' she said, a note of alarm in her voice. 'You don't think I—'

'Think you what, Mrs Latham?'

'You can't be thinking I'd kill him. I'd never hurt a

fly. Even if my husband behaved worse than an animal I couldn't kill him.'

'But do you know who did kill him?'

'No, of course I don't – I don't know anything about it. Now look, there's nothing more I can tell you, and I'd like you to go, please.'

'Very well, Mrs Latham. I'm sorry to have distressed you, but if you find there's anything more you'd like to tell me, please get in touch.'

CHAPTER TWENTY-FOUR

'That's a bit of a turn-up for the book, isn't it, guv'nor?' said Cradock as they set off to walk back to Baring and Sons, where they'd left the car. 'What she said about that dog, I mean. Puts Lucky Les in a different light, doesn't it? Explains what her mum said about his mean streak too – no wonder she said ask her about Bob.'

'It does, yes – if what Rose said is true. Unfortunately we can't get Latham's side of it now. But I'm prepared to accept it at face value – for the time being, at least.'

'That savings book was a surprise too, wasn't it? All that money – that's about a year's wages on six pounds a week. Where'd it all come from, I wonder?'

'That's something else that only Mr Latham might've been able to tell us – it's certainly a lot to save up on the money he's been earning. He could've inherited it, of course, but you'd think his wife might've known about that.'

'Could he have been blackmailing someone, or working a fiddle at work, do you think, sir? All that chocolate, and he's meeting all sorts of shopkeepers who might be keen to sell a bit extra on the side, no questions asked.'

'It's a possibility. We'll be up in Cambridge all day tomorrow, so I think when we get to Albert Street we'd better pop back into Baring and Sons and check with Mr Baring – see what he has to say.'

'Righto, sir. And about that savings book – it was interesting how Mrs Latham reacted to her husband's little nest egg, wasn't it? Especially when she came out with that stuff about him maybe saving up so he could run off with someone else. That suggests their marriage was a bit rocky, doesn't it? She said herself they'd grown apart.'

'Indeed it does, Peter.' Jago put a hand to his trouser pocket. 'By the way,' he said, 'I was forgetting – there were some bits of paper in the back of that savings book. I've got them here – let's have a quick look at them.'

He took the slips of paper out and leafed through them. 'IOUs,' he said, 'from people who owed Latham money. That's interesting.'

Cradock peered at them. 'Was he running a money-lending racket, do you think?'

'No way of knowing. They don't say what the money's owed for, only how much they owe him and who they are. They're all in the same handwriting, so I assume Latham wrote them, but they're all signed by different people.' He scrutinised the signatures. 'And look at this one.'

He passed the IOU to Cradock. Its signature was

clumsy and unformed, like that of a child, but it was clear.

'Well, well,' said Cradock. 'J. Trent. So his old pal owed him money.'

'Yes, and it's for seventy-two pounds. That's a lot of boat trips up the canal at three quid a go. If Latham was on the fiddle, he seems to have been making enough to lend to other people too – if he managed to get these redeemed his bank balance would've been even fatter.'

They paused to let a red double-decker bus lumber noisily by, then crossed Camden High Street at the Buck's Head pub.

'One other thing, sir,' said Cradock. 'I've been wondering about what that Trent bloke said about the Russians. Bowen said they were spies, didn't he?'

'He said there were rumours that they were spies, Peter, which isn't quite the same thing.'

'Yes, but no smoke without fire, is there? I mean, suppose they did give Latham a bit of petrol or whatever, and suppose they asked him to do them a favour or two in return, like a little business arrangement. Do you think he could've been a spy?'

'Spying on what? The chocolate industry?'

'I don't know. I just thought, you know, maybe . . .' His voice trailed away as he realised he couldn't think of anything to support his supposition.

Jago felt sorry for him. 'Maybe he was, maybe he wasn't,' he conceded. 'The truth is, I haven't the faintest idea. But I know someone who probably does, so we'll ask him.'

'Who's that, sir?'

'Mr Ford. I'll call him as soon as we're back at the

station and see whether we can take a few minutes of his time when we get back from Cambridge so you can explain your thinking to him.'

'Me, sir?' Past experience told him that explaining his thinking on any subject even to his own mother would be a daunting prospect, but the thought of presenting his suspicions to the Chief Constable of the CID bordered on terrifying. 'Wouldn't it be better if you did that, sir?' he said.

'No, I think it'll be good experience for you. But don't worry – I'll bail you out if you start sinking.'

Cradock could imagine himself sinking and quite possibly drowning in such a situation only too vividly, so he clutched at the offer. 'Thank you, sir – I appreciate that.' He gulped and wished, like all drowning men no doubt, that he'd kept his mouth shut.

When they called at Baring and Sons they found the managing director at work in his office, looking tired. He remained seated at his desk.

'Good afternoon, gentlemen,' he said, inviting them to sit. 'I didn't expect you to be here again so soon.'

'Neither did we, Mr Baring,' said Jago, 'but since we spoke to you this morning something's come to light which may have a bearing on the company.'

'I see. In that case you'd better tell me what it is.'

'Thank you. The thing is, we've found a savings book belonging to Mr Latham, and it shows that he'd been paying in considerable sums of money on a regular basis – more than we might reasonably expect him to be able to deposit given his salary. We're obliged to consider the

190

possibility that he was involved in some irregular financial transactions, and that means we have to ask you whether you're aware of any such activity that he may've been involved in.'

'Well, I'm very concerned to hear that, Inspector. I have to confess that that sort of behaviour seems only too possible these days. It's always distressing to come across disloyalty, especially in a company that tries to do the best for its staff, but somehow as I get older I find there's less honour in business than there used to be. Perhaps I'm just too old for the modern world – by rights it should be my son sitting here, but sadly we lost him in the Great War.'

'I'm sorry.'

'Thank you. So many fine young men lost.' He paused, lost in thought. 'So I'm still here, soldiering on as best I can. But to answer your specific question, I must say it comes as something of a surprise – Mr Latham was one of our best representatives. I find it difficult to believe he was involved in any, er, irregular activity, but I'm sure you wouldn't suggest such a thing without good reason.'

'Have you noticed anything in particular of that nature going on in the company?'

Baring lowered his voice. 'What I'm going to tell you is strictly confidential, but I'm afraid the fact is we find ourselves in a slightly embarrassing situation. We had the auditors in recently, and they said they'd found certain discrepancies in our stock figures. That implies that there's something slack in our procedures, but we're convinced that's not the case. Nevertheless, we're reviewing them now and hoping to find they're still robust – but if it turns out we've got stock going missing, we'll be facing another threat to our reputation.'

'Are you thinking your products may be finding their way onto the black market?'

'It's a possibility we have to keep in mind. The thing is, these are very challenging times for our industry. The public's demand for chocolate is greater than ever, because it's such a convenient food, but the war means our supplies of the fresh milk and sugar we need to make it are restricted. The products themselves aren't rationed in the shops yet, but our raw materials are, and at the same time we have big government contracts to fulfil, so we're having to ration how much we make available to the customers ourselves. I believe it's almost impossible to find slab chocolate in the shops now.'

'And so opportunity knocks at the black-market trader's door?'

'Yes, I'm afraid so. It's a very undesirable situation, but it's the way things are these days, and the black market seems to present an irresistible temptation to unscrupulous people, so I suppose our products are as likely as anyone else's to find themselves being traded illegally. There may be nothing we can do to stop it, but I still feel it reflects adversely on our reputation, so if we find any malpractice we'll put a stop to it.'

'Do you think it's possible this might've had something to do with Mr Latham?'

'I really couldn't say. If stock is unaccounted for, there could be any number of reasons. It could be damaged stock that was disposed of without being correctly recorded, or goods dispatched with inaccurate paperwork.'

'Those would be accidental discrepancies, I suppose.'

'Yes, it can happen, I'm afraid, even with the most rigorous procedures. It's simply human error.'

'But it could be the result of some deliberate action? Pilfering, for example?'

'Of course, yes – in principle anyone in the supply chain could misappropriate an amount of stock, but normally we'd detect it.'

'Was Mr Latham part of what you call your supply chain?'

'Not directly in what one might call our primary supply chain, which is our physical delivery of stock to our retail customers – shops and so on. But he was part of it in the sense that he took orders from shopkeepers.'

'I don't mean to cast aspersions on your company, Mr Baring, but I believe it's not unknown for an employee in some lines of business to take an order for a certain number of boxes of goods, for example, but then supply a few extra boxes at a cheaper rate and pocket the additional money for himself while falsifying the records.'

'Are you suggesting Mr Latham might have engaged in some such fraud?'

'No. I'm asking you whether he could have.'

'Well, I don't know. We've never had any reason to believe Mr Latham was not an utterly trustworthy employee, and nothing's come to light to suggest he wasn't. All the auditors have found is a discrepancy, not a specific case of individual wrongdoing, and nothing to point the finger of blame at him in particular. I suppose in your profession you're obliged to suspect the worst of everyone, but for my part I'm reluctant to pass judgement on any man alive, let alone dead. Nevertheless, if you do come across any evidence of unprofessional behaviour by Mr Latham, I shall be obliged if you'll let me know.'

'Of course, Mr Baring. We'll do that. And now I think we'd better be on our way – I expect you have things to do before you go home.'

Jago got out of his chair, ready to go, but Baring came out from behind his desk and took him to one side. 'Indeed I do, Inspector,' he said. 'But before you go, I wonder . . . would it be possible for me to speak to you sometime on another matter, privately? Not here in the office, I mean.'

'Of course. It's a police matter, I assume?'

'Yes, I rather think it is, or at least it could be. It's something I'm concerned about. My wife and I don't do a lot of entertaining these days, but would you care to join us for dinner this evening? Only if it's not inconvenient for you, of course. We live in Hampstead, so it's only two or three miles from here. Do you have a car?'

'Yes, I do.'

'In that case it won't take you long. Are you a married man? I don't want to disrupt any domestic arrangements you may have.'

'No, sir, I'm not married, and I have no prior engagements for this evening.'

'And your constable – is he a family man?'

'No, sir, he's a bachelor like myself, and as far as any domestic arrangements are concerned, we're currently both lodging in a boarding house near Kentish Town police station, so we won't be missing anything much.'

'Well, in that case do bring him along too. I can speak in confidence to both of you, can I?'

'That rather depends on what you say, sir, but Detective Constable Cradock is subject to the same rules as I am, so you needn't worry on that score.'

'Good. It'll only be simple fare, the times being what they are, but I imagine you might both enjoy some home cooking. We may end up sharing an air-raid shelter for the evening – that's out of our hands, of course – but I'm pleased to say we had something a little more substantial than the Anderson shelter built before the war started. Oh, and we won't be dressing for dinner, so do come just as you are.'

'What time would you like us?'

'We eat a little earlier than we used to – would seven o'clock be all right?'

'Yes, that should be fine. Can you give us some directions to your house?'

'Yes. It's a bit difficult to find but I'll draw you a map – it's on West Heath Road, and the house is called Laburnum Lodge. We have a sign at the gate in white paint, so you should be able to spot it when you get close enough.'

Baring turned back to his desk and sketched a map and some notes on a sheet of paper. 'Here you are,' he said, handing it to Jago. 'And I've written our telephone number at the bottom there, in case you get delayed for any reason and happen to be somewhere near a telephone box.'

'Thank you,' said Jago. 'We'll see you later. Can you tell me what it is you'd like to talk about?'

'I think perhaps not, Inspector, if you don't mind. It's more of a personal matter, you see, and as I said, I'd rather not discuss it here in the office. I'll explain everything later, but it's a rather complicated situation. The thing is, you see, I think I may have been unwise . . .'

CHAPTER TWENTY-FIVE

Hampstead was not a part of London that Jago was familiar with, and his knowledge of the area was scarcely increased by driving through it in the blackout with just the regulation single masked headlamp to light their way. He knew of its famous heath, of course, and of its popularity among the capital's well-to-do as a place to live, but this evening it was simply another series of dark roads. The only visible feature to distinguish it was the size of the houses silhouetted in the moonlight: they were appreciably bigger than anything to be seen in his native West Ham. With Cradock using a carefully screened torch to read Baring's directions, they made slow but steady progress.

'Now then,' said Jago, not taking his eyes off the short patch of road he could make out ahead of them, 'I can't imagine the managing director of Baring and Sons living anywhere too poky, so it'll probably be a big house, but if it is, don't gawp. And even though Mr Baring said they don't dress for dinner, it might still be a bit of a posh do. How are you with your knives and forks?'

'Sir?'

'You might find there's more than one set by your plate, but if you do, just start with the outside ones and work your way in – if in doubt, follow me.'

'Yes, sir.' Cradock sounded puzzled. 'How do you know things like that, sir?'

'Because back in the Great War the army started running out of proper officers from the landed gentry and had to give commissions to oiks like me from the ranks. They packed us off to Officer Cadet Battalions and taught us a few social graces so we wouldn't make fools of ourselves when we were dining in the officers' mess. Not that it made gentlemen of us, of course, but it rubbed a few rough edges off – just enough so they could designate us as what they called "temporary gentlemen".'

'How long did that take?'

'Four months.'

'Not much chance of me picking up many social graces between here and Baring Towers then, is there?'

'I shouldn't worry if I were you – just don't talk with your mouth full and try not to wipe your mouth on your sleeve. Besides, I shouldn't exaggerate – it wasn't only about knives and forks. They did teach us things that were actually of some use on the battlefield too, like map reading and tactics, so it wasn't a complete waste of time.'

'And then they made you an officer?'

'Yes. But I don't think anyone ever regarded us as equal to the ones who'd gone to the right schools and been through the Officer Training Corps. They were the real officers – they'd been trained to command from an early age.'

'Not people like me, then.'

'No, Peter, not people like you. Now, how are we doing?'

'Well, sir, maybe I could do with a bit of training in map reading too, but as far as I can make out from these directions, if we turn left at the next T junction we'll be in West Heath Road, and the house'll be on the left-hand side, so we'll just have to look out for the name.'

'Very good. I'll keep my eyes on the road, then, while you look for that.'

Moments later, Cradock spotted the sign. Jago turned the car into an open gateway and onto a gravelled drive, the length of which from road to house suggested it was a secluded property. When they stopped outside the front porch, the shadowy outline of Laburnum Lodge gave the impression of a substantial family house rather than a mansion, but even so, when the man who opened the door ushered them in, Cradock's eyes widened. Clearly, thought Jago, he was finding it hard to comply with his instruction not to gawp. The hall was more than spacious – in fact a quick glance convinced him that more than half of his own modest house would fit into it.

'Good evening, gentlemen,' said Baring, entering the hall from a door on the opposite side, accompanied by a woman of similar age to himself. She was wearing a dark dress almost to her ankles with a sash at the waist, and her grey hair was cut in a short bob. 'This is my wife, Olive.'

She smiled at them. 'Welcome to our home. I'm so pleased you could join us. My husband tells me you're in temporary lodgings, so I hope we'll be able to provide you with a more congenial evening, Mr Goering and his air force permitting.'

'Thank you very much for inviting us,' Jago replied. 'And from what Mr Baring's told us, if Herr Goering does choose to come visiting this evening, your air-raid shelter's more comfortable than most.'

'Ah, yes,' Baring interjected. 'We're fortunate enough to have a basement, so we're a lot better off than the people living in those blocks of flats in Camden Town – I understand that for some years London County Council regulations have prohibited the construction of basements under blocks of flats, for hygienic reasons, so they're having to rely on public shelters in the street, which are not very safe. We've made the most of ours – we've strengthened it and had heating and electricity installed, so if the sirens go off while we're eating we can simply go down there.'

'And your staff?'

'They come with us, of course – what did you think they would do?'

Jago could imagine some men in Baring's position consigning their domestic staff to an Anderson shelter while enjoying their own comforts elsewhere, but he kept this thought to himself. 'How's the bombing been around here?' he said.

'Oh, nothing like as bad as it's been for those poor souls in the East End,' said Mrs Baring. 'But I've even heard of people sleeping out in the open on the Heath here to get away from the bombing. A lot of people shelter in our local

Tube station, too – apparently Hampstead's the deepest one in London. We did think about using it ourselves as it's only about a mile from here, but that's a bit too far for us to run in an emergency at our age, so we thought we'd better make sure we could shelter safely at home. But let's hope we don't have to go down to the basement just yet. Now, would you like to come through to the dining room?'

They followed the Barings to a room at the back of the house. It was panelled with dark wood from floor to ceiling, with a large fire blazing in the grate. On the far wall there was a heavy antique sideboard, on which stood a framed photograph of a young army officer, and in the middle of the room a dining table was neatly laid with silver cutlery and linen napkins. There were four chairs at the table, although it was long enough to take more.

Baring invited them to sit. 'In happier times we'd have offered you some good old-fashioned roast beef, but I'm afraid with the meat rationing being what it is, we can't. However, my wife has managed to obtain some nice fish from the local fishmonger.'

Jago suspected that given the Ministry of Food's stories of butchers buying more than they could sell to their customers, a couple like this would've had no difficulty paying over the odds to obtain a good joint of beef off the ration. Baring's comment suggested either that they were skinflints or that flouting the rationing rules went against their conscience. To be fair, he thought, from what he knew of Baring so far it was probably the latter.

A door at the far end of the dining room opened, and a maid brought in serving dishes for their dinner, placing them on the table with a polite smile.

'Thank you, Jane,' said Mrs Baring. 'This, gentlemen, is baked mackerel in parsley sauce, served, as you can see, with potatoes and carrots – not exotic, but available. I'm very thankful that we're an island – at least while we still have trawlers we can eat our fill of fish, and our cook uses any leftovers to make excellent kedgeree and fish cakes.'

They began eating. Jago was relieved to find that their plates were not flanked by rows of cutlery, so there was little danger of Cradock embarrassing himself. The talk at the table was light. Like most conversations these days, especially between strangers, it focused on the war, air raids and rationing. The Barings proved to be well informed and considerate hosts, even gently coaxing a few words out of Cradock, who was clearly nervous about speaking in such company. By the time they moved on to the second course, however, Jago was running out of small talk.

He noticed Cradock's eyes lighting up when the next course arrived; it looked like a real pudding.

'This,' said Mrs Baring, 'is mock apricot flan and custard. The key word in that name is of course "mock". I haven't seen an apricot since last year, but our cook, who's a very resourceful woman, uses carrots instead and adds just a few spoonfuls of plum jam to give it a better flavour. Fortunately, we have a large garden here with a number of fruit trees, so this year we took advantage of the extra sugar ration for jam-making and made as much as we could. One of the government's more sensible ideas, in my humble opinion.'

They made a start on the flan. Jago enjoyed it, and as far as he could tell, Cradock did too, but then he'd formed the impression long ago that eating was Cradock's favourite pastime. He was wondering how long he'd have to keep up this level of polite conversation before Baring finally got onto the private matter he wanted to discuss, but it looked as though their host wanted to wait until they'd finished eating. His heart sank when Cradock's beaming gratitude secured him a second helping of pudding.

At last the dinner ended, and Jago almost breathed a sigh of relief. 'Thank you, Mrs Baring,' he said. 'It was a delightful meal.'

'You're too kind,' Mrs Baring replied. 'The pleasure is ours.' She rose from the table. 'Now, I'll leave you men to get on with whatever you've come to discuss.'

'No, my dear,' said Baring, 'please stay. My wife and I have no secrets from each other, Inspector.'

Mrs Baring sat down again, and her husband cleared his throat. 'Let me explain what I wanted to talk to you about, Inspector. Many years ago, Baring and Sons set up a charitable foundation. The company donates part of its profits, and I also make occasional donations in a personal capacity. I was contacted recently by a gentleman who was fundraising for a good cause – it happens from time to time, as we're known in those circles as charitable donors. We met, and he explained that he was engaged in a project to raise money for one of the major London teaching hospitals – St George's, at Hyde Park Corner. It seemed he'd been treated there during the Great War when he was wounded and felt he owed them a debt of gratitude, but he also knew their teaching was of the highest standard and he wanted to support them in what have been difficult times of late. He'd made a donation himself and was encouraging others to do the same, so I said if he could tell me more we'd certainly consider it. He did, and my wife and I made a modest donation to the hospital and had a kind letter of thanks from the appeal committee.'

'And this donation – is that what you were referring to in your office when you said you thought you might've been unwise?'

'No, it's to do with what happened later, and that's why I wanted to speak to you away from the office. He seemed a very decent, well-bred sort of man – he was an ex-officer and walked with a stick because of a war wound, but he hadn't a word of complaint about it. He'd served on the Western Front with the Middlesex Regiment and won a DSO on the Somme. When I asked him how he got it, he said he and his company had come under fire from a machine-gun post as they advanced on the enemy lines, and he was wounded himself. But when he realised he was still alive he thought there was no point stopping now, so he continued leading them forward and knocked out the post with a Mills bomb, and they took their objective. He laughed when he told me – he said looking back it was the folly of youth, a crazy thing to do, and now he was older and wiser, but the stick was his daily reminder.'

'A bit of a hero, then?'

'Yes, but a very modest and unassuming sort of chap – a down-to-earth type. Every inch an old-fashioned gentleman, I suppose one could say. I liked him.' His voice faltered as he looked at the photograph across the room. 'He reminded me of my son.'

Jago nodded in silent sympathy.

'Anyway,' said Baring, pulling himself together, 'the next time we met I asked him how he'd got involved in charitable fundraising. He said he'd been born into quite a wealthy family, but a lot of their money was invested in Argentina and they lost it in a revolution there in 1890. The family fell on hard times, but he was determined to restore their fortunes, and having no capital of his own to speak of, he'd done that by making money for other people. He said his inspiration came from the Bible. You know the parable of the talents? He said it spoke to him so clearly – the money he made shouldn't just sit in the bank, he should put it to work by investing it, boosting businesses, creating jobs for people, generating more tax revenue for the government, and using the profits he made on those investments to support good causes. He'd been so successful that he'd been able to help friends and relatives to do the same, and eventually he'd decided to act as a private investment broker for anyone who shared that vision. It was simple, he said – if you left your money in the bank you might get two-and-a-half per cent interest, but in the last six months, despite the war, by astute investment decisions he'd managed to get his clients an average return of ten per cent. I asked him how he found his clients, and he said it was usually by word of mouth, but he also approached people who were known to be charitable and who might have some spare capital that they'd like to put to work in this way.'

'Did he say why he'd approached you in particular?'

'Yes, I asked him that. He said he'd recently run into a man he used to know in the army, who'd told him I was the kind of chap who might support a charitable project.'

'Was that man Mr Latham, by any chance?'

Baring looked surprised. 'I don't know – I didn't ask

him for the man's name. Why? Do you think it could have been?'

'I don't know, Mr Baring. It's just that you said this man served in the Middlesex Regiment, and I happen to know that was Mr Latham's regiment too. It may mean nothing, but in a case like this any potential connection is of interest.'

'Well, in that case I'm sorry I neglected to ask.'

'That's all right, Mr Baring. Now, with regard to perhaps being unwise – did you check this man's credentials?'

'Yes. He mentioned that one of his investors was the chairman of a competitor of ours, Glaisters Confectionery, and I know him of course, so I got on the phone and asked him if he could vouch for the man, and he said he'd no reason to doubt him. Glaister had made a personal investment of five thousand pounds as a trial. His first half-year return had been four hundred pounds, which is eight per cent, not quite the average quoted, but that suggests some other investors were making even more. So I went ahead and invested five thousand of my own – in a personal capacity, you understand, because the company trust doesn't make investments, it simply disburses funds. In the first half-year I got a return almost as good as Glaister's, three hundred and fifty pounds, and I gave it to a children's home that we support, but after that I had occasion to ring him and found the phone was dead. I wrote to him and got no reply, so in the end I visited his office address and it was closed – "Closed and gone away," the caretaker said. I've never heard a word since, and I think you can see why I've been unwise, Inspector – unwise to the tune of five thousand pounds, or four thousand six hundred and fifty if I allow for the income I received. I don't think I'll ever see that money again. I didn't go to the police at the time, because I was worried that it might get out and embarrass the company, but you strike me as a man who can keep a confidence, and I just wonder whether there's anything you can do to track this man down and hold him to account. I don't want anyone else to suffer the same fate as me.'

'Well, Mr Baring, I'll certainly look into it. What's this man's name?'

'It's Fortescue – Major Edmund Fortescue.'

CHAPTER TWENTY-SIX

It was still dark when the train pulled out of Liverpool Street station in a hissing cloud of steam and a chorus of chuffing, clanking and squealing. Taking the Tube across London from their makeshift lodgings in Kentish Town to Liverpool Street had meant an early start after a night disrupted by sirens, and Jago was already feeling tired. But at least, he thought, there was a chance of some rest on their way before they started the day's work in Cambridge.

They'd found seats towards the front of the train and now sat facing each other as it gradually began to pick up speed. Cradock had brought the brown leather attaché case known as the murder bag – not that they were expecting to find anyone murdered, but it contained fingerprinting equipment and other items that might prove useful. Now it lay innocuously in the luggage net above them, its exotic contents hidden from public view.

Jago, hoping to leave Cradock to his own devices on the journey, had bought himself a newspaper at the station, but he could see his companion was still looking distressed. It seemed he hadn't known until they got on board that there'd be no food on the train. From what Jago had heard, even when there was, you might have to pay a shilling for a sandwich, and considering his old friend Rita only charged tuppence for one at her cafe in West Ham, this struck him as little short of daylight robbery. Perhaps Cradock would have been willing to pay an inflated price for the chance to eat something, but the fact that there was nothing to buy had come as a shock to him. Now Jago feared the boy would spend the whole journey pining for food.

Their fellow passengers in the compartment appeared to be hoping for a quiet journey too. All three of them were in uniform: a soldier in a greatcoat with the collar turned up, smoking in the corner and clearly not interested in conversation, and two young men in RAF blue who looked as though they were already settling down for a sleep. A bit early in the day to be snoozing, thought Jago, but he guessed they were probably on their way back to base after a 48-hour pass in London. He knew from his own early days in the army in the Great War, before they sent him to France, that if you managed to get a spot of leave you didn't want to waste it on sleeping.

He pulled the newspaper from his overcoat pocket, pleased to see that there was enough light to read by. The last time he'd used a main-line train he'd struggled with the dim blue lighting decreed by the government early in the war, but now it seemed things had improved. This train at least had been fitted with blackout blinds, and the proper white lights were on, so he was looking forward to a little relaxed reading.

Cradock, however, was fidgeting. 'When will we get there, sir?' he said.

Jago was about to give him a brusque reply, but then remembered this was the first time since Cradock had been assigned to him that they'd taken a long train journey together. The way the boy was acting made him wonder whether he'd ever been on such a trip at all. There was no reason why he should have done. It was perfectly possible to be born in London, go to school in London, train to be a policeman in London and stay there all your life. There must be young men in their tens of thousands up and down the country these days who were only having their first taste of long-distance travel because they'd been called up into the forces and dispatched to some remote camp for their basic training. That was how it had been for him, and it had been a shock to the system, although nothing like the shock of being sent overseas.

'Sir?' Cradock repeated.

'Sorry, Peter, my mind was wandering. According to the timetable, we should be there in an hour and a half from now, but I wouldn't bet on it. I imagine the timetable's subject to variation if the Luftwaffe happens to turn up, and if there's any bomb damage to the line we'll probably have to get off and hope we can find a bus. Apart from that we should be fine.'

'What if they machine-gun us? They do that, don't they?'

'So I've heard, yes. If that happens, Peter, you'll just have to hope their aim's not very good. I don't think a railway carriage roof's going to stop a machine-gun bullet, and a window certainly won't.'

'Oh, right,' Cradock replied, and lapsed into silence for a moment, but his face suggested another question was forming in his mind.

Jago saw his chances of a quiet read fading. He folded the newspaper and stuffed it back into his coat pocket. 'Actually, Peter, I think I'm going to follow the example of those young airmen over there and shut my eyes. It's going to be a busy day, so if we can manage not to get bombed or machine-gunned I might be able to snatch a little nap on the way. Feel free to do the same.'

Without waiting for a reply, he tipped his hat down over his eyes and did his best to get comfortable as the train clattered over a set of points and swayed on towards Cambridge.

CHAPTER TWENTY-SEVEN

They arrived only three minutes late and found a constable from the Cambridge Borough Police waiting for them at the ticket barrier. Jago's first action was to enquire where the nearest sandwich kiosk was, and his second was to buy enough sustenance to keep Cradock going for the time being. This humanitarian deed accomplished, they left the station with the policeman, who took them to a car that he explained was for them to use with the compliments of the town's chief constable. It was a little Morris of some considerable age and didn't look suitable for pursuing criminals at more than thirty miles an hour, but Jago judged it more than adequate for a day's motoring in and around Cambridge. He obtained directions from the constable to their first port of call, the village of Bassingbourn, and got into the driver's seat. Cradock squeezed himself into the passenger seat, with the attaché case balanced on his knees.

'Right,' said Jago. 'Time for a nice little drive out into the country. Have you got Latham's journey book handy?'

'Yes, sir,' Cradock replied, taking the notebook from the case.

'Good. We'll see if we can find that first customer he was due to visit on the day he died. The name's Carter, isn't it?'

Cradock checked the book. 'That's right, sir – Henry Carter, at Carter's Village Stores, Bassingbourn High Street.' He thought for a moment. 'Odd, though, isn't it? That's the only visit he's written in his book – Latham, I mean. You'd think he had more than one customer to see in the day – I imagined he'd be going round as many of them as possible. What was he going to do for the rest of the day?'

'I've no more idea than you, Peter. But I suppose he may've had other duties to attend to that he didn't need to write in his book, or perhaps there were other customers to see but he hadn't decided which ones yet and was going to jot their details down before he set off. If that's what he was planning to do, of course, he didn't live to do it – in which case, we'll probably never know.'

'Hmm – other duties to attend to. Do you think that might've included visiting a lady friend?'

'Well, anything's possible, but let's not condemn the poor man without evidence. He's not in a position to defend himself, is he?'

'No, sir.'

Jago headed south from the railway station, and soon they were out of the town and driving through flat, open countryside, each twig of the leafless trees etched finely against the cold blue November sky.

'So,' he said, 'what did you make of yesterday evening?'

'At Mr and Mrs Baring's, you mean? I thought that flan and custard was very nice. I'm not a big fan of mackerel, though.'

'Yes, but leaving aside the food, what did you think about Baring and his wife?'

'Oh, they both seemed nice too. I'm not used to posh people, but they made us welcome, didn't treat me like I was common, and they sounded like they cared about people less fortunate than themselves – like me.'

'But a little unwise, perhaps?'

'You mean about that money? Do you think Mr Baring was right about that? I mean, the fact that that Major Fortescue's office was closed and the caretaker said he'd gone away doesn't necessarily make him a villain, does it? He could've had an accident and be lying unconscious in a hospital somewhere, or maybe he'd had a family emergency and had to go away at short notice. And he did make a donation to the hospital, didn't he?'

'He told Baring he had, but we don't know for sure. I think we'd better check that before we draw any conclusions about his generosity. What about Fortescue's investment scheme – how did that strike you?'

'Well, I've never had any money to invest, so I don't know what that kind of thing involves, except that it seems to make money for people who do it. But he paid Baring a good return on his investment, didn't he, like he said he would. Eight per cent's a lot. Maybe Fortescue was the genuine article but something just went wrong for him – I mean, if you're going to steal someone's money, why would you give them some first?'

'I'll tell you why, Peter. It's called setting a sprat to catch a mackerel.'

'Sir?'

'Bait, Peter – have you ever been fishing?'

'No, sir. Not much chance of that where I grew up.'

'Well, let me explain, then. A sprat's a small fish, and you could eat a few for your tea, but if you use one for bait instead, you might land a bigger fish, like a mackerel.'

'I'm not very keen on mackerel, sir.'

'So you said. But that's not the point – I'd lay a pound to a penny that's exactly what this Fortescue fellow's been doing. He shells out some cash to impress his client, but it's only so they'll take the bait. Then when he's got them on the hook, he reels them in. It's called a get-rich-quick scheme, but the only person who gets rich is the fraudster running it, and that's why I told Mr Baring we're going to look into it.'

'Ah, I see. So Mr Baring's the mackerel.'

'Exactly, Peter – well done. And there's definitely something a bit fishy about Major Fortescue.'

They drove on past fields, hedgerows and the occasional farmhouse. Bassingbourn was about twelve miles south-west of Cambridge, and with the constable's directions it was easy to find. As they entered it, Jago noted what seemed to him the typical features of an English village high street: a couple of pubs, a neat little school, modest cottages in a variety of styles, some with a degree of charm and some without, and the usual collection of small shops. Cradock spotted Carter's Village Stores among them, and they parked outside it.

A bell jangled over the door as they went in, and a

portly man in a white grocer's coat greeted them from behind the counter.

'Good morning, gentlemen,' he said, rubbing his hands together. 'I don't believe I've had the pleasure of meeting you before.'

'Good morning,' Jago replied. The shopkeeper seemed pleased to see them, but then customers who weren't local were probably a rarity in a place like this. 'Excuse me, but are you Mr Carter?'

'I certainly am. How can I help you?'

'I'm hoping you might be able to assist us with a little information, Mr Carter. It's about a police matter – I'm Detective Inspector Jago and this is Detective Constable Cradock. We've come up from London in connection with an investigation concerning Mr Leslie Latham, who I understand was due to pay you a visit on Tuesday.'

'Ah, right, yes. He didn't turn up, but I thought he must've been delayed or had to change his plans – you know what it's like these days. It didn't bother me, but normally if he can't make an appointment he'll call me, so when it got to yesterday and I'd still seen neither hide nor hair of him I phoned his head office. They said the poor fellow had died. I was sorry to hear that, but it's happening all the time now, isn't it? Seems like life's getting cheaper.' He paused, as if moved by the profundity of his own words. 'But anyway, what is it you're investigating that means you have to come all the way up here to see me? Was he getting his fingers in the till or something?'

'No, it's not that. I'm afraid it's because we're treating his death as a case of suspected murder.'

Carter looked shocked. 'Murder? My goodness – they didn't mention that. When did it happen?'

'It was on Tuesday morning.'

'And was that down in London?'

'Yes, it was.'

Carter shook his head and tutted. 'I suppose that's London for you, isn't it? Some people say Bassingbourn's a bit of a backwater, but at least we don't get that kind of thing happening here.'

'I'm glad to hear it.'

'Do you know who did it yet?'

'We're still pursuing our enquiries. Tell me, Mr Carter, how well did you know Mr Latham?'

'Not what you'd call well,' Carter replied. 'I was just one of his customers. We'd have a little chat when he visited, but it wasn't like we were pals or anything.' He raised an open hand to signal a temporary halt to their conversation. 'Forgive me, Inspector, I haven't offered you anything to drink. Would you like a cup of tea?'

'Actually, that would be most kind of you, Mr Carter. We came up on the train, and there were no refreshments available.'

'In that case, if you'll bear with me for a moment I'll go and make you one. I'm on my own here this morning, but the kettle's on the range so it won't take two ticks. Are you from Scotland Yard?'

'We are, yes.'

'That should be all right, then – if I can't rely on two Scotland Yard detectives to mind the shop for a couple of minutes, who can I?' He chuckled at his own wit. 'And would you like a biscuit, or a piece of fruit cake? You can see I've got plenty in stock, and it's not rationed.'

Jago knew what Cradock would be thinking and took pity on him. 'Thank you, Mr Carter. I'm sure we'd both appreciate a piece of cake.'

'Oh, yes,' Cradock added with conviction, 'that would be wonderful.'

Carter disappeared into the back of the shop and reappeared as promptly as he'd promised, bearing two steaming mugs of tea, a bowl of sugar, and two slices of cake big enough, Jago thought, to impress even Cradock.

Jago thanked him again and stirred a spoonful of sugar into his tea. 'Now then, Mr Carter, I wonder if you could tell me when Mr Latham last visited you.'

'Certainly,' Carter replied. 'That'd be about a month ago. He used to come once a month to take orders and deliver some stock – I believe he kept a supply in a warehouse or something in Cambridge for his customers in this area. It was never very much.' He waved his arm across the packed shelves behind him. 'You can see I've got this place stuffed with just about anything anyone in the village might want to buy, so there's not much room. My orders were never big, but he was always a pleasant enough man to do business with.'

'What else can you tell me about Mr Latham?'

'Well, let me see. His suits were a bit snappier than you'd normally see in a place like this, but he was representing his company, so I expect they said he had to look smart. He was always polite and friendly – took an interest, like – but then again, he was a salesman, so I suppose he had to. It never pays to get too pally with his sort, or you find yourself buying four times as much stock as you wanted. I was always firm with him, ordered what I needed, no more, and he accepted that. Better to get a small order than no order at all, I suppose.'

'Yes. Now, I hope you don't mind me saying this, but I was wondering whether a small shop in a village would be . . . well, would be worth his while visiting, in terms of sales.'

'Well you might, Inspector, but he probably had some bigger fish to make up for us tiddlers – I know he had Woolworths in Cambridge on his books, because he mentioned it once. But most shops selling sweets are small, aren't they, and I suppose he reckoned a lot of small orders added up to something big too. He certainly always seemed pleased to be here – he used to say Bassingbourn was an up-and-coming place, and business could only get better.'

'Why do you think he said that?'

'He reckoned we'd see more people moving out to places like this, away from the likes of London – not just because of the bombing, but because it'd be nice to live somewhere with peace and quiet. He was quite surprised when I told him we'd been bombed too.'

'Really?'

'Well, just the once, but that's once too many as far as I'm concerned. We've got a new airfield, you see, just outside the village – the RAF built it a couple of years ago. They could see the war coming, I suppose. Anyway, back in April it got bombed – just one German plane came over, but it hit the airfield and eleven men were killed. Terrible business.'

'But quiet since then?'

'Yes, thank the Lord – and I hope it stays that way.

I'd be happy if the village stayed just the way it is. But Mr Latham – well, he was a townie, I suppose, and more used to change, and I got the impression he was a very optimistic kind of chap – you know, the "glass half full" type. He said he could see that airfield turning into an airport once the war's over – he thought this place had a lot of potential to grow and get more prosperous.'

'So he saw Bassingbourn as some kind of future boom town?'

Carter laughed. 'I don't know about that. People here've heard that before – we had a bit of a boom back in the last century, and that didn't end well. Mind you, we did get connected to the electricity three or four years ago, so things are looking up again. And the airfield's very good for business – the RAF's keeping us well supplied with customers.'

'Good. You said Mr Latham could see people wanting to move out from London to places like this. Did he ever suggest he'd like to do that himself?'

'No, not as I recall. I think it was only what he thought other people might do.'

'And you said he was here every month, so do you know if he became friendly with anyone round here or spent time with anyone in particular?'

'No, I don't, I'm afraid. I think he covered quite an area in Cambridgeshire, as well as the town itself, so I don't suppose he had much time left for socialising.'

'Do you know whether he ever had any trouble with a customer?'

'What kind of trouble?'

'Anything that might've given someone cause to wish him harm.'

'What, you mean murder him?'

'Possibly.'

'Oh, no, I don't think so. I can't imagine anyone round here wanting to kill him. More likely he was mixed up with some crooks down your way, I'd say.'

'What makes you say that?'

'Oh, nothing really – it was just something he said last time he was here.'

'Could you tell me more, please?'

'Of course – can't do any harm now the poor fellow's dead, can it? It was when he'd taken my order last time and we were chatting over a cup of tea. We were talking about cars – he was always interested in cars – and I asked him how he was managing for petrol, what with the rationing and him having to drive round all over the place. I just wondered whether he was getting enough. He said yes, no problem – quite the opposite, really. Then he asked me how I was doing. Well, I've got an old wreck of a car I've been driving for years. It's big and heavy and just drinks petrol, so I can't get about as much as I used to, and I was having a bit of a moan. I was just making conversation really, but blow me down if he didn't say well, there's no need for you to worry, old chap. If you're short, I know where to lay my hands on a few extra coupons.'

'What did you say to him?'

'Well, I turned him down flat, didn't I? It was like I'd suddenly seen a completely different side to the man – I was shocked, really I was. I'm an honest tradesman with a reputation to think about here in the village, and if I did

221

something like that and word got out, my business would be ruined. I dare say things are different where you come from, but it's not something I'd dream of doing. In fact I even rang up his boss the next day and complained.'

'Really? And what did he say?'

'He said he'd look into it, but of course I've no idea whether he did anything about it. But I couldn't in all conscience just let it go without saying something, could I?'

'Can you remember what his boss was called?'

'Yes, it was a Mr Todd. I told him all about it.'

CHAPTER TWENTY-EIGHT

'That Mr Carter was the second person to say Latham was an optimist, wasn't he?' said Cradock as he joined Jago in the Morris once they'd said goodbye to the shopkeeper and left the village stores. 'Sounds like he was a bit of go-getter.'

'Yes,' said Jago, 'and everyone seems to agree he was ambitious. The sort of man who'd have plans. But I'm beginning to wonder whether some of those plans might've extended beyond his career as a commercial traveller. Offering to supply one of your company's customers with petrol coupons would certainly fall outside his official responsibilities, and I don't imagine for a moment that it's something Mr Baring would countenance.'

'Funny that Todd didn't mention it when we spoke to him, though, isn't it? He said he trusted Latham to do an honest job, and he'd never caught him on the fiddle. Shows how much he knows about his staff, I suppose.'

'Possibly – if Mr Carter's account is accurate. I think

we'd better have another word with Mr Todd and see if we can jog his memory.'

'That other stuff Carter was saying was interesting too.'

'Which particular stuff do you have in mind?'

'What Latham said to him about Bassingbourn, and people wanting to move out to places like that for the peace and quiet.'

'Carter didn't seem to think Latham was having thoughts about doing that himself, though. Do you think he was?'

'I'm not sure, but his wife was certainly willing to believe he might've been planning to run off with someone else. I don't suppose many wives would think that, let alone say it, so maybe there was something in it.'

Jago doubted that Cradock's qualifications to pronounce on what wives might think were any more credible than his own, but he let it pass. 'I wonder,' he said. 'It sounds like he'd have needed to invest in one or two tweed suits to blend in, but if he was as optimistic and confident as people say, I suspect he'd have pulled it off. We've no evidence that that was in his plans, but it's worth bearing in mind. But now I think we should go back to Cambridge and visit his digs – see if his landlady can tell us anything about what he got up to on his trips up here.'

After a stop for a more than agreeable lunch at a pub on the road back to Cambridge, they arrived at the Fairview Commercial Hotel in St Barnabas Road, not far from the railway station. As Jago had suspected, despite the grand impressions that the word 'hotel' might create, the establishment proved in reality to be merely a largeish private house converted into lodgings.

'Did you speak to that Mrs Roberts or whatever her

name was herself when you phoned this place about Latham, sir?' said Cradock as the car came to a halt.

'Yes, I did,' Jago replied, switching off the engine.

'What's she like?'

'It was only a brief conversation, but she sounded a lot more pleasant than our current landlady in Kentish Town. Why? Not scared, are you?'

'Course not, sir. I was just thinking it'll be nice if she's not like that dragon Mrs Minter – means we might get something out of her.'

'Well, we'll see if my impression's correct, won't we?'

They got out of the car, and Jago rang the bell on the hotel's front door. It was opened moments later by a woman in her forties wearing a royal blue dress and cardigan. Her first reaction when he introduced himself and Cradock was to smile, which he took as an encouraging improvement on their initial encounter with their own temporary landlady.

'Ah, yes,' she said. 'You called about poor Mr Latham, didn't you? Suspected murder, you say.' She shook her head slowly and sighed. 'Well, do come in.' She led them to a small parlour that looked as though it served as both a sitting room and an office. 'Can I get you anything?'

'That's very kind, Mrs Roberts, but we've not long had lunch. We'd just like to ask you one or two things about Mr Latham, so we shouldn't be long.'

'By all means. What would you like to know?'

'I wonder if you could tell us what sort of person he was – how he struck you.'

'Right. Well, I'd say he was quite a lively character, but in a nice way. Some of the commercial travellers can be rather too boisterous, especially the younger ones, and I have to keep them on a tight leash, but he was a bit older, more responsible. I appreciate that, because I've been running this place on my own for the last three years, since my husband passed away – he was gassed in the last war and never really recovered properly, poor thing.'

'I'm sorry to hear that. You say Mr Latham was a lively character – can you tell me more about what you mean by that?'

'Well, he was always cheerful, for a start. I never saw him looking down in the dumps, as they say, unlike some of the other commercial travellers I get here – they can be a bit glum. But perhaps they're the ones who aren't doing so well in their work. I always got the impression Mr Latham was one of the more successful ones. He was very well turned out and he seemed to enjoy his work. I believe he represented a chocolate manufacturer – he, er, used to pass me the odd free sample, which was very nice, although I was never too sure whether he was supposed to.' She paused. 'I hope that's not illegal, is it?'

'I think that'd be more a question of his company's regulations, Mrs Roberts.'

'Oh, I see. Well, I'm sure he wouldn't do anything against the law. He seemed too nice for that.'

'So you'd say he was easy to get on with?'

'Oh, yes, but I suppose if you want to get on as a salesman you have to be, don't you? He had a nice way to him – very sociable, like. What I believe people call an outgoing personality.'

'Did he have any local contacts here, people he was friendly with?'

'There were some men he used to get together with

in the evening sometimes – they'd come round here for a game of cards.'

'And what about lady friends?'

'No – he was a married man, wasn't he?'

'Yes, but—'

'I know what you're thinking, Inspector, and it's true – there are some men in his line of work who like to let their hair down when they're away from home and have a little fun, but I don't think he was like that. Not that I allow any goings-on under my roof, you understand – I don't stand for any funny business. But I never saw anything to suggest he was carrying on with anyone, if that's what you mean. The only time I ever saw him with a woman was when his niece was visiting. She's doing war work somewhere round here. Munitions, I expect – that's what most people seem to be doing these days.'

'Do you remember her name?'

'No, sorry. I only met her the once. A smart dresser, like him, nice hair, but a bit too much of that mascara stuff for my liking. Makes a girl look too forward by half, if you ask me. But you know what girls are like these days.'

Jago wasn't sure he did, but he took her question as rhetorical. 'You mentioned some men used to come round here to play cards with him. So these other men weren't staying here – is that right?'

'Yes – they'd just visit for the evening.'

'Was that a regular activity when he was here?'

'Yes, pretty much every time he stayed here they'd get together. I used to let them play in his room – I even provided some extra chairs so they could all sit down at the table. It always sounded like they were enjoying themselves, but in the end I had to put a stop to it.'

'Why was that?'

'It just got a bit out of hand. It was last time he was here, about a month ago. I mean, I don't mind men having a good time and enjoying a drink or two together, but that night, well, it sounded like some almighty row had broken out. I could hear it down here and I was worried what the other guests might think, so I went out and listened on the stairs. One of them shouted out "I'll kill you," and it sounded like there was some shoving about going on, and then I heard something like a glass smashing on the floor. I wasn't having that, so I went straight up there and told them to pack it in and behave themselves, otherwise I'd call the police. That shut them up, and they were all apologetic, but I gave them their marching orders, and off they went. Not Mr Latham, of course, but the rest.'

'And did you know these other men?'

'Only one of them. He's called Swanson – George Swanson, I think. He runs an estate agent's in Mill Road, up near the Parker's Piece end – it's called Swanson and Catchpole. I don't know what the row was all about, but he didn't look at all pleased when he left – something had put his nose out of joint, I reckon.'

'Thank you, Mrs Roberts – you've been very helpful.'

'Well, I hope so. Poor Mr Latham – it's so sad. Cut off in his prime like that, with so much to live for. And him a regular customer too – I'll miss him.'

CHAPTER TWENTY-NINE

The premises of Swanson and Catchpole, auctioneers and estate agents, on Mill Road were only a couple of minutes' drive from the Fairview Commercial Hotel. When Jago and Cradock walked in through the door, the place was silent. A young man was seated at a desk, a pen in his hand and a sheet of paper on the blotter in front of him, but whether he was working out the details of a lucrative property deal or simply doodling, it was impossible to tell. He looked up and gave the visitors a half-hearted smile. 'Good afternoon. Can I help you?'

Jago wondered whether the man's bored tone was due to lack of customers or lack of interest. He tried to be charitable: perhaps the property business was going through hard times because of the war. 'Yes,' he said. 'We'd like a word with Mr Swanson, if he's here.'

'Certainly. Are you wishing to buy, or to sell?'

'Neither. We're police officers and we need to talk to Mr Swanson for a few minutes.'

'OK, I'll go and tell him you're here. What name shall I say?'

'Detective Inspector Jago and Detective Constable Cradock.'

The young man hauled himself up from his desk and ambled to the back of the office, where he knocked on a door and put his head round it to speak to someone inside. An older, shorter man in a dark suit emerged and approached Jago at a more business-like pace.

'I'm Swanson – George Swanson,' he said. 'I understand you want a word. Come into my office.'

The office proved to be more like a cupboard, into which Jago and Cradock squeezed themselves and sat down. It suggested that Swanson and Catchpole's estate agency might not be the most profitable of businesses.

'So you're police officers, right?' Swanson continued.

'That's correct,' said Jago. 'We won't take too much of your time, though – I'm sure you're busy.'

'Not a bit of it. Business is pretty slack at the moment.'

'Because of the war?'

'Yes. It's thrown the whole market into confusion. When people buy a house, they want to have some sort of certainty about the future, but nothing's certain now, is it? A year ago estate agents in London were saying move to a safe area, buy a house somewhere quiet like Folkestone, on the coast.' He snorted. 'That was a joke, wasn't it? Those same houses are within range of the German guns in France now.'

'But what about Cambridgeshire? Would that still be seen as a safe area?'

'As much as anywhere can, I suppose. We've had a few air raids on the town this year – nine people were killed in Vicarage Terrace in the summer, and that's not far from where we're sitting now, just the other side of the Mill Road cemetery. It's generally been much quieter away from the town, though, and we still get enquiries about country cottages – broadly speaking, the more remote it is, the better price you're likely to get, which is the opposite of the way things were before the war started. I suppose people are still thinking they'd like to live somewhere the German bombers aren't likely to find, but experience shows those bombs can drop anywhere, especially when the pilot's keen to get home before his fuel runs out. And now I suppose people are wondering whether they can find somewhere to live that the Germans won't find when they invade, but with those parachute troops, who knows where that might be?'

'That's interesting – I'd like to ask you something more about that before we go, but first there's a more important matter. It's to do with Mr Les Latham – a friend of yours, I believe.'

'Well, he's more of an acquaintance, really – but what's that got to do with the police?'

'I'm sorry to have to tell you this, Mr Swanson, but we're here because Mr Latham has been killed.'

'Oh, that is a shock – was this in London?'

'Yes – the day before yesterday.'

Swanson shook his head slowly. 'So many people

dying. This bombing's dreadful. But I'm not his next of kin or anything, so why—'

'I'm afraid Mr Latham's death wasn't due to enemy action. We're treating it as a case of suspected murder.'

'Murder? My goodness – so what do you want from me?'

'We're talking to people who knew Mr Latham, and I understand you used to play cards with him from time to time. Is that correct?'

'Yes. I got chatting to him in the local pub when he was up on one of his visits, and we discovered we had a common interest in cards. After that we used to get together to have a drink and play a few games.'

'At his lodgings, I believe.'

'Yes, that's right.'

'With another couple of gentlemen?'

'Yes – they run local businesses, like me. One's got a dry-cleaning shop and the other's a men's outfitter – they've both got premises just down the road from here. They like a game of cards too, so we made up a foursome. But I don't suppose that's of much interest to you.'

'In a case like this, Mr Swanson, we take a particular interest in identifying anyone who might've wished harm to the deceased.'

'I see. I don't think I can help you there – I didn't know him well enough, and I certainly don't know anyone who might've wanted to harm him.'

'The thing is, though, we've been talking to Mr Latham's landlady, and she mentioned that at your last little gathering there was some kind of altercation – the precise term she used was an "almighty row".'

'Well, yes, there was a disagreement, now you come to mention it. But it was nothing serious.'

'She also says she heard someone shouting "I'll kill you."'

'Ah, yes.' He paused, thinking. 'I can see how that might arouse your interest, Inspector, but I can assure you it was only said in the heat of the moment.'

'Was it you who said it?'

'Yes.'

'And who did you say it to?'

'It was, er . . . Latham. I'm sorry to have to say this of a man who's not long dead, but the truth of the matter is I'd just caught him cheating.'

'You're sure of that?'

'Absolutely – allow me to explain. Are you aware of the Observer Corps?'

'Yes, of course. The "eyes on the skies" people – that's what they say, isn't it?'

'Correct. I'm a member of the local unit – we've got a little observation post out on the Gog Magog hills, south-east of the town, and we send information about the movements of any enemy aircraft to the reporting centre so that our fighter boys can intercept them.'

'And what does this have to do with your card game?'

'Well, at the risk of stating the obvious, I'm in the Observer Corps because I'm observant. It's all in the detail, you see – if you want to identify a plane correctly when it's flying over you've got to know everything to look out for. We're all civilian volunteers, but we're all experts. Long before this war started we were working hard to learn all the identifying features of all the planes, friend and foe. And we did it all in our own time, because we have a passionate interest in aircraft. So you see I'm observant by nature, and I've got a sharp eye for detail.'

'So you're saying you were observing Mr Latham?'

'Exactly. I didn't know much about him, and when I'm playing cards with people I don't know very well, I keep a close watch on their hands. Some of them are very clever, but I'm not easily distracted, and if a man's dealing from the bottom or playing some other trick, I'm going to see it. I reckon I can spot a cheat as well as I can tell a Heinkel from an Anson.'

'I take it you were playing for money.'

'We were. Not enormous amounts, but serious nonetheless, and he'd just taken a considerable sum from me. I was angry.'

'Angry enough to threaten to kill him, it seems.'

'Now wait a minute. That was just words – a few strong ones, in the heat of the moment, and the fact that I said it doesn't mean I killed Latham or had the slightest intention of doing so. For goodness' sake, Inspector, I'm a respectable businessman. I'm a member of the Cambridge Chamber of Commerce.'

'Can you tell me where you were on Tuesday morning?'

'Here of course – the property market may be in the doldrums, but I still have a business to run. In any case, you said he was killed in London – I haven't been down there for months. You should be talking to people there.'

'Oh, we are, Mr Swanson, but I'm also interested in people who knew him here. Do you know of any friends he had in this area?'

'No – as I said, I was only acquainted with him through

our card sessions, so the only men I know who knew him here were my two business colleagues that I mentioned earlier.'

'And lady friends?'

'I certainly didn't know him well enough to discuss matters like that with him. I'm afraid I can't help you on that score. Now, is that all, Inspector?'

'Almost, Mr Swanson, but as I said, there's one small question I'd like to ask you before we go – it's to do with houses for sale in this area.'

'What?' Swanson laughed. 'Don't tell me you're looking for a place to buy.'

'No. This is still to do with Mr Latham. We found a photograph in the bag he was going to take for his visit up here today.' He took the picture from his pocket and passed it to Swanson. 'I'm curious to know why he was bringing it with him to Cambridge. I don't know whether the house is in this area, but as you're an estate agent I wondered whether you might recognise it.'

Swanson took the photo from Jago, eyeing him cautiously. 'As a matter of fact, I do – I gave him this picture myself.'

'In your professional capacity?'

'Of course. He said his mother was terrified of the bombing and wanted to buy a cottage out in the country, preferably somewhere off the beaten track, so I showed him the details of one or two we've got on our books at the moment. This one's south of here, in the middle of nowhere off the road between Duxford and Ickleton. The owners were away, but they'd left me a key, so I took him over to have a look. He seemed to like it and said he thought his mother would too, but I never heard back from him, so that was the end of that.'

'How much would a place like that cost these days?'

'That particular one's on the market at four hundred pounds.'

'And is that your writing on the back?'

Swanson turned the photograph over. 'No, not mine. Maybe it's Latham's, but I wouldn't know.'

'Is Shangri-La the name of the property?'

'No – it's called Rose Cottage.'

'I see. And you said the owners were away – it hasn't been burgled, has it?'

'No, not as far as I know. Why?'

'No special reason – it's just that I suppose a cottage standing empty in an out-of-the-way place might be an attractive proposition to a burglar.'

'Well, it has been known to happen, but not to that one, as far as I know. I must say I was rather hopeful of a sale – Latham appeared to be quite taken with it. A missed opportunity. But I suppose that's all irrelevant now that he's dead.'

'Yes, I rather think it is.'

'I do hope you catch whoever did it, Inspector.'

'We will, Mr Swanson, don't you worry – we will.'

CHAPTER THIRTY

It was time to head back to London. Cradock had established that the five-thirty non-stop service to London was still running, so they returned the Morris in good time to Cambridge police station. This was an ornate Victorian building in St Andrew's Street, close to the town centre, a distinctly more refined edifice than its Kentish Town counterpart.

Jago handed over the car keys to the desk sergeant and left a note of thanks for the chief constable. When he then asked for the police station's copy of the railway timetable, Cradock looked disappointed.

'It is still running, sir – that half-past five train,' he said, thinking perhaps Jago didn't trust him.

'Yes, I know,' said Jago, thumbing through the timetable. 'There's something else I wanted to check, that's all.'

He studied it for a moment and handed it back. 'Thank you, Sergeant, and goodbye. Come on, Peter. It's not far to the station – we'll walk.'

The five-thirty arrived on time. As it pulled into the station Jago could see it wasn't crowded, and the number of passengers waiting on the platform to board wasn't excessive. Maybe people were reluctant to travel in the evening, he thought, what with the blackout and the air raids, but whatever the reason, he was pleased to find an empty compartment towards the rear of the train, and even more pleased when no one else joined them before a whistle blew and the train began to chug out of the station.

'Well,' he said as they settled into their seats, facing each other across the compartment, 'I'd say that's been a very interesting and fruitful day, wouldn't you?'

'Yes, sir,' said Cradock.

'And what about that George Swanson? He's the only person we've met so far who admits to actually threatening to kill Latham.'

'Yes. It's not very sensible to say that in public if you really plan to do it, though, is it?'

'True, but it's not beyond the bounds of possibility. He's provided us with a motive, too – he said Latham had cheated him out of a considerable sum of money with his card tricks.'

'He's got an alibi, though, hasn't he? Could he really've killed Latham in Camden Town at a quarter to eight in the morning and then got all the way back up to Cambridge in time for work?'

'I'm not sure. I was checking the morning trains in that

timetable at Cambridge nick, and I saw there's one that leaves London at eight-thirty and gets in to Cambridge by ten. On the face of it that's cutting it a bit fine, but with a bit of luck and a following wind he could've got to Liverpool Street and caught it.'

'That would've made him late for work, though.'

'Yes, but it's his business, so he can turn up late if he likes with no questions asked. I dare say he could persuade that lad who works for him to back him up if necessary, or his pals down the road from the chamber of commerce, for that matter.'

'Even so, guv'nor, it's not exactly an open and shut case, is it?'

'Maybe you're right.'

'That business about the cottage was interesting, though, wasn't it? I mean, Rose Cottage – Rose Latham? Do you think Latham was looking at it because of the name? It'd be just right if he was thinking of somewhere nice for him and his wife to live.'

'If he was – but she didn't seem too convinced that's what he was planning to spend the money on, did she? Besides, there's probably a Rose Cottage in every village in England, so it could well be just a coincidence. We'll have to find out whether she knew he was viewing houses for sale, but I'm beginning to suspect there were a few things he was getting up to that she didn't know about. That thing his landlady said about his niece visiting, for example – I'd take more than a pinch of salt with that. I'm surprised Mrs Roberts seemed so ready to believe him, but then I suppose she didn't know what we know.'

'What's that, sir?'

'Don't you remember? His wife told us he was an only child, so where would he get a niece from? And she said she was too, so on the face of it he couldn't have been talking about a niece-in-law either, if there is such a thing. No, I'm thinking perhaps the relationship between him and her, whoever she is, wasn't a family one. Talking of which, what about Latham's mum, who's apparently so interested in buying a country cottage? According to Rose Latham she's dead. So why was he going and viewing rural properties on behalf of a mother who doesn't exist?'

'Is that why you asked Swanson whether the cottage had been burgled?'

'Yes.'

'So do you think I was right about those tools in Latham's boot?'

'You mean that he might've been doing a bit of quiet burglary on the side?'

'That's it – I wasn't sure you thought too much of the idea at the time.'

'As I said, Peter, Latham was a man of many parts, just as you're a man of many ideas, some perhaps less bad than others.'

Cradock wasn't entirely sure what this meant. 'Do you mean that was a good idea?'

'Possibly. We'll see.'

Before Cradock could press him further, there was a clanking and clattering from the railway carriage buffers as the train braked and slowed down, finally squealing to a halt. Jago didn't want to incur the wrath of the railway staff by attempting to move the blackout curtain, but there was no noise of doors banging to suggest they'd made an unscheduled stop at a station. Outside there was only silence.

'Could it be an air-raid alert, sir?' said Cradock. 'Don't they stop trains if there's a raid on?'

'I'm not sure, Peter. I know they used to in the last war, but I'm sure I heard somewhere that now they're supposed to keep going, only slowly – fifteen miles an hour, I think it was. If that's right, this should mean there isn't a raid coming – I hope.'

There was another reason why Jago hoped they hadn't run into an enemy air raid, but it was one he kept to himself: his desire that nothing should make them late for their dinner engagement with Dorothy. But as the minutes ticked by and the train remained immobile, his relief at the absence of bomb blasts was overshadowed by the increasing risk of a significant delay.

Cradock sat in silence, looking nervous. Finally the train gave a lurch and stuttered forward. His expression relaxed a little as it steadied into a more regular motion, albeit still proceeding slowly.

Jago smiled. 'Do you feel happier now we're moving again?'

'I don't know, sir – I suppose I am if it means there's no problem, but not if it means there's bombers on their way over.'

'People do say a moving target's harder to hit.'

'Yes, but it depends, doesn't it? I mean, if you're sitting still, a bomb might hit you or it might miss, and if you're moving, you might be moving away from where it's going to land or right into it. It just feels safer, somehow. Was it like that when you were in the trenches?'

'I think sometimes it was, yes. When the enemy's doing

an artillery bombardment, you know they're aiming at you, so if their aim's good you're going to be in trouble. You think if only you could move you might be safer, but on the other hand . . . well, you just can't tell. All you know is you're in a war and you might win or you might lose.'

The train picked up speed and was soon going as fast as it had before their unexplained stop. Cradock settled back into his seat. 'Do you think we'll win this war, sir?'

Jago smiled again. 'That's a big question. We're a long way off winning at the moment – even the prime minister admits that. You heard what he said the other day, didn't you?'

'Er, I'm not sure, sir.'

'He said between intermediate survival and lasting victory there's a long way to tread. Good with words, isn't he? I think "intermediate survival" describes our present state pretty well, but as for getting to a lasting victory, to be honest I don't know whether we'll win, any more than I know whether it'll rain next Wednesday. But I hope we will, and I think we've got a good chance, if we're lucky.'

Cradock seemed unsure. 'But there's no way of knowing whether you really will be lucky, is there? It's like what that Henderson bloke said about Latham – he thought life was a game and he was lucky, so he'd win. But he didn't, did he?'

'No, but there are plenty of people who think like that, whether it's about life or a war.'

Cradock thought for a few moments. 'When I was at school, sir, one of the teachers told us some of our soldiers went into battle in the Great War kicking footballs to each other as if it was some sort of game. Is that true?'

'Well, I didn't see it myself, but I heard about it. I believe it was a young captain in the East Surreys who gave the order.'

'Would you've done that, sir?'

'Given the order? No, not if I'd had a choice. But things were different in those days – a lot of officers thought war was like a noble game, and dying for the Empire was part of it. And who knows, maybe the footballs helped take those lads' minds off what they were doing. I'm just glad I wasn't one of them.'

'And what about Latham? What kind of game do you think he was playing?'

'That's the question, isn't it? But whatever kind of game it was, I don't think he was playing it for the greater good of the Empire. And I'm not so sure what he thought about playing by the rules, either.'

CHAPTER THIRTY-ONE

The rhythmic clickety-clack of the wheels on the rail joints eased off as the train slowed again. As before, it came to a halt, but this time the sound of whistles, Tannoy announcements and banging doors confirmed that they'd reached the end of their journey, mercifully neither bombed nor machine-gunned, and were at Liverpool Street station. Jago glanced at his watch and allowed himself a brief smile. Despite their enforced stop on the way, whatever its reason, the driver had managed to make up the lost time, and they were only two minutes late. Now he could look forward to making up some lost time with Dorothy.

He and Cradock took the Tube to Piccadilly Circus, then walked to the nearby backstreet where the restaurant she had invited them to was located. Inside he saw her sitting at a corner table, deep in conversation with Rita and oblivious to their arrival. He hoped she was grilling

Rita for working-class Londoners' perceptions of the Blitz and not, as he considered equally likely, discussing him. He gave a theatrical cough as he approached them.

'Ah,' said Dorothy, swinging round to greet them, 'how lovely to see you both. Happy Thanksgiving! Come and sit down here with us.'

They pulled out the two remaining seats at the table and sat down. Jago glanced round the room: it was a small establishment, and crowded with people who seemed to be having a good time. In the general buzz of conversation he could make out more than one transatlantic accent, and the American flag was draped on the wall behind them.

Dorothy seemed to have gained the ability to read his mind. 'You're right, John – you've stepped into a little corner of the USA, right here in London, and tonight these fellow diners of ours are planning on celebrating.'

'Until the sirens put paid to that idea, I suppose.'

'Well, yes, but I get the impression they're becoming a bit blasé about the bombs – they think there's nothing we can do about them, so we might as well just get on with it and enjoy yourselves. Especially the young people – they don't want to spend their best years cooped up in a damp, smelly air-raid shelter when they could be out dancing with their friends.'

'I imagine London doesn't have much to offer in the way of night life these days. It's probably not quite the magnet for rich American tourists that it used to be either.'

Dorothy laughed. 'That's true. Some people I know back home think I'm crazy to want to be here in the middle of a terrible war, but then again, a lot of them have never set foot outside their own country – even Canada feels foreign to them. But most of my American friends here love it.'

She paused while a waiter placed a jug of water on the table and a glass for each of them. 'There,' she continued when he'd gone, 'a touch of home for American visitors. Restaurants in the States always give you water, and as like as not it'll be iced. But over here there's hardly ever water on the table, and if you ask for some they look at you like you're from a different planet.'

'Perhaps you are,' said Jago.

'Maybe you're right. It certainly feels like it sometimes. What do you think, Rita?'

Rita raised her eyebrows as if surprised by the question. 'People who come to my cafe don't want a glass of water with their meal, dear – they want a nice cup of tea, so that's what I give them, and I'm sure if I ever went to America, which I never will, that's what I'd do there. But anyway, it's very sweet of you to invite us here – I don't get out much these days, especially up the West End, and I've never been to an American place before. It all looks every nice in here.'

'I'm glad you like it. I thought it was time I repaid your hospitality.' She glanced at Jago. 'And yours too, of course, John – all those interesting English pie shops and fish and chip shops you've taken me to.'

'Thank you,' he replied. 'I appreciate it too. This looks a bit smarter than those places, though.'

'It's very popular – I was lucky to get a table.'

'And will we be having real American food?'

'Of course – I promised, didn't I? At least, it'll be as American as the guys here can manage in London in the middle of a war. They're doing a traditional Thanksgiving dinner today, so I thought you might all like to have that.

It'll be roast turkey with chestnut stuffing and cranberry sauce, Brussels sprouts and mashed potatoes. Brussels sprouts aren't quite as traditional as some of the other ingredients, but I guess they're on the menu because you grow plenty of them over here.'

'Ooh, that sounds lovely,' said Rita. 'I do like a nice Brussels sprout.'

'Me too,' said Cradock eagerly. 'Anything else?'

'Well, back home we might follow that with something like a romaine and orange salad, but I don't suppose there's much romaine to be found in London these days, not to mention oranges, so our salad course will be whatever the restaurant can rustle up. Then we'll have pumpkin pie, and coffee with after-dinner mints.'

'Pumpkin pie?' said Jago. 'That sounds very American. Can you get pumpkins here in November?'

'I'm not sure, but in any case back home nowadays we mostly get our pumpkin from a can. I imagine if there's any difficulty with supply the people who run this place have probably managed to get some through the US Embassy. It's all about who you know, isn't it?'

'That's what they say, yes, but generally speaking if you want one of life's luxuries these days and it has to come from another country, well, you can whistle for it.'

She laughed. 'I know. I wrote a piece for my paper on Tuesday about your government's latest decision.'

'Which one would that be?'

'Bananas. All imports of bananas to stop, says the Colonial Office. Great for headlines like "Banana ban" and "British ban bananas", but not so good for people who like to eat them, not to mention the folks in Jamaica who grow them. I found out your banana imports have already fallen by half since the war began, but it looks like now they're going to be zero, because you need the cargo space for war materials. The only good news is that your government's still going to buy millions of bananas a year to support the growers – just too bad you won't see any of them here.'

Cradock looked glum. 'I like a banana,' he said.

'You'll just have to cherish their memory,' said Jago. 'And be thankful you can still have your Brussels sprouts.'

Cradock's face suggested this was little consolation.

The waiter returned, and Dorothy gave him their orders. When he left, she noticed that Rita looked troubled.

'Is something bothering you, Rita? The bananas?' she asked.

'No, it's not that,' Rita replied. 'Well, I mean I'll miss them for sure, but it was about this Thanksgiving thing. Pardon me for asking, dear, but what's it all about?'

Dorothy laughed again. 'I'm sorry, Rita, I should have explained. It's a tradition that goes back to when the first people from here were sailing to America. The Pilgrim Fathers settled in Massachusetts, where I'm from, and at the end of their first year they held a special feast to give thanks for their harvest.'

'Oh, that's nice.'

'Yes, but it's a bit controversial right now. It used to be on the last Thursday in November, but then last year President Roosevelt decided to move it a week earlier. The country was divided over it, and it's the same this year – some states are having Thanksgiving on the twenty-first and some on the twenty-eighth. Massachusetts decided to stick with the twenty-eighth, which is today.'

Rita looked a little confused.

'Don't worry, Rita,' said Jago, coming to her rescue. 'I don't think it matters too much to us. Besides, I think I can see our food coming.'

As the waiter brought their meals to the table, Dorothy opened her handbag, took out a scrap of paper and unfolded it, then stood up. 'I hope you don't mind if I get a bit serious just for a moment. I've got something here that's precious to me because it was written by one of my ancestors, a man called Ebenezer Appleton. He left England back in the sixteen-hundreds looking for religious freedom with a new life in a new world, and I find it kind of moving because now I've sailed back to see you fighting for your freedom in the old world. It's a simple Thanksgiving prayer, and I guess he was probably a simple man, but it's been handed down through the generations in our family. My father used to read it to us every year at Thanksgiving, so I'd like to read it now, for you.'

She cleared her throat and read from the paper.

*We thank Thee, Lord, that Thou hast brought us
    safe across the sea
And landed us upon a shore where men might yet be
    free.
We thank Thee for Thy mighty wind that blew us
    straight and true,
That we might serve our holy Lord, who maketh all
    things new.
We thank Thee for this food, and as Thy people,
    Thine alone,*

May we now dwell in peace, and love our neighbour
    as our own.
O help us Lord to bring not curse but blessing to this
    place,
And by Thy mercy grant we might be vessels of Thy
    grace.
Amen.

The others at the table murmured 'Amen' and observed a respectful moment's silence. Then Dorothy invited them all to eat, which they did.

Rita was the first to speak. 'Thank you again, dear – I thought that little prayer was very nice. You don't meet many people with a name like Ebenezer nowadays, do you? I don't think I ever have, anyway.'

'I think more people used to have religious names in those days,' Dorothy replied. 'My father told me it means "Hitherto hath the Lord helped us," so it's always seemed to me kind of appropriate that he should write a prayer of thanks like that. It's just a pity that if we look back now we can see it didn't quite work out the way he hoped.'

'What do you mean?'

'I mean we ended up driving out the people who were already living there, and instead of brotherly love we had slavery and a terrible civil war.'

'So was that what he meant by "curse", do you think?'

'Who can say? I guess maybe he knew enough about human nature to understand that going to a new place doesn't mean everything's going to be hunky-dory, just like that. Maybe he could see trouble ahead and could only pray it wouldn't happen.'

'Like this war, I suppose. But between you and me, I sometimes think the whole world could be praying and Hitler would still do whatever he wants.'

'We all do that, in one way or another – I guess it's the way we're made.'

'Well,' said Rita, resting her knife and fork on the rim of her plate, 'I'm still praying old Adolf'll get run over by a bus or something and give us all a bit of peace and quiet. I'm very happy to love my neighbour, as long as he's not called Hitler.'

Rita sat back in her chair, as if resting her case. She cast an affectionate glance at Jago, more in hope than expectation, but he was looking in another direction.

'Actually,' said Dorothy, 'I have my own little thanksgiving to add. It won't be in the papers until tomorrow because of the censorship, but since the last time I saw you all, my home's been bombed.'

Rita's eyes widened. 'They haven't gone and started bombing America, have they?'

'No,' Dorothy replied with a reassuring smile. 'I don't think Mr Hitler's planes can fly that far yet. I mean my home here in London.'

'The Savoy?' Jago cut in. 'Why didn't you—'

He was about to say 'tell me', but stopped short for fear of appearing more attached to her than he wanted Rita and Cradock to think.

'What happened?' he asked instead, not quite managing to suppress the anxiety in his voice.

'The same thing as everywhere else, I guess. A high-explosive bomb hit the hotel during the night a week or so ago. A few rooms were wrecked, but apart from that the building didn't come off too badly. The Savoy has dozens of its own staff trained as ARP wardens, so they were able to handle the whole incident themselves.'

'Was anyone hurt?'

'Sadly two people were killed as they slept in their bedroom.'

'I'm sorry. And you?'

'That's why I'm thankful – I was away on assignment, otherwise I might not be sitting here now.'

'Well, I'm sure we're all pleased to hear that. But you should've told us sooner.'

'I don't want to be a bomb bore – we've all heard enough narrow escape stories by now. But I am thankful.'

'So are we, dear,' said Rita. 'And it's lovely to be here tonight. I'm sure we're all very glad they didn't get you.'

'Thanks, Rita,' said Dorothy. 'Now, come on, don't let this dinner get cold.'

The food was good, and the conversation ambled along agreeably through the meal. Jago was pleased that Rita and Dorothy seemed to get on so well: two very different women from different countries and backgrounds, unexpectedly thrown together by a war. Watching them chatting, he realised these were the two most important women in his life. Rita, a friend for more years than he cared to remember, and Dorothy, whom he'd only met for the first time the month before last but who already . . . well, even in his own unspoken thoughts he wasn't quite sure how to put it, but he knew she'd won a special place in his heart. This evening he had to share her, but it was pleasure enough to be at the same table.

Cradock, meanwhile, was torn between his delight at being treated to such a hearty meal and his fear that Dorothy might ask him how things were going with Emily while that young lady's mother was sitting not three feet away. He was confident that Dorothy would never be that indiscreet, but while it remained even a hypothetical possibility it put his enjoyment of the evening at risk.

At length he made it to the end of the meal, untroubled by the feared inquisition. Savouring his last mouthful of pumpkin pie, he put his spoon down, declaring to Dorothy that the dinner had been amazing, and was rewarded with a smile. His heart sank, however, when Rita, announcing that she couldn't risk drinking coffee this late in the evening, excused herself for a moment while she went to powder her nose.

As soon as Rita was out of earshot, Dorothy leant conspiratorially across the table towards Cradock. 'So, Peter, how's it all going with your Emily? Still moving forward?'

He resigned himself to his fate, desiring only to get it over and done with. 'Actually,' he said, glancing in the direction that Rita had gone in case she'd changed her mind, 'I'm not sure I could say it's moving forward at all. Things seem to have got a bit stuck.'

'Stuck? How do you mean? You still like her, don't you?'

'Oh, yes, I do, but—'

'And she likes you?'

'Er, well, she hasn't said she doesn't, but nothing much seems to be happening.'

'And whose fault is that?'

'I don't know.'

Jago turned away to spare the poor boy embarrassment and gazed across the room as if he were fascinated by everything else that was happening in the far recesses of the restaurant rather than by the conversation proceeding at his own table.

Dorothy, meanwhile, sat back in her chair and fixed Cradock with a look that reminded him of the strict schoolmistress who'd ruled over his class when he was nine years old. 'Peter, I know I told you before you mustn't rush her, but I did say you had to take the initiative. You can't just sit around hoping she'll invite you out somewhere – she might if she thinks you'll never summon up the strength to do it, but she shouldn't have to do that.'

'I know,' he said glumly.

'So take her out – and to something romantic that a girl's going to like, not another crime caper movie like you did before. What was it? *The Saint Takes Over*? No – you can do better than that. OK?'

'Yes.' It was all Cradock could do to stop himself adding 'Miss' to his monosyllabic replies.

'Now,' said Dorothy, 'this is what you need to do. There's a new movie out – *Pride and Prejudice*. It's made in Hollywood, but the stars are British – Greer Garson and Laurence Olivier. What could be better than that? And it's romantic. Tell Emily you'd like to take her to see it.'

Cradock nodded his assent, hoping the interrogation was over.

'Good,' said Dorothy. 'And here's another thing – what have you done about gifts?'

'Gifts?'

'Yes. Have you bought her any?'

'Not yet, no – but that's only because I don't know what she'd like, and I don't want to give her something she doesn't like. Have you got any suggestions?'

'Well, the traditional answer is flowers, but there's not so many around nowadays – I believe your government's told the growers to plough their land for vegetables instead. Not very romantic, but necessary, I suppose.'

'Dig for Victory, you mean?'

'Exactly, but even so, you don't want to give her a bunch of Brussels sprouts. But don't worry – if you can't get flowers, there's always chocolates. You won't go far wrong with those lovely English chocolates of yours. Give her a box of Black Magic – they're my favourite, anyway, although you'd need to find out what Emily likes and make sure you get the right ones.'

'Thanks,' said Cradock.

'And one last question,' said Dorothy.

'Yes?'

She lowered her voice. 'Have you kissed her yet?'

Cradock lowered his own in reply, but knew that Jago could still hear. 'Well, no, I didn't want to rush her, you see, like you said, but I'm just wondering – how do you know when's the right time?'

'Peter, I don't think I can tell you that – it's not like a mathematical formula you can apply. How long have you been seeing her?'

'Since about the beginning of the Blitz.'

'Well, I can't say "in ten days' time" or anything as precise as that. You just have to feel it – if the thought of it makes you feel a bit dizzy, then maybe it's the time. Just don't force it on her. A little peck on the cheek is OK, but if you want to kiss her on the lips, that's getting serious, so you'd better be sure she's happy for you to do that.' She looked over his shoulder. 'Now, I see Rita coming back, so will that be enough?'

Cradock gulped. 'Er, yes, thanks – more than enough.'

CHAPTER THIRTY-TWO

Jago's last meeting with Chief Constable Ford had been when he was investigating a case in Pimlico, and on that occasion he'd been required to present himself at eight o'clock in the morning. Now he was here again, this time with an appointment at seven-thirty, and he wondered whether the start of Ford's working day was creeping steadily earlier as the full weight of his new responsibilities bore down on his shoulders. The fact that a man hurried out of the office with the briefest of nods to him as he and Cradock arrived suggested that even this was not his boss's first meeting of the day and seemed to confirm Jago's impression. He knew, however, from his experience of working for the then Detective Superintendent Ford during his secondment to Special Branch in 1936 that the chief constable's shoulders were broad.

'Come in, take a seat,' said Ford. 'Good to see you, John. Now, you said you wanted to know if I could tell you whether your murder victim in Camden Town could have been a spy, is that right?'

'Yes, sir. It was actually Detective Constable Cradock here who raised the possibility, so I'd like him to explain his thinking to you.'

Cradock felt a stab of panic as he contemplated the prospect of having to account for his thinking, and the austere expression on Ford's face did little to calm him.

'Well,' said Ford, 'let's hear it, Detective Constable.' He glanced at the clock on the wall behind Cradock's head as if to signal that he'd be timing him.

'Er, yes, sir,' Cradock began, stumbling into his explanation. 'It's nothing much, really, just that the man who was murdered – Mr Latham, that is – he was a commercial traveller, and he had a friend, a boatman on the canal called Trent – I mean he was called Trent, not the canal – and this friend told us Latham might've had some connection with a Russian company that had a place on a wharf up the canal, and, er . . .'

'Just take your time, Detective Constable,' said Ford. 'This isn't an exam.'

'No, sir. Yes, sir,' Cradock gabbled, then took a deep breath and continued. 'The thing is, sir, one of the Russians working for this company asked him – Trent, that is – to tell him all about the canal and the locks and show him round, so he did. The Russian offered to give him some petrol in return, but he didn't need any, so he said no. But then later on, when the war started, Trent's friend Latham was complaining about never having enough petrol, so Trent mentioned it to the Russian at the wharf, and the Russian said he might be able to help, so Trent put Latham in touch with him.'

He stopped and took another deep breath to steady himself.

'And did this result in any contact between Latham and the Russians?' said Ford.

'Ah, well, sir, that's the thing – Trent said Latham never said. But one of Latham's other friends, a garage owner called Bowen, he said there were rumours that the Russians working for this company were all spies.'

'So you think that means Latham might have been spying for the Russians.'

Cradock lowered his head, preparing for the chief constable to wipe the floor with him. 'Er, yes, sir. But perhaps not, sir.'

'It's a reasonable question to ask,' said Ford.

Cradock's head shot back up. 'Really, sir?' he beamed.

'Of course. After all the years I spent in Special Branch it doesn't surprise me at all to hear someone suggesting that a Russian company's scope might extend beyond purely commercial activities. What was the name of the company?'

'Russian Oil Products, sir.'

'Ah, yes, ROP – I remember them. A couple of their directors were expelled back to Russia by the Home Office in 1927 – before my time, of course, but it was the kind of organisation that had an eye kept on it even as long ago as that. Not that that was anything unusual – there were suspicions about anyone who was over here representing the Soviets in any official way. And there still are, especially now they've got that non-aggression pact with Hitler. The thing about these companies is that they're all officially here to promote trade between the USSR and Britain, but they're all owned and run by the Soviet state and they're also a front for Soviet intelligence work.'

'You mean they are all spies, sir?'

'Not necessarily everyone who works for them, but my colleagues in the Security Service would tell you gathering intelligence is part of what these businesses are here for. None of this is secret, by the way – the Home Secretary himself told the House of Commons years ago that the Soviet trade delegation here was what he called a nefarious spy system. There was always a concern too that ROP might be involved in planning and organising sabotage operations, which could be very serious in a time of war. But tell me more about this man Latham – he was a commercial traveller, you say?'

Jago decided to spare Cradock the stress of being cross-examined by the chief constable. 'That's right, sir,' he said, noticing the relief on Cradock's face. 'He works for a chocolate company, and as DC Cradock said, he's an old friend of Trent.'

'Yes, the man who showed the Russian round the canal locks. That was naive, to say the least – canals are strategic objects.'

'Yes, sir, but Trent's a boatman, and they live a very isolated life. He's barely literate, and the only time he's ever strayed more than a few miles from the canal was when he was in the army in the last war, and then he ended up in France – and later in North Russia, of all places.'

'So there's another Russian connection, eh? And this Latham – a chocolate company doesn't sound a very likely hotbed of espionage, but did his travelling take him near any sensitive defence areas where Russian visitors might be a bit too conspicuous?'

'I'm not sure – his sales patch was Cambridge and the villages around it.'

Ford thought for a moment. 'Hmm, well, there's a lot of airfields up that way – Duxford, of course, Bassingbourn, and a string of others. They might've been interested in that. The powers that be are certainly a bit paranoid about it – only a few weeks ago a civil servant in the Air Ministry was sent down for three years just because he was found in possession of a list of airfields being built for the RAF. No previous convictions, either.' He paused again. 'This fellow of yours wasn't a bird watcher by any chance, was he?'

'Not as far as we know, sir. Why do you ask?'

'Oh, just because one or two of those bird-loving types like to go out into the countryside and hang around near airfields with binoculars because they say that's the best place to spot them. They're a bit suspicious – especially the ones who happen to be keen photographers too and take a camera with them. If he'd been caught at that game, the Defence Regulations would've had something to say about it. The Germans aren't the only ones keen to get information about our ports and airfields and arms factories – that sort of stuff's right up those Soviet agents' street too. Recruiting some willing British subject to take photos of airfields is exactly what they do, and they'll pay a bit of cash for it. Still, no risk of that now that the poor blighter's dead.'

'Indeed, sir, and given that he's been murdered, I'm wondering whether they'd kill someone who was providing them with information.'

'Well, I wouldn't put it past them. They reward people who are loyal, but if you cross them, the consequences can be very severe. Look what happened to Trotsky in August – he'd got on the wrong side of Stalin and thought he was safe living in Mexico, but they caught up with him and stuck an ice pick in his head. I'm not saying that your man was another Trotsky – far from it – but if he was working for them and cheated them in some way, they might well have decided to terminate his contract, in a manner of speaking. Have you got any more evidence of this connection of his with the Russians that might suggest that was the case?'

'No sir, I don't think so. The only other thing was that we found an empty petrol can near the scene of the fire, and it was an ROP one.'

'Well, I know you have a suspicious mind, John, like me, so I'm sure you'll be thinking that could be significant if the Russians brought some of their own petrol to start a fire with. But the fact that it's a Russian can doesn't mean it was a Russian using it. Any prints on it?'

'No, sir – looks like it may've been wiped clean.'

'Any other evidence to connect it with the fire?'

'No, sir, except that the garage man who services the car thinks Latham had an ROP can.'

'Along with a few thousand other people, I imagine.'

'Yes, sir. I think we need to know more before we can reach any firm conclusions.'

'You're right – keep digging. This Latham fellow's dead now, so he's beyond our reach, but if he was mixed up in some kind of spying there'll be other people who were involved who might still be alive and active. So let me know if you come up with anything that might link him with someone like that – I imagine Special Branch and the Security Service would both be interested in following up any leads you could provide.'

CHAPTER THIRTY-THREE

It was still well before the start of normal office hours
when they emerged from their meeting with Chief
Constable Ford, but Jago had a phone call to make,
and he hoped that in wartime the Middlesex Regiment
would have someone up and dressed to answer. He
found an unoccupied desk with a phone and called
the regimental headquarters, and was reassured when
a voice came on the line, identifying himself as the
duty officer. Jago left with him a request on behalf
of Scotland Yard that they check their records for a
Major Edmund Fortescue, who had served with the
regiment in the Great War. He was unable to tell them
when or in which battalion, but said he understood
the major had served on the Western Front and won
the DSO, and had survived the war. The duty officer
assured him that they should be able to complete this

task within the hour and invited him to call back.

Jago thanked him and put the phone down. 'Right, Peter,' he said. 'I think we'll head back to Camden Town now, and on the way we'll call in at St George's Hospital. If Dr Gibson's in, he might be able to suggest someone who can tell us what they know about the gallant major and his fundraising efforts on their behalf. Unless you need a lie down, that is, to recover from being interrogated by Mr Ford.'

'No, I'm all right, guv'nor . . . I think. He knows a lot about all sorts of things, doesn't he?'

'Indeed he does – there's no flies on him. But you don't get to be chief constable of the CID without knowing a thing or two, and I imagine his work in Special Branch must've brought some very interesting people across his path, including one or two Russian characters.'

'I've been thinking about those Russians, though, and there's something I don't understand.'

'I wouldn't worry too much about that, Peter. Most people find it a bit difficult to understand what goes on in the Soviet Union. Maybe it's best just to accept that it's different there.'

'Yes, sir, but this is about the war. I mean, we declared war on Germany because they invaded Poland, didn't we?'

'That's correct.'

'But then Russia invaded Poland from the other side, but we didn't declare war on them, did we?'

'I think that's actually quite easy to explain. Mr Chamberlain gave Hitler an ultimatum that if he didn't withdraw his troops we'd declare war, because we'd signed an agreement with Poland to help them. But he didn't give Stalin an ultimatum, so we didn't declare war on Russia.'

'But that doesn't make sense, sir. If we'd promised to help Poland, why did we only help them against the Germans and not against the Russians?'

'Ah, well, there you have me, Peter. I suspect you'd have to ask Mr Chamberlain, had he not unfortunately passed away three weeks ago. All he said at the time was that he wasn't going to be rushed into anything. It's a mystery to me. As far as I'm concerned, all those dictators are the same – Hitler, Stalin, Mussolini, they all like strutting around, throwing their weight about and picking fights with smaller countries. Look at what Stalin was doing to Finland this time last year – he wanted to grab some territory from them, so he just invaded the place. He must've thought it'd be a walkover, but the way they fought back, he nearly bit off more than he could chew.'

'That's something else I don't understand, sir – why do all these blokes want to take bits of land?'

'I don't know, Peter – I suppose it's like moving your fence so you can pinch a few inches of your next-door neighbour's garden. Hitler says he needs more room for his people to live in, Stalin says he's not safe unless he's got a bit of Finland, and as for what Mussolini's been saying to the Greeks these last few weeks, I can't imagine.'

They arrived at the car and Jago got the key out of his pocket, but as he reached for the door handle he stopped and turned to Cradock. 'Talking about all those dictators strutting around's just reminded me of something. You know the way they are in their photos – chin up, staring ahead – and the photographers are always pointing their cameras up at them?'

'Yes, sir.'

'They all do it, don't they? I suppose they think it makes them look strong and frightening, like conquering heroes. Mosley too, although I should think the only thing he might be in a position to annex at the moment is a corner of the exercise yard at Brixton Prison.'

'Sir?'

'Sorry, Peter, what I mean is thinking of them striking those daft poses reminded me of that photo we've got of Latham – you know, the one of him standing on the front steps where he lived. Have you still got it on you?'

'Yes, sir.' Cradock got the two photos of Latham out of his pocket and handed one to Jago. 'Here it is.'

'There,' said Jago, brandishing it in Cradock's direction. 'See what I mean? Standing on the top step, hands on hips, staring into the distance with his chin up, and the angle makes it look like whoever took it must've been squatting on the pavement.'

'His wife did say he liked the idea of being king of the castle.'

'King of the castle? He looks more like the Mussolini of Camden Town.'

'Do you think maybe he was a fan, then, sir?'

'It's impossible to say, isn't it? Maybe those dictators did inspire him in some way, or maybe it was some sort of private joke, taking a picture that made him look like them. From what people've said so far, my impression is that whatever motivated Latham, it was more likely to be financial than ideological, but if he really did think of himself as some sort of Viking conqueror, who knows what might've been going through his mind at the time?'

'Pity we can't ask him.'

'Yes, but we can talk to the photographer. And do you recall who Mrs Latham said took that picture?'

'Yes, sir – it was his mate, Jack Henderson.'

'Precisely.'

CHAPTER THIRTY-FOUR

On their previous visits to St George's Hospital, Jago and Cradock had been expected, and so had used what Dr Gibson called the tradesmen's entrance, at the back of the building. Today, however, they were not, and Jago thought it might be more appropriate to use the front entrance, as other visitors presumably did. They climbed the steps beneath the grand classical facade and went in to enquire whether Gibson was on the premises. A telephone call by the porter brought him up to meet them.

'Well, this is an unexpected pleasure,' said Gibson. 'Is it a social visit, or business?'

'Business, I'm afraid,' said Jago. 'I'm wondering whether you can help us with some information.'

'I'll do my best. But look, I started early today and I was just thinking about popping into the refectory for a spot of breakfast. Would you like to join me?'

The meeting with Ford had meant getting up at an unearthly hour, too early on this occasion for their landlady to provide anything more than a cup of tea and some toast before they set off, so Jago didn't need to look to know that Cradock would be excited at the prospect. 'Yes,' he said, 'that would be very nice.'

The refectory was buzzing with hospital staff, but Gibson managed to secure a table. The St George's cooked breakfast proved to be a hearty affair, more than a match for what they'd enjoyed at Mrs Minter's on Wednesday morning, and in Cradock's estimation a jolly sight better than yesterday's sandwich at Cambridge station.

'So what is this information you'd like to extract from me?' said Gibson. 'Something medical? Nothing too complex, I hope, at this time of day.'

'No, nothing medical,' Jago replied, 'except indirectly, I suppose, in that it's to do with the hospital. But it's more about money than medicine.'

'Aha. Two subjects that are nevertheless closely related, in my experience.'

'Indeed. But this is about raising money for the hospital.'

'Well, that's not exactly my patch, but try me.'

'It's to do with our investigation.'

'The demise of the unfortunate Mr Latham, you mean?'

'Yes. We'd like to find out about a man who's been doing a bit of fundraising for St George's, or so we've been told.'

'Is he a suspect?'

'At this stage everyone we come across in the course of the investigation is a potential suspect, but no, we don't have any reason to suppose this man is. He's just someone we have one or two doubts about for a different reason, so I'd like to check his credentials, as it were, with the hospital.'

'Well, I doubt whether I'd have anything useful to contribute, but . . .' He scanned the room. 'Yes, there she is. If you look over there, to that column with a clock on it, there's a woman at the table next to it – the confident-looking lady facing you and talking animatedly to someone with their back to you.'

Jago followed his directions and saw a well-dressed woman who fitted the description of confident and animated perfectly. 'I see her – who is she?'

'She's not just any lady. She's a Lady with a capital L – Lady Cynthia Melville, a very enthusiastic volunteer on our appeal committee and by all accounts a woman of dynamic personality. I think she's the daughter of a marquess or something, so she's very well connected socially, and I understand that by lending her name to our fundraising effort she helps to bring it to the attention of people who may be in a position to support it. She's often here by breakfast time, which I suppose is an indication of how keen she is. Do you think she's the kind of person who might be able to help you?'

'I should imagine so, yes.'

'Would you like me to introduce you?'

'Yes, please – but probably best not to say the police are here wanting to talk to her. I wouldn't want to embarrass her in front of her friends.'

'Don't worry, I'll be tactful. Wait here.'

Jago watched as Gibson went over to the other table and spoke to the woman. He saw her nod vigorously and excuse herself from her companions, then stride

270

purposefully towards them with Gibson. He rose from his chair when she arrived, prodding Cradock to show similar good manners. Gibson introduced them to her.

'Well, Inspector,' she said, taking a chair at the table, 'Dr Gibson says you'd like a word with me – how can I help?'

Jago resumed his seat, together with Cradock and Gibson. 'Thank you, Lady Cynthia,' he said. 'I'm trying to find out a bit more about the hospital's fundraising, and I understand you're quite involved with it.'

'Oh, yes, very. My elder brother was treated for wounds here during the Great War, you see, and my parents were so impressed with the way he was cared for that they became patrons of the hospital. When I grew up I followed in their footsteps, and I do a little voluntary work to help with the fundraising.'

'More than a little, from what I've heard.'

'Well, I suppose so, yes, but then the needs are very great. This building's been standing here since 1829, you know, and to be perfectly frank, it's falling apart. We've got walls shored up because the fabric's crumbling, and we've so little space we can't keep up with the latest advances in medicine and surgery. On top of that, our staff were having to work in almost impossible conditions even before the war came along. I'm sure Dr Gibson can vouch for that.'

Gibson hadn't been expecting to be called as a witness in support of Lady Cynthia's testimony. 'Er, yes, well,' he said, 'I suppose it would be fair to say that the conditions can be somewhat trying.'

'The good doctor is too tactful by far,' she replied. 'I call a spade a spade, and that's probably why I'm a fundraiser and not a doctor. When I diagnose a problem, I don't put it in Latin so no one will understand what I'm talking about – I prefer plain English. Not to put too fine a point on it, the whole damned business has been a mammoth challenge for years, and in the end the hospital's governing body decided the only solution was to rebuild the entire institution, one section at a time, right here on the same site.'

'That does sound a rather expensive project.'

'It is, and as you may be aware, St George's is a voluntary hospital, which means it's funded entirely by charitable donations and legacies, so raising money is hugely important. The only way we'd be able to do something on this scale would be to mount a huge fundraising effort, so the upshot was that in 1935 we launched an appeal for what we call our rebuilding fund – we worked out we need to raise a million pounds.'

'My goodness. And how's it going?'

'Our supporters have been magnificent, and over the past five years we've raised more than a third of that, but everything's rather been on hold since the war started. As things stand, we're not sure how it's going to work out.'

'But the work of fundraising goes on, I assume.'

'Oh, yes – that never stops.'

'I'd like to ask you about one supporter in particular. He's a Major Edmund Fortescue – do you recognise that name?'

She thought for a moment. 'Yes, I do – he came here, just the once, I think, and we had a brief meeting.'

'Did he make a donation?'

'Yes – he wrote a cheque on the spot, for about a hundred pounds, I think.'

'And the cheque was honoured?'

'Yes, as far as I recall. Why, do you think he's the kind of man whose cheques might not be?'

'No, but let's just say questions've been raised, so I'm interested to find that wasn't your experience. How did he strike you?'

'Well, he seemed a decent enough chap. I must say, though, that I tend not to look a gift horse in the mouth.' She gave him a broad smile. 'I don't concern myself with how a donor made their money, for example, otherwise I might have to turn down donations from some of the grandest families in the land.'

'Indeed you might. Did Major Fortescue say why he wanted to support St George's Hospital in particular? There are plenty of hospitals to choose from in London alone.'

'Yes. He said he'd been treated here during the Great War, when he was recovering from wounds he sustained at the front.'

'The same as your brother.'

'Yes, a coincidence, isn't it? But I suppose a lot of men passed through here for the same reason back then. He seemed to know about my brother, but I can't remember how – our family's quite well known, though, so his wounding would have been in the papers.'

'He didn't claim he knew your brother, then?'

'I can't be sure, but I don't think so. Is it important?'

'Not necessarily – it's just that in my job I'm expected not to take coincidences at face value. Did you by any chance check to see whether the major had indeed been a patient here?'

'No. I'm afraid it never occurred to me to trawl through the records to see if he was telling the truth. He wasn't someone I knew socially, but he was so well-mannered and so appreciative of the care he'd had here that I'm afraid I took him at his word. Besides, it wasn't a critical factor in agreeing to accept a donation, and that was what our meeting was about. If you need to know, though, I can ask for someone here to check and then let you know.'

'Thank you – that would be helpful if it's not too much trouble.'

'By all means. I can contact you at Scotland Yard? Whitehall 1212, isn't it?'

'Yes, that's right. If you call that number they'll put you through, or take a message if I'm out.'

'Good. Now,' she added brusquely, 'I assume you've a busy day ahead of you, and I know I have, so if that's all, I'll bid you good day.'

'Yes, that'll be all, thank you.'

Jago rose from his chair again, but she was already striding away across the refectory, ready for her next challenge.

'There,' said Gibson, 'I told you she was a dynamic woman, didn't I?'

'Yes,' said Jago. 'The confidence of her class. Now, I wonder if I could use your telephone – I need to make a call in private.'

'Of course. I'll take you to my office and leave you to it – I have to be in the laboratory. Can you find your own way out?'

274

'I'm sure we'll manage.'

'Good.'

Gibson led them through a maze of corridors to his office and left them. Jago picked up the phone and asked the operator for the Middlesex Regiment headquarters. After some silence punctuated by occasional clicking a woman's voice answered. He asked to speak to the duty officer, and after a further wait he heard the same voice he had spoken to earlier.

'Detective Inspector Jago here,' he said. 'You kindly offered to check your records for a Major Edmund Fortescue, so I'm calling to find out whether you've managed to trace him . . . Yes, that's right . . . No, I don't . . . Ah, well, thank you for trying . . . Really? Yes, that is interesting . . .'

Cradock, hearing only one end of the conversation, could make no sense of it, but he was intrigued. There was another silence, then Jago suddenly banged his fist on the desk. 'Ha!' he exclaimed into the handset. 'Of course – that's it! . . . Is he? . . . Hmm, most interesting . . . Well, well, well . . . Thank you very much – you've been very helpful. Goodbye.'

He put the phone down, and Cradock looked at him expectantly.

'A very revealing conversation,' said Jago. 'I knew in my bones that man was a scoundrel – and he is.'

'So, er, what did they say, sir? It wasn't very revealing at this end.'

'They said they had no record of a Major Edmund Fortescue, but the nearest they could find was a man whose name was Edmund Fortescue Hale. That's it – don't you see?'

Cradock looked blank at first, but a glimmer of understanding began to appear in his eyes as he made the connection. 'Ah, yes,' he replied slowly. 'I see it. Like the singer – Binnie Hale. That must be what they called him, mustn't it? Like a nickname.'

'That's right – not very original, perhaps, but the sort of name you're likely to end up with at school, and in the army too.'

'But Binnie Hale's a girl. Why would they call him that?'

'We can only surmise, but I expect it seemed very witty to whoever decided to do it.'

'So we should actually be looking for a Major Hale, then.'

'Yes, but on the other hand no, not exactly. They told me something else. They said this man wasn't a major, he was only a lieutenant – so if he's our Fortescue, he's promoted himself too. And that's only the half of it. They also said unfortunately there was no record of the lieutenant getting a DSO, or any other medal apart from the standard ones we all got, and their records of decorations for gallantry like the DSO were meticulous. I was beginning to wonder whether this chap Hale might not be our man after all, but then they mentioned another rather important fact, which is that after the war he was brought before a general court-martial and cashiered.'

Cradock's face suggested he wasn't familiar with the term.

'It's a military thing, Peter. According to the Army Act, it's a punishable offence for a commissioned officer to misbehave – to quote, if I recall correctly, "behaving in a scandalous manner unbecoming the character of an officer and a gentleman". The punishment's called being cashiered, and it's very serious – you lose your commission, so that means he's not even a lieutenant any more.'

'Blimey – so the whole set-up's phoney.'

'That's right.'

Cradock was embarrassed to ask, but his curiosity got the better of him. 'And, er . . . did they say what he'd done that was so . . . er, scandalous?'

'They did, Peter. He was found guilty of presenting dud cheques – writing a cheque to someone when he knew he didn't have enough money in the bank to meet it.'

'But he didn't do that here, did he? Lady Cynthia said the cheque he wrote for the hospital was honoured.'

'Yes, but that doesn't mean all his cheques were. I suspect this one was another sprat – he'd have known Baring might very well check up with the hospital on his story of a donation, so he'd have to make a genuine one to ensure they confirmed it. But the others – well, we must assume there's evidence that he wrote some that bounced. In the army's eyes that's precisely the kind of thing that's scandalous and unbecoming of an officer and gentleman, because it's dishonourable. He must have a lot to regret.'

'Too true. It's harsh, but I suppose the army has to be harsh.'

'Maybe, but now I need to make another quick call. I want to get my hands on this Fortescue or Hale or whatever his name is, and the Yard's got those new-fangled teleprinters now, so they can send a message to every police station in London. I'm going to ask them to put one out to see if anyone knows the whereabouts of a person of interest calling himself Major Edmund Fortescue.'

'Does that mean we'll have to wait here until we hear back from them?'

'No, we haven't got time for that. I want to see whether Jimmy Trent can tell us any more about this fellow, and then I want to call on Mr Todd at Barings about that business of Carter's complaint about Latham, but I'll give the Yard Barings' number, and if they don't ring me there I'll call them back later. Let's go.'

CHAPTER THIRTY-FIVE

They headed north from the hospital along Park Lane, with the luxurious homes and apartments of Mayfair on their right and the green open space of Hyde Park on their left. The Lane itself seemed to have escaped fresh bomb damage during the previous night, but Londonderry House, the Marquess of Londonderry's elegant mansion on the corner of Hertford Street, still looked in a sorry state after taking a hit earlier in the Blitz, and the papers had reported damage to numerous other parts of Mayfair farther back from the road. The most shocking sight, however, came as they drove down Oxford Street and passed the remains of the once-great John Lewis store, which had taken a direct hit in September and of which all they could see now was a charred and gutted shell.

On arriving in Camden Town they went straight to where Jimmy Trent had his narrowboat, still moored where it had been two days ago. A woman was standing on the cabin roof, washing it with a mop, and as they drew nearer they recognised her as Annie Trent, but when Jago climbed onto the boat she turned away without acknowledging him. Guessing that she might be better left alone, he knocked gently on the cabin doors, and her husband poked his head out.

'Hello again,' he said. 'You've come to talk to me?'

'That's right, Mr Trent,' Jago replied. 'We just want to check a couple of things with you.'

'All right, then, but we'd better talk on the bank.' He nodded his head slightly in the direction of his wife, as if to signify that it would be better not to disturb her with their conversation. 'We'll go for a little stroll, shall we?'

The three men walked slowly along the canalside towpath together.

'Your wife's still suffering?' Jago asked.

'Yes, it's like she can't snap out of it. I think what happened to her in Coventry . . .' His voice trailed off as he seemed to picture her experience. 'I don't know what to say. We've seen a bit of bomb damage on the canal, but nothing like that. I've heard there's been narrowboats taking loads of flat-packed coffins up there – so many people killed, they've been having mass funerals. Annie's cousin told me there were women standing in the street, screaming, fainting. People didn't know what to do – they were just trying to get out of the city any way they could, trying to find somewhere safe, sleeping in hedges and ditches. I can't imagine what Annie was thinking – it must've seemed like the end of the world to her. And it wasn't just the shock – I think it's brought back everything bad that's happened in her life, like losing our Daisy and Bobby. She's in a sort of daze, and I can't get through to her. I'm worried about what this might've done to her on the inside – she's not the same person she used to be, and I . . . well, I just don't know what she might do next.'

Trent looked close to tears. He turned his head away from Jago, towards the canal. When he turned back, his eyes were dry. 'Thanks for asking, though, Inspector. I don't suppose there's anything more I can do to help her – she'll just have to find her own way through it. So, what is it you want from me?'

'Well, first of all, I just wanted to let you know it looks like we've identified that officer you mentioned – the lieutenant you said Les Latham had overhead talking to the lieutenant-colonel at battalion headquarters.'

'I remember, yes – Lieutenant Binnie. Unusual name, isn't it? That's why I remembered him saying it – unless I misheard him, of course.'

'I think you probably heard correctly, Mr Trent. We've talked to the Middlesex Regiment, and they say there was no one by that name amongst their officers during the war, but there was a Lieutenant Hale, so we think it's very likely it was him.'

Trent thought for a moment, then his face lightened with a hint of a smile. 'Ah, yes, I see – like the singer. Very clever – the sort of thing some of those posh officers would think was funny, I suppose.'

'I wondered whether you'd ever come across him yourself, since you were in that regiment too.'

Trent looked as though he was thinking hard, but eventually shook his head. 'No, sorry, it doesn't ring a bell – but there were thousands of us out there, umpteen battalions of the Middlesex alone. I certainly don't recall a Lieutenant Hale in my battalion, but the officers came and went pretty quickly when we were at the front, and it was the young lieutenants and captains that got killed the most. Besides, all that business of Les and him was after I'd gone off to be a batman – I didn't know anything about it until he told me after the war. Sorry I can't be of more help – is it important?'

'No, it's all right – I just wondered, that's all.'

'Anything else?'

'Yes, I'd like to bring you up to date concerning what you told us about Mrs Latham having discovered something that upset her.'

'Oh, yes? What was it?'

'It was a Post Office savings book, Mr Trent. It seems that Mr Latham had been putting some money aside for a while.'

'I'll bet he was,' said Trent, with a sudden note of bitterness in his voice.

'What do you mean?'

'I mean it doesn't surprise me to hear he was salting money away. He was probably earning enough to do that, knowing Les – not the sort of thing I've ever been able to do. We just about scrape by, Annie and I, and always have done.'

'I see. I'd be interested to know what you can tell me about Mr Latham's attitude to money – you mentioned before that he was an ambitious man, so how important do you think making money was in his ambitions?'

'How important? I'd say it probably came next after living and breathing. There was no way he was ever going to be happy with just scraping by. He used to laugh at me and that old boat of mine, said I was living in the past. He'd say what's the point of being in the transport business if you're up against lorries and trains and all you've got is a barge that can only go as fast as the old horse can pull it? All you can promise your customers is that you'll deliver their goods at a fairly slow walking pace. It was like I'd got a one-horsepower lorry, he said, and even his little car was eight horsepower.'

'But you were friends. Was that just his way of pulling your leg?'

'It didn't feel like that. I used to think he pitied me, but he wasn't the sort of fellow to have much pity for man or beast. No, it was more like he looked down on me – used to say I'd got no ambition, that I'd be stuck walking a horse up and down the towpath till the day I died.'

'And how did you feel about that?'

'Well, I suppose I didn't understand, really. I mean, I couldn't see what was wrong with that. I belong on the canal and I'd be happy to live like this for the rest of my days. People know me and respect me, and they care about me. He came on the boat once, and when he saw the cabin he laughed and said I lived in a cupboard – not enough room to swing a rat, never mind a cat, he said. That felt like he was looking down his nose at me too – the way he laughed, it was sort of sarcastic, not friendly.'

'Scornful?'

'Yes, that's a good word for it. I suppose he had a point

– my home's only seven foot wide, but if it was any bigger it wouldn't get up and down the canal. I'm used to living in a small place, and it's all right if you keep everything tidy. Les's little flat wasn't exactly a palace, but he was different to me – he used to talk about having a proper big house out in the country somewhere one day. He said some of them have electric bells you can ring to tell the maid to bring you a cup of tea or whatever. I've never seen nor heard of such a thing.'

'But Mr Latham had?'

'I don't know, but he certainly talked like he had. Maybe he had friends with big houses – I don't know. Personally, I can't see the point. I knew he was money mad, but I used to think good luck to you, mate, if money's what you want. I'm happy with my life and I don't need it. But then—'

Jago waited for him to continue, but Trent seemed to be fighting some deeper feeling. 'But then what?' he asked.

'Then . . . then Annie took that trip up to Coventry. You've seen the state she's in, haven't you? A bottle of tonic won't fix what's wrong with her. My old mum used to talk about the things that money can't buy, bless her, but now I know there's things it *can* buy, and one of them's doctors. She needs to see someone who can really help her, and I thought maybe if I could pay for a proper doctor to take a look at her, well, she'd get better. I haven't got two ha'pennies to rub together, though, so there was no chance of that happening, but then I thought maybe Les . . .'

'Maybe he could help you?'

'Yes . . . But there was a problem.'

'Something to do with this?' Jago reached into his

pocket and pulled out a slip of paper. He unfolded it and handed it to Trent.

'Ah, right,' said Trent. 'Where did you get this?'

'It was tucked in the back of that Post Office savings book. It says you owed Mr Latham seventy-two pounds, and the fact that the IOU was still in his possession suggests that you still owed him that when he died. Is that correct?'

Trent's voice was expressionless. 'Yes.'

'Quite a sum for a man who barely earns enough to scrape by. What happened?'

'It was the cards. I lost.'

'But you told us yourself that you couldn't afford to play for money.'

'Yes, but I had once or twice, and that was all it took. We were drinking too, you see, or at least I was – I had a few more than I should have one night when we were playing, and somehow I lost far more than I ever would normally. I think the drink affected my judgement, and I just couldn't stop. Next thing I knew Les was making me sign that blasted bit of paper. I thought maybe it was a joke – I mean, we were old pals and I thought he'd let me off, especially considering the drink. But no, he was serious, said I'd used up my credit and I owed him. I said he couldn't do that, but he said if the boot had been on the other foot I'd have expected him to pay up and no mistake. He said he could wait if I was short of cash, but a debt was a debt, and it was only right for me to pay it back if we were going to stay friends.'

'So it was unlikely that he'd help you when you needed money for Annie. Did you ask him?'

'Yes, I did. I thought even if he wouldn't do it for me,

he'd do it for her. But he said sorry, he couldn't – he had expenses of his own to meet, and I already owed him. He didn't quite say it'd be throwing good money after bad, but I knew that's what he was thinking. I couldn't believe it.'

Jago waited for him to continue, but Trent fell silent and kicked a stone on the edge of the path into the canal, his hands thrust deep into his trouser pockets.

'So, Mr Trent,' Jago said quietly, 'If Mrs Latham hadn't found this IOU, her husband's death might've turned out rather convenient for you.'

'What do you mean?'

'I mean it would've let you off the hook. If he dies and no one knows you owe him that money, you don't have to repay it, do you? The secret dies with him.'

'But that's crazy. I wouldn't kill an old pal just for that, would I?'

'I don't know. As you said yourself, when your time's up, there's nothing you can do about it – maybe you decided his time was up.'

Trent stared at him, then gave a nervous laugh. 'You're joking, aren't you? You can't be serious.'

'Murder is a very serious matter, Mr Trent.'

'Yes, well, if you think I killed Les Latham you're very much mistaken – and I'll thank you not to go around accusing decent people who were his friends.'

'I'm not accusing you, Mr Trent, I'm simply discussing one possible interpretation of the situation you've described concerning that IOU. Can you tell me where you were on Tuesday morning, between the hours of seven and eight?'

'Here on the boat, of course.'

'And can anyone corroborate that?'

'Only Annie – she was here with me.'

'Your wife. Anyone else?'

'No, just her.'

'I see. That'll be all for now, then, Mr Trent. Don't go too far up or down this canal without letting me know, though – I may need to speak to you again.'

CHAPTER THIRTY-SIX

Jago had only met Todd once, but that meeting had left the impression of a man who was a keen advocate of the company he worked for and of its products. As he and Cradock arrived at Baring and Sons' head office, he was therefore curious to know why a man so apparently dedicated to his employer's business would not have mentioned a complaint against a subordinate whose murder the police were investigating. As they approached the entrance, however, their path converged with that of Jack Henderson.

'Ah, good morning, Inspector,' he said. 'Just popping into the office to pick up a few things before I go out to see what I can do for some of my loyal customers in Middlesex. Were you looking for me?'

'I'm actually on my way to see Mr Todd, and we were going to come back this afternoon in the hope of catching you, but while you're here, perhaps we could have a quick word with you too.'

'Of course. Would out here suit you? There'll be other chaps in the office, so it won't be very private.'

'Yes, that'll be fine.'

'This way, then.' Henderson took them a few yards down the road to a small alleyway that afforded some privacy and shelter from the chilly breeze that was blowing down Albert Street. 'How can I help?'

'There's just two things. First of all, you've been very helpful filling in some of the detail about Mr Latham's working life for us, but I'd be interested to know what you can tell us about his home life – as a friend.'

'Well, the answer's not a lot, I suppose – you never really know, do you, with somebody else's marriage. It can't have been too bad – they'd been married for about twenty years – but to be honest I don't think everything in the garden was rosy. Then again, it can't be easy for any woman to be married to a commercial, because we're away on the road so much of the time.'

'I suppose the same could be said for some of the husbands – they probably miss their wives when they're travelling.'

'Maybe – not being married, I wouldn't know. But the thing is, Les was really enthusiastic about the job, so when he was away he'd be busy, working hard, meeting people, having a bit of fun perhaps – he'd be enjoying it. But for Rose at home on her own, well, I think she probably got a bit bored when he was away. And absence doesn't always make the heart grow fonder.'

'Do you know if she had friends, a social life?'

'Sorry, I don't, and I don't recall Les ever mentioning what she was doing or who she was pally with. The only person I've ever seen when I was visiting the flat was her mother. Have you met her?'

'Mrs Crow? Yes, we have.'

'Well, I can't say I envied Les, having his mother-in-law living just round the corner, in and out of his place all the time – especially a woman like that. A nasty piece of work, if you ask me.'

'Really? In what way?'

Henderson lowered his voice slightly, as though he were confiding a trade secret. 'I'd say she was a troublemaker. She had this habit of whispering in her daughter's ear, but it wasn't nice – it looked sly, if you know what I mean. I dropped by once, at the flat, to see if Les was in. He wasn't, but she was there – Mrs Crow, that is. When I asked after him, Rose said she didn't know where he was, and her mum started doing it – you know, sort of whispering in her ear as though she was making some snide comment about him.'

'How did Mrs Latham react?'

'Oh, she didn't react at all. Maybe she was used to it, I don't know. All I do know is when I come across a mother-in-law like that it makes me glad I'm not married.'

Jago suppressed a smile, he could think of a number of times in his life when he'd felt the same way. He wondered whether like himself, Henderson might also sometimes think the risk worth taking, given the disadvantages of the unwed state, but the thought was distracting, and he banished it.

'You said absence doesn't always make the heart grow fonder,' he continued. 'Was there any tension between Mr and Mrs Latham?'

'To be perfectly frank with you, I think there was, yes. It was just odd things he'd say to me now and again – he wasn't as respectful as he used to be. That's not the way a man ought to speak about his wife, in my book.'

'Do you know why he was doing that?'

'No, but it wasn't right. I don't think it was fair.'

'You mentioned visiting their flat. Was that something you did often?'

'No, just once in a while – sometimes I'd pop round for a cup of tea.'

'With Mr Latham?'

'Yes. Or with both of them if Rose was in.'

'Did you ever see any of that tension when they were at home together?'

'Only once – it was a couple of weeks ago. I reckon they must've been having a row just before I arrived – there was something in the air, and they were looking daggers at each other. I didn't say anything, of course. Rose offered me a cup of tea, so I stayed, but it was all very frosty. Afterwards I wondered whether she'd done that so I'd stay and keep Les off her back. Sort of protect her, I suppose.'

'That must've felt strange, given that he was your friend.'

'You're right, it did. After that I tried to keep out of it – it's not my place to get involved in other people's domestic tiffs, any more than it's yours.'

'Indeed.'

Henderson looked at his watch. 'You said two things. What was the other one?'

'It was to do with something you said when we spoke to you the day before yesterday – about company cars. You said Mr Latham would've liked a Rover, because he thought they were a cut above the Standards and the Austins, just like he was a cut above the average salesman. Was that just part of his ambitious nature that you talked about before?'

'Oh, yes, without a doubt – he wasn't one to settle for mediocrity. I'd even go so far as to say he was always dissatisfied – whatever he might have, it wasn't good enough, and he was always going to have something better.'

'You said you thought the Viking ship that Rovers have on their radiator badge took his fancy. What did you mean by that?'

Henderson laughed. 'I suppose I meant I got the impression sometimes he saw himself as some sort of Viking warrior. Les was a very confident man, you see. Tall, blond hair, blue eyes – the Nazis would've loved him for breeding, I should think. Very Aryan, by their book. He reckoned he had Viking blood in him – his grandad came from somewhere up north, Yorkshire I think, and he used to say Latham was an old Norse name. He said his people were winners, conquerors, and that's what he was going to be in his business – always a winner.'

'The Vikings had some unsavoury ways of asserting themselves, didn't they? Slaughter and pillage?'

'Yes, but I'm not saying he went around killing people. He was ambitious, yes, but that's no bad thing in a salesman – like I said before, you've got to believe in your product, but you've got to believe in yourself too.'

'I see. And something else you mentioned was how

292

even with the extra ration that commercial travellers are entitled to it can be difficult to get as much petrol as you need. Do you think it's possible Mr Latham might've come into possession of petrol coupons that he perhaps wasn't strictly entitled to?'

'That's a strange question. You mean stolen ones? What makes you think that?'

'We found some coupons in his flat and we think there's a possibility they may've been subject to some illegal trading, and since you're a friend and colleague of his, I thought you might be able to shed some light on it.'

'Well, he never told me about anything like that, if that's what you mean. It's true we're always short of petrol these days in our business, so I suppose if he'd been offered one or two he might've been tempted, but if it's evidence you're looking for I can't help you.'

'You've said yourself he was a born salesman. I'm wondering whether he might've been tempted to trade in petrol coupons too.'

'Selling stolen coupons? Not a chance.'

'You sound very sure. Why's that?'

'Because it's a mug's game, that's why, and I'd bet you anything you like that's what Les would've said too.'

'A mug's game?'

'Yes. I know there are people who sell stuff like sugar on the black market to get round the rationing, but those petrol ration books have serial numbers, don't they? That means they're traceable, not like a bit of cheese or a few rashers of bacon. I can't see Les getting mixed up in a racket like that. He was a salesman, not a criminal. So, all right if I go now?'

'Forgive me, Mr Henderson, I don't want to delay you, but there is just one more thing. We've been told Mr Latham used to play card games, and I'm interested to know who might've been involved in those games. Did you ever play cards with him?'

'Yes, but not regularly – just once in a while.'

'And can you tell me anyone else who did?'

'Well, I don't know who he might've been playing with when I wasn't there, but I remember one bloke – I think he worked on the canal. Les called him Jimmy, but I never heard his surname. The only other one I recall was a younger lad. I only saw him the once, but he sticks in my mind because he didn't seem like a very experienced player – still a bit wet behind the ears, I thought – and he had a terrible apology for a moustache.'

'And his name?'

Henderson screwed up his face in concentration, then shook his head. 'No, sorry – can't remember. All I know is he wasn't very strong at cards.'

'And Mr Latham was?'

'Yes, although he put it down to luck. I'm no judge, mind, but he was certainly better than me – that's all I can say.'

'And how was he with the ladies?'

'What do you mean?'

'Well, I mean did he take an interest in women other than his wife?'

'I see, right. Well, he had a roving eye, that's for sure, but I don't know whether it ever came to anything more than that. He didn't talk about that sort of thing, you see, but like I said, I don't think things were too good at home. "Lucky at cards, unlucky in love" – that's what they say, isn't it? Maybe that's how it was with Les.' He smiled, then looked at his watch again. 'Now, if you'll excuse me, I really must dash.'

'Thank you,' said Jago, but before the words were off his lips Henderson was lost to them, striding urgently back the way they'd come, into the world of Baring and Sons.

CHAPTER THIRTY-SEVEN

When Henderson had disappeared round the corner, Jago and Cradock continued at their own pace into the Baring and Sons building and made their way up to Todd's office, where they found his secretary filing papers in a cabinet.

'Good morning, Miss Edwards,' said Jago.

'Good morning, Inspector,' she replied, her voice bright and perky but somehow forced, as if someone had trained her to greet visitors in this way. 'How can I help you?'

'I'm just calling in on the off-chance that Mr Todd might be here – I'd like a quick word with him if I may.'

She moved to her desk and reached out her hand towards a Bakelite intercom that stood beside her typewriter. 'I'll buzz him for you.'

'Thank you – but before you do, I'd like to say I'm sorry for upsetting you last time we were here. It must've been a shock for you when I said Mr Latham had been murdered.'

'That's all right, Inspector – I'm fine now, thank you.

It was a shock, yes, to hear out of the blue that someone had murdered him, but that's all it was, so there's no need to apologise.'

As if to signal that the matter was closed, she pressed a button on the intercom and reported their arrival to Todd, then ushered them through the connecting door to his office.

Todd came out from behind his desk to greet them and invited them to sit. 'To what do I owe the pleasure of this visit, gentlemen? I assume it's something to do with poor Latham's death.'

'That's right, Mr Todd, and I'm sorry to disturb you like this, but I'd like to have a brief word with you about something that's cropped up since we last saw you.'

'Of course. I am pretty busy today, so the briefer the better, if you don't mind, but I'm very happy to help you if I can. Such a terrible business, him being killed like that. So what's this new development?'

'Well, it's quite simple, really. We've been talking to one of your customers, and we've discovered that he lodged a complaint about Mr Latham – with you.'

For the briefest of moments Todd's businesslike manner seemed to falter, but he recovered himself quickly. 'Oh, yes, and, er, who was that?'

'It was a Mr Carter.'

'Who?'

'Mr Todd, does your company receive so many complaints about its representatives from your customers that you can't remember their names?'

'Of course not – we're a highly regarded company and we take any complaint seriously. This particular gentleman's name just seems to have slipped my mind, that's all.'

'Mr Carter's a shopkeeper in Cambridgeshire.'

'Ah, yes, of course – sorry. Now I remember. Stuck out in some little village that time forgot, isn't he?'

'He does live in a village, yes – it's called Bassingbourn. According to what he says, he and Mr Latham were having a conversation about the difficulties of getting enough petrol in rural areas like that, and Mr Latham said there was no need to worry, because he knew where he could lay his hands on some extra petrol ration coupons. You didn't mention this when we were talking about him the day before yesterday.'

'Well, you never asked me anything about that, so I didn't think of mentioning it. Besides, as far as I was concerned it was all a storm in a teacup.'

'Really? So did you take up the shopkeeper's complaint?'

'Yes, of course I did. I spoke to Latham about it. What's the meaning of this, I said – have you been bringing Baring and Sons into disrepute by offering to supply our clients with extra petrol coupons? Certainly not, he said – he was most emphatic. He said it was all a misunderstanding.'

'A misunderstanding?'

'Yes, he said he wasn't offering to supply this man with coupons, he was simply making a general comment about the availability of petrol. You know, something like yes, it may be tricky getting enough petrol in places like that, but down here there always seems to be someone in the pub who can get hold of whatever you want – coupons for anything that's on ration, including petrol. Not that he was condoning the black market, of course – he said it was merely an observation on what life's like closer to London.'

'And you were satisfied with his explanation?'

'Yes, I was. Anyway, it was all just one man's word against another, and people can say the most extraordinary things when the fancy takes them. I had no reliable evidence that Latham had done anything wrong, so I had no reason to take any disciplinary action. I did have a quiet word with him, though – I said I'm all for our representatives building up a warm and friendly relationship with the clients, but even so you need to watch your step. I just reminded him to be careful what he said, not to give the wrong impression. I mean it's not exactly "Careless talk costs lives", but careless talk can certainly cost a business money.'

'How did Mr Latham respond to that?'

'He took my point – said he understood, and that he'd be more careful in future.'

'And that was that?'

'Yes. That was the end of it. He went back to work, and I didn't hear any more about it.'

'I see,' said Jago, leaning back in his chair. 'Now, Mr Todd, would you be surprised to learn that among Mr Latham's effects we found some petrol coupons that might be termed "off the record"?'

Todd looked puzzled. 'Off the record?'

'Let's just say they appeared to be of potentially dubious provenance, and I think he might've had difficulty in explaining them away if he were still alive.'

'Well, that's shocking, I must say. But look – I can't imagine he'd be involved in anything irregular. I mean, why would he need to? Like I said, he was one of our best salesmen, if not the best, and he was earning very good money – nine pounds a week.'

Jago raised an eyebrow. 'Nine pounds, you say?'

'Yes. So that's my point – why would he risk that for a few extra bob on the side? No, it defies all logic.' He paused, his brow furrowed. 'Is it possible he just found them somewhere and hadn't handed them in yet?'

'That is possible, but unfortunately all we have to go by is the evidence that's available, and we have nothing to suggest that was the case.'

'Well, I'm sorry, but you've heard everything I know on the subject, so that's probably all the evidence I can provide. All I can say is I find it difficult to believe Latham would ever have considered getting involved in something like that.'

The phone rang on Todd's desk. 'Excuse me, Inspector,' he said, putting the handset to his ear. 'Todd.' He listened for a moment. 'Yes, he's here. I'll hand you over.'

He passed the handset across the desk to Jago. 'It's one of your colleagues at Scotland Yard.'

'Hello,' said Jago into the mouthpiece, 'Jago speaking.' He listened. 'Thank you, that's very interesting . . . Yes, we'll get over there straightaway . . . Yes, that's good . . . Thanks very much. Goodbye.' He passed the handset back to Todd, who replaced it on its cradle. 'I'm sorry, Mr Todd, we need to be on our way. Thank you for giving us your time.' He rose from his chair. 'We'll leave it at that for now, but if you do recall anything else that might help us, please get in touch.'

Todd also got to his feet and shook Jago's hand. 'Of course, yes.'

'Good day to you then, Mr Todd.'

'Good day to you, Inspector.'

CHAPTER THIRTY-EIGHT

Cradock had to walk briskly to keep up as Jago strode back towards Baring and Sons' front entrance. It was only when they were out of the building that Jago spoke, and his voice was urgent. 'Come along, Peter, we need to get to Islington as fast as we can.'

'Islington, sir?' Cradock thought perhaps he'd missed something: he could recall no previous mention of the neighbouring borough.

'Yes, that was the Yard on the phone – they've had a reply to their teleprinter message from Islington nick. Seems our gallant major's over there – he was arrested this morning.'

'Really? So what's he got up to now? The same old fundraising caper?'

'Sounds like his old caper all right, but this time not fundraising – one of their men picked him up for presenting a dud cheque.'

'Old habits run deep, eh, sir?'

'Well, strictly speaking it's still waters, Peter, but I think I know what you mean. Anyway, they say he's just been released on bail and he's staying at a cheap hotel in Islington. They're sending a man round straight away to make sure he stays put until we get there.'

They hurried to the car and set off for the hotel. When they arrived, they found what looked from the outside a drab building in a drab street. The inside was no better. The only person they could see was an unshaven man in an open-necked shirt who was slouching behind what purported to be the reception desk and who gave the impression that he'd only recently woken from a snooze. They managed to extract the number of Fortescue's room from him and dashed up the stairs.

The room was conspicuously marked by the presence of a uniform police constable at the door. He gave a smart salute when Jago identified himself. 'He's in there, sir,' he said. 'Do you want me to come in with you, or should I stay here?'

'Come with us, please,' said Jago. 'We might need an extra pair of hands.'

Jago didn't bother knocking. He opened the door and walked in, followed by Cradock and then the constable. What greeted his eyes was not quite the accommodation he might have expected for a man of Fortescue's claimed background. In fact it made his own modest billet at Mrs Minter's establishment seem quite salubrious in comparison. The room was badly in need of decoration and sparsely furnished: a single unmade bed with a raincoat draped across it, a wardrobe with one door hanging limply open, and a wash-stand with a chipped china bowl and a jug of water. The only other item of furniture was an armchair, in which lounged a gaunt-looking man in a crumpled suit with a cigarette in one hand and a box of Swan Vestas in the other. Upon seeing his visitors enter, he took a match from the box, casually flicked his thumbnail against the head to spark it into flame, and lit the cigarette. He slipped the box into his pocket, drew on the cigarette and rose to his feet, leaning heavily on a stick. Slowly exhaling the smoke, he looked down his nose at Jago.

'Are you the odd job man?' he drawled contemptuously. He jabbed his cigarette in the direction of the wall behind him. 'There's a draught from that window.'

Jago recognised the look of condescending arrogance that he'd become all too familiar with during his army service in the Great War. 'No, Mr Fortescue, I'm not the odd job man. I'm a police officer, and my name is Detective Inspector Jago.'

Fortescue moved his head slightly to one side as though this was a matter of distaste and indifference to him. 'I called for the odd job man, not a policeman.'

'Well, I'm afraid you've got me, and I've got a few questions for you. You might like to sit down.'

'I prefer to stand.'

'As you please. I understand you've been fundraising for St George's Hospital.'

If Fortescue was surprised by this question, he didn't show it. His voice sounded tired, as if disdainful of his own philanthropy. 'Yes, one does what one can to help those less fortunate in life. It's not something I flaunt, however – one doesn't want to draw attention to oneself.'

'I'll bet you don't. I don't suppose you like to have too much attention drawn to certain other aspects of your life either, especially from people like me.'

'Forgive me, Inspector, but I don't know what you're talking about.'

'I'm talking about your business activities as, what I believe you call, a private investment consultant.'

For the first time the man before him looked apprehensive. 'I assure you, Inspector,' he said cautiously, 'my professional life is entirely respectable.'

Jago thought it was time to annoy him. 'Respectable my eye,' he said with a dismissive laugh. 'Let's start with a few biographical details. I've been told you served with distinction in the war and were decorated – the DSO, no less.'

'Yes, I was leading an assault on a German trench, but they beat us back. The citation said something about bravery under fire, but I tell you, it was my men who showed true courage – that medal was for them. All I had to do was rally them, inspire them to risk everything for the sake of victory, and then lead them to it. Suffice it to say, we took the trench.'

'That sounds very impressive.'

'Well, one did one's duty. What can I say?'

'What can you say, indeed? I might say I was so impressed with your exploits that I checked with your regiment. I discovered not only that you were never awarded a DSO, but also that you don't exist. Not under the name of Fortescue, at any rate, but only perhaps under the name of Hale.'

'Well, yes, my full name is Edmund Fortescue Hale, but I dropped the Hale when I left the army because I preferred to be known as Fortescue.'

'And I'm afraid I began to lose faith in you when I discovered you were not a major – you were only a lieutenant. Is that correct?'

'Well, technically, I suppose. But with my length of service I'd have been a major if I hadn't been deliberately overlooked for promotion. There was a conspiracy against me, to block my progress despite my having all the qualities and experience required. You might disapprove, but I felt I'd earned it, and besides, it's better for business to have a more senior rank.'

'Ah, yes, your business. I've no doubt it helps if people know you as an officer and a gentleman.'

'I suppose it does, yes.'

'But according to your regiment, you have little claim to be known as either. They told me you were cashiered for issuing dud cheques. That's not exactly the way an officer or a gentleman behaves, is it? In my day it was what we called "conduct unbecoming". I'm not even convinced you were treated at St George's Hospital for wounds. I've asked them to check their records, but I suspect they're not going to find you in them.'

Hale said nothing, but maintained his contemptuous stare.

'By the way,' Jago continued, 'what can you tell me about a man called Latham?'

Hale looked him blankly. 'Latham? I don't believe I know anyone by that name.'

'I'm talking about Mr Les Latham, who served with you on the Western Front in the Middlesex Regiment.'

'I'm sorry, Inspector, he may have served in the same regiment as me, but that doesn't mean I knew him. I knew the men under my command, and a few more besides, but really, you surely don't expect me to have known every man in the regiment. That's absurd. Was he an officer?'

'No, a private.'

'There you are, then – I rest my case. I'm afraid the name means nothing to me.'

'It's been suggested to us that he served in the same company as you.'

Hale shook his head. 'No. No recollection of the name at all. Besides, back then a company was four platoons, a couple of hundred men. If he wasn't in the platoon I commanded, he might have known who I was but I doubt whether I would have known him. In any case, who told you that?'

'A man who said Mr Latham had told him so, after the war.'

'Pure hearsay, then. One or both of them must be mistaken – or lying.'

'Well, we'll see whether we can jog your memory later. In the meantime you have some financial questions to answer.'

'You mean that silly little cheque yesterday? Five pounds? An honest misunderstanding, that's all. I'm sure the magistrate will understand, if he's a decent chap.'

'No, Mr Hale, I'm not here to talk about your grubby little cheque fraud. I've got something more serious in mind – and I think you'll find the court takes a very dim view of it. You've been defrauding people of their savings, thousands of pounds, by worming your way into their confidence. I know what you've been getting up to as a so-called investment adviser, and I've heard all about what happened to anyone who took your advice.'

'I don't know what you mean.'

'Yes, you do, Mr Hale. You've been fraudulently obtaining sums of money by falsely representing that you could secure a high return on funds your clients would invest when in fact there was no return, because there was no investment. You pocketed their money and paid them their so-called return from the funds invested by your next client. In other words, robbing Peter to pay Paul. You're under arrest on suspicion of obtaining money under false pretences, with intent to defraud, and of fraudulently converting money to your own use.'

As Jago uttered these words, Hale's composure cracked. With an angry roar he leapt from his chair, flung his stick to one side and bolted for the door. He was still a yard from it when Cradock stepped into his path, bracing himself for a head-on collision. Hale smashed into him, cursed loudly and sprang back, staring as if mesmerised at a small tongue of flame and a billow of smoke pouring from his jacket pocket.

'Oh! Oh!' he cried in panic, slapping his hand ineffectively against his jacket. 'Help – I'm on fire!'

He stepped back again, tripping over the rug, and fell to

the floor. Jago grabbed the water jug from the wash-stand and tipped its contents in the general direction of Hale's jacket, then took the disgraced officer's raincoat from the bed and used it to smother any residual fire. 'Don't worry, Mr Hale, you're all right now. You can get up – and I don't think you'll need the assistance of that stick, will you? So much for your war wound.'

Hale struggled to his feet, and Cradock pushed him firmly back into the armchair before standing guard over him. The uniform constable took up a position beside him, to deter any further thought of escape. Hale pulled dispiritedly at his pocket, which now had a hole burnt into it.

'A word of advice, Mr Hale,' said Jago. 'If you're planning any such violent antics in the future, don't use Swan Vestas to light your cigarettes. They're designed to strike on any surface, including police constables that don't get out of your way. I think you'd be better off all round with safety matches.'

Hale scowled at him resentfully but had nothing to say.

'Now, as I was saying,' Jago continued, 'you're under arrest. You're coming with us to the station. And another word of advice – in case you're thinking of awarding yourself a bar to your DSO, I'd say after that little display of bravery under fire I don't think you're eligible.'

CHAPTER THIRTY-NINE

Jago delivered Hale to the safe keeping of Kentish Town police station, with instructions for him to be held for further questioning and charging.

'You're not going to question him now, then, sir?' said Cradock.

'No, I'll let him stew for a bit and talk to him later – we've still got a murder case on our hands, so he can wait. First I want to see Mrs Latham again. In view of what the chief constable said about airfields and photographers, I'd like to find out whether Latham was much of a snapper himself.'

'Right, sir. And that reminds me – Todd said Latham was getting paid nine pounds a week, but Mrs Latham said—'

'Yes, I know.' Jago completed the sentence for him. 'Mrs Latham said he earned six pounds a week. That hadn't escaped my attention, Peter.'

'So do you reckon she didn't know?'

'That's difficult to say – it's certainly possible that he didn't tell her.'

'Maybe that's how he managed to save up all that money – if he was putting away three quid a week from his wages he'd be able to save a hundred and fifty a year.'

'Yes, although that would depend on what other financial commitments he might've had.'

'You mean like . . . girls in every port, for example?'

'It's something to bear in mind. Even one girl in one port could be expensive to maintain, let alone any kiddies who might have an absent daddy.'

'You mean keeping another family somewhere?'

'It has been known, Peter. As I told you, that fellow Rouse said he had a harem of women around the country – and harems can cost you a pretty penny.'

'Really? I wouldn't know, sir.'

'And neither would I, Peter, I'm glad to say. But perhaps Mr Latham did.'

They drove to Belmont Street and found Rose Latham at home, looking tired. 'Come in,' she said, and took them up to her flat. 'Take a seat. Can I get you a cup of tea?'

Jago checked his watch. 'Actually, yes – that would be very nice.'

She left the room and returned shortly with tea for them both, and a cup for herself. 'So,' she said, leaning forward in her chair, 'have you got anywhere with your investigation? It's awful not knowing. Every time I pass someone on the street I think to myself it could be him. I don't think I'll sleep properly until I know you've caught whoever did it.'

'We're doing our best, Mrs Latham.'

'I'm sure you are. But when I opened the door just now and saw it was you, I suppose it just sort of got my hopes up. Do you have any news?'

'No – I just wanted to ask you one or two questions, if you feel up to it.'

'Yes, of course. What is it you want to know?'

'Well, I was just wondering – was your husband interested in photography?'

'No, not particularly – I mean, he used to have one of those old Box Brownie things for taking snaps on holiday, but they never came out very well, and I think he gave up in the end. I don't think he's taken a photo for years – certainly not of me. Why do you ask?'

'Oh, I'm just trying to tie up a few loose ends, that's all. I remember you mentioned that the photo you lent me – the one of your husband standing on the steps outside the house – was taken by his friend Mr Henderson. That was rather better quality than you'd get with a Box Brownie.'

'Yes, but his pal brought his own camera with him for that – some fancy foreign one it was.'

'Do you remember what it was?'

'Yes, I do, actually. Only because I asked him what it was called and I thought he said Fred. I said that was a funny name for a camera, but he said no, it's Fed – F, E, D. He said it was made in Russia and it was named after the bloke in charge of their secret police – they were his initials. I'm still not sure whether he was joking or not, but I'm not interested, really.'

'Did he happen to say how he'd come by the camera?'

'I think he said he picked it up second-hand in a camera

shop, but I can't remember if he said where. You'd have to ask him.'

'Yes – thank you. Now, there's another little thing I'd like to get straight too, if you don't mind.'

'Of course – what is it?'

'I'd just like to clarify something you said on Tuesday. Could you remind me how much you said your husband earned?'

'Yes, it was six pounds a week. Les always looked after the money, but he said after a pound a week for the rent it left us plenty to live on, so we never had any money worries. Well, I suppose I should say I never had any, because if there were any he'd have dealt with them. I used to feel a bit in the dark as far as money was concerned, but he always said it was his job to provide for me. Why do you ask?'

'Well, it's just that I've had information that he didn't actually earn that much.'

A look of anxiety flashed across her face. 'What – you're not going to tell me he was making it up, are you? He was a proud man, you know, just the sort who might've said he earned more than he did to impress me, or even to stop me worrying. Has he gone and left me with a load of unpaid bills?'

'You misunderstand me, Mrs Latham. The fact is, according to what I've been told, he was on a salary of nine pounds a week.'

Jago expected her to look surprised, but instead her reaction was muted. She opened her mouth as if to speak, but said nothing, and her head dropped as she stared down into her lap.

'Is something the matter?' asked Jago.

She remained silent.

'Did you know that already?' he added.

'No,' she replied quietly. 'All I knew for sure was that we were managing fine on six, but something happened a while ago that puzzled me.'

'Yes?'

'He was away, and I had to take one of his suits down to the dry cleaners. I checked the pockets, as you do, although there was never anything in them, but this time I found something. It was a pay slip that he must've left there by accident – it was the first time I'd ever seen one. I thought maybe it was just that he'd been paid a bit extra that week for some reason, or maybe not, but either way I don't think I was supposed to find it.'

'That must've been quite a surprise for you.'

'Yes and no, Inspector. At that actual moment it was a surprise, but then again, over the years I've found out quite a few things about Les, and it got to the point where nothing really surprised me.'

'And he was still telling you he only earned six pounds?'

'Yes – or at least, he'd never told me he'd had a rise.'

'Did you challenge him about it?'

'No. It was weak of me, I suppose, but I thought whatever the reason, it was something he didn't want me to know about, and I think I was afraid to ask. Better not to know, I thought.' Her voice caught, and she wiped her eyes quickly with her finger.

'Mrs Latham, DC Cradock and I have been up to Cambridge in connection with our enquiries and we talked to an estate agent there who was acquainted with your

313

husband. Do you remember that photo I found in your husband's suitcase?'

'The one of the cottage?'

'Yes, that's the one.'

'Well, I remember you found it, but like I said at the time, I'd never seen it before.'

'I showed it to the estate agent, and he recognised the property. He said it was for sale and he'd taken your husband to view it. Were you aware of that?'

'A cottage? No, I wasn't. Why would he be doing that?'

'There was something written on the back of the photo – Shangri-La. My colleague here tells me it refers to some kind of perfect place where no one can find you and everyone's kind – what some people would call a utopia. Is that a name your husband ever referred to?'

'Not that I recall, no.'

'Had you and he been talking about possibly moving up towards Cambridgeshire, getting away from London? It's a safer part of the country than here, and it's where a lot of his work is.'

'No, we hadn't.'

'Could he've been planning a surprise for you? Had you ever said you'd like to live somewhere like that, a little cottage in the countryside?'

'No. I've no desire to go and bury myself out in the wilds, and anyway, this war won't go on for ever. It wouldn't have been a nice surprise for me, and to tell you the truth, if that's what he was doing, I wouldn't be at all surprised if he had it in mind as a nice little present for someone else.'

'You mean another woman?'

She drew a deep breath. 'Look, I wish I could say no, that's a ridiculous suggestion, but I can't, and you might as well know. I've no idea what he was thinking, but I know I didn't trust him, and I had good reason not to. I'd found out, you see – he'd got involved with someone else.'

'And who was that?'

'It was that girl Violet from the regional manager's office – a common little madam, but she knew how to catch his eye, if you know what I mean. He was old enough to be her father, but she probably reckoned he was just a fool who'd spend his money on her – and she was probably right.'

'Do you have any evidence for this?'

'No. I just know.'

'So how do you know?'

'His boss told me.'

'Mr Todd?'

'Yes. I asked him the same question – what's your evidence, I said. He said he knew because he'd seen how the two of them were when Les visited the office. It seems she'd found an excuse once or twice to visit the Cambridge area while Les was up there too.'

'Why do you think Mr Todd told you?'

'I can't say that I know why. Perhaps he just thought the decent thing was to let me know what was going on.'

'Is it possible he had some other motive – a personal motive – for telling you?'

'I don't think so, but how would I know?'

'When we spoke to you the day before yesterday, I asked you whether you'd found someone who paid you more attention than your husband, and you said yes. Now, we had a little misunderstanding at that point, because you talked about your dog, whereas I was thinking in terms of a man, but we didn't return to the question. I'm just wondering now whether when Mr Todd did the decent thing, as you say, and told you about your husband's association with Violet Edwards, it created some sort of connection between you and him.'

'Connection? I don't know what you mean.'

'I mean some sort of emotional connection – let's say emotional support.'

'With Todd?' She laughed. 'Good gracious, no – he's the last person I'd go to for that. Definitely not him.'

'But there is someone else you'd go to? Another man?'

Rose looked uncertain about how to respond to Jago's gentle probing. In the end she gave him a timid smile. 'Well, yes, there was someone, if you must know. I don't think I could've got through it without him.'

'And who was that?'

'It was George – George Bowen.'

'I see.'

'Do you? Or are you just sitting there judging me? You don't know what I've had to put up with all these years, unloved and unappreciated. George is different. He's a good friend and he cares about me. He's been very supportive, very kind to me.'

'Forgive me, Mrs Latham, but I have to ask you – how kind was he?'

'Very kind, like I said.' She hesitated. 'Look, we're grown-ups, aren't we? George was the only person who valued me and respected me – he's devoted to me.'

'So your relationship was more than just emotional support?'

Her voice sank. 'Yes. Les is away all week, you see, and I've been finding things very difficult. These air raids've been ruining my nerves, and on top of that I've got a husband I can't trust. So I've . . . well, I've gone over to George's place a few times at night, in the blackout. I feel safe with him, and no one can see me.'

Jago suspected there was more she wanted to say, so he remained silent and waited for her to continue.

'You probably think I'm weak, Inspector. I know plenty of people who'd say I should've had it out with Les, done whatever it took to make him see what he was doing was wrong and I wasn't prepared to put up with him. But my problem was simple – I hated what Les was doing, but I was scared of losing him. I was going through hell thinking of him with another woman, but I was afraid it might be even worse without him. I turned a blind eye when he insulted me with the things he was doing – I kept telling myself I could win him over by being nice to him and keep him when I knew I meant nothing to him. I was hoping for something to happen that I knew was impossible.'

'Are you saying you didn't tell your husband that you knew about his association with Miss Edwards?'

'No, I'm not. That was my big mistake. In the end I couldn't take it any more – I told Les I knew exactly what he was up to. He went crazy – told me he was going to throw me out. I thought he was going to kill me. I was scared, and I ran to George for protection.'

'Were you hoping that he'd deal with your husband in some way?'

'What, like a knight in shining armour? No, of course not.' She squeezed her eyes shut, as if fighting to control her feelings. 'Look, Inspector, all I wanted to do was get away from Les while he was in a rage. I didn't want to hurt him – I just wanted to make sure he didn't hurt me or George. And I came back, didn't I? I didn't stay with George. I couldn't just run away from everything. Besides, I think Les was just angry that I'd found out. I came back because I thought we could work something out. I don't know – I'm confused.'

'Very well, Mrs Latham. That'll be all for now, but I shall speak to you again.'

There was pain in her eyes and anger in her voice. 'All right,' she said, 'but for pity's sake just go away – now!'

CHAPTER FORTY

'Well, well,' said Jago as they left Rose Latham's flat. 'That's something else Mr Todd didn't think of mentioning to us, isn't it? I'm beginning to think there's more to him than meets the eye.'

'Me too, guv'nor,' said Cradock. 'I mean, did he think he was being kind, telling Mrs Latham his secretary'd been having a fling with her old man? It sounds like all he did was set the cat among the pigeons and wreck the Lathams' marriage.'

'It certainly didn't seem very tactful of him. I'd like to know what he thought he was doing, telling her that.'

'Yes, and what about that thing she said about the camera? Jack Henderson having a Russian one, I mean – Mr Ford said something about the Russians paying people to take photos of airfields, didn't he? You don't think Henderson's a spy, do you?'

'I wouldn't necessarily jump to that conclusion. There must be plenty of people who have Russian cameras, but that doesn't make them spies. But on the other hand not so many of them would have friends whose work involves driving around in areas with lots of RAF airfields.'

'Should we ask him, then?'

'I think we should, yes, but I'll check with Mr Ford first. He might prefer to pass it on to Special Branch rather than have us blundering into it in our size twelve boots. They'll probably have someone who knows all about Soviet cameras, and if they don't, they'll know someone in MI5 who does. For the moment, I think our talents'll be better employed with Mr Todd – let's go and disturb him again.'

They drove to Barings in Albert Street and went straight to Todd's office, where they could hear the rapid clattering of a typewriter coming from behind the door. They knocked and went in, to find Violet Edwards seated at the machine, her fingers clicking rhythmically on the keyboard. She stopped when she saw them.

'Hello again,' she said.

'Is Mr Todd in?' asked Jago.

'Through there,' she replied, gesturing towards the connecting door. 'Is he expecting you?'

'No.'

'I'll see if he's free, then.'

She reached for the intercom, but Jago placed his hand over the switch before she could press it. 'Wait. There's something I want to ask you first.'

'Yes? How can I help you?'

'I don't have much time, Miss Edwards, so I won't beat about the bush. I'd like to know whether you were having an affair with Les Latham.'

She responded by calmly patting the hair on the side of her head into place. 'Well, that is a bold question to ask a poor girl at this time of the day,' she said. 'I hardly know what to say. But since you're in such a hurry, I'll answer you in one word – no.'

'We've been told otherwise.'

'It's not true – it never happened.'

'Mrs Latham told us she knew about your affair with her husband.'

'She's lying.'

'It's easy to say that, Miss Edwards, but then you would, wouldn't you?'

'How dare you!' She glared at him. 'All right,' she hissed, keeping her voice down. 'Maybe she thinks that, but it's not true. You want to know who's lying?' She jerked her head in the direction of Todd's door. 'Ask that man in there – ask him where he really was on Tuesday morning.'

'Are you suggesting Mr Todd knows something about what happened to Les Latham?'

'I'm not suggesting anything. I just don't like being accused of something that's not true.'

'Well, we'll see what Mr Todd has to say. Will you tell him we'd like a word, please?'

Violet turned in haughty silence to the intercom and spoke to Todd, then motioned them towards his door with as much dignity as she could muster.

They entered Todd's office, and Cradock shut the door behind them.

'Hello, gentlemen,' said Todd. 'Back so soon? Take a seat.'

'Thank you,' Jago replied. 'I'm sorry to interrupt you again, but there's something I'd like to get straight.'

'Fire away.'

'I'd like to know whether you told Rose Latham that her husband was conducting some sort of affair with your colleague, Miss Edwards.'

'Oh. Who told you that?'

'Mrs Latham.'

'I see. Well, yes, I did. I have to tell you, that girl Violet has no scruples – I saw her flirting with Latham here in the office, right under my nose. She was deliberately trying to . . .'

His voice trailed off into silence.

'Trying to what, Mr Todd?'

'To provoke me,' he mumbled.

'Provoke you?'

'Yes – I don't know, maybe make me jealous or something? I probably ought to feel sorry for poor Latham – any man who gets entangled with her is making a big mistake.'

'Are you speaking from personal experience?'

'What do you mean?'

'I mean are you entangled with her in some way?'

'I might've been once, but not now. I've seen through her games.'

'Is there any connection between that and the fact that she's no longer confirming your alibi?'

'Alibi? What are you talking about?'

'When we were here the day before yesterday she appeared to confirm that you were both here in the office on Tuesday morning at the time Mr Latham was murdered. But now she's intimated that that wasn't true.'

'Well, if I haven't got an alibi, neither has she. Ask her where she was.'

'I'd like to start with you, if you don't mind. First of all, why did you tell Rose Latham her husband was having an affair with your secretary?'

'Because I thought she was entitled to know her husband was being unfaithful to her.'

'Did you have any designs on Mrs Latham yourself?'

'Designs? Of course not. What sort of man do you think I am?'

'I'm not sure, Mr Todd. I think there may be more to it than you trying to do the decent thing for Mrs Latham. Is it to do with Miss Edwards? You're covering something up, and I'd like to know what it is.'

'No, that's not true.'

'You've just told us you were once entangled with Miss Edwards yourself.'

'Yes, but that ended weeks ago.'

'So tell me where it went wrong.'

'All right. It was my own stupid fault. I should've seen her for what she was – a cunning little minx, a schemer. My biggest mistake was falling for her. She played with me like a cat with a mouse, just to get what she could out of me, but love's blind – that's what they say, isn't it? I was so infatuated I couldn't see the truth staring me in the face. Before long she'd got me obsessed with her.'

'So when you saw her with Latham it made you jealous?'

'Of course – but that's just what she wanted. It was all intended to make me more desperate to please her.'

'And when you told Mrs Latham about Miss Edwards and her husband, that was to scare Latham off, wasn't it? So you could have Miss Edwards all to yourself.'

'Yes.'

'Did it work?'

'I don't know. All I know is one day she dropped a hint

that she might come away with me for a weekend in the country. Said she fancied being driven in my nice big car to some cosy little place where we could get away from everything and just be the two of us together for a couple of days. She knew about this place down in Sussex where no one would know us. Very soon I couldn't think about anything else. But I knew if I wanted to use the car for private travel on a journey that long I'd have to get hold of some extra petrol that the company couldn't find out about.'

'I see. So how did you solve that small problem?'

'I made one or two discreet enquiries, and Jack Henderson said he thought Latham might be able to help me out – said he always had a lot of useful contacts. I ended up buying some coupons from Latham.'

'So how did Mr Latham have petrol coupons to sell? Mr Henderson told me that commercial travellers don't have enough petrol to get round all their customers as often as they should these days, even with the extra allowance.'

'Yes, well, I think Latham had some unorthodox way of obtaining them.'

'You mean some illegal way?'

'I think so, yes.'

'Were they stolen?'

His voice dropped. 'Yes, I believe they were.'

'So when you said you had no reliable evidence that Latham was doing anything wrong with regard to stolen petrol coupons you were lying to us.'

'I suppose so, yes.'

'I see. And did you tell him you needed them so you could take Miss Edwards away for a weekend in the country?'

'Of course not – I didn't want him to know about me and Violet. But from that moment on I was at his mercy. I used the coupons and had the weekend with Violet, but I should've known there'd be a price to pay. He soon made it clear there was a little favour I could do him, and I knew I was heading for trouble. He said he'd discovered some of his stock was missing and he knew I was due to do a stock-check soon, so he'd be obliged if I'd adjust my report to show that everything was duly accounted for. He didn't fool me, of course – I knew what he must be up to.'

'And what was that?'

'A trick that I've seen travellers trying to pull before. They take orders for whatever products they're selling and supply the customer with the goods, but they issue a fake receipt and mark the invoice as paid. Then they pocket the money the customer's handed over and keep it for themselves. It's one of the oldest fiddles in the business.'

'And did you do what he said?'

'Yes.' Todd's voice was bitter. 'I know I was stupid, but I did it. Later on I saw what an idiot I'd been and I told him I wasn't going to do it again, but by then it was too late, of course. He said that would be very unwise, because he might have to disclose what would otherwise remain our little secret.'

'So he was blackmailing you?'

'That's the long and the short of it, yes.'

'For money?'

'Yes.'

'Didn't you consider going to Mr Baring and telling

him the whole story? Then Mr Latham might not've had anything to blackmail you with.'

'I did think about that, but not for long. It would've meant telling Mr Baring I'd broken the law by buying petrol coupons on the black market, I'd falsified the stock records to cover up a crime, and to put the tin lid on it I'd had an affair with my secretary. Mr Baring's a good man, but he wants his company to maintain high moral standards. He would've sacked Les for sure, but he would've sacked me too.'

'So what happened next?'

'I paid Latham some money to keep him quiet, but then he wanted more – that's what always happens, isn't it? But what could I do? He'd got me trapped.'

'So you murdered Latham to get him off your back?'

Todd stared at him with a look of shocked disbelief. 'No, absolutely not! That's an outrageous thing to say – what evidence have you got?'

'Well, your secretary seems less willing than she was to vouch for your being here early on the morning Mr Latham was killed.'

'But that doesn't mean I killed him – she's just bitter because I blew the gaff on her sordid little affair with Latham. She hates me now, and this is her way of getting back at me.'

'But you had plenty of motive to get rid of him – you've just said yourself that you were facing the sack.'

'I was facing it if I went to the managing director and made a clean breast of it, but like I said, I didn't think about that for long. I was still reckoning I'd find some way of buying Latham off or shutting him up. I certainly wasn't thinking of killing him. I tell you I was here in the office on Tuesday morning, trying to sort out this mess with the stock. Surely you can see I had to do that to save my job? Now, if you don't mind, I need to get back to work on that stock.'

Jago stood up. 'I'm afraid the stock will have to wait, Mr Todd. There's the small matter of you having received petrol coupons knowing them to have been stolen. I must ask you to accompany us to the station.'

CHAPTER FORTY-ONE

Todd put his coat and hat on, opened the connecting door to his secretary's office, and muttered something to her about going to help the police and possibly being out for the rest of the day, then hurried out of the building with Jago and Cradock without speaking to anyone else on the way. He remained silent as they drove to Kentish Town police station, where Jago entrusted him to the care of the uniform sergeant. 'Find Mr Todd somewhere to wait for us, will you?' said Jago. 'We need to pop out, but we'll be back in a bit to question him.'

'Yes, sir,' said the sergeant. 'But you might like to know we've got another gentleman here waiting to see you – a Mr Bowen. He seems anxious to speak to you as soon as possible.'

'OK. You look after Mr Todd, and we'll go and have a word with Mr Bowen.'

They found Bowen sitting in an interview room, dressed

in his work overalls and clutching a green flat cap in both hands. He jumped up nervously when they entered.

'Do sit down, Mr Bowen,' said Jago, pulling up a chair opposite him, with Cradock doing the same by his side. 'I trust your pigeons are well.'

The question seemed to catch Bowen off guard. 'Oh, er, yes, thank you, they are. Actually, one of them – Snowball, he's called – came back with a message in his canister. You remember I said every RAF bomber has two pigeons on board in case it gets shot down? Well, this message was from a crew, saying they'd come down in the North Sea and giving their rough position. So I took it straight down to the Post Office – that's the procedure, see, and then they send a telegram to the Air Ministry. I heard this morning that they'd been rescued, and it was all thanks to my Snowball.'

'Congratulations – you must be very proud of him.'

'Oh, yes. It makes all the work with the birds worthwhile, and it makes me feel like I'm helping those poor boys on the planes and making a contribution to the war effort that's saving lives.'

'I understand. But I don't suppose you've come to tell us that, have you?'

Bowen looked down into his lap for a few seconds, fiddling with his cap, then raised his head. There was an almost imperceptible quiver in his lips. 'No,' he said. 'There's something else I want to tell you. I want to make a statement.'

'Very well, Mr Bowen. DC Cradock will write down whatever you want to tell us.'

Cradock fetched some paper and began to write as

Bowen confirmed his name, age, occupation and address.

'So,' said Jago, 'what is it you want to say?'

'It's, er, about my business,' Bowen began hesitantly.

'Yes?'

'When you came to my garage the other day I told you times were hard for the motor trade because of the war, and it was really hitting businesses like mine. Well, the long and the short of it is that I've been struggling, and I did something to make a bit of extra cash – something illegal.'

He stopped.

'I see,' said Jago. 'I must caution you, Mr Bowen, that you are not obliged to say anything, but anything you say may be given in evidence. Do you want to continue with your statement?'

'I do.'

'You've said you did something illegal. What exactly was it?'

'I let people have extra petrol coupons – for money.'

'You mean you sold petrol coupons?'

'Yes, that's right.'

'And were these your own?'

'No – they were stolen.' Bowen's voice dropped to a whisper. 'I didn't set out to do it, but, well, it just happened.'

'Was one of these people you sold them to Mr Latham?'

Bowen looked surprised. 'What, Les? No, it was him who gave them to me. He told me I could do what I liked with them, but to be careful, because they were nicked.'

'So you sold stolen petrol coupons supplied to you by him? How much did you pay him?'

'No, it wasn't like that. I didn't pay him – like I said, he gave them to me. He said it was a sort of thank-you gift for putting a bit of business his way.'

'What did he mean by that?'

'Well, the thing is, he'd been in the garage a few weeks ago asking me if I could get him any extra coupons – you know, did I have some suitable contacts in the trade and so on. I said why did he want them – I knew he already qualified for a supplementary allowance on account of being a commercial traveller. But he said he needed a bit more on top of that for his private use – for travelling round when he was on his business trips, seeing the local sights and what have you. That sounded a bit suspicious to me, but it was none of my business, so I didn't press him on the subject. I just said I didn't have any contacts like that and couldn't help him. But then a week or two later a bloke came into the garage and said he'd found some petrol coupons and did I want to buy them – you know, cash in hand, no questions asked. Said he could let me have enough coupons for two thousand gallons – maybe even more if I wanted, and I could make myself a few quid selling them on to my regular customers or anyone else who needed a bit of extra fuel.'

'How much was he asking?'

'Sevenpence a unit – and of course I could sell them on at whatever price I liked. A better return than I'd get on war bonds, he said.'

'And you bought them?'

'No. I said I didn't want to, and in any case they were no use to me, because they hadn't been stamped. No petrol station's going to accept a coupon that hasn't been stamped. He said he'd get them stamped by a pal of his in the Post Office, no problem, but I didn't want to get involved in anything like that. But then I thought of Les, so I just told this bloke he might want some and how he could get in touch with him. I swear to God that's all I did, and I heard no more about it, never saw him again. But then a bit later Les gave me that little present, as I said, and I guessed they'd done a deal. So I kept a few for myself and sold the rest to some of my regular customers.'

'The last time I spoke to you, you said you'd never heard of Mr Latham being involved in anything to do with stolen petrol coupons.'

'Yes, well, you caught me on the back foot, didn't you? I didn't have time to think. I'm sorry about that.'

'So what's made you decide to tell me all this now?'

'I suppose it's what you'd call conscience. The thing is, you see, when my pigeon came back and I heard he'd saved an RAF crew, I began to feel bad about myself. I mean, there's those brave young lads risking their lives for all of us, and even my blinking little pigeon doing his bit for the war effort, and what am I doing? Profiteering, that's what they call it, isn't it? I feel ashamed of myself, Inspector, and I just had to get it off my chest.'

'And this man who came to the garage – who was he?'

'I don't know. He didn't give a name, and even if he had done, I suppose it would've been a false one.'

'What did he look like?'

'Just an ordinary young bloke, tallish, slim, a bit shifty-looking – you know, collar turned up, flat cap pulled down. I was about to close up shop for the day when he turned up, so it was getting a bit dark too.'

'Right, so how many coupons did Mr Latham give you?'

'Fifty.'

'And how many of those have you sold?'

Bowen hesitated.

'I should remind you,' said Jago, 'that under the new Motor Fuel Rationing Order we're authorised to inspect any premises used in connection with the business of supplying motor fuel, so it would save us all time if you just told me.'

'All right,' Bowen replied. 'I've sold all of them.'

'Thank you. Now, is there anything else you want to add?'

'No. That's it.'

'In that case there's something else I want to ask you, Mr Bowen.'

'Yes?'

'It concerns Mrs Latham.'

A hint of apprehension came into Bowen's eyes, and he began to fiddle with his cap again. 'What do you want to know?'

'I'd like to know about your relationship with her.'

'Relationship? She was Les's wife, and I used to look after his car for him.'

'I can understand your discretion, but in the light of information I've received, I'm under the impression that you took care of Mrs Latham too.'

'What are you getting at?'

'Rose Latham's told us her husband threatened her and she came to you for protection, and that was because she was already in an emotional relationship with you.'

'Oh,' said Bowen, his voice flat.

'Is that all you have to say?'

'No, it's just, well, it sounds a bit clinical when you put it like that. The fact is, Inspector, she's a very fine woman, and he didn't deserve her. He just went off and did whatever took his fancy, but always expected her to be waiting for him with a hot meal and clean shirts whenever he got back. He didn't appreciate her, but I did. I couldn't bear to see a beautiful, sensitive woman like her being bullied by the man she was married to. She knew that, and I was the only person she could turn to. So yes, if you want to know, I did take care of her. I know what it's like to be lonely – I've never had a wife, and it's always been just me and my work and the pigeons. But with Rose I began to realise she was someone I could love, and who might love me back. You probably think I'm just a silly old fool, but being with Rose – it made me feel young again, in a way that I didn't even really feel when I was young. She means everything to me now, and I'd do anything for her.'

'Anything? Even murdering her husband so you could "take care of her"?'

A look of shock flashed across Bowen's face. 'No!' he said. 'How could you think that? I could no more do that than fly to the moon. What do you take me for?'

'I don't take you for anything, Mr Bowen, but you lied to me, didn't you? When I asked you if you knew Mrs Latham, you said you'd only met her once or twice when her husband brought the car in to you and she was with him.'

'Yes, well, you'd only just told me the poor fellow was dead. I didn't want you to think there was anything going on between me and his missus, did I?'

'But there was.'

'Yes, but . . . I'm sorry, I shouldn't have said that. I suppose it was the shock – I wasn't thinking straight.'

'Yes, well, that's as may be, but now I want the truth.'

'Look, he drove off in his car on Tuesday morning and I never saw him again – and I never laid a finger on him either. That's the honest truth, I swear it.'

'Very well, Mr Bowen, we'll see whether your account of events holds water. In the meantime I'm arresting you on suspicion of receiving petrol coupons, knowing them to have been stolen. You'll be taken to the cells and charged later.'

'Wait!' said Bowen. 'Don't lock me up. What'll happen to my pigeons? They need feeding and looking after – and what happens if another one comes back with a message and I'm not there? Please let me look after them.'

'We'll decide later whether to release you on bail. I understand your concern, but you should've thought about that before you started selling stolen coupons. I'm afraid the law must take its course, and you may need to find someone else to look after your pigeons.'

CHAPTER FORTY-TWO

Jago closed the door of the interview room behind them, leaving Bowen inside, and took Cradock a few steps down the corridor. 'Right, Peter,' he said, 'I want you to deal with Bowen while I go and check something with Rose Latham. He said he put the man with the stolen ration books in contact with her husband, but Latham's dead now and can't confirm or deny whether he bought them, so I want to find out whether she knows anything that might help us.'

'Very good, sir. But speaking of ration books, I've been thinking about what Jack Henderson said. When you asked him whether Latham might've been selling stolen petrol coupons, he said no. He came straight out with it too, didn't he? Denied it flat – not a chance, he said. I believed him. I mean he's been so friendly and helpful – he seemed like a nice bloke. But now Todd's told us it was Henderson who sent him Latham's way when he wanted to buy some. So Henderson lied to you, didn't he?'

'I'm afraid he did, yes.' Jago paused, pondering what action to take next. 'Unless it was Todd who wasn't telling the truth. We know he lied to us when he said he didn't know Latham was mixed up with stolen petrol coupons. So now he says Henderson did know, but maybe that's a lie too. We'll need to find out more, but first I must see Rose Latham. I'll be straight back.'

She was still at home when Jago arrived. 'Hello, Mrs Latham,' he said. 'I'm sorry to disturb you again, but something's come up since we last spoke, and I need to have a word with you.'

'You'd better come in, then,' she replied, opening the door wider, and stood aside for Jago to enter. 'Can I take your coat?'

'No, thank you,' he said as she closed the door behind him. 'This won't take a moment.'

'Before you start, Inspector, I want to apologise for being rude to you – telling you to go away like that. I was just getting very upset about the whole thing – not just Les being killed, but what you were saying about me and Mr Todd, and me having to rake over the whole business of George when all he'd done was be kind to me. I don't think anyone's ever been kind to me like he has, not even my own mother. It was all too much for me, but even so, you didn't deserve to have me shouting at you, so I'm sorry.'

'That's all right, Mrs Latham. I'm afraid sometimes I have to ask some blunt questions.'

'I understand – it's your job to do that. But what is it you want to talk to me about now? I promise I won't shout.'

'Well, it's just that it's come to our attention that your

husband may've been involved in buying and selling petrol coupons.'

'That's against the law, isn't it?'

'Yes, it is.'

'Well, he never said anything to me, but I wouldn't put it past him. Who told you?'

'It was Mr Bowen, actually. So he never mentioned it?'

'What, George? No, he didn't. I can't believe he'd get mixed up in anything like that, though – but Les I can, only too well.'

'Did your husband say anything?'

She gave a bitter laugh. 'Les? No, but then he deceived me about that little floozy of his in the office, so I reckon he could've lied to me just as easily about anything else too. There was one thing, though, now you mention it. I'm not sure exactly what was going on, but it looked like it might've had something to do with buying and selling.'

'Tell me about it then, please.'

'Yes, of course. It was the weekend before last. There was a bloke on the doorstep saying he had a delivery for Mr Latham – he had a cardboard box under his arm and said Les was expecting him, so I let him in. Les said he had to have a quick word with him and took him into the bedroom. Well, I thought that was a bit strange, but there's nowhere else private in this little flat. So I hung around for a bit and then the bloke came out again – this time without the cardboard box, but he had a little envelope that was open and he was looking into it, as if he was checking. I reckoned it must've had some money in it, but I didn't like to be too nosey in case Les got cross. When the bloke had gone I asked Les what it was all about, and he said it was just a work thing. Do you think that could've been something to do with it?'

'It's possible, I suppose. Have you seen this man again since then?'

'No, I haven't.'

'Could you describe him?'

'Yes, I think so. He was youngish, and skinny – no meat on him at all. I couldn't tell you what he was wearing, but I do remember he had a flat cap on, and I could see a bit of ginger hair sticking out. He had a bit of a moustache as well – that was ginger too.'

'Did he give a name?'

'Yes. He said it was Smith.'

'Thank you, Mrs Latham, you've been very helpful. I'll see myself out.'

CHAPTER FORTY-THREE

Jago returned to Kentish Town police station, where he found Cradock ensconced in the canteen, armed with a mug of tea and halfway through a large currant bun.

'Hello, sir,' said Cradock as Jago approached his table. 'Bowen's making himself cosy in a cell, so ready when you are.'

'Bowen will have to wait,' said Jago, 'and so will your little tea break. Rose Latham's just told me that a man delivered a package to her husband the weekend before last and left with what she thought was an envelope full of money. What's more, he told her his name was Smith, and her description of him sounded very much like our friend Mr Hepworth, so we're going straight down to that Ministry of Transport depot to see what he has to say for himself.'

Cradock gulped down as much of the tea as he could. 'Righto, guv'nor. All right if I finish my bun on the way? The government says we're not to waste food, doesn't it?'

'It does, Peter,' Jago sighed. 'And you're commendably diligent in your compliance with that instruction. Now, let's get a move on.'

Jago strode briskly to the door as Cradock took another gulp from his mug, put it down, and then hastened after his boss, currant bun in hand, to the car. Jago drove as quickly as the traffic allowed to the depot, where they found Sarah Mallard in her office with her secretary, as before.

'Hello again, Inspector,' she said as they entered. There was a weariness in her voice that he hadn't noticed in their previous meeting. 'How can I help you today? I can't be long, I'm afraid – we're terribly busy at the moment.'

'I understand, Miss Mallard,' Jago replied. 'But actually we've come to have a word with Mr Hepworth. Is he here?'

'Yes, he is. But is it absolutely necessary? He's got a lot of work to do, you know.'

'I'm afraid it is – oh, and that's a word in private again, if you don't mind.'

'Of course, if you insist, but I'm concerned about you whisking him away to interrogate him in secret. I am his manager, you know, and that doesn't just mean I tell him what to do – I have a responsibility for his welfare too. He's not the most reliable of men, and he can be a little . . . well, nervous, if you know what I mean.'

'There's no need to worry – he won't come to any harm with us. Now, if you don't mind . . .'

'Very well, I'll send for him.' She turned to her secretary. 'Miss Shanks, please take these two gentlemen to the chief clerk's office – he's not here today, so it'll be empty – then find Mr Hepworth and take him to them.'

'Yes, Miss Mallard,' the young woman replied meekly, and led the detectives away.

Minutes after installing them in the empty office, she returned with Hepworth and then departed.

'Take a seat, Mr Hepworth,' said Jago. 'This won't take long.'

'Oh, er, right – yes,' Hepworth replied, sitting down as bidden at a small table. 'Is this something to do with vehicle log books?'

'No, we're here to talk to you about something else – about petrol coupons.'

'Petrol coupons? But I told you I don't deal with those.'

'Not in an official capacity, perhaps, but we have reason to believe you've been engaged in some unofficial dealings.'

'I don't know what you mean.'

'I think you do. There are one or two questions I need to ask you, and before I do, I must caution you that you are not obliged to say anything, but anything you say may be given in evidence.'

'What?' The astonishment in Hepworth's voice suggested not just nervousness but something more like fear. 'What is this?'

Jago spoke calmly. 'As I said, Mr Hepworth, I just need to ask you a few questions.' He took from his pocket the three unstamped books of petrol coupons he'd found in Latham's flat and placed them on the table. 'Do you recognise these?'

'Of course I do,' said Hepworth. 'They're motor spirit ration books. But so what? We see them by the truckload in here.'

'I don't mean do you recognise them in general, I

342

mean do you recognise them in particular.'

'No. Why should I?'

'Because these are part of the batch that's gone missing from the stock in this depot.'

'Missing? That's nothing to do with me.'

'But we have information that it is to do with you, Mr Hepworth – or is it Mr Smith? You stole these coupons, didn't you?'

'No, that's absurd – of course I didn't. It'd be more than my job's worth. And anyway, what's all this about Mr Smith? I don't know what you're talking about.'

'Come, now, I'd be prepared to believe your protestations of innocence, but we have a witness who can confirm that a man matching your description offered to sell two thousand gallons' worth of petrol coupons to a garage owner. I'm sure I don't need to tell you that stealing government property is a very serious offence. You're on your way to court, and you could be looking at a stretch of hard labour.'

Hepworth leant towards him, his eyes wide and imploring. 'No, no, you've got it all wrong – you don't understand.'

'What don't I understand?'

'It wasn't me. You have to believe me. I didn't steal them – I didn't steal anything.'

'We have witnesses, Mr Hepworth.'

'All right, yes, but it wasn't me. It was her – she made me do it.'

'Oh, really? And who would that be?'

'Miss Mallard, of course. What choice did I have? I'm just a pen-pusher, a thirty-bob-a-week clerk, and she's the boss.'

'You're trying to tell me she made you steal them?'

'No – that's not it. I've just told you I didn't steal anything. I was just the delivery boy. She's the one you should be talking to, not me. All I've done is obey her instructions.'

'And she made you go to a garage and offer two thousand gallons' worth of coupons for sale to the owner?'

'I was only delivering a message.'

'Did you sell any to him?'

'No – he said he didn't want any.'

'Did he tell you how to contact a man who might be interested in buying them?'

'He might've done.'

'Come, Mr Hepworth, you're too young to be that forgetful. Did he?'

'All right. Yes, he did – but I just passed the information on to Miss Mallard.'

'So she made you do all these things – but you could've said no, couldn't you?'

'I tried to, but she threatened me – she said if I wasn't careful I'd find myself out of a job. I'm supposed to be getting married next spring, and I can't afford to risk that. I'm in a reserved occupation too, so if I lose my job I'll be called up and might not be able to get married at all. There was no way out – I had to do what she said.'

'Were you selling these coupons?'

'No, all I did was deliver them.'

'Who was doing the selling, then?'

'I don't know. Miss Mallard didn't say – she just told me where to take them.'

'Are you sure that's the truth?'

'Yes, of course it is.'

'Do you play cards, Mr Hepworth?'

'Cards? What that got to do with anything?'

'It's just that someone's told us they were playing cards for money with someone who sounded remarkably like you.'

'Well, I can assure you it wasn't me.'

'Does the name Les Latham mean anything to you?'

'No.'

'You're sure?'

'Absolutely. Why should it?'

'Because he was the potential customer whose details you were given by the garage owner, and I can't believe he omitted to include the man's name. And not only that – Mr Latham's wife says a man matching your description delivered a package to their home and said it was for him. We have reason to believe that package contained a quantity of stolen petrol coupons, and we also believe you left those premises in possession of a sum of money.'

'Well, I don't remember, so I don't know. That woman must've got me mixed up with someone else. And anyway, even if I did say I had something for him, it would only be because Miss Mallard must've told me to say that – I swear it.'

'We'll have to see what Miss Mallard says about that, then, won't we? In the meantime I'm arresting you on suspicion of handling stolen goods. Detective Constable Cradock will escort you to the police station while I go and have a word with her. And if I find out you've told me a pack of lies you'll be in even more trouble, my lad.'

CHAPTER FORTY-FOUR

Jago told Cradock to phone Kentish Town police station and get a car sent down to pick up him and Hepworth, then left them and returned to Sarah Mallard's office.

'Ah, you're back,' she said, looking up from her desk as he entered the room. Her voice sounded tired. 'Have you finished with Mr Hepworth?'

'Yes, I have, thank you,' he replied, glancing at her secretary. He pulled a chair towards the desk and sat down. 'And now I need a word with you, Miss Mallard. A private word.'

The secretary got to her feet and hovered uncertainly, notebook and pencil in hand, looking to her superior for instructions.

'Thank you, Miss Shanks,' the latter replied. 'Leave us for a moment – I'm sure this won't take long.'

Miss Shanks put her notebook and pencil down on her desk and left the office with a brief nod of acquiescence.

'Now, what's all this about, Inspector?' Miss Mallard continued.

'It's about your missing petrol coupons. You might like to know that I've just arrested Mr Hepworth on suspicion of handling stolen goods.'

'Stolen goods? Hepworth? What on earth do you mean?'

'I mean we have evidence that he's been supplying stolen motor fuel ration books to members of the public.'

'My goodness. That's shocking – he's a civil servant. I know I said he was unreliable, but I never imagined he'd get involved in something like that. It's dreadful news.' She paused. 'So did he steal them from here, the depot? Right from under my nose?'

'I didn't actually say he'd stolen them,' Jago replied. 'I said he'd been handling them. That's a different matter.'

She looked puzzled. 'So then—'

'So then who did? Is that what you were going to say?'

'I, er . . . well, yes, I suppose . . .'

'Our conversation with Mr Hepworth was very revealing. He was indeed somewhat nervous, as you said, and I suspect he may be one of those men who don't cope easily with pressure. Whatever the reason, he was quite forthcoming.'

'What exactly did he say?'

'He admitted delivering some petrol ration books to a private address in Camden Town, and we believe those books to have been stolen. What's more, he told us that he delivered them on your instruction. And before we go any further, I must caution you that you are not obliged to say anything, but anything you say may be given in evidence.'

She muttered something under her breath that Jago couldn't quite make out, then looked down at the floor, silent again, chewing her lip as though trying to think of a way out. Before Jago could speak, she straightened up and looked him in the eye. Her face hardened. 'All right, I admit it. I took a few of those blasted coupons and supplied them to people who needed them – but it wasn't my fault. You have to understand – I was forced into it. I've got a demanding job here that pays me a pittance, and my mother's been so frail she couldn't look after herself any more. The Public Assistance Committee put her into a council old people's home, and that was cruel – it made her feel ashamed. She was an educated woman, you know, what good it did her – she deserved better. It was humiliating for her. There was a private home for gentlewomen just down the road from her, and I wanted her to live out her last days in comfort there, but that required money – money that she didn't have, and neither did I.'

She pulled a handkerchief from her pocket and dabbed her eyes, looking annoyed at herself for doing so. 'I don't want to bore you, Inspector, but to be frank I've had to learn to look after myself, because no one else is going to help. I've given twenty-two years of my life to the Civil Service, and I've worked my way up entirely by my own efforts. But I know what'll happen when this war ends – it'll be just like the last time. The men'll come back and I'll be out of a job.'

Jago listened but didn't rise to the bait. The sympathy he felt for her in those circumstances was not relevant to the job he had to do. 'You said you took a few coupons,' he continued calmly, 'but Mr Hepworth's told me you instructed him to offer to sell two thousand gallons' worth to a garage owner – Mr Bowen. He also says you told him to deliver a quantity of coupons to a private address in the area. That's hardly a few, is it?'

'All right, then, so I took more than a few. So what? They're just bits of paper, and there are millions of them – it's not going to make any difference if a few go missing.' She gave a deep sigh of resignation. 'To be honest, Inspector, I don't care any more. Time was pressing – the new three-month ration period started on the first of November, so the coupons were delivered to the depot in October, and I had to make a quick decision. I was desperate for the money, so it was only worth taking the risk if I could get my hands on a decent number of coupons.'

'So how did you come to know Mr Bowen?'

She snorted contemptuously. 'Know him? Why would I know a garage owner? You think I can afford to run a car on what they pay me? You must be joking. I didn't know him – I just told Hepworth to try the first garage he came to. Most men who sell second-hand cars are crooks anyway, aren't they?'

Again, Jago didn't allow himself to be distracted. 'Mr Bowen says he declined to buy any. Is that correct?'

Her reply was sullen. 'Yes.'

'But he told you how to contact a man who might want to?'

'Yes – a man who could sell ice cream to Eskimos, he said.'

'His name was Latham?'

'Yes. We met up, and he said if I was interested in selling, he was interested in buying. Simple as that. Not that doing business with him was simple – he drove a hard bargain. I suppose he knew he had me over a barrel when it came to haggling a price, and he beat me right down. But like I said, I don't care any more. I've had enough.'

'How many ration books did you sell to him?'

'He took all of them.'

'That's more than he could've needed for his private motoring.'

'Yes – but I'm sure there's plenty of other people who need them. They still have to pay for the petrol, of course, but they can't buy it without coupons, and it seems there's no shortage of them willing to pay a bit for a few more. Latham was a salesman, so I'm sure he'd have had no trouble selling them on.'

'And you used Mr Hepworth as your assistant in these transactions to protect yourself?'

'Yes – more fool me.'

'So how did you manage to exert such control over your young colleague?'

'That wasn't difficult. He's not a strong character, and I found out he'd been on the fiddle already.'

'Doing what?'

'Taking bribes. There's always a list of people waiting to get a replacement log book, and some of them don't want to wait. He'd take a bit of cash and push their application up to the top – only small sums of money, I expect, but still a criminal act. I threatened to report him, and that was that – he was putty in my hands, as they say.'

'And what made you willing to risk your career by stealing ration books?'

'Career? I've already told you what I think of my long-term career prospects. Once this war's over I'll be heading back to the bottom of the heap in no time.' She hesitated, as if distracted by this thought. 'No, my career didn't come into it. If you must know, I did it for my mother – I just wanted to have enough money to make sure she could live out her final days in a place where she was properly cared for and respected, not in that council home. But I was a fool to think it'd be that easy.'

'What do you mean?'

'I mean I didn't realise who I was dealing with. It was easy getting Hepworth to do my bidding, but a man like Latham isn't the sort you can control. I think he must've realised he could make easy money by flogging coupons to people as crooked as him, and he wanted me to keep up a regular supply. I'm sure that would've suited him, because I'd be the one taking all the risks. But I began to get cold feet – I was worried about what would happen to my mother if I got caught. I wanted to stop, leave it at that, but Latham wouldn't take no for an answer. He demanded to meet me, so I agreed – I still thought if I explained my situation he'd see reason and let me be. I was nervous about being alone with him, though, so I took Hepworth along too.'

'You didn't consider going to the police?'

'How could I? That would mean revealing what I'd done. He hadn't forced me – I was the one who'd gone looking for someone to sell those damned coupons to.'

'So what happened when you met?'

'He said he was going to be out of London on business for a few days, so I'd have to meet him before he set off on Tuesday morning. He told me the time and the place.'

'In Baynes Street?'

'Yes. He was in a car, and he told us to get in. I sat in the front seat next to him, and Hepworth sat in the back. I tried to make him see that I couldn't continue with our arrangement, but he wouldn't have it. We got into an argument. He got angry and threatened to expose me and ruin me. I thought he was going to hit me and I was frightened, so the only thing I could think of was to get out of the car and run away. I tried to, but he lunged towards me. I was desperate by then, so I elbowed him in the face and tried to open the door, but he pulled me back in. Then he just went mad and began to attack me. Hepworth couldn't do much to stop him from the back seat, so I suppose he did the only thing he could think of – he got hold of Latham from behind and banged his head forward against the steering wheel. Latham went quiet – it looked as though the blow had knocked him out. But I was scared of what he might do to me if he came round, so I grabbed his flat cap and pressed it over his face until he stopped breathing. I don't know what came over me – it was a stupid thing to do, but before I could think about it he was dead. It was just pure fear that drove me.'

'And the fire?'

'That was a snap decision. I didn't think anyone had seen us, but I knew we had to destroy the evidence. We got out, and Hepworth found a can of petrol in the boot, so I told him to burn the car. He was still splashing it over the inside when I ran, but as I went I heard a big whooshing noise and looked round to see the car on fire. I didn't wait for Hepworth – I just got away as fast as I could, and then once I was out of Baynes Street I slowed down and walked along as normally as I could manage, so as not to attract attention.'

'Did you see any police officers on your way?'

'No. There was no one about, so I don't think anyone saw me.'

'And what became of the petrol can?'

'I didn't see what happened to it, but when I saw Hepworth here at the depot later that morning he told me he'd wiped his fingerprints off it and got rid of it. He'd had to go back to his flat and change his clothes in case they smelt of petrol, so he was a bit late for work, but since I'm the manager I'm the one who'd take him to task for it, and that was nobody else's business.'

Jago studied her face: she seemed quite composed, perhaps resigned to her fate. 'There's one thing that puzzles me,' he said. 'When we asked you about the ration books, you were helpful – you didn't try to block us, in fact you confirmed that they might've been stolen. Why did you do that?'

'That's simple,' she replied wearily. 'I wanted to be the one controlling the information you had – if I hadn't co-operated, you'd have gone over my head, and that would've been more dangerous.'

She fell silent, looking down into her lap.

'Is there anything else you wish to say?' said Jago.

'No, I don't think so – I expect you've got as much as you need. But there is one thing.' She lifted her head. 'It's just – well, you didn't ask how my mother was.'

'I'm sorry – how is she?'

There was a pause, during which the only sound Jago

could hear was a man whistling tunelessly in the street outside. Sarah Mallard sighed, her expressionless eyes fixed straight ahead as if to stare through him, the wall and the world.

'I had a telegram this morning,' she replied, her voice flat. 'It said she died last night, in her sleep.'

CHAPTER FORTY-FIVE

Jago placed Sarah Mallard under arrest and escorted her discreetly out of the depot: he had no desire to humiliate her in front of her subordinates. She said nothing further and remained silent throughout their journey in the car to the police station. Only when they arrived did she ask him what would happen next, and Jago explained that she'd be charged and brought up before the police court, which would decide whether she should be remitted for trial to the Central Criminal Court. She nodded meekly, and he led her into the station. After handing her over to the uniform sergeant he went in search of Cradock.

His guess that he'd find his colleague in the canteen proved correct. Time was pressing, so he grabbed a quick cup of tea and drank it while updating him on Sarah Mallard's confession and arrest. As soon as this was done he jumped to his feet. 'Get your coat, now, Peter – I want to nip back to Rose Latham and tell her we've got someone under arrest.'

They drove to Belmont Street for the third time that day and found Mrs Latham at home.

'Not you again,' she said when she opened the door. 'Haven't you got anything better to do than come round here all the time?'

'I'm very sorry to disturb you again, Mrs Latham, but there's been a new development.'

'Oh, yeah? I suppose you'd better come in, then.'

They followed her up to the flat and she let them in.

'So what is it this time?' she said. 'To be honest with you, I'm getting a bit fed up with this running up and down the stairs all the time.'

'We're here because I thought we should let you know that we've made an arrest.'

'Oh, right.' This news seemed to mollify her. 'Does that mean you've caught whoever did that terrible thing to Les?'

'It means we believe we have sufficient evidence to charge someone.'

'I see. So who was it? Did that little bit of skirt at Barings turn out to have a jealous husband?'

'No. It's not someone connected with Barings. We've discovered that your husband was involved in some illegal handling of motor fuel ration books.'

'You mean those petrol coupons that fell out of his journey book when you were here the other day?'

'That's right. We now know that they'd been stolen, and it seems there was some sort of falling-out between him and his accomplice. She's been arrested on suspicion of murder.'

'A woman, then, eh? Don't tell me – is she another one of his young admirers?'

'We've no evidence of any romantic association between them.'

'Romantic? That's a nice way to put it. Not the word I'd use, though. What's her name?'

'I'm afraid I can't go into any more detail at the moment. I just wanted to keep you up to date with our progress and to make sure you heard it from us, not from anyone else.'

'That's all right. I suppose I should thank you, but quite frankly I'm not sure I'm all that interested anyway. Just another fool of a woman, I imagine – probably no more of a fool than I am. I've been thinking a lot in the last few days, you know, and the way I see it, it's quite simple – he got what he wanted, and then he got what he deserved. I'm sorry if that sounds callous, but that's about all there is to it in the end. The only thing that still puzzles me is exactly what it was he really wanted, deep down.'

Jago gazed round the room and remembered the first time he'd been here, when she'd spoken of her husband's pleasure in being the king of the castle. He wondered now whether Latham had come to see this flat not as his castle but as his prison. 'I remember you saying your husband wanted to get everything he could out of life,' he said. 'Do you think that explains his actions?'

'I suppose so, yes – that just about sums him up. He said to me once we only have one life, so why go through it poor and miserable if you can get your hands on a bit of money and enjoy some of its pleasures? People used to say he had a real appetite for life, but I don't think that was right – with him it was more like a greed for life, an all-consuming greed. He definitely wanted everything – he was never content.' She paused, and for the first time there was a hint of sadness in her eyes. 'And now he's lost everything, hasn't he? Even his own life. What a stupid waste.'

CHAPTER FORTY-SIX

'Is that it, then, guv'nor?' said Cradock as they left Rose Latham to her thoughts and returned to the car. 'All done and dusted?'

His words, and the cheery tone in which they were uttered, jarred on Jago. Their work on the case might be almost over, but 'done and dusted' seemed a heartlessly inadequate way to describe its end. Those closest to Les Latham would be left to deal with the consequences of his actions, and of his murder, for the rest of their lives. But he knew Cradock didn't mean to sound cynical. He was young, and in a few years' time he'd probably be more measured in his judgements.

'Not quite,' he replied. 'Before we pack up for the day I think we should let Mr Baring know that we've made an arrest too. We'll just go and see if he's in.'

They drove to Baring and Sons and were shown to the managing director's office. Baring rose from his desk as they entered, with an anxious look on his face.

'Detective Inspector,' he said. 'I've been told you've arrested Mr Todd. Is this true? I've been terribly worried.'

'No, Mr Baring, we haven't actually arrested him. Mr Todd's at Kentish Town police station, helping us in our enquiries, and we're going to be interviewing him.'

'About what? Mr Latham's death?'

'Not directly, no. We want to talk to him in connection with a matter we're investigating concerning the theft of some motor fuel ration books.'

'You mean stolen by Todd?'

'No, but we believe some of them may have come into his possession.'

'So this is nothing to do with Latham's death?'

'Only in the sense that we believe Mr Latham supplied them to him, knowing them to have been stolen, and that Mr Todd was also aware that they were stolen property.'

Baring slumped back into his chair and motioned vaguely with his hand to invite his visitors to sit too. He shook his head slowly. 'My goodness. That's terrible.'

'Yes, I'm sorry to be the bearer of bad news – I knew you'd be concerned about the possible damage to your company's reputation.'

'No, that's not what I mean – I told you when you first came here that your getting to the truth of the matter was more important than any embarrassment to our company. No, what concerns me is Latham's poor wife. How's she going to cope if it turns out her husband was a criminal?'

'I appreciate your concern, sir, but when a man's

murdered we're duty bound to investigate the possible causes and motives, and that can sometimes mean we uncover things that he'd kept secret. Mrs Latham seems to be quite a resilient woman, though, and I hope that'll help her to cope with the consequences. And with regard to Baring and Sons, I think once we've finished with Mr Todd it might be worth your while to have a word with him about your auditors' findings. From what he's told us, it sounds as though Latham was fiddling his stock records and coercing Todd into falsifying his own stocktaking report to cover up for him.'

Baring looked deflated. 'I suppose I must thank you, Inspector, for helping to bring this to light, but it really is depressing to think that sort of thing could be going on in Baring and Sons. I can see we'll have our own little war to fight to get the company back on the right track – but we will.' He gave a sigh that suggested grim determination. 'Yes, we will. Now, is that all?'

'It is as far as Mr Todd's concerned, but I thought you might like to know where we've got to with regard to Mr Fortescue.'

'Ah, yes – you've looked into it?'

'Of course, and we've made some interesting discoveries. The gallant major turns out to have been a rather less than gallant lieutenant, and his name's not Fortescue either. And the Middlesex Regiment has no record of that DSO he so modestly mentioned to you.'

'I see. It just goes to show you can't judge a book by its cover.'

'Indeed not, Mr Baring.'

'So have you managed to track him down yet?'

'Oh, yes – he's currently cooling his heels in a cell, awaiting our return.'

'Well, in that case I suppose I mustn't keep you – I'm very grateful to you, Inspector. Now I must get to grips with what to do about Mr Todd. Is there anything else?'

'There is just one other thing, if you don't mind. I'd like to have a word with Mr Todd's secretary.'

'By all means – you know the way to her office now, do you?'

'Yes, thank you. We'll find our own way.'

They left Baring alone to grapple with the responsibilities of executive leadership and took the stairs down to where Violet Edwards acted out her own more mundane dramas. When they entered her office she was reading a magazine.

'Oh, hello,' she said, looking up. 'What brings you back? Is there something I can do for you?' She smiled and added breezily, 'I know you can't be looking for Mr Todd, because you took him away, didn't you?'

This might be her way of fishing for information, Jago thought, but if it was, she wasn't going to get it from him.

'Good afternoon, Miss Edwards. I'm here because there's something I'd like to ask you – something of a personal nature.'

'Sure – fire away.'

'Last time we were here I asked you whether you'd been having an affair with Mr Latham, and you denied it. But I have a witness who says you were, so I'm asking you again – did you have an affair with Mr Latham? Yes or no?'

She glared at him. 'Yes, I did. So what? He was all right, was Les – he knew how to look after a girl and give her a good time. And if you're going to tell me he was old enough to be my father, I don't care – it's none of your business. Maybe he was, but older men, well, sometimes they have a bit more money to spend on a girl and a bit less sense about spending it. He was married, of course, but I didn't mind. It's not as if I saw us going on for ever together –it was just a bit of fun while it lasted.'

'Was he planning to leave his wife?'

'I don't know. He said he was, of course – they always do. He used to talk about him and me running away together and living in some beautiful cottage in the middle of nowhere, just the two of us in a little love nest. It was a nice romantic idea, but honestly, I couldn't really see him doing it. For one thing it costs a lot of money, and he was spending his on little treats for me, so I couldn't see him buying a house just like that. And from what I know of old Mr Baring, I don't imagine he'd have kept Les in a job for a moment if he left his wife. I'd have been out on my ear too, I'm sure. Besides, what kind of girl my age wants to go and bury herself out in the country for ever? I like a good time as much as the next girl, and to be fair, Les gave me a good time, but it was never going to last. I want more than that.'

'I understand from Mr Todd that you were involved with him too, before you took up with Mr Latham. Is that correct?'

'Yes, it is – that's my business too.'

'Who was it who ended that relationship?'

'Me, of course. He just started annoying me – he was

my boss here at work, fair enough, but he wanted to be my boss outside the office too, and I wasn't having that. It wasn't fun any more, so I told him it was over.'

'But you continued to work here?'

'Yes, well, a job's a job, isn't it? I wasn't going to pack it in just because of him.'

'And when you suggested that he was lying about being here in the office with you at the time of Mr Latham's death – why did you say that?'

'I don't know, I just said it because he'd been annoying me again – taking me for granted. I thought I'd annoy him for a change.'

'So he *was* here.'

She gave a casual shrug. 'Yes.'

'Well, let me remind you, Miss Edwards, for future reference, that it's an offence to obstruct the police in the execution of their duty. You understand?'

'Yes,' she said with a pout. 'I'm very sorry, Inspector, but I just wanted a bit of fun. It's not much to ask, is it? This stupid war's made everything go all serious, but I'm young and I deserve some fun. What's the point of sitting around hoping for a good time in the future when I might be dead by the morning?'

Jago had no answer for her, but he found himself wondering how long her ambitions and Latham's would have remained compatible. In the end, he mused, the two pleasure-seekers had probably deserved each other.

'So,' she continued, 'am I going to be in trouble with the law?'

'No, I don't think so, Miss Edwards,' he replied.

She gave him a cheeky wink. 'Oh, that's very kind of

you, Inspector, and you too, Detective Constable – you're both so nice. I bet you have some fascinating tales to tell with your job, don't you? I just love detective stories. If ever you'd fancy going out for a drink and—'

'Thank you, Miss Edwards, but I think not – once we're finished here we'll be back to Scotland Yard and very busy.'

'Oh, well, never mind. All the best, then, and here's to a bit more fun for all of us in the future, eh?'

Cradock opened the door for Jago as they left the Baring and Sons building. The clouds were thinning, and a hint of winter sunshine was breaking through again.

'She's a bit of a handful, isn't she, sir?' he said. 'I reckon she was right about being out on her ear if Mr Baring found out what she was getting up to with Latham, never mind Todd. I can't imagine her lasting long in the company now.'

'Perhaps not,' said Jago. 'But who knows? Maybe Mr Baring'll give her another chance, maybe he won't. Either way, we won't be charging her with anything, and she's the kind of confident girl who'll probably land on her feet. Either that or she'll come a serious cropper, but even if she does I dare say she'll think she can charm her way out of it. No, he's the one I feel sorry for – Baring, I mean.'

'Me too. Got a lot on his plate, hasn't he? And now with Todd and Latham and all that it feels like we've just slipped a couple of incendiary bombs into his in-tray. I don't think I'd like his job, even if I did get free chocolates.'

Jago laughed. 'Put you off getting to the top, has it? Imagine being Chief Constable of the CID – all that grief, but without the free chocolates. You know what they say – with great power comes great responsibility. Better off as a bobby with a boot allowance, eh?'

'I'm not saying that, sir – I just don't think I want to get too far up the greasy pole.'

'Very wise, Peter, and I'd say if you apply yourself diligently, you might just be able to avoid that fate.'

Cradock looked askance at Jago, uncertain about the precise meaning of this advice. Meeting only with an inscrutable smile in reply, however, he shrugged his shoulders and followed his boss to the car.

CHAPTER FORTY-SEVEN

Jago sat beside Dorothy on a bench in Hyde Park, watching other Saturday-afternoon visitors strolling beside the Serpentine. There was a nip in the air, but the morning mist had cleared quickly, and now the bright blue sky made it seem warmer than it was. He found it somehow reassuring to see that even though it was late November and there was a war on, people were still rowing on the lake for pleasure. He took in a deep breath and felt refreshed: he was relaxed, no longer preoccupied with the investigation. Now, as long as he remembered not to leave behind the brown paper bag he'd deposited on the bench beside him, all he had to think about was being here with Dorothy. He'd enjoyed the Thanksgiving dinner on Thursday evening, but there he'd had to share her with Rita and Cradock. It had made him realise how much he appreciated his time alone with her.

'This is a nice place,' said Dorothy. 'It's good to slow down and see some greenery instead of just staring at paper on a typewriter.'

'You've been busy, then?'

'As ever. There's never a shortage of things to write about in a war, even with the censorship.'

'That must be difficult for you, I imagine – being censored, I mean.'

'It's a challenge, I guess, but it's like a kind of game we have to play. If I want to keep working here as a foreign correspondent, any copy I file back to my paper in Boston has to comply with your Ministry of Information's censorship. So this week I wrote about that terrible air raid you had on Bristol last Sunday night, but your censors say I can't name the city – all I'm allowed to say is "a West of England town", so that's what my paper has to print. I even said that the censor won't let me name the place. But I am allowed to quote the German High Command in Berlin saying it was an attack on Bristol in the same article.'

'It sounds a bit crazy when you put it like that.'

'You bet. But it gets even crazier – I heard even the local newspaper in Bristol itself couldn't say the attack was on Bristol, so they had to do the same thing. I can't imagine what the people who live there thought.'

'It wasn't like that with Coventry, though – that was all over the front pages and on the BBC the next day.'

'Yes, but that was an exception – it was such a terrible attack, I think your government probably wanted the whole world to know. They even supplied photos for us to use in the American press. They didn't do it for

Bristol, though, so they seem to have gone back to their old ways.'

'I suppose it all makes sense to someone in the Ministry of Information.'

'No doubt, but not to me. I think the papers here are getting a bit sick of it too – I noticed a couple of days ago one of your national dailies was saying the whole system's absurd. The idea seems to be that the Germans might not know what city they hit, so you don't confirm or deny it, but when the target's as big as Bristol they must surely have known where they were.'

Jago was about to murmur his agreement when he was distracted by the sight of a squirrel scampering down the broad trunk of an oak tree and across the grass in front of them.

'Look at that little fellow,' he said. 'An invader from your country.'

'What, a squirrel?'

'A grey squirrel. Some well-meaning Englishmen brought a few over from America, but they've settled in rather too well, and since the last war they've been taking over from our good old red ones. Ten years ago we were shooting hundreds of the grey ones a year in the London parks to try and keep the numbers down, but now the red squirrels've almost disappeared from the whole London area.'

'So the Nazis aren't the only invaders you've got to worry about – it's the Americans too.'

'I wouldn't go that far – I think some Americans are very welcome here.'

Dorothy turned to him with a smile. 'That's very sweet of you.'

He felt a twinge of embarrassment at having come out with what had felt like a smooth-tongued riposte as soon as it left his lips. Perhaps he'd been mixing with too many smooth-talking salesmen, he thought.

'So,' he continued, 'what news is there from across the pond?'

'Well, let me see now – your ambassador and ours have both been hitting the headlines. Our big rival paper in Boston, the *Globe*, did an interview with Joe Kennedy – you know, the US ambassador to London. They quoted him as saying democracy's finished in England and the idea that you're fighting for democracy is bunkum. That doesn't sound very diplomatic, but he's disavowed the interview and said any comments he might have made were strictly off the record. I don't think that will have gone down very well with the president, and the word from home is that Mr Kennedy will probably be resigning pretty soon.'

'And what's our ambassador to America been up to?'

'Lord Lothian? He's been out passing the hat. Apparently this war's costing your country nine million pounds a day, so the ambassador's trying to get the US government to extend more credit – he says you're nearly out of cash to pay for the ships and planes and war supplies you need from us. The papers back home are saying it looks like your government's scraping the bottom of the financial barrel, so it's a pretty serious situation.'

'Hmm . . . too serious for an afternoon like this, I'd

say. In any case, I've never understood high finance. We ran into a man this week who claimed he did, but he was just a crook – he was persuading people to let him invest their money, then tricking them by paying them a good return out of the next investor's cash. He must've known it couldn't last, but he was making easy money out of it for a while.'

'That sounds like what we call a Ponzi scheme in the States. Charles Ponzi wasn't the first to work that kind of racket, but he's certainly the most notorious – he took in ten million dollars from investors by promising a fifty per cent return, paid out eight million dollars, and kept a cool two million for himself. I'm sorry to say he was from Boston, like myself – but we're not all cheats and criminals. In fact it was my paper that investigated him and brought the whole thing tumbling down. He ended up in jail.'

'So I should think. I suspect that's where our gentleman's going to land up too. But that's enough about financial trickery for me – what do you say to having a cup of tea somewhere agreeable instead?'

'That sounds like a good idea. Where do you have in mind?'

'There's a place called the Ring Tea House over that way,' he said, jerking his thumb over his shoulder. 'The Ring's that track we crossed when we came into the park – it's where the rich and fashionable used to drive their carriages. I've heard they make a decent cup of tea there – shall we try it?'

'Yes, let's do that.'

They walked northwards through the park until

the tea house came into view. It was a quaint-looking structure nestling among the trees, with a graceful veranda running round its front. Inside, they found a window table with a view into the park and an atmosphere that was quietly soothing. The customers were scattered thinly across the room, and their conversations were hushed.

Jago ordered afternoon tea for two, and the young waitress delivered it to their table with a smile. It wasn't an elaborate affair, but here in the peaceful tea room, secluded by the trees and the park from the noise and bustle of a city at war, he felt a sudden sense that all was well. The rigours of his job were far from his mind, but as he stared out of the window he found himself thinking about Les Latham. He wondered whether the salesman, with all his schemes and ambitions, had ever had space in his life for simplicity and contentment.

'You look as though your mind's somewhere else, John,' said Dorothy quietly. 'What are you thinking about?'

'Oh, I'm sorry,' he said, turning back to face her. 'Just something to do with the case I've been working on. Have you ever heard of a place called Shangri-La?'

'Yes, I read the book a year or so ago – *Lost Horizon*. It's about an Englishman and an American who find themselves in a lost world somewhere in the wilds of Tibet. Don't tell me Hyde Park reminds you of that.'

'No, not exactly. I'd never heard of it, but young Peter told me about the film and explained it to me. The thing is, the case was about the murder of a commercial traveller, and when we looked in his suitcase we found a photo – it was a picture of an idyllic English country cottage, with "Shangri-La" written on the back of it. Later we discovered he'd been to look at that very cottage, which was up for sale, and also that he'd salted away a lot of money that his wife didn't know about.'

'So he had a secret?'

'I think he had a lot of secrets. I asked her whether he might've been saving up to buy a place like that as a surprise for her, but she seemed to think it was more likely the surprise would be that he'd decided to run off with another woman.'

'He wouldn't be the first.'

'Yes. But anyway, I was just thinking about how nice it is, sitting here in the quiet. It makes me wonder whether that's what he was looking for – a better life in a better place, somewhere he could hide away from a world that's trying to destroy itself.'

'I guess that description could fit a lot of people these days – not just getting away from the bombs, but finding someplace where you can live in safety and be at peace with the world and with yourself. Do you ever feel that way?'

He laughed. 'I used to think like that, especially when I was being shelled and shot at in the war. I thought if we could just win it, everything would be all right – but then we did, and it wasn't. It's the same now – we keep going because we think if we can win this one, there'll be peace, and everything'll be good. But I'm not so sure – once bitten, twice shy, I suppose. I don't think we can ever just draw a line under the past and say it's all finished. What happened yesterday always affects today and tomorrow too.'

'You mean the past comes back to haunt you, right?'

'That's it, yes. It seems the man in our case had quite a few skeletons in the cupboard. He was good at his job, but he was ambitious, he wanted more of the good things in life. That meant he needed money, but I guess he never had enough – a bit like the British government, I suppose.' Dorothy smiled at the allusion, and he continued. 'And from what we've heard, he wasn't too particular about how he made it. He might've thought he could create a perfect life for himself in his Shangri-La, but the trouble is once he got there it wouldn't have been perfect any more. It's probably that ambition that got him killed in the end.'

'And greed?'

'I think so, yes – one of the seven deadly sins, isn't it? According to his wife he wanted everything, but she said in the end he lost everything, even his own life.'

'What shall it profit a man if he gains the whole world and loses his own soul?'

'Exactly. That just about sums him up, I fear. Not my idea of how to live – I prefer the simple life. I'm happy enough just sitting here drinking a cup of tea in the park.'

'But we probably shouldn't sit here indefinitely – they may want to close the park at some point.'

'Ah, yes. Now, before we go, there's something I mustn't forget.' He reached under his chair and picked up the brown paper bag he'd brought with him. 'Here,' he said, handing it to her, 'this is for you.'

'Really? What is it?'

'Just a little something.'

Dorothy reached into the bag and pulled out a black cardboard box. 'English chocolates!' she said. 'For me?'

'Of course they're for you. A little token of appreciation from me.'

'Appreciation of what?'

'Of . . . er, well, of your friendship.'

'Thank you – that's very kind.'

She opened the box to reveal two densely packed layers of dark chocolates. 'That's perfect – and Black Magic too.' She gave him a sly look. 'They're my favourite. How did you— ' She interrupted herself. 'Ah, yes, of course, I told Peter, didn't I? Fancy you noticing that – how sweet of you.'

'Oh, I don't know about that. Maybe it's just something policemen and journalists have in common – we both spend a lot of our time listening carefully to what other people say.'

'Well, maybe it is – but it's still very kind of you. And is there anything else *you* wanted to say? I'm listening carefully.'

He hesitated, sensing that having perhaps passed one test he was about to fail another.

'Well,' she continued, as if giving up hope of him replying, 'There's something I'd like to ask you.'

Jago tried to suppress the uncertainty in his voice. 'Yes?'

Dorothy put the box of chocolates down on the table and fixed him with a disarming smile. 'There's a new movie out that I'd like to see.'

A nervous tension gripped Jago's stomach at

the thought that her next words might be *Pride and Prejudice*, the romantic drama she'd recommended to Cradock, but there was no way to avoid the obvious question. He braced himself. 'Really? Er, which one would that be?'

'It's called *North West Mounted Police*, starring Gary Cooper and Madeleine Carroll. It's about the Mounties – you know, the Royal Canadian Mounted Police?'

'Yes, I know them, of course.'

'Well, I thought it might be right up your street, you see, and one of your papers says it's the best picture of the year. It's on at the Carlton, in Haymarket, and the last showing today's at five, so we can make it if we leave pretty soon. How about you take me to see it?' She paused and looked at him in a way that made it feel like a challenge. 'Will you?'

Jago was caught on the hop. He'd been happy to be an amused bystander when Dorothy encouraged Cradock to take Emily to the pictures, because that was something that young people did. Cradock, he'd thought, might make a fool of himself and the whole thing might backfire on him, but that too was part of being young, and he'd get over it. But the thought of himself taking Dorothy to the pictures was a very different matter. They were both mature adults. For them – or for him at least – this would be a significant step, and if he were honest with himself, he was scared. His mouth opened, but no words came out. All he could think was that suddenly, out of nowhere, he was hurtling towards a junction in the road, with no signposts and no time to think. He took a deep breath. 'Yes,' he gulped at last. 'I, er . . . I will.'

She lowered her voice and spoke slowly and deliberately, holding his gaze. 'Good. That'll be very nice – and maybe we could share some of those chocolates while we watch it. Thank you, John.'

She smiled at him, then leant across the table and planted the lightest of kisses on his cheek.

For a fleeting but exquisite moment, Jago felt dizzy.

ACKNOWLEDGEMENTS

Camden Town in north London, with its picturesque Regent's Canal and celebrated Camden Lock market, is today a magnet for tourists and visitors. But in 1940, when Jago's latest case took him there, it was very different. Described by contemporary commentators as 'drab' and 'dreary', this was the smoke-shrouded world of dismal lodgings evoked so exquisitely in John Betjeman's poem 'Business Girls'.

The convergence of canal, roads and railways at Camden Town also made it a major transport hub, and when war came it was an obvious target for enemy air raids. The place and its people were changed for ever.

As I endeavour to recreate that lost world of wartime London known simply as 'the Blitz', I always feel a debt of gratitude to those who in years gone by took the trouble to record life as it was then, never knowing who might read their words and probably unaware of how fascinating the details of their experience might be to later generations. In the case of *The Camden Murder*, two books that I found particularly interesting were Sheila Stewart's *Ramlin Rose: The Boatwoman's Story*, an account of working lives on the canals in the first half of the twentieth century, and *Fifty Years on the Road*, by Nick Nickols, about the life of a commercial traveller in the nineteen-twenties, thirties and forties.

I also examined the Rouse case, to which Jago refers, a real-life 'blazing car' mystery involving commercial traveller Alfred Rouse, whose trial at the Northampton Assizes in January 1931 was a sensation. In echoing it in this book I'm following humbly in the footsteps of Dorothy L Sayers, who referenced it in her 1939 Lord Peter Wimsey story *In the Teeth of the Evidence*.

Some of the other historical details in *The Camden Murder* are more obscure, and you might suspect I've made them up – this is, after all, a work of fiction. To save you unnecessary perplexity, therefore, I should note that a bomb did hit the Savoy Hotel in November 1940, and a zebra reportedly escaped from London Zoo after an air raid. A man did suffer burns when a box of strike-anywhere matches in his pocket burst into flames because of friction, and the British government did pledge to pay for up to 12 million stems of Jamaican bananas to protect the industry. Finally, a selling point of the pre-war Rover Ten Special was indeed the possibility of having it sprayed on the inside with asbestos for safety. If you're curious about any other historical references, do drop me a line via the Blitz Detective website.

My thanks go, as always, to Roy Ingleton for his advice

on policing as it was done in those far-off days, Rudy Mitchell for his on American English, and David Love for his efforts to keep me on track medically. I'm grateful to Dr Julia Ahvensalmi, archivist at St George's, University of London, for sharing some fascinating memoirs of the wartime years at the hospital, to Pete Warner for his advice on matters mechanical, and to Clifford White, former divisional officer in Kent Fire Brigade, who helped me with my questions about fire but sadly passed away before this book was published. Thanks also to Cass and Ted Staines for so kindly sharing their memories of the old days in Camden Town.

Lastly, my special thanks to Margaret, Catherine and David, without whose unstinting encouragement, support and love I wouldn't be writing these words.

MIKE HOLLOW was born in West Ham, on the eastern edge of London, and grew up in Romford, Essex. He studied Russian and French at the University of Cambridge and then worked for the BBC and later Tearfund. In 2002 he went freelance as a copywriter, journalist, editor and translator, but now gives all his time to writing the Blitz Detective books.

blitzdetective.com   @MikeHollowBlitz